John Galt was born in 1779 in the town of Irvine on the Ayrshire coast where his father was a shipowner and sea captain trading with the West Indies. The family moved to Greenock when Galt was 10, and much of his later writing came from this corner of the West of Scotland. Leaving his job as a junior clerk in Greenock, Galt set out for London at the age of 25. When his business plans did not work out he went on a tour of the Mediterranean and the near east. It was during this time that he met and befriended Byron.

Having published a *Life of Cardinal Wolsey* and a volume of tragedies in 1812, Galt turned to writing full-time after his marriage in 1813. He proposed *Annals of the Parish* but Constable rejected the concept as too local. A second novel, *The Majolo* (1816) was published but met with little success. Galt found his metier with *The Ayrshire Legatees* (1820), purporting to be letters home from a family of Scots visiting London. Appearing anonymously in monthly instalments in *Blackwoods Magazine*, this work led directly to the publication of *Annals of the Parish* (1821), now properly recognised as a gently ironic masterpiece. This was followed in the same vein by *The Provost* (1822), while *The Entail* and *Sir Andrew Wylie* (both 1822) had similar strengths, although structured as more conventional novels. These and other 'Tales of the West' made Galt's reputation as a writer of humour and subtle social observation, but *Ringan Gilhaize* (1823) took a darker turn in a unique psychological and historical study of Covenanting fervour and the 'killing times' in the 17th century.

Becoming involved with the development of Canada, he became a supervisor for the Canada Company. Galt helped to settle Ontario and founded the town of Guelph. He was badly treated by the Directors, however, and after four years abroad his health failed and he returned to London to face bankruptcy and a spell in a debtors' prison. His *Life of Lord Byron* (1830), was a controversial success and the novels *The Member* and *The Radical* (both 1832) took a searching look at his country's political life. After suffering a disabling series of strokes he worked on his *Autobiography* (1833) followed by *Literary Life and Miscellanies* (1834). He returned to Greenock in 1834 and died there five years later.

JOHN GALT

Ringan Gilhaize, or The Covenanters

Edited with an introduction by
PATRICIA J. WILSON

CANONGATE
CLASSICS
64

This edition first published as a Canongate Classic in 1995 by Canongate Books Ltd, 14 High Street, Edinburgh EHI ITE. Introduction copyright © Patricia J. Wilson 1995.

The publishers gratefully acknowledge general subsidy from the Scottish Arts Council towards the Canongate Classics series and a specific grant towards the publication of this title.

Set in 10pt Plantin by Palimpsest Book Production Limited, Polmont, Stirlingshire. Printed and bound in Finland by WSOY.

Canongate Classics
Series Editor: Roderick Watson
Editorial Board: Tom Crawford, John Pick,
Cairns Craig

British Library Cataloguing in Publication Data
A catalogue record for this volume
is available on request from the
British Library.

ISBN 086241 552 7

Contents

Introduction

Galt's novel *Ringan Gilhaize* is a splendid example of realistic folk history, bringing the enormous social and religious changes which shook Scotland between 1558 and 1696 into the same frame as the story of a single family and its changing fortunes over more than three generations. The tale is told by Ringan Gilhaize (pronounced Gillies), the Covenanter grandson of old Michael Gilhaize who had lived through the Reformation. In a unique act of psychological insight Galt enters into the mind of Ringan, imaginatively repossessing the faith in which he was reared, and the veneration the child felt for a grandfather who had served so well the Protestant cause. In old Michael's time the Reformation was supported by pious noblemen who protected him for his service and rewarded him with a farm called Quharist ('Whaur is't?') in Ayrshire. But two generations later, Ringan finds himself in a harsher world, with much less influential support for those who find themselves caught up in renewed religious dispute and the struggle for spiritual and political power.

It is a hard battle, and in time Ringan will lose everything but his belief in his own mission. And if the reader cannot share Ringan's obsession, then Galt's skill makes sure that he never loses our sympathy. We come to know what made him the Cameronian fanatic he becomes. We have seen him change from an affectionate and deeply religious man to one who breaks the sixth commandment and kills in the belief that he is thus fulfilling the mission Providence had assigned him and delivering his native land from bondage. We are fully aware of the extent of his delusion but grant him our pity. It is he who narrates the whole story and yet long before the end of the novel the reader knows more than Ringan, and can watch his gradual and increasing alienation from those with whom he comes in contact.

Writing about *Ringan* in his *Literary Life*, Galt says that it 'is no doubt a fiction, and as such may be called a novel, but memory does not furnish me with the knowledge of a work of the same kind'.[1] In actual fact, Galt's own earlier works had already paved the way, for *Annals of the Parish* and *The Provost* were written in the first person, and both were studies of ironic self-revelation, as well as being examples of social history. In these books, events of world importance such as the American War of Independence, the French Revolution, and the coming of industry are registered through their effect on a small part of Ayrshire and its people, most notably the Reverend Micah Balwhidder in his parish and Provost Pawkie of Gude Town (a thinly disguised Irvine). Then again immediately preceding *Ringan*, Galt produced *The Entail*, a full three-volume novel dealing with roughly the same period as that covered by *Annals* and *The Provost* but showing what Galt calls the 'progress of improvement', this time on the larger town of Glasgow and its environs, thus adding another work to the group he wanted to call his 'Tales of the West', classified by their author as 'theoretical histories of society'. *Ringan* is another in the same vein. In it Galt looks back in time to examine the beginnings and growth of that Calvinist way of thought which produced his minister, his provost, and his thriving cloth merchant, Claud Walkinshaw of *The Entail*. Thus it can be seen that in *Ringan*, Galt was using skills of which he was already a master, and materials with which he was deeply preoccupied, hoping, as he told his publisher, that his latest novel 'is to be my best'.

In the first instance, as Galt explained in his *Literary Life*, *Ringan Gilhaize* was prompted by Sir Walter Scott's *Old Mortality*, in which, not surprisingly, he had disliked Scott's treatment of the Covenanters. Indeed, Galt had long kept a wary eye on Scott's fiction and had made the Rev. Dr. Pringle in *The Ayrshire Legatees* (1821) remark of *Waverley* that it was 'no so friendly to protestant principles as I could have wished', and a character in *The Steam-Boat* (1822) comments that when Scott 'put out his tale of Old

Mortality, true Presbyterians conceived that he had laid an irreverent hand on the ark of our great national cause, the Covenant'.[2]

Galt objected to *Old Mortality* on two counts: first because he thought that in it Scott 'treated the defenders of the Presbyterian Church with too much levity, and not according to my impressions derived from the history of that time'; and secondly, Galt said that he had been 'hugely provoked' by the fact that Sir Walter—

> ... the descendant of Scott of Harden, who was fined in those days forty thousand pounds Scots for being a Presbyterian, or rather for countenancing his lady for being so, should have been so forgetful of what was due to the spirit of that epoch, as to throw it into what I felt was ridicule. (*Literary Life*, I, 254)

Unlike Scott, Galt wanted to pay respectful homage to 'the spirit of that epoch' and admits:

> I am not myself quite a disinterested person on the subject of the Covenant. ... A collateral ancestor of mine, [a grand-uncle of his father] namely, John Galt of Gateside, was banished, in 1684, to Carolina, for refusing to call the affair of Bothwell Bridge a rebellion, and to renounce the Covenant ... In a proclamation of Charles the Second, dated the 5th May, 1684, another ancestral relation, William Galt, of Wark, in the parish of Stewarton, was also proscribed. (*Literary Life*, I, 254–55)

Galt recalled in his *Autobiography*[3] that he had experienced religious enthusiasm himself, for at the age of four or five, in company with many other children, he had been moved to run away with the Buchanites, a religious sect that was eventually driven out of Irvine for their charismatic teachings:

> ... but my mother in a state of distraction pursued

and drew me back by the lug and the horn. I have
not the slightest recollection of Mrs. Buchan's heresies,
– how could I? – but the scene and more than once
the enthusiasm of the psalm singing has risen on my
remembrance, especially in describing the Covenanters
in Ringan Gilhaize. (*Autobiography* I, 6–7)

Thus it is that *Ringan Gilhaize* conveys what Scott could
not, for it shows how a man could become a Covenanter,
and it claims, too, that the spirit which animated those
who took part in the religious struggles of the sixteenth
and seventeenth centuries was the same spirit that moved
those who fought under Wallace and Bruce. In this con-
text Galt wanted to define the special characteristics of
his own people, for as he noted in his Postscript to
Ringan:

The English are a justice-loving people, according to
charter and statute; the Scotch are a wrong-resenting
race, according to right and feeling: and the character of liberty among them takes its aspect from that
peculiarity.

It is in *Ringan Gilhaize* that Galt illustrates what the
Scots understand by liberty, going beyond matters of
Catholic or Protestant doctrine to deal with the nature
of democracy itself. In the situation that obtained in
1558 Galt saw that the authority of rulers and church
had become arbitrary and oppressive. A powerful and
corrupt Church supported by a foreign and autocratic
Queen Regent is shown to be ignoring the higher law
which should bind rulers and ruled alike. Infringement of
that higher law by those in authority was bound to provoke
the resistance of the oppressed, just as when, more than
two centuries earlier, the nation had risen under Wallace
to oppose foreign domination in the struggle for national
independence. This was the spirit in which the Covenanters
sought once more to rouse the nation against Charles II,
the mansworn king, and Archbishop Sharp, the apostate
prelate.

Galt appended to *Ringan* a translation of the Remonstrance that the Scots sent to the Pope in 1320 because he thought, as Magna Carta illustrated the English attitude to authority, the Remonstrance illustrated the Scottish. It warned the Pope against encouraging Edward of England to turn greedy eyes on Scotland, who now had her own king. To him the Scots swore to be loyal but only for as long as he did not attempt to subvert his own and their rights. If he did, they would not hesitate to expel him as an enemy.

The liberty which alone the Scots had fought for and would not lose but with their lives was that same liberty which Galt showed the Lords of the Congregation defending. What they were exercising in the Reformation era was the divine right to resist the arbitrary imposition of authority by a Church and a Queen Regent grown arrogant in the abuse of their power. But by the seventeenth century, when Charles II failed to honour the Covenant and sought to meddle with the Scottish Kirk, the nobles no longer resisted Erastian encroachment. Even the strength of the gentry was 'sookit awa' by fines' to make them conform to Charles's demands. But liberty was not lost, for people of Ringan's degree, who now bore the burden of persecution and suffering, so resented their wrongs that they were roused, even without the protection of noble leaders, to preserve their birthright of the divine right of resistance. Galt sees passive obedience in the face of oppression as abhorrent to the Scot, for whom eternal vigilance was ever the proper price of liberty.

In *Ringan Gilhaize* Galt deals with just such a man of vigilance, a man who comes to feel that he is the instrument Providence has chosen for a great mission. Ringan's whole heritage led him to believe that some great task was in store for him. His grandfather foresaw it for the child. His father confirmed it, and at the age of fifty-eight Ringan comes to see his sufferings and the loss of wife and home and family as God's way of moulding him into the instrument that is to bring down the Stuarts and liberate his country. To this cause he sacrifices his last surviving son.

But Galt also shows how suffering and persecution have

alienated Ringan from reality, driving a man of strong natural affections to feel that in killing Claverhouse he was 'animated by Heaven in a righteous cause'. The book finishes at a peak of elation for Ringan. He feels that when God allows him to fire the fatal shot, the bolt of justice that summons Claverhouse to the audit of his crimes, he has crowned his mission with success. But the reader can feel only compassion for Ringan's delusion, for we cannot regard the deed or its probable outcome as he does. With Ringan Galt may well have achieved his early ambition, recorded in *Stories of the Study*, of showing that when an honest man is consumed by a ruling passion, his 'conscientious sincerity is no proof of the virtue of [his] actions'.

Ringan Gilhaize is historical fiction of a highly individual kind, but it did not have the success that Galt had hoped for. The inevitably sombre colouring of the whole may have militated against the book's popularity, especially for the readers who knew Galt only in the sunnier mood of *Annals of the Parish*, or who had enjoyed the vivid Scots dialogue of *The Entail*. Furthermore, considering the period and the scale of events to be covered, there are many more characters than the average novel could ever attempt to develop. Nevertheless, Galt gives us a whole succession of tantalising vignettes, for he is adept at setting a character before us in a few lightning strokes. We never forget James Coom who had 'the honour and glory of ca'ing a nail intil the timber hip o' the Virgin Mary' after her leg 'had sklintered aff'; nor Tobit Balmuto 'toasting an oaten bannock on a pair of tormentors, with a blue puddock-stool bonnet on his head, and his grey hose undrawn up'. We could happily stay longer in the company of such worthies but Galt has to leave them behind to satisfy the demands of his novel, and he moves steadily forward to the climactic moment when Ringan launches the bolt he was ordained 'by the Almighty avenger' to hurl, and so to 'overthrow the oppressor and oppression of my native land'.

Galt was philosophical about the contemporary lack of interest in *Ringan*: 'whatever may be the blindness of the present age, thank God there will be a posterity' (*Literary*

Life I, 258); and slowly posterity has justified his faith. Sir George Douglas, in his foreword to the 1899 edition of the novel, writes that in *Ringan* 'Galt laid bare the soul of the Covenanting movement [which] . . . Scott in *Old Mortality* most signally failed to do'. More recently Ian Gordon thought Galt's 'the most sympathetic recreation in literature of the harshly independent, dour yet admirable spirit of Scottish Calvinism'. Ian Jack found 'a technical expertise or sophistication about *Ringan Gilhaize* which is seldom to be found in Scott', and Francis Hart noting their different approaches to characterisation concludes that 'Scott belongs with the older mode of allegorical fable and Galt with the newer romantic one of symbolic naturalism'.[4]

In *Ringan* there is much to admire, such as the innate fairmindedness, which allows Ringan to admit of the Bishop of Edinburgh, 'take Patterson all in all for a prelate, he was . . . not void of the charities of human nature'. Then there is Galt's interest in the ordinary people who lived through the struggles he depicts and who have their own thoughts and opinions: people like Tobit Balmuto who looks forward in pre-Reformation days to a time when, for hiring out horses, he will be paid in white money and not fobbed off with a benison; and people like Jaddua Fyfe later, who, one suspects, favours the accession of William of Orange for its likely effect on trade rather than on the future of the Presbyterian church.

More remarkable for his time, however, is the way Galt imposes unity on a story that covers 138 years by having one theme run through it, the theme of the abuse of authority and the need to resist it; argued first by the Lords of the Congregation against Marie of Lorraine, then by Knox against Mary, and latterly by commoners like Ebenezer Muir, Gideon Kemp and Ringan himself against the inequitable laws of the later Stuarts.

Galt also links his Reformation and Covenanting periods by the use of contrast and comparison. He shows the contrasting attitudes of the two ages to carnality, but where possible he deliberately draws parallels between earlier and later events: the descent of the Highland Host on Ayrshire is likened to the Massacre of St Bartholomew's Eve; the riots in St Giles Cathedral when the new liturgy is read for the first time are compared to the breaking of the idols at Perth that heralded popular involvement in the Reformation cause. He skilfully makes the burning of Walter Mill and reactions to it the core of the first volume. Central to the other two is the idea that Ringan is destined to undertake a mission. We see the incidents that determine what that mission will be and the sacrificing of everything to its accomplishment. Galt shows the divided loyalty of Scotland's common people in the divided homes in which Ringan is forced to seek shelter and risk betrayal. These households are usually fictitious. But when he wants to show in its most extreme form the lack of leadership, the divided counsels and the internal strife that the Covenanting movement latterly suffered from, he manages to epitomise it in an actual historical event – Argyle's abortive rising of 1685.

Perhaps even more remarkable, however, is the way Galt makes Ringan's behaviour mirror that of the late conventiclers. Just as he suffers periods of apathy and increasing alienation followed by outbursts of feverish activity, so the Covenanting movement in its latter phases was characterised by spells of reluctant obedience and passive resistance followed by outbreaks of violence. Altogether *Ringan Gilhaize* is an achievement worthy the attention of that posterity of whose favourable judgement Galt had such high hopes. No other novel in our tradition has taken on both the historical scale and the inner psychology of the Covenanting times with such conviction and such compassion.

Patricia J. Wilson

NOTES

1 *The Literary Life and Miscellanies of John Galt*, 3 vols (Edinburgh, 1834), I, Patricia J. Wilson 251.

2 See Galt's *The Ayrshire Legatees; or, The Pringle Family* (Edinburgh, 1821), p. 15; and *The Steam-Boat* (Edinburgh and London, 1822), p. 318.

3 *The Autobiography of John Galt*, 2 vols (London, 1833), page references relate to this edition, and are given in parentheses in the text.

4 See Ian A. Gordon, *John Galt: the Life of a Writer* (Edinburgh, 1972), p. 67; Ian Jack, *English Literature 1815 –1833* (Oxford, 1963), p. 231; and Francis Russell Hart, *The Scottish Novel* (London, 1978), p. 50.

Volume I

Their constancy in torture and in death,—
These on Tradition's tongue still live, these shall
On History's honest page be pictured bright
To latest times.

GRAHAME'S SABBATH

It is a thing past all contesting, that, in the Reformation, there was a spirit of far greater carnality among the champions of the cause, than among those who in later times so courageously, under the Lord, upheld the unspotted banners of the Covenant. This I speak of from the remembrance of many aged persons, who either themselves bore a part in that war with the worshippers of the Beast and his Image, or who had heard their fathers tell of the heart and mind wherewith it was carried on, and could thence, with the helps of their own knowledge, discern the spiritual and hallowed difference. But, as I intend mainly to bear witness to those passages of the late bloody persecution in which I was myself both a soldier and a sufferer, it will not become me to brag of our motives and intents, as higher and holier than those of the great elder Worthies of 'the Congregation.' At the same time it is needful that I should rehearse as much of what happened in the troubles of the Reformation, as, in its effects and influences, worked upon the issues of my own life. For my father's father was out in the raids of that tempestuous season, and it was by him, and from the stories he was wont to tell of what the government did, when drunken with the sorceries of the gorgeous Roman harlot, and rampaging with the wrath of Moloch and of Belial, it trampled on the hearts and thought to devour the souls of the subjects, that I first was taught to feel, know, and understand, the divine right of resistance.

He was come of a stock of bein burghers in Lithgow; but his father having a profitable traffic in saddle-irons and bridle-rings among the gallants of the court, and being moreover a man who took little heed of the truths of religion, he continued with his wife in the delusions of the papistical idolatry till the last, by which my grandfather's

3

young soul was put in great jeopardy. For the monks of that
time were eager to get into their clutches such men-children
as appeared to be gifted with any peculiar gift, in order to
rear them for stoops and posts to sustain their Babylon,
in the tower and structure whereof many rents and cracks
were daily kithing.

The Dominican friars, who had a rich howf in the
town, seeing that my grandfather was a shrewd and sharp
child, of a comely complexion, and possessing a studious
observance, were fain to wile him into their power; but he
was happily preserved from all their snares and devices, in
a manner that shows how wonderfully the Lord worketh
out the purposes of His will, by ways and means of which
no man can fathom the depth of the mysteries.

Besides his traffic in the polished garniture of horse-gear,
my grandfather's father was also a ferrier, and enjoyed a
far-spread repute for his skill in the maladies of horses;
by which, and as he dwelt near the palace-yett, on the
south side of the street, fornent the grand fountain-well,
his smiddy was the common haunt of the serving-men
belonging to the nobles frequenting the court, and as
often as any new comers to the palace were observed in
the town, some of the monks and friars belonging to the
different convents were sure to come to the smiddy to
converse with their grooms and to hear the news, which
were all of the controversies raging between the priesthood
and the people.

My grandfather was then a little boy, but he thirsted
to hear their conversations; and many a time, as he was
wont to tell, has his very heart been raspet to the quick by
the cruel comments in which those cormorants of idolatry
indulged themselves, with respect to the brave spirit of
the reformers; and he rejoiced when any retainers of the
protestant lords quarrelled with them, and dealt back to
them as hard names as the odious epithets with which
the hot-fed friars reviled the pious challengers of the papal
iniquities. Thus it was, in the green years of his childhood,
that the same sanctified spirit was poured out upon him,
which roused so many of the true and faithful to resist
and repel the attempt to quench the re-lighted lamps of

the gospel, preparing his young courage to engage in those great first trials and strong tasks of the Lord.

The tidings and the bickerings to which he was a hearkener in the smiddy, he was in the practice of relating to his companions, by which it came to pass that, it might in a manner be said, all the boys in the town were leagued in spirit with the reformers, and the consequences were not long of ripening.

In those days there was a popish saint, one St Michael, that was held in wonderful love and adoration by all the ranks and hierarchies of the ecclesiastical locust then in Lithgow; indeed, for that matter, they ascribed to him power and dominion over the whole town, lauding and worshipping him as their special god and protector. And upon a certain day of the year they were wont to make a great pageant and revel in honour of this supposed saint, and to come forth from their cloisters with banners, and with censers burning incense, shouting and singing paternosters in praise of this their Dagon, walking in procession from kirk to kirk, as if they were celebrating the triumph of some mighty conqueror.

This annual abomination happening to take place shortly after the martyrdom of that true saint and gospel preacher Mr George Wishart, and while kirk and quire were resounding, to the great indignation of all Christians, with lamentations for the well-earned death of the cruel Cardinal Beaton, his ravenous persecutor, the monks and friars received but little homage as they passed along triumphing, though the streets were, as usual, filled with the multitude to see their fine show. They suffered, however, no molestation nor contempt, till they were passing the Earl of Angus' house, on the outside stair of which my grandfather, with some two or three score of other innocent children, was standing; and even there they might, perhaps, have been suffered to go by scaithless, but for an accident that befell the bearer of a banner, on which was depicted a blasphemous type of the Holy Ghost in the shape and lineaments of a cushy-doo.

It chanced that the bearer of this blazon of iniquity was a particular fat monk, of an arrogant nature, with the crimson complexion of surfeit and constipation, who, for many causes and reasons, was held in greater aversion than all the rest, especially by the boys, that never lost an opportunity of making him a scoff and a scorn; and it so fell out, as he was coming proudly along, turning his Babylonish banner to pleasure the women at the windows, to whom he kept nodding and winking as he passed, that his foot slipped, and down he fell as it were with a gludder, at which all the thoughtless innocents on the Earl of Angus' stair set up a loud shout of triumphant laughter, and from less to more began to hoot and yell at the whole pageant, and to pelt some of the performers with unsavoury missiles.

This, by those inordinate ministers of oppression, was deemed a horrible sacrilege, and the parents of all the poor children were obligated to give them up to punishment, of which none suffered more than did my grandfather; who was not only persecuted with stripes till his loins were black and blue, but cast into a dungeon in the Blackfriars' den, where for three days and three nights he was allowed no sustenance but gnawed crusts and foul water. The stripes and terrors of the oppressor are, however, the seeds which Providence sows in its mercy, to grow into the means that shall work his own overthrow.

The persecutions which from that day the monks waged, in their conclaves of sloth and sosherie, against the children of the town, denouncing them to their parents as worms of the great serpent and heirs of perdition, only served to make their young spirits burn fiercer. As their joints hardened and their sinews were knit, their hearts grew manful, and yearned, as my grandfather said, with the zealous longings of a righteous revenge, to sweep them away from the land as with a whirlwind.

After enduring for several years great affliction in his father's house, from his mother, a termagant woman, who was entirely under the dominion of her confessor, my grandfather entered into a paction with two other young lads to quit their homes for ever, and to enter the service of some of those pious noblemen who were then active in procuring adherents to the protestant cause, as set forth in the first covenant. Accordingly, one morning in the spring of 1558, they bade adieu to their fathers' doors, and set forward on foot towards Edinburgh.

'We had light hearts,' said my grandfather, 'for our trust was in Heaven; we had girded ourselves for a holy enterprise, and the confidence of our souls broke forth into songs of battle, the melodious breathings of that unison of spirit which is alone known to the soldiers of the great Captain of Salvation.'

About noon they arrived at the Cross of Edinburgh, where they found a crowd assembled round the Lucken-booths, waiting for the breaking up of the States, which were then deliberating anent the proposal from the French king, that the Prince Dolphin, his son, should marry our young queen, the fair and faulty Mary, whose doleful captivity and woful end scarcely expiated the sins and sorrows that she caused to her ill-used and poor misgoverned native realm of Scotland.

While they were standing in this crowd, my grandfather happened to see one Icener Cunningham, a servant in the household of the Earl of Glencairn, and having some acquaintance of the man before at Lithgow, he went towards him, and after some common talk, told on what errand he and his two companions had come to Edinburgh. It was in consequence agreed between them, that this Icener should speak to his master concerning them; the which he did as soon as my Lord came out from the Parliament; and the Earl was so well pleased with the looks of the three young men, that he retained them for his service on the spot, and they were conducted by Icener Cunningham home to his Lordship's lodgings in St Mary's Wynd.

Thus was my grandfather inlisted into the cause of the Lords of the Congregation; and in the service of that great champion of the Reformation, the renowned, valiant, and pious Earl of Glencairn, he saw many of those things, the recital of which kindled my young mind to flame up with no less ardour than his, against the cruel attempt that was made, in our own day and generation, to load the neck of Scotland with the grievous chains of prelatic tyranny.

The Earl of Glencairn, having much to do with the other Lords of the Congregation, did not come to his lodging till late in the afternoon; when, as soon as he had passed into his privy chamber, he sent for his three new men, and entered into some conversation with them concerning what the people at Lithgow said and thought of the Queen-dowager's government, and the proceedings at that time afoot on behalf of the reformed religion. But my grandfather jealoused that in this he was less swayed by the expectation of gathering knowledge from them, than by a wish to inspect their discretion and capacities; for, after conversing with them for the space of half an hour, or thereby, he dismissed them courteously from his presence, without intimating that he had any special service for them to perform.

One evening as the Earl sat alone at supper, he ordered my grandfather to be brought again before him, and desired him to be cup-bearer for that night. In this situation, as my grandfather stood holding the chalice and flagon at his left elbow, the Earl, as was his wonted custom with such of the household as he, from time to time, so honoured, entered into familiar conversation with him; and when the servitude and homages of the supper were over, and the servants were removing the plate and trenchers, he signified, by a look and a whisper, that he wished him to linger in the room till after they were gone.

'Gilhaize,' said he, when the serving men had retired, and they were by themselves, 'I am well content with your prudence, and therefore, before you are known to belong to my train, I would send you on a confidential errand, for which you must be ready to set forth this very night.'

My grandfather made no reply in words to this mark of

trust, but bowed his head, in token of his obedience to the commands of the Earl.

'I need not tell you,' resumed his master, 'that, among the friends of the reformed cause, there are some for policy, and many for gain; and that our adversaries, knowing this, leave no device or stratagem untried to sow sedition among the Lords and Leaders of the Congregation. This very day the Earl of Argyle has received a mealy-mouthed letter from that dissolute papist, the Archbishop of St Andrews, entreating him, with many sweet words, concerning the ancient friendship subsisting between their families, to banish from his protection that good and pious proselyte, Douglas, his chaplain; evidently presuming, from the easy temper of the aged Earl, that he may be wrought into compliance. But Argyle is an honest man, and is this night to return, by the Archbishop's messenger and kinsman, Sir David Hamilton, a fitting and proper reply. It is not however to be thought, that this attempt to tamper with Argyle is the sole trial which the treacherous priest is at this time making to breed distrust and dissension among us, though as yet we have heard of none other. Now, Gilhaize, what I wish you to do, and I think you can do it well, is to throw yourself in Sir David's way, and, by hook or crook, get with him to St Andrews, and there try by all expedient means to gain a knowledge of what the Archbishop is at this time plotting – for plotting we are assured from this symptom he is – and it is needful to the cause of Christ that his wiles should be circumvented.'

In saying these words the Earl rose, and, taking a key from his belt, opened a coffer that stood in the corner of the room, and took out two pieces of gold, which he delivered to my grandfather, to bear the expenses of his journey.

'I give you, Gilhaize,' said he, 'no farther instructions; for, unless I am mistaken in my man, you lack no better guide than your own discernment. So God be with you, and His blessing prosper the undertaking.'

My grandfather was much moved at being so trusted, and doubted in his own breast if he was qualified for the duty which his master had thus put upon him. Nevertheless he took heart from the Earl's confidence, and, without saying any thing either to his two companions or to Icener Cunningham, he immediately, on parting from his master, left the house, leaving his absence to be accounted for to the servants according to his lord's pleasure.

Having been several times on errands of his father in Edinburgh before, he was not ill-acquainted with the town, and the moon being up, he had no difficulty in finding his way to Habby Bridle's, a noted stabler's at the foot of Leith Wynd, nigh the mouth of the North Loch, where gallants and other travellers of gentle condition commonly put up their horses. There he thought it was likely Sir David Hamilton had stabled his steed, and he divined that, by going thither, he would learn whether that knight had set forward to Fyfe, or when he was expected so to do; the which movement, he always said, was nothing short of an instinct from Heaven; for just on entering the stabler's yard, a groom came shouting to the hostler to get Sir David Hamilton's horses saddled outright, as his master was coming.

Thus, without the exposure of any inquiry, he gained the tidings that he wanted, and with what speed he could put into his heels, he went forward to the pier of Leith, where he found a bark, with many passengers on board, ready to set sail for Kirkcaldy, waiting only for the arrival of Sir David, to whom, as the Archbishop's kinsman, the boatmen were fain to pretend a great outward respect; but many a bitter ban, my grandfather said, they gave him for taigling them so long, while wind and tide both served, – all which was proof and evidence how much the hearts of the common people were then alienated from the papistical churchmen.

Sir David having arrived, and his horses being taken aboard, the bark set sail, and about day-break next morning she came to anchor at Kirkcaldy. During the voyage, my grandfather, who was of a mild and comely aspect, observed that the knight was more affable towards him than to the lave of the passengers, the most part of whom were coopers going to Dundee to prepare for the summer fishing. Among them was one Patrick Girdwood, the deacon of the craft, a most comical character, so vogie of his honours and dignities in the town-council, that he could not get the knight told often enough what a load aboon the burden he had in keeping a' things douce and in right regulation amang the bailies. But Sir David, fashed at his clatter, and to be quit of him, came across the vessel, and began to talk to my grandfather, although, by his apparel, he was no meet companion for one of a knight's degree.

It happened that Sir David was pleased with his conversation, which was not to be wondered at; for in his old age, when I knew him, he was a man of a most enticing mildness of manner, and withal so discreet in his sentences, that he could not be heard without begetting respect for his observance and judgment. So out of the vanity of that vogie tod of the town-council, was a mean thus made by Providence to further the ends and objects of the Reformation, in so far as my grandfather was concerned; for the knight took a liking to him, and being told, as it was expedient to give a reason for his journey to St Andrews, that he was going thither to work as a ferrier, Sir David promised him not only his own countenance, but to commend him to the Archbishop.

There was at that time in Kirkcaldy one Tobit Balmuto, a horse-setter, of whom my grandfather had some knowledge by report. This Tobit being much resorted to by the courtiers going to and coming from Falkland, and well known to their serving-men, who were wont to speak of him in the smiddy at Lithgow as a zealous reformer, – chiefly, as the prodigals among them used to jeer and say, because the priests and friars, in their journeyings atween St Andrews and Edinburgh, took the use of his beasts without paying for them, giving him only their feckless benisons instead of white money.

To this man my grandfather resolved to apply for a horse, and such a one, if possible, as would be able to carry him as fast as Sir David Hamilton's. Accordingly, on getting to the land, he inquired for Tobit Balmuto, and several of his striplings and hostlers being on the shore, having, on seeing the bark arrive, come down to look out for travellers that might want horses, he was conducted by one of them to their employer, whom he found an elderly man, of the corpulent order, sitting in an elbow-chair by the fireside, toasting an oaten bannock on a pair of tormentors, with a blue puddock-stool bonnet on his head, and his grey hose undrawn up, whereby his hairy legs were bare, showing a power and girth such as my grandfather had seen few like before, testifying to what had been the deadly strength of their possessor in his younger years. He was thought to have been an off-gett of the Boswells of Balmuto.

When he had made known his want to Tobit, and that he was in a manner obligated to be at St Andrews as soon as Sir David Hamilton, the horse-setter withdrew the bannock from before the ribs, and seeing it somewhat scowthert and blackent on the one cheek, he took it off the tormentors, and scraped it with them, and blew away the brown burning, before he made any response; then he turned round to my grandfather, and looking at him with the tail of his eye, from aneath his broad bonnet, said,—

'Then ye're no in the service of his Grace, my Lord the Archbishop? and yet, frien', I think na ye're just a peer to Sir Davie, that ye need to ettle at coping with his braw mare, Skelp-the-dub, whilk I selt to him mysel; but the de'il a bawbee hae I yet han'let o' the price; howsever that's neither here nor there, a day of reckoning will come at last.'

My grandfather assured Tobit Balmuto, it was indeed very true he was not in the service of the Archbishop, and that he would not have been so instant about getting to St Andrews with the knight, had he not a dread and fear that Sir David was the bearer of something that might be sore news to the flock o' Christ, and he was fain to be there as soon as him, to speak in time of what he jealoused, that any of those in the town, who stood within the reverence of the Archbishop's aversion, on account of their religion, might get an inkling, and provide for themselves.

'If that's your errand,' said the horse-setter, 'ye s'all hae the swiftest foot in my aught to help you on, and I redde you no to spare the spur, for I'm troubled to think ye may be owre late – Satan, or they lie upon him, has been heating his cauldrons yonder for a brewing, and the Archbishop's thrang providing the malt. Nae farther gane than yesterday, auld worthy Mr Mill of Lunan, being discovered hidden in a kiln at Dysart, was ta'en, they say, in a cart, like a malefactor, by twa uncircumcised loons, servitors to his Grace, and it's thought it will go hard wi' him, on account of his great godliness; so mak what haste ye dow, and the Lord put mettle in the beast that bears you.'

With that Tobit Balmuto ordered the lad who brought my grandfather to the house, to saddle a horse that he called Spunkie; and in a trice he was mounted and on the road after Sir David, whom he overtook, notwithstanding the spirit of his mare, Skelp-the-dub, before he had cleared the town of Pathhead, and they travelled onward at a brisk trot together, the Knight waxing more and more pleased with his companion, in so much, that by the time they had reached Cupar, where they stopped to corn, he lamented that a young man of his parts should think of following the slavery of a ferrier's life, when he might rise to trusts and fortune in the house of some of the great men of the time, kindly offering to procure for him, on their arrival at St Andrews, the favour and patronage of his kinsman, the Archbishop.

It was the afternoon when my grandfather and Sir David Hamilton came in sight of St Andrews, and the day being loun and bright, the sky clear, and the sea calm, he told me, that, when he saw the many lofty spires and towers and glittering pinnacles of the town rising before him, he verily thought he was approaching the city of Jerusalem, so grand and glorious was the apparition which they made in the sunshine, and he approached the barricadoed gate with a strange movement of awe and wonder rushing through the depths of his spirit.

They, however, entered not into the city at that time, but, passing along the wall leftward, came to a road which led to the gate of the castle where the Archbishop then dwelt; and as they were approaching towards it, Sir David pointed out the window where Cardinal Beaton sat in the pomp of his scarlet and fine linen to witness the heretic Wishart, as the knight called that holy man, burnt for his sins and abominations.

My grandfather, on hearing this, drew his bridle in, and falling behind Sir David, raised his cap in reverence and in sorrow at the thought of passing over the ground that had been so hallowed by martyrdom. But he said nothing, for he knew that his thoughts were full of offence to those who were wrapt in the errors and delusions of popery like Sir David Hamilton; and, moreover, he had thanked the Lord thrice in the course of their journey for the favour which it had pleased Him he should find in the sight of the kinsman of so great an adversary to the truth as was the Archbishop of St Andrews, whose treasons and treacheries against the church of Christ he was then travelling to discover and waylay.

On reaching the castle-yett they alighted: my grand-father springing lightly from the saddle, took hold of Sir David's mare by the bridle-rings, while the knight went forward, and whispered something concerning his Grace to a stalwart hard-favoured grey-haired man-at-arms, that stood warder of the port leaning on his sword, the blade of whilk could not be shorter than an ell. What answer he got was brief, the ancient warrior pointing at the same time with his right hand towards a certain part of the city, and giving a Belial smile of significance; whereupon Sir David turned round without going into the court of the castle, and bidding my grandfather give the man the beasts and follow, which he did, they walked together under the town wall towards the east, till they came to a narrow sallyport in the rampart, wherewith the priory and cathedral had of old been fenced about with turrets and bastions of great strength against the lawless kerns of the Highlands, and especially the ships of the English, who have in all ages been of a nature gleg and glad to mulct and molest the sea-harbour towns of Scotland.

On coming to the sallyport, Sir David chapped with his whip twice, and from within a wicket was opened in the doors, ribbed with iron stainchers on the outside, and a man with the sound of corpulency in his voice, looked through and inquired what they wanted. Seeing, however, who it was that had knocked, he forthwith drew the bar and allowed them to enter, which was into a pleasant policy adorned with jonquils and jelly-flowers, and all manner of blooming and odoriferous plants, most voluptuous to the smell and ravishing to behold, the scents and fragrancies whereof smote my grandfather for a time, as he said, with the very anguish of delight. But, on looking behind to see who had given them admittance, he was astounded when, instead of an armed and mailed soldier, as he had thought the drumly-voiced sentinel there placed was, he saw a large elderly monk, sitting on a bench with a broken pasty smoking on a platter beside him, and a Rotterdam greybeard jug standing by, no doubt plenished with cordial drink.

Sir David held no parlance with the feeding friar, but

going straight up the walk to the door of a lodging, to the which this was the parterre and garden, he laid his hand on the sneck, and opening it, bade my grandfather come in.

They then went along the trance towards an open room, and on entering it they met a fair damsel in the garb of a handmaid, to whom the knight spoke in familiarity, and kittling her under the chin, made her giggle in a wanton manner. By her he was informed that the Archbishop was in the inner chamber at dinner with her mistress, upon which he desired my grandfather to sit down, while he went ben to his Grace.

The room where my grandfather took his seat was parted from the inner chamber, in which the Archbishop and his lemane were at their festivities, by an arras partition, so that he could hear all that passed within, and the first words his Grace said on his kinsman going ben were—

'Aweel, Davie, and what says that auld doddard Argyle, will he send me the apostate to mak a bonfire?'

'He has sent your Grace a letter,' replied Sir David, 'wherein he told me he had expounded the reasons and causes of his protecting Douglas, hoping your Grace will approve the same.'

'Approve heresy and reprobacy!' exclaimed the Archbishop; 'but gi'e me the letter, and sit ye down, Davie. – Mistress Kilspinnie, my dauty, fill him a cup of wine, the malvesie, to put smeddum in his marrow: he'll no be the waur o' t, after his gallanting at Enbro. – Stay! what's this? the auld man's been at school since him and me hae swappit paper. My word, Argyle, thou's got a tongue in thy pen neb! but this was ne'er indited by him; the cloven foot of the heretical Carmelite is manifest in every line. Honour and conscience truly! – braw words for a hieland schore, that bigs his bield wi' other folks gear!'

'Be composed, your sweet Grace, and dinna be so fashed,' cried a silver-tongued madam, the which my grandfather afterwards found, as I shall have to rehearse, was his concubine, the Mrs Kilspinnie – 'what does he say?'

'Say! why that Douglas preaches against idolatry, and he remits to my conscience forsooth, gif that be heresy – and he preaches against adulteries and fornications too – was ever sic varlet terms written in ony nobleman's letter afore this apostate's time – and he refers that to my conscience likewise!'

'A faggot to his tail would be owre gude for him,' cried Mrs Kilspinnie.

'He preaches against hypocrisy,' said his Grace, 'the which he also refers to my conscience – conscience again! Hae, Davie, tak thir clishmaclavers to Andrew Oliphant. It'll be spunk to his zeal. We maun strike our adversaries wi' terror, and if we canna wile them back to the fold, we'll e'en set the dogs on them – Kind Mistress Kilspinnie, help me frae the stoup o' sherries, for I canna but say that this scalded heart I hae gotten frae that auld shavling-gabbit hielander has raised my corruption, and I stand in need, my lambie, o' a' your winsome comforting.'

At which words Sir David came forth the chamber with the letter in his hand; but seeing my grandfather, whom it would seem he had forgotten, he went suddenly back and said to his Grace—

'Please you, my Lord, I hae brought with me a young man of a good capacity and a ripe understanding, that I would commend to your Grace's service. He is here in the outer room waiting your Grace's pleasure.'

'Davie Hamilton,' replied the Archbishop, 'ye sometimes lack discretion – what for did ye bring a stranger into this house – knowing as ye ought to do, that I ne'er come hither but when I'm o' a sickly frame, in need o' solace and repose? Howsever, since the lad's there, bid him come ben.'

Upon this, Sir David came out and beckoned my grandfather to go in; and when he went forward, he saw none in that inner chamber but his Grace and the Mrs Kilspinnie, with whom he was sitting on a bedside, before a well-garnished table, whereon was divers silver flagons, canisters of comfits, and goblets of the crystal of Venetia.

He looked sharp at my grandfather, perusing him from head to foot, who put on for the occasion a face of modesty and reverence, but he was none daunted for all his eyes

were awake, and he took such a cognition of his Grace
as he never afterwards forgot. Indeed, I have often heard
him say, that he saw more of the man in the brief space of
that interview, than of others in many intromissions, and
he used to depict him to me as a hale black-avised carl, of
an o' ersea look, with a long dark beard inclining to grey;
his abundant hair, flowing down from his cowl, was also
clouded and streaked with the kithings of the cranreuch of
age – there was, however, a youthy and luscious twinkling
in his eyes, that showed how little the passage of three
and fifty winters had cooled the rampant sensuality of
his nature. His right leg, which was naked, though on the
foot was a slipper of Spanish leather, he laid o' er Mistress
Kilspinnie's knees, as he threw himself back against the
pillar of the bed, the better to observe and converse with my
grandfather; and she, like another Delilah, began to pattle it
with her fingers, casting at the same time glances, unseen by
her papistical paramour, towards my grandfather, who, as I
have said, was a comely and well-favoured young man.

After some few questions as to his name and parentage,
the prelate said he would give him his livery, being then
anxious, on account of the signs of the times, to fortify
his household with stout and valiant youngsters; and
bidding him draw near and to kneel down, he laid his
hand on his head, and mumbled a benedicite; the which
my grandfather said, was as the smell of rottenness to
his spirit, the lascivious hirkos, then wantoning so openly
with his adulterous concubine, for no better was Mistress
Kilspinnie, her husband, a creditable man, being then
living, and one of the bailies of Crail. Nor is it to be
debated, that the scene was such as ought not to have been
seen in a Christian land; but in those days the blasphemous
progeny of the Roman harlot were bold with the audacious
sinfulness of their parent, and set little store by the fear of
God, or the contempt of man. It was a sore trial and a
struggle in the bosom of my grandfather that day, to think
of making a show of homage and service towards the mitred
Belial and high priest of the abominations wherewith the
realm was polluted, and when he rose from under his paw,
he shuddered, and felt as if he had received the foul erls

of perdition from the Evil One. Many a bitter tear he long after shed in secret for the hypocrisy of that hour, the guilt of which was never sweetened to his conscience, even by the thought that he may be thereby helped to further the great redemption of his native land, in the blessed cleansing of the Reformation.

Sir David Hamilton conducted my grandfather back through the garden and the sallyport to the castle, where he made him acquainted with his Grace's seneschal, by whom he was hospitably entertained when the knight had left them together, receiving from him a cup of hippocras, and a plentiful repast, the like of which, for the savouriness of the viands, was seldom seen out of the howfs of the monks.

The seneschal was called by name Leonard Meldrum, and was a most douce and composed character, well stricken in years, and though engrained with the errors of papistry, as was natural for one bred and cherished in the house of the speaking horn of the Beast, for such the high priest of St Andrews was well likened to, he was nevertheless a man of a humane heart and great tenderness of conscience.

The while my grandfather was sitting with him at the board, he lamented that the Church, so he denominated the papal abomination, was so far gone with the spirit of punishment and of cruelty, as rather to shock men's minds into schism and rebellion, than to allure them back into worship and reverence, and to a repentance of their heresies. A strain of discourse which my grandfather so little expected to hear within the gates and precincts of the guilty castle of St Andrews, that it made him for a time distrust the sincerity of the old man, and he was very guarded in what he himself answered thereto. Leonard Meldrum was, however, honest in his way, and rehearsed many things which had been done within his own knowledge against the reformers, that, as he said, human nature could not abide, nor the just and merciful Heavens well pardon.

Thus, from less to more, my grandfather and he fell into

frank communion, and he gave him such an account of the bloody Cardinal Beaton, as was most awful to hear, saying, that his then present master, with all his faults and prodigalities, was a saint of purity compared to that rampagious cardinal, the which to hear, my grandfather thinking of what he had seen in the lodging of Madam Kilspinnie, was seized with such a horror thereat, that he could partake no more of the repast before him; and he was likewise moved into a great awe and wonder of spirit, that the Lord should thus, in the very chief sanctuary of papistry in all Scotland, be alienating the affections of the servants from their master, preparing the way, as it were, for an utter desertion and desolation to ensue.

They afterwards talked of the latter end of that great martyr, Mr George Wishart, and the seneschal informed him of several things concerning the same, that were most edifying, though sorrowful to hear.

'He was,' said he, 'placed under my care, and methinks I shall ever see him before me, so meek, so holy, and so goodly was his aspect. He was of tall stature, black hair'd, long bearded, of a graceful carriage, elegant, courteous, and ready to teach. In his apparel he was most comely, and in his diet of an abstemious temperance. On the morning of his execution, when I gave him notice that he was not to be allowed to have the sacrament, he smiled with a holiness of resignation that almost melted me to weep. I then invited him to partake of my breakfast, which he accepted with cheerfulness, saying—

'"I will do it very willingly, and so much the rather, because I perceive you to be a good Christian, and a man fearing God."

I then ordered in the breakfast, and he said—

'"I beseech you, for the love you bear to our Saviour, to be silent a little while, till I have made a short exhortation, and blessed this bread we are to eat."

He then spoke about the space of half an hour of our Saviour's death and passion, exhorting me, and those who were present with me, to mutual love and holiness of life; and giving thanks, brake the bread, distributing a part to those about him; then taking a cup, he bade us remember that Christ's blood was shed to wash away our sins, and, tasting it himself, he handed it to me, and I likewise partook of it: then he concluded with another prayer, at the end of which he said, "I will neither drink nor eat any more in this world," and he forthwith entered into an inner chamber where his bed was, leaving us filled with admiration and sorrow, and our eyes flowing with tears.'

To this the seneschal added, 'I fear, I fear, we are soon to have another scene of the same sort, for to-morrow the Bishops of Murray, and Brechin, and Caithness, with other dignitaries, are summoned to the cathedral, to sit in judgment on the aged priest of Lunan, that was brought hither from Dysart yestreen, and from the head the newfangled heresies are making, there's little doubt that the poor auld man will be made an example. Woes me! far better would it be an they would make an example of the like of the Earls of Argyle and Glencairn, by whom the reprobates are so encouraged.'

'And is this Mill,' inquired my grandfather with diffidence, for his heart was so stung with what he heard, that he could scarcely feign the necessary hypocrisy which the peril he stood in required – 'Is this Mill in the castle?'

'Sorry am I to say it,' replied the seneschal, 'and under my keeping; but I darena show him the pity that I would fain do to his grey hairs and aged limbs. Some of the monks of the priory are with him just now, trying to get him to recant his errors, with the promise of a bein provision for the remainder of his days in the abbey of Dunfermline, the whilk I hope our blessed Lady will put it into his heart to accept.'

'I trust' said my grandfather in the core of his bosom, 'that the Lord will fortify him to resist the temptation.'

This, however, the seneschal heard not, for it was ejaculated inwardly, and he subjoined—

'When the monks go away, I will take you in to see him, for truly he is a sight far more moving to compassion than displeasure, whatsoever his sins and heresies may be.'

In this manner, for the space of more than an hour, did my grandfather hold converse and communion with Leonard Meldrum, in whom he was often heard to say, there was more of the leaven of a sanctified nature, than in the disposition of many zealous and professing Christians.

When the two shavlings that had been afflicting Master Mill with the offer of the wages of Satan were departed from the castle, the seneschal rose, and bidding my grandfather to come after him, they went out of the room, and traversing a narrow dark passage with many windings, came to the foot of a turnpike stair which led up into the sea-tower, so called because it stood farthermost of all the castle in the sea, and in the chamber thereof they found Master Mill alone, sitting at the window, with his ancient and shrivelled lean hand resting on the sole and supporting his chin, as he looked through the iron stainchers abroad on the ocean that was sleeping in a blessed tranquillity around, all glowing and golden with the schimmer of the setting sun.

'How fares it with you?' said the seneschal with a kindly accent; whereupon the old man, who had not heard them enter, being tranced in his own holy meditations, turned round, and my grandfather said he felt himself, when he beheld his countenance, so smitten with awe and admiration, that he could not for some time advance a step.

'Come in, Master Meldrum, and sit ye down by me!' said the godly man. 'Draw near unto me, for I am a thought hard of hearing. The Lord has of late, by steeking the doors and windows of my earthly tabernacle, been admonishing me that the gloaming is come, and the hour of rest cannot be far off.'

His voice, said my grandfather, was as the sound of a mournful melody, but his countenance was brightened with a solemn joyfulness. He was of a pale and spiritual complexion; his eyes beamed as it were with a living light, and often glanced thoughts of heavenly imaginings, even as he sat in silence. He was then fourscore and two years old; but his appearance was more aged, for his life had been full of suffering and poverty; and his venerable hands and skinny arms were heart-melting evidences of his ineffectual power to struggle much longer in the warfare of this world. In sooth, he was a chosen wheat-ear, ripened and ready for the garnels of salvation.

'I have brought, Master Mill,' said the seneschal, 'a discreet youth to see you, not out of a vain curiosity, for he sorrows with an exceeding grief that such an aged person should be brought into a state of so great jeopardy; but I hope, Master Mill, it will go well with you yet, and that ye'll repent and accept the boon that I hae heard was to be proffered.'

To these words the aged saint made no reply for the space of about a minute; at the end of which he raised his hands, and casting his eyes heavenward, exclaimed—

'I thank thee, O Lord, for the days of sore trial, and want, and hunger, and thirst, and destitution, which thou hast been pleased to bestow upon me, for by them have I, even now as I stand on the threshold of life, been enabled, through thy merciful heartenings, to set at nought the temptations wherewith I have been tempted.'

And, turning to the seneschal, he added mildly, 'But I am bound to you, Master Meldrum, in great obligations, for I know that, in the hope you have now expressed, there is the spirit of much charitableness, albeit you discern not the deadly malady that the sin of compliance would bring to my poor soul. No, sir, it would na be worth my while now, for world's gain, to read a recantation. And blessed be God, it's no in my power to yield, so deeply are the truths of his laws engraven upon the tablet of my heart.'

They then fell into more general discourse, and while they were speaking, a halberdier came into the room with a paper, whereby the prisoner was summoned to appear in the cathedral next day by ten o'clock, to answer divers matters of heresy and schism laid to his charge; and the man having delivered the summons, said to the seneschal, that he was ordered by Sir Andrew Oliphant, to bid him refrain from visiting the prisoner, and to retire to his own lodging.

The seneschal to this command said nothing, but rose, and my grandfather likewise rose. Fain would be have knelt down to beg the blessing of the martyr, but the worthy Master Meldrum signified to him with a look to come at once away; and when they were returned back into his chamber where the repast had been served, he told him, that there was a danger of falling under the evil thoughts of Oliphant, were he to be seen evidencing any thing like respect towards prisoners accused of the sin of heresy.

The next day was like a cried fair in St Andrews. All the country from ayont Cupar, and many reformed and godly persons, even from Dundee and Perth, were gathered into the city to hear the trial of Master Walter Mill. The streets were filled with horses and men with whips in their hands and spurs at their heels, and there was a great going to and fro among the multitude; but, saving in its numbers, the congregation of the people was in no other complexion either like a fair or a tryst. Every visage was darkened with doure thoughts; none spoke cheerfully aloud; but there was whispering and muttering, and ever and anon the auld men were seen wagging their heads in sorrow, while the young cried often 'Shame! shame!' and with vehement gestures clave the air with their right hands, grasping their whips and staffs with the vigour of indignation.

At last the big bell of the cathedral began to jow, at the doleful sound of which there was, for the space of two or three minutes, a silence and pause in the multitude, as if they had been struck with panic and consternation; for till then there was a hope among them that the persecutors would relent; but the din of the bell was as the signal of death and despair, and the people were soon awakened from their astonishment by the cry that 'the bishops are coming;' whereat there was a great rush towards the gates of the church, which was presently filled, leaving only a passage up the middle aisle.

In the quire a table was spread with a purple velvet cloth, and at the upper end, before the high place of the mass, was a stool of state for the Archbishop; on each side stood chairs for the Bishops of Murray, Brechin, and Caithness and his other suffragans, summoned to sit in judgment with him.

My grandfather, armed and wearing the Archbishop's

livery, was with those that guarded the way for the cruel
prelates, and by the pressure of the throng in convoying
them into their place, he was driven within the skreen of
the quire, and saw and heard all that passed.

When they had taken their seats, Master Mill was
brought before them from the prior's chamber, whither
he had been secretly conducted early in the morning, to
the end that his great age might not be seen of the people
to work on their compassion. But, notwithstanding the
forethought of this device, when he came in, his white
hair, and his saintly look, and his feeble tottering steps,
softened every heart; even the very legate of antichrist, the
Archbishop himself, my grandfather said, was evidently
moved, and for a season looked at the poor infirm old man
as he would have spared him, and a murmur of universal
commiseration ran through the church.

On being taken to the bottom of the table, and placed
fornent the Archbishop, Master Mill knelt down and
prayed for support, in a voice so firm, and clear, and
eloquent, that all present were surprised; for it rung to the
farthest corner of that great edifice, and smote the hearts
of his oppressors as with the dread of a menacing oracle.

Sir Andrew Oliphant, who acted as clerk and chancellor
on the occasion, began to fret as he heard him thus
strengthened of the Lord, and cried, peevishly—

'Sir Walter Mill, get up and answer, for you keep my
lords here too long.'

He, however, heeded not this command, but continued
undisturbed till he had finished his devotion, when he rose
and said—

'I am bound to obey God more than man, and I serve a
mightier Lord than yours. You call me Sir Walter, but I
am only Walter. Too long was I one of the Pope's knights:
but now say what you have to say.'

Oliphant was somewhat cowed by this bold reply, and he
bowed down, and turning over his papers, read a portion of
one of them to himself, and then raising his head, said—

'What thinkest thou of priests' marriage?'

The old man looked bravely towards the bishops, and
answered with an intrepid voice—

'I esteem marriage a blessed bond, ordained by God, approved by Christ, and made free to all sorts of men; but you abhor it, and in the meantime take other men's wives and daughters; you vow chastity, and keep it not.'

My grandfather at these words looked unawares towards the Archbishop, thinking of what he had seen in the lodging of Mistress Kilspinnie; and their eyes chancing to meet, his Grace turned his head suddenly away as if he had been rebuked.

Divers other questions were then put by Oliphant, touching the sacraments, the idolatry of the mass, and transubstantiation, with other points concerning bishops, and pilgrimages, and the worshipping of God in unconsecrated places; to all which Master Mill answered in so brave a manner, contrary to the papists, that even Oliphant himself often looked reproved and confounded. At last the choler of that sharp weapon of persecution began to rise, and he said to him sternly—

'If you will not recant, I will pronounce sentence against you.'

'I know,' replied Master Mill, with an apostolic constancy and fortitude, 'I know that I must die once; and therefore, as Christ said to Judas, What thou doest do quickly. You shall know that I will not recant the truth; for I am corn and not chaff. I will neither be blown away by the wind, nor burst with the flail, but will abide both.'

At these brave words a sough of admiration sounded through the church, but, instead of deterring the prelates from proceeding with their wicked purpose, it only served to harden their hearts and to rouse their anger; for when they had conferred a few minutes apart, Oliphant was ordered to condemn him to the fire, and to deliver him over to the temporal magistrates to see execution done.

No sooner was the sentence known, than a cry like a howl of wrath rose from all the people, and the provost of the town, who was present with the bailies, hastily quitted the church and fled, abhorring the task, and fearful it would be put upon him to see it done, he being also bailie of the archbishop's regalities.

When the sentence was pronounced, the session of

the court was adjourned, and the bishops, as they were guarded back to the castle, heard many a malison from the multitude, who were ravenous against them.

The aged martyr being led back to the prior's chamber, was, under cloud of night, taken to the castle; but my grandfather saw no more of him, nor of Master Meldrum the seneschal; for there was a great fear among the bishop's men that the multitude would rise and attempt a rescue; and my grandfather, not being inclined to go so far with his disguise as to fight against that cause, took occasion, in the dusk of the evening, to slip out of the castle, and to hide himself in the town, being resolved, after what he had witnessed, no longer to abide, even as a spy, in a service which his soul loathed.

All the night long there was a great commotion in the streets, and lights in many houses, and a sound of lamentation mingled with rage. The noise was as if some dreadful work was going on. There was no shouting, nor any sound of men united together, but a deep and hoarse murmur rose at times from the people, like the sound of the bandless waves of the sea when they are driven by the strong impulses of the tempest. The spirit of the times was indeed upon them, and it was manifest to my grandfather, that there wanted that night but the voice of a captain to bid them hurl their wrath and vengeance against the towers and strongholds of the oppressors.

At the dawn of day the garrison of the castle came forth, and on the spot where the martyrdom of Mr George Wishart had been accomplished, a stake was driven into the ground, and faggots and barrels of tar were placed around it, piled up almost as high as a man; in the middle, next to the stake, a place was left for the sufferer.

But when all things were prepared, no rope could be had – no one in all the town would give or sell a cord to help that sacrifice of iniquity, nor would any of the magistrates come forth to see the execution done, so it was thought for a time that the hungry cruelty of the persecutors would be disappointed of its banquet. One Somerville, however, who was officer of the Archbishop's guard, bethought himself, in this extremity, of the ropes wherewith his master's pavilion was fastened, and he went and took the same; and then his men brought forth the aged martyr, at the sight of whom the multitude set up a dreadful imprecation, the roar and growling groan of which was as if a thousand furious tigresses had been robbed of their young. Many of Somerville's halberdiers looked cowed, and their faces were aghast with terror; and some cried, compassionately, as they saw the blessed old man brought, with his hands tied behind him, to the stake, 'Recant, recant!'

The monks and friars of the different monasteries, who were all there assembled around, took up the word, and bitterly taunting him, cried likewise, 'Recant, recant and save thyself!' He, however, replied to them with an awful austerity—

'I marvel at your rage, ye hypocrites, who do so cruelly pursue the servants of God. As for me, I am now fourscore and two years old, and by course of nature cannot live long; but hundreds shall rise out of my ashes who shall scatter you, ye persecutors of God's people.'

Sir Andrew Oliphant, who was that day the busiest high priest of the horrible sacrifice, at these words pushed him forward into the midst of the faggots and fuel around the stake. But, nothing moved by this remorseless indignity, the martyr looked for a moment at the pile with a countenance full of cheerful resignation, and then requested permission to say a few words to the people.

'You have spoken too much,' cried Oliphant, 'and the bishops are exceedingly displeased with what you have said.'

But the multitude exclaimed, 'Let him be heard! let him speak what he pleases! – speak, and heed not Oliphant.' At which he looked towards them and said—

'Dear friends, the cause why I suffer this day is not for any crime laid to my charge, though I acknowledge myself a miserable sinner, but only for the defence of the truths of Jesus Christ, as set forth in the Old and New Testaments.'

He then began to pray, and while his eyes were shut, two of Somerville's men threw a cord with a running-loop round his body, and bound him to the stake. The fire was then kindled, and at the sight of the smoke the multitude uttered a shriek of anguish, and many ran away, unable to bear any longer the sight of that woful tragedy. Among others, my grandfather also ran, nor halted till he was come to a place under the rocks on the south side of the town, where he could see nothing before him but the lonely desert of the calm and soundless ocean.

CHAPTER SIX

Many a time did my grandfather, in his old age, when all things he spoke were but remembrances, try to tell what passed in his bosom while he was sitting alone, under those cliffy rocks, gazing on the silent and innocent sea, thinking of that dreadful work, more hideous than the horrors of winds and waves, with which blinded men, in the lusts of their idolatry, were then blackening the ethereal face of heaven; but he was ever unable to proceed for the struggles of his spirit and the gushing of his tears. Verily it was an awful thing to see that patriarchal man overcome by the recollections of his youth; and the manner in which he spoke of the papistical cruelties was as the pouring of the energy of a new life into the very soul, instigating thoughts and resolutions of an implacable enmity against those ruthless adversaries to the hopes and redemption of the world, insomuch that, while yet a child, I was often worked upon by what he said, and felt my young heart so kindled with the live coals of his godly enthusiasm, that he himself has stopped in the eloquence of his discourse, wondering at my fervour. Then he would lay his hand upon my head, and say, the Lord had not gifted me with such zeal without having a task in store for my riper years. His words of prophecy, as shall hereafter appear, have greatly and wonderfully come to pass. But it is meet that for a season I should rehearse what ensued to him, for his story is full of solemnities and strange accidents.

Having rested some time on the sea-shore, he rose and walked along the toilsome shingle, scarcely noting which way he went, – his thoughts being busy with the martyrdom he had witnessed, flushing one moment with a glorious indignation, and fainting the next with despondent reflections on his own friendless state. For he looked upon himself as adrift on the tides of the world, believing that his patron, the Earl of Glencairn, would to a surety condemn his lack of fortitude in not enduring the servitude of the Archbishop, after having been in so miraculous a manner accepted into it, even as if Providence had made him a special instrument to achieve the discoveries which the Lords of the Congregation had then so much at heart. And while he was walking along in this fluctuating mood, he came suddenly upon a man who was sitting, as he had so shortly before been himself, sad and solitary, gazing on the sea. The stranger, on hearing him approach, rose hastily, and was moving quickly away; but my grandfather called to him to stop and not to be afraid, for he would harm no one.

'I thought,' said the melancholy man, 'that all his Grace's retainers were at the execution of the heretic.'

There was something in the way in which he uttered the latter clause of the sentence, that seemed to my grandfather as if he would have made use of better and fitter words, and therefore, to encourage him into confidence, he replied—

'I belong not to his Grace.'

'How is it then that you wear his livery, and that I saw you, with Sir David Hamilton, enter the garden of that misguided woman?'

He could proceed no farther, for his heart swelled, and his utterance was for a while stifled, he being no other than the misfortunate Bailie of Crail, whose light wife had sunk into the depravity of the Archbishop's lemane. She had been beguiled away from him and her five babies, their children, by the temptations of a Dominican, who, by habit and repute, was pandarus to his Grace, and the poor man had come to try if it was possible to wile her back.

My grandfather was melted with sorrow to see his great affection for the unworthy concubine, calling to mind the scene of her harlotry and wanton glances – and he reasoned with him on the great folly of vexing his spirit for a woman so far lost to all shame and given over to iniquity. But still the good man of Crail would not be persuaded, but used many earnest entreaties that my grandfather would assist him to see his wife, in order that he might remonstrate with her on the eternal perils in which she had placed her precious soul.

My grandfather, though much moved by the importunity of that weak honest man, nevertheless withstood his entreaties, telling him that he was minded to depart forthwith from St Andrews and make the best of his way back to Edinburgh, and so could embark in no undertaking whatever.

Discoursing on that subject in this manner, they strayed into the fields, and being wrapt up in their conversation, they heeded not which way they went, till turning suddenly round the corner of an orchard, they saw the castle full before them, about half a mile off, and a dim white vapour mounting at times from the spot, still surrounded by many spectators, where the fires of martyrdom had burnt so fiercely. Shuddering and filled with dread, my grandfather turned away, and seeing several countrymen passing, he inquired if all was over.

'Yes,' said they, 'and the soldiers are slockening the ashes; but a' the waters of the ocean-sea will never quench in Scotland the flame that was kindled yonder this day.'

The which words they said with a proud look, thinking my grandfather, by his arms and gabardine, belonged to the Archbishop's household, – but the words were as manna to his religious soul, and he gave inward praise and thanks that the self-same tragical mean which had been devised to terrify the Reformers, was thus, through the mysterious wisdom of Providence, made more emboldening than courageous wine to fortify their hearts for the great work that was before them.

Nothing, however, farther passed; but, changing the course of their walk, my grandfather and the sorrowful Master Kilspinnie, for so the poor man of Crail was called, went back, and entering the bow at the Shoegate, passed on towards a vintner's that dwelt opposite to the convent of the Blackfriars; for the day was by this time far advanced, and they both felt themselves in need of some refreshment.

While they were sitting together in the vintner's apartment, a stripling came several times into the room, and looked hard at my grandfather, and then went away without speaking. This was divers times repeated, and at last it was so remarkable that even Master Kilspinnie took notice of him, observing, that he seemed as if he had something very particular to communicate if an opportunity served, offering at the same time to withdraw, to leave the room clear for the youth to tell his errand.

My grandfather's curiosity was, by this strange and new adventure to him, so awakened, that he thought what his companion proposed a discreet thing; so the honest bailie of Crail withdrew himself, and going into the street, left my grandfather alone.

No sooner was he gone out of the house than the stripling, who had been sorning about the door, again came in, and coming close up to my grandfather's ear, said with a significance not to be misconstrued, that if he would follow him he would take him to free quarters, where he would be more kindly entertained.

My grandfather, though naturally of a quiet temperament, was nevertheless a bold and brave youth, and there was something in the mystery of this message, for such he rightly deemed it, that made him fain to see the end thereof. So he called in the vintner's wife and paid her the lawin', telling her to say to the friend who had been with him, when he came back, that he would soon return.

The vintner's wife was a buxom and jolly dame, and before taking up the money, she gave a pawkie look at the stripling, and as my grandfather and he were going out at the door, she hit the gilly a bilf on the back, saying it was a ne'er-do-weel trade he had ta'en up, and that he was na blate to wile awa' her customers, – crying after him, 'I redde ye warn your madam, that gin she sends you here again, I'll may be let his Grace ken that her cauldron needs clouting.' However, the graceless gilly but laughed at the vintner's wife, winking as he patted the side of his nose with his fore-finger, which testified that he held her vows of vengeance in very little reverence; and then he went on, my grandfather following.

They walked up the street till they came to the priory yett, when, turning down a wynd to the left, he led my grandfather along between two dykes, till they were come to a house that stood by itself within a fair garden. But instead of going to the door in an honest manner, he bade him stop, and going forward he whistled shrilly, and then flung three stones against a butt, that was standing at the corner of the house on a gauntrees to kep rain water from the spouting image of a stone puddock that vomited what was gathered from the roof in the rones, – and soon after an upper casement was opened, and a damsel looked forth; she however said nothing to the stripling, but she made certain signs which he understood, and then she drew in her head, shutting the casement softly, and he came back to my grandfather, to whom he said it was not commodious at that time for him to be received into the house, but if he would come back in the dark, at eight o'clock, all things would be ready for his reception.

To this suggestion my grandfather made no scruple to assent, but promised to be there; and he bargained with the lad to come for him, giving him at the same time three placks for a largess. He then returned to the vintner's, where he found the Crail man sitting waiting for him; – and the vintner's wife, when she saw him so soon back, jeered him, and would fain have been jocose, which he often after thought a woful immorality, considering the dreadful martyrdom of a godly man that had been done that day in the town; but at the time he was not so over straitlaced as to take offence at what she said; indeed, as he used to say, sins were not so heinous in those papistical days as they afterwards became, when men lost faith in penance, and found out the perils of purchased pardons.

My grandfather having, as I have told, a compassion for the silly affection wherewith the honest man of Crail still regarded his wanton wife, told him the circumstantials of his adventure with the stripling; without, however, letting wot he had discovered that the invitation was from her; the which was the case, for the damsel who looked out at the window was no other than the giglet he had seen in her lodging when he went thither with Sir David Hamilton, – and he proposed to the disconsolate husband that he should be his friend in the adventure; meaning thereby to convince the unhappy man, by the evidence of his own eyes and ears, that her concubinage with the Antichrist was a blessed riddance to him and his family.

At first Master Kilspinnie had no zest for any such frolic, for so it seemed to him, and he began to think my grandfather's horror at the martyrdom of the aged saint but a long-fac't hypocrisy; nevertheless he was wrought upon to consent; and they sat plotting and contriving in what manner they should act their several parts, my grandfather pretending great fear and apprehension at the thoughts of himself, a stranger, going alone into the traps of a house where there were sic forerunners of shame and signs of danger. At last he proposed that they should go together and spy about the precincts of the place, and try to discover if there was no other entrance or outgate to the house than the way by which the stripling conducted him, though well he remembered the sallyport, where the fat friar kept watch, eating the pasty.

Accordingly they went forth from the vintner's, and my grandfather, as if he knew not the way, led his companion round between the priory and the sea, till they came near the aforesaid sallyport, when, mounting upon a stone, he affected to discover that the house of the madam stood in the garden within, and that the sallyport could be no less than a back yett thereto.

While they were speaking concerning the same, my grandfather observed the wicket open in the gate, and guessing therefrom that it was one spying to forewarn somebody within who wanted to come out unremarked, he made a sign to his companion, and they both threw themselves flat on the ground, and hirsled down the rocks to conceal themselves. Presently the gate was opened, and then out came the fat friar, and looked east and west, holding the door in his hand; and anon out came his Grace the Antichrist, hirpling with a staff in his hand, for he was lame with that monkish malady called the gout. The friar then drew the yett to, and walked on towards the castle, with his Grace leaning on his arm. In the meantime the poor man of Crail was grinding the teeth of his rage at the sight of the cause of his sorrow, and my grandfather had a sore struggle to keep him down, and prevent him from running wud and furious at the two sacerdotal reprobates, for no lightlier could they be called.

Thus, without any disclosure on my grandfather's part, did Master Kilspinnie come to jealouse that the lemane who had trysted him was no other than his own faithless wife, and he smote his forehead and wept bitterly, to think how she was become so dreadless in sin. But he vowed to put her to shame; so it was covenanted between them, that in the dusk of the evening the afflicted husband should post himself near to where they then stood, and that when my grandfather was admitted by the other entrance to the house, he should devise some reason for walking forth into the garden, and while there admit Master Kilspinnie.

Accordingly, betimes my grandfather was ready, and the stripling, as had been bargained, came for him to the vintner's, and conducted him to the house, where, after giving the signals before enumerated, the damsel came to the door and gave him admittance, leading him straight to the inner chamber before described, where her mistress was sitting in a languishing posture, with the table spread for a banquet.

She embraced my grandfather with many fond protestations, and filled him a cup of hot malvesie, while her handmaid brought in divers savoury dishes; but he, though a valiant young man, was not at his ease, and he thought of the poor husband and the five babies that the adultress had left for the foul love of the papist high-priest, and it was a chaste spell and a restraining grace. Still he partook a little of the rich repast which had been prepared, and feigned so long a false pleasance, that he almost became pleased in reality. The dame, however, was herself at times fearful, and seemed to listen if there was any knocking at the door, telling my grandfather that his Grace was to be back after he had supped at the castle. 'I thought,' said she, 'to have had you here when he was at the burning of the heretic, but my gilly could not find you among the troopers till it was owre late; for when he brought you my Lord had come to solace himself after the execution. But I was so nettled to be so balked, that I acted myself into an anger till I got him away, not, however, without a threat of being troubled with him again at night.'

Scarcely had Madam said this, when my grandfather started up and feigned to be in great terror, begging her to let him hide himself in the garden till his Grace was come and gone. To this, with all her blandishments, the guilty woman made many obstacles; but he was fortified of the Lord with the thoughts of her injured children, and would not be entreated, but insisted on scogging himself in the garden till the Archbishop was sent away, the hour of his coming being then near at hand. Seeing him thus peremptory, Madam Kilspinnie was obligated to conform; so he was permitted to go into the garden, and no sooner was he there than he went to the sallyport and admitted her husband; – and well it was that he had been so steadfast in his purpose; for scarcely were they moved from the yett into a honeysuckle bower hard by, when they heard it again open, and in came his Grace with his corpulent pandarus, who took his seat on the bench before spoken of, to watch, while his master went into the house.

The good Bailie of Crail breathed thickly, and he took my grandfather by the hand, his whole frame trembling with a passion of grief and rage. In the lapse of some four or five minutes, the giglet damsel came out of the house, and by the glimpse of a light from a window as she passed, they saw she had a tankard of smoking drink in her hand, with which she went to the friar; and my grandfather and his companion taking advantage of this, slipped out of their hiding-place and stole softly into the house, and reached the outer chamber, that was parted from Madam's banquet bower by the arras partition. There they stopped to listen, and heard her complaining in a most dolorous manner of great heart-sickness, ever and anon begging the deluded prelate Hamilton to taste the feast she had prepared for him, in the hope of being able to share it with him and the caresses of his sweet love. To which his Grace as often replied, with great condolence and sympathy, how very grieved he was to find her in that sad and sore estate, with many other fond cajoleries, most odious to my grandfather to hear from a man so far advanced in years, and who, by reason of the reverence of his office, ought to have had his tongue schooled to terms of piety and temperance.

The poor husband meanwhile said nothing, but my grandfather heard his heart panting audibly, and three or four times he was obligated to brush away his hand, for, having no arms himself, the bailie clutched at the hilt of his sword, and would have drawn it from the scabbard.

The Antichrist seeing his lemane in such great malady as she so well feigned, he at last, to her very earnest supplications, consented to leave her that night, and kissed her as he came away; but her husband broke in upon them with the rage of a hungry lion, and seizing his Grace by the cuff of the neck, swung him away from her with such vehemence, that he fell into the corner of the room like a sack of duds. As for Madam, she uttered a wild cry, and threw herself back on the couch where she was sitting, and seemed as if she had swooned, having no other device so ready to avoid the upbraidings and just reproaches of her spouse. But she was soon roused from that fraudulent dwam by my grandfather, who, seizing a flagon of wine, dashed it upon her face.

Mrs Kilspinnie uttered a frightful screech, and, starting up, attempted to run out of the room, but her husband caught her by the arm, and my grandfather was empowered, by a signal grant of great presence of mind, to think that the noise might cause alarm, whereupon he sprung instanter to the door that led into the garden, just as the damsel was coming up, and the fat friar hobbling as fast as he could behind her, – and he had but time to say to her, as it was with an inspiration, to keep all quiet in the garden, and he would make his escape by the other door. She, on hearing this, ran back to stop the pandarus, and my grandfather closed and bolted fast that back-door, going forthwith to the one by which he had been himself admitted, and which, having opened wide to the wall, he returned to the scene of commotion.

In the meantime, the prelatic dragon, that was so ravished from the woman, had hastily risen upon his legs, and, red with a dreadful wrath, raged as if he would have devoured her husband. In sooth, to do his Grace justice, he lacked not the spirit of a courageous gentleman, and he could not, my grandfather often said, have borne himself more proudly and valiantly had he been a belted knight, bred in camps and fields of war, so that a discreet retreat and evasion of the house was the best course they could take. But Master Kilspinnie fain would have continued his biting taunts to the mistress, who was enacting a most tragical extravagance of affliction and terror; my grandfather, however, suddenly cut him short, crying, 'Come, come, no more of this; an alarm is given, and we must save ourselves.' With that he seized him firmly by the arm, and in a manner harled him out of the house, and into the lane between the dykes, along which they ran with nimble heels. On reaching the Shoegate they slackened their speed, still, however, walking as fast as they could till they came near the port, when they again drew in the bridle of their haste, going through among the guards that were loitering around the door of the wardroom, and passed out into the fields as if they had been indifferent persons.

On escaping the gate, they fell in with divers persons going along the road, who, by their discourse, were returning home to Cupar, and they walked leisurely with them till they came to a cross-road, where my grandfather, giving Master Kilspinnie a nodge, turned down the one that went to the left, followed by him, and it happened to be the road to Dysart and Crail.

'This will ne'er do,' said Master Kilspinnie, 'they will pursue us this gait.'

Upon hearing this reasonable apprehension, my grandfather stopped and conferred with himself, and received on that spot a blessed experience and foretaste of the protection wherewith, to a great age, he was all his days protected. For it was in a manner revealed to him, that he should throw away the garbardine and sword which he had received in the castle, and thereby appear in his simple craftsman's garb, and that they should turn back and cross the Cupar road, and go along the other, which led to the Dundee water-side ferry. This he told to his fearful companion, and likewise, that as often as they fell in with or heard any body coming up, the bailie should hasten on before, or den himself among the brechans by the road-side, to the end that it might appear they were not two persons in company together.

But they had not long crossed the Cupar road, and travelled the one leading to the ferry, when they heard the whirlwind sound of horsemen coming after them, at which the honest man of Crail darted aside, and lay flat on his grouff ayont a bramble bush, while my grandfather began to lilt as blithely as he could, 'The Bonny Lass of Livingston,' and the spring was ever after to him as a hymn of thanksgiving; but the words he then sang was an auld ranting godless and graceless ditty of the grooms and serving-men that sorned about his father's smiddy, – and the closer that the horsemen came he was strengthened to sing the louder and the clearer.

'Saw ye twa fellows ganging this gait?' cried the foremost of the pursuers, pulling up.

'What like were they?' said my grandfather in a simple manner.

'Ane of them was o' his Grace's guard,' replied the man, 'but the other, curse tak me gin I ken what he was like, but he's the bailie or provost of a burrough's town, and should by rights hae a big belly.'

To this my grandfather answered briskly, 'Nae sic twa hae past me; but as I was coming along whistling, thinking o' naething, twa sturdy loons, ane o' them no unlike the hempies of the castle, ran skirring along, and I hae a thought that they took the road to Crail or Dysart.'

'That was my thought too,' cried the horseman, as he turned his beast, and the rest that were with him doing the same, bidding my grandfather good-night, away they scampered back; by which a blessed deliverance was there wrought to him and his companion, on that spot, in that night.

As soon as the horsemen had gone by, Bailie Kilspinnie came from his hiding-place, and both he and my grandfather proved that no bird-lime was on their feet till they got to the ferry-house at the water-side, where they found two boats taking passengers on board, one for Dundee and the other for Perth. Here my grandfather's great gift of foreknowledge was again proven, for he proposed that they should bargain with the skipper of the Dundee boat to take them to that town, and pay him like the other passengers at once, in an open manner; but that, as the night was cloudy and dark, they should go cannily aboard the boat for Perth, as it were in mistake, and feign not to discover their error till they were far up the river, when they should proceed to the town, letting wot, that by the return of the tide they would go in the morning by the Perth boat to Dundee, with which Master Kilspinnie was well acquainted, he having had many times, in the way of his traffic as a plaiding merchant, cause to use the same, and thereby knew it went twice a-week, and that the morrow was one of the days: –

all this they were enabled to do with such fortitude and decorum, that no one aboard the Perth boat could have divined that they were not honest men, in great trouble of mind at discovering they had come into the wrong boat.

But nothing showed more that Providence had a hand in all this than what ensued, for all the passengers in the boat had been at St Andrews to hear the trial and see the martyrdom, and they were sharp and vehement not only in their condemnation of the mitred Antichrist, but grieved with a sincere sorrow, that none of the nobles of Scotland would stand forth in their ancient bravery, to resist and overthrow a race of oppressors more grievous than the Southrons that trode on the neck of their fathers in the hero-stirring times of the Wallace wight and King Robert the Bruce. – Truly there was a spirit of unison and indignation in the company on board that boat, every one thirsting with a holy ardour to avenge the cruelties of which the papistical priesthood were daily growing more and more crouse in the perpetration; – and they made the shores ring with the olden song of

> 'O for my ain king, quo' gude Wallace,
> The rightfu' king of fair Scotlan';—
> Between me and my sovereign dear
> I think I see some ill seed sawn.'

It was the grey of the morning before they reached Perth; and as soon as they were put on the land, the bailie took my grandfather with him to the house of one Sawners Ruthven, a blanket-weaver, with whom he had dealings, a staid and discreet man, who, when he had supplied them with breakfast, exhorted them not to tarry in the town, then a place that had fallen under the suspicion of the clergy, the lordly monks of Scoone taking great power and authority, in despite of the magistrates, against all that fell under their evil thoughts anent heresy. And he counselled them not to proceed, as my grandfather had proposed, straight on to Edinburgh by the Queensferry, but to hasten up the country to Crieff, and thence take the road to Stirling. In this there was much prudence; but Bailie Kilspinnie was in sore tribulation on account of his children, whom he had left at his home in Crail, fearing that the talons of Antichrist would lay hold of them, and keep them as hostages till he was given up to suffer for what he had done, none doubting that Baal, for so he nicknamed the prelatic Hamilton, would impute to him the unpardonable sin of heresy and schism, and leave no stone unturned to bring him to the stake.

But Sawners Ruthven comforted him with the assurance that his Grace would not venture to act in that manner, for it was known how Mistress Kilspinnie then lived at St Andrews as his concubine. Nevertheless, the poor man was in sore affliction; and, as he and my grandfather travelled towards Crieff, many a bitter prayer did his vexed spirit pour forth in its grief, that the right arm of the Lord might soon be manifested against the Roman locust, that consumed the land, and made its corruption naught in the nostrils of Heaven.

Thus was it manifest, that there was much of the ire of a selfish revenge mixt up with the rage which was at that time kindled in so unquenchable a manner against the Beast and its worshippers; for in the history of the honest man of Crail there was a great similitude to other foul and worse things which the Roman idolaters seemed to regard among their pestiferous immunities, and counted themselves free to do without dread of any earthly retribution.

My grandfather and his companion hastened on in their journey; but instead of going to Stirling they crossed the river at Alloa, and so passed by the water-side way to Edinburgh, where, on entering the West-port, they separated. The bailie, who was a fearful man, and in constant dread and terror of being burned as a heretic for having broke in upon the dalliance of his incontinent wife and the carnal-minded primate of St Andrews, went to a cousin of his own, a dealer in serge and temming in the Lawn-market, with whom he concealed himself for some weeks; but my grandfather proceeded straight towards the lodging of the Earl of Glencairn, to recount to his lordship the whole passages of what he had been concerned in, from the night that he departed from his presence.

It was by this time the mirkest of the gloaming, for they had purposely tarried on their journey that they might enter Edinburgh at dusk. The shops of the traders were shut, for in those days there was such a resort of sorners and lawless men among the trains of the nobles and gentry, that it was not safe for honest merchants to keep their shops open after nightfall. Nevertheless the streets were not darkened, for there were then many begging-boxes, with images of the saints, and cruisies burning afore them, in divers parts of the High-street and corners of the wynds, insomuch that it was easy, as I have heard my grandfather tell, to see and know any one passing in the light thereof. And indeed what befell himself was proof of it; for as he was coming through St Giles' kirk-yard, which is now the Parliament-close, and through which at that time there was a style and path for passengers, a young man, whom he had observed following him, came close up just as he reached a begging image of the Virgin Mary with its lamp, that stood on a pillar at the south-east corner of the cathedral, and touching him on the left shoulder at that spot, made him look round in such a manner that the light of the Virgin's lamp fell full on his face.

'Dinna be frighted,' said the stranger, 'I ken you, and I'm in Lord Glencairn's service; but follow me and say nothing.'

My grandfather was not a little startled by this salutation; he however made no observe, but replied, 'Go on then.'

So the stranger went forward, and after various turnings and windings, led him down into the Cowgate, and up a close on the south side thereof, and then to a dark timber stair, that was so frail and creaking, and narrow, that his guide bade him haul himself up with the help of a rope that hung down dangling for that purpose.

When they had raised themselves to the stair-head, the stranger opened a door, and they went together into a small and lonesome chamber, in the chimla-nook of which an old iron cruisie was burning with a winking and wizard light.

'I hae brought you here,' said his conductor, 'for secrecy; for my Lord disna want that ye should be seen about his lodging. I'm ane of three that hae been lang seeking you; and, as a token that ye're no deceived, I was bade to tell you, that before parting from my Lord he gi'ed you two pieces of gold out of his coffer in the chamber where he supped.'

My grandfather thought this very like a proof that he had been so informed by the Earl himself; but, happening to remark that he sat with his back to the light, and kept his face hidden in the shadow of the darkness, Providence put it into his head to jealouse that he might nevertheless be a spy, one perhaps that had been trusted in like manner as he had himself been trusted, and who had afterwards sold himself to the perdition of the adversaries' cause; he was accordingly on his guard; but replied with seeming frankness, that it was very true he had received two pieces of gold from the Earl at his departure.

'Then,' said the young man, 'by that token ye may know that I am in the private service of the Earl, who, for reasons best known to himsel', hath willed that you should tell me, that I may report the same secretly to him, what espionage you have made.'

My grandfather was perplexed by this speech, but distrust having crept into his thoughts, instead of replying with a full recital of all his adventures, he briefly said, that he had indeed effected nothing, for his soul was sickened by the woeful martyrdom of the godly Master Mill to so great a disease that he could not endure to abide in St Andrews, and therefore he had come back.

'But you have been long on the way – how is that? – it is now many days since the burning,' replied the stranger.

'You say truly,' was my grandfather's answer, 'for I came round by Perth; but I tarried at no place longer than was needful to repair and refresh nature.'

'Perth was a wide bout-gait to take frae St Andrews to come to Edinburgh; I marvel how ye went so far astray,' said the young man curiously.

'In sooth it was; but being sorely demented with the tragical end of the godly old man,' replied my grandfather, 'and seeing that I could do the Earl no manner of service, I wist not well what course to take; so, after meickle tribulation of thought, and great uncertainty of purpose, I e'en resolved to come hither.'

Little more passed: the young man rose and said to my grandfather, he feared the Earl would be so little content with him, that he had better not go near him, but seek some other master. And when they had descended the stair, and were come into the street, he advised him to go to the house of a certain Widow Rippet, that let dry lodgings in the Grass-market, and roost there for that night. The which my grandfather in a manner signified he would do, and so they parted.

The stranger at first walked soberly away; but he had not gone many paces when he suddenly turned into a close leading up to the High-street, and my grandfather heard the pattering of his feet running as swiftly as possible, which confirmed to him what he suspected; and so, instead of going towards the Widow Rippet's house, he turned back and went straight on to St Mary's Wynd, where the Earl's lodging was, and knocking at the yett, was speedily admitted, and conducted instanter to my Lord's presence, whom he found alone, reading many papers which lay on a table before him.

'Gilhaize,' said the Earl, 'how is this? why have you come back? and wherefore is it that I have heard no tidings from you?'

Whereupon my grandfather recounted to him all the circumstantials which I have rehearsed, from the hour of his departure from Edinburgh up till the very time when he then stood in his master's presence. The Earl made no inroad on his narrative while he was telling it, but his countenance often changed, and he was much moved at different passages – sometimes with sorrow and sometimes with anger; and he laughed vehemently at the mishap which had befallen the grand adversary of the Congregation and his concubine. The adventure, however, with the unknown varlet in the street appeared to make his Lordship very thoughtful, and no less than thrice did he question my grandfather, if he had indeed given but those barren answers which I have already recited; to all which he received the most solemn asseverations, that no more was said. His Lordship then sat some time cogitating, with his hands resting on his thighs, his brows bent, and his lips pursed as with sharp thought. At last he said—

'Gilhaize, you have done better in this than I ought to have expected of one so young and unpractised. The favour you won with Sir David Hamilton was no more than I thought your looks and manners would beget. But you are not only well-favoured but well-fortuned; and had you not found yourself worthily bound to your duty, I doubt not you might have prospered in the Archbishop's household. The affair with Madam Kilspinnie was a thing I reckoned not of; yet therein you have proved yourself not only a very Joseph, but so ripe in wit beyond your years, that your merits deserve more commendation than I can afford to give, for I have not sufficient to bestow on the singular prudence and discernment wherewith you have parried the treacherous thrusts of that Judas Iscariot, Winterton, for so I doubt not is the traitor who waylaid you. He was once in my service, and is now in the Queen Regent's. In sending off my men on errands similar to yours, I was wont to give them two pieces of gold, and this the false loon has gathered to be a custom, from others as well as by his own knowledge, and he has made it the key to open the breasts of my servants. To know this, however, is a great discovery. But, Gilhaize, not to waste words, you have your master's confidence. Go therefore, I pray you, with all speed to the Widow Rippet's, and do as Winterton bade you, and as chance may require. In the morning come again hither; for I have this night many weighty affairs, and you have shown yourself possessed of a discerning spirit, that may, in these times of peril and perjury, help the great cause of all good Scotchmen.'

In saying these most acceptable words, he clapped my grandfather on the shoulder, and encouraged him to be as true-hearted as he was sharp-witted, and he could not fail to earn both treasure and trusts. So my grandfather left him, and went to the Widow Rippet's in the Grass-market; and around her kitchen fire he found some four or five discarded knaves that were bargaining with her for beds, or for leave to sleep by the hearth. And he had not been long seated among them when his heart was grieved with pain to see Winterton come in, and behind him the two simple lads of Lithgow that had left their homes with him, whom, it appeared, the varlet had seduced from the Earl of Glencairn's service, and inveigled into the Earl of Seaton's, a rampant papist, by the same wiles wherewith he thought he had likewise made a conquest of my grandfather, whom they had all come together to see; for the two Lithgow lads, like reynard the fox when he had lost his tail, were eager that he too should make himself like them. He feigned, however, great weariness, and indeed his heart was heavy to see such skill of wickedness in so young a man as he saw in Winterton. So, after partaking with them of some spiced ale, which Winterton brought from the Salutation tavern opposite the gallows-stone, he declared himself overcome with sleep, and per force thereof obligated to go to bed. But when they were gone, and he had retired to his sorry couch, no sleep came to his eyelids, but only hot and salt tears; for he thought that he had been in a measure concerned in bringing away the two thoughtless lads from their homes, and he saw that they were not tempered to resist the temptations of the world, but would soon fall away from their religious integrity, and become lewd and godless roisters, like the wuddy worthies that paid half price for leave to sleep on the widow's hearth.

At the first blink of the grey eye of the morning my grandfather rose, and, quitting the house of the Widow Rippet, went straight to the Earl's lodgings and was admitted. The porter at the door told him, that their master having been up all night had but just retired to bed; but, while they were speaking, the Earl's page, who slept in the antechamber, called from the stair-head to inquire who it was that had come so early; and being informed thereof, he went into his master, and afterwards came again and desired my grandfather to walk up, and conducted him to his Lordship, whom he found on his couch, but not undressed, and who said to him, on his entering, when the page had retired—

'I am glad, Gilhaize, that you have come thus early, for I want a trusty man to go forthwith into the west country. What I wish you to do cannot be written, but you will take this ring;' and he took one from the little finger of his right hand, on the gem of which his cipher was graven, and gave it to my grandfather. 'On showing it to Lord Boyd, whom you will find at the Dean Castle, near Kilmarnock, he will thereby know that you are specially trusted of me. The message whereof you are the bearer is to this effect, – That the Lords of the Congregation have, by their friends in many places, received strong exhortations to step forward and oppose the headlong fury of the churchmen; and that they have in consequence deemed it necessary to lose no time in ascertaining what the strength of the Reformed may be, and to procure declarations for mutual defence from all who are joined in professing the true religion of Christ. Should he see meet to employ you in this matter, you will obey his orders and instructions whatsoever they may be.'

The Earl then put his hand aneath his pillow, and drew out a small leathern purse, which he gave to my grandfather, who, in the doing of this, observed that he had several other similar purses ready under his head. In taking it my grandfather was proceeding to tell him what he had observed at the Widow Rippet's, but his Lordship interrupted him, saying—

'Such things are of no issue now, and your present duty is in a higher road; therefore make haste, and God be with you.'

With these words his Lordship turned himself on his couch, and composed himself to sleep; which my grandfather, after looking on for about a minute or so, observing, came away; and having borrowed a frock and a trot-cozey for the journey from one of the grooms of the hall, he went straight to Kenneth Shelty's, a noted horse-setter in those days, who lived at the West-port, and bargained with him for the hire of a beast to Glasgow, though Glasgow was not then the nearest road to Kilmarnock; but he thought it prudent to go that way, in case any of the papistical emissaries should track his course.

There was, however, a little oversight in this, which did not come to mind till he was some miles on the road, and that was, the obligation it put him under of passing through Lithgow, where he was so well known, and where all his kith and kin lived; there being then no immediate route from Edinburgh to Glasgow but by Lithgow. And he debated with himself for a space of time, whether he ought to proceed, or turn back and go the other way, and his mind was sorely troubled with doubts and difficulties. At last he considered, that it was never deemed wise or fortunate to turn back in any undertaking, and besides, having for the service of the Saviour left his father's house and renounced his parents, like a bird that taketh wing and knoweth the nest where it was bred no more – he knit up his ravelled thoughts into resolution, and, clapping spurs to his horse, rode bravely on.

But when he beheld the towers of the palace, and the steeples of his native town, rising before him, many remembrances came rushing to his heart, and all the

vexations he had suffered there were lost in the sunny
recollections of the morning of life, when every one was
kind, and the eyes of his parents looked on him with the
brightness of delight, in so much, that his soul yearned
within him, and his cheeks were wetted with fast-flowing
tears. Nevertheless, he overcame this thaw of his fortitude,
and went forward in the strength of the Lord, determined
to swerve not in his duty to the Earl of Glencairn, nor in
his holier fealty to a far greater master. But the softness
that he felt in his nature, made him gird himself with a
firm purpose to ride through the town without stopping.
Scarcely, however, had he entered the port, when his
horse stumbled and lost a shoe, by which he was not only
constrained to stop, but to take him to his father's smiddy,
which was in sight when the mischance happened.

On going to the door, he found, as was commonly the
case, a number of grooms and flunkies of the courtiers, with
certain friars, holding vehement discourse concerning the
tidings of the time, the burden of which was, the burning
of the aged Master Mill, a thing that even the monks durst
not, for humanity, venture very strenuously to defend. His
father was not then within; but one of the prentice lads,
seeing who it was that had come with a horse to be shod,
ran to tell him; and at the sight of my grandfather, the
friars suspended their controversies with the serving-men,
and gathered round him with many questions. He replied,
however, to them all with few words, bidding the foreman
to make haste and shoe his horse, hoping that he might
thereby be off and away before his father came.

But, while the man was throng with the horse's foot,
both father and mother came rushing in, and his mother
was weeping bitterly, and wringing her hands, chiding him,
as if he had sold himself to the Evil One, and beseeching
him to stop and repent. His father, however, said little, but
inquired how he had been, what he was doing, and where
he was going; and sent the prentice lad to bring a stoup of
spiced ale from a public hard by, in which he pledged him,
kindly hoping he would do well for himself and he would
do well for his parents. The which fatherliness touched my
grandfather more to the quick than all the loud lament

and reproaches of his mother; and he replied, that he had entered into the service of a nobleman, and was then riding on his master's business to Glasgow; but he mentioned no name, nor did his father inquire. His mother, however, burst out into clamorous revilings, declaring her dread, that it was some of the apostate heretics; and, giving vent to her passion, was as one in a frenzy, or possessed of a devil. The very friars were confounded at her distraction, and tried to sooth her and remove her forth the smiddy, which only made her more wild, so that all present compassionated my grandfather, who sat silent and made no answer, wearying till his horse was ready.

But greatly afflicted as he was by this trial, it was nothing to what ensued, when, after having mounted and shaken his father by the hand, he galloped away to the West-port. There, on the outside, he was met by two women and an old man, parents of the lads whom he had taken with him to Edinburgh. Having heard he was at his father's smiddy, instead of going thither, they had come to that place, in order that they might speak with him more apart, and free from molestation, concerning their sons.

One of the women was a poor widow, and she had no other child, nor the hope of any other bread-winner for her old age. She, however, said nothing, but stood with the corner of her apron at her eyes, sobbing very afflictedly, while her friends, on seeing my grandfather coming out of the port, stepped forward, and the old man claught the horse by the bridle, and said gravely—

'Ye maun stop and satisfy three sorrowful parents! What hae ye done with your twa thoughtless companions?'

My grandfather's heart was as if it would have perished in his bosom; for the company he had seen the lads with, and the talk they had held, and above all their recklessness of principle, came upon him like a withering flash of fire. He, however, replied soberly, that he had seen them both the night before, and that they were well in health, and jocund in spirit.

The mother that was standing near her husband was blithe to hear this, and reminded her gudeman, how she had often said, that when they did hear tidings of their son her words would be found true, for he had ever been all his days a brisk and a valiant bairn.

But the helpless widow was not content, and she came forward, drying her tears, saying, 'And what is my poor fatherless do-na-gude about? I'm fearfu, fearfu, to be particular; for, though he was aye kind-hearted to me, he was easily wised, and I doubt, I doubt, he'll prove a blasting or a blessing, according to the hands he fa's among.'

'I hope and pray,' said my grandfather, 'that he'll be protected from scaith, and live to be a comfort to all his friends.' And, so saying, he disengaged his bridle with a gentle violence from the old man's hold, telling them, he could not afford to stop, being timed to reach Glasgow that night. So he pricked the horse with his rowals, and shot away; but his heart, all the remainder of his day's journey, was as if it had been pierced with many barbed arrows, and the sad voice of the poor anxious widow rung in his ears like the sound of some doleful knell.

Saving this affair at Lithgow, nothing befell him till he came to the gates of Glasgow; by which time it was dark, and the ward and watch set, and they questioned him very sharply before giving him admission. For the Queen Regent was then sojourning in the castle, and her fears and cares were greatly quickened at that time, by rumours from all parts of the kingdom, concerning the murder, as it was called, of Master Mill. On this account the French guards, which she had with her, were instructed to be jealous of all untimeous travellers, and they being joined with a ward of burgers, but using only their own tongue, caused no small molestation to every Scotsman that sought admission after the sun was set; for the burgers not being well versed in military practices, were of themselves very propugnacious in their authority, making more ado than even the Frenchmen. It happened, however, that there was among those valiant traders and craftsmen of Glasgow one Thomas Sword, the deacon of the hammermen, and he having the command of those stationed at the gate, overheard what was passing with my grandfather, and coming out of the wardroom, inquired his name, which when he heard, and that he was son to Michael Gilhaize, the Lithgow ferrier, he advised to let him in, saying, he knew his father well, and that they had worked together, when young men, in the King's armory at Stirling; and he told him where he lived, and invited him, when his horse was stabled, to come to supper, for he was glad to see him for his father's sake.

CHAPTER ELEVEN

At this time an ancient controversy between the Arch-
bishops of St Andrews and of Glasgow, touching their
respective jurisdictions, had been resuscitated with great
acrimony, and in the debates concerning the same the
Glasgow people took a deep interest; for they are stout-
hearted and of an adventurous spirit, and cannot abide to
think that they or their town should, in any thing of public
honour, be deemed either slack or second to the foremost
in the realm; and none of all the worthy burgesses thereof
thought more proudly of the superiority and renown of
their city than did Deacon Sword. So it came to pass,
as he was sitting at supper with my grandfather, that
he enlarged and expatiated on the inordinate pretensions
of the Archbishop of St Andrews, and took occasion to
diverge from the prelate's political ambition to speak
of the enormities of his ecclesiastical government, and
particularly of that heinous and never-to-be-forgotten act,
the burning of an aged man of fourscore and two years,
whose very heresies, as the deacon mercifully said, ought
rather to have been imputed to dotage than charged as
offences.

My grandfather was well pleased to observe such vigour
of principle and bravery of character, in one having such
sway and weight in so great a community as to be the
chief captain of the crafts who were banded with the
hammermen, namely, the cartwrights, the saddlers, the
masons, the coopers, the mariners, and all whose work
required the use of edge-tools, the hardiest and buirdliest
of the trades – and he allowed himself to run in with
the deacon's humour, but without letting wot either in
whose service he was, or on what exploit he was bound;
sowing, however, from time to time, hints as to the need

that seemed to be growing of putting a curb on the bold front wherewith the Archbishop of St Andrews, under the pretext of suppressing heresies, butted with the horns of oppression against all who stood within the reverence of his displeasure.

Deacon Sword had himself a leaning to the reformed doctrines, which, with his public enmity to the challenger of his own Archbishop, made him take to those hints with so great an affinity, that he vowed to God, shaking my grandfather by the hand over the table, that if some steps were not soon taken to stop such inordinate misrule, there were not wanting five hundred men in Glasgow, who would start forward with weapons in their grip, at the first tout of a trump, to vindicate the liberties of the subject, and the wholesome administration, by the temporal judges of the law against all offenders as of old. And giving scope to his ardour, he said there was then such a spirit awakened in Glasgow, that men, women, and children, thirsted to see justice executed on the churchmen, who were daily waxing more and more wroth and insatiable against every one who called their doctrines or polity in question.

Thus out of the very devices, which had been devised by those about the Queen Regent to intercept the free communion of the people with one another, was the means brought about whereby a chosen emissary of the Congregation came to get at the emboldening knowledge of the sense of the citizens of Glasgow, with regard to the great cause which at that period troubled the minds and fears of all men.

My grandfather was joyfully heartened by what he heard; and before coming away from the deacon, who, with the hospitality common to his townsmen, would fain have had him to prolong their sederunt over the gardevine, he said, that if Glasgow were as true and valiant as it was thought, there could be no doubt that her declaration for the Lords of the Congregation would work out a great redress of public wrongs. For, from all he could learn and understand, those high and pious noblemen had nothing more at heart than to procure for the people the free exercise of their right to worship God according to their conscience, and the doctrines of the Old and New Testaments.

But though, over the liquor-cup, the deacon had spoken so dreadless, and like a manly citizen, my grandfather resolved with himself to depart betimes for Kilmarnock, in case of any change in his temper. Accordingly, he requested the hostler of the hostel where he had taken his bed, to which his day's hard journey early inclined him, to have his horse in readiness before break of day. But this hostel, which was called the Cross of Rhodes, happened to be situated at the Waterport, and besides being a tavern and inn, was likewise the great ferryhouse of the Clyde when the tide was up, or the ford rendered unsafe by the torrents of speats and inland rains – the which caused it to be much frequented by the skippers and mariners of the barks that traded to France and Genoa with the Renfrew salmon, and by all sorts of travellers, at all times, even to the small hours of the morning. In short it was a boisterous house, the company resorting thereto of a sort little in unison with the religious frame of my grandfather. As soon, therefore, as he came from the deacon's, he went to bed without taking off his clothes, in order that he might be fit for the road as he intended; and his bed being in the public room, with sliding-doors, he drew them upon him, hoping to shut out some of the din, and to win a little repose. But scarcely had he laid his head on the pillow, when he heard the voice of one entering the room, and listening eagerly, he discovered that it was no other than the traitor Winterton's, the which so amazed him with apprehension, that he shook as he lay, like the aspen leaf on the tree.

Winterton called like a braggart for supper and hot wine, boasting he had ridden that day from Edinburgh, and that he must be up and across his horse by daylight in the morning, as he had need to be in Kilmarnock by noon. In this, which vanity made him tell in bravado, my grandfather could not but discern a kind Providence admonishing himself, for he had no doubt that Winterton was in pursuit of him; and thankful he was that he had given no inkling to any one in the house as to whence he had come, and where he was going. But had this thought not at once entered his head, he would soon have had cause to think it; for while Winterton was eating his supper he began to converse with their host, and to inquire what travellers had crossed the river. Twice or thrice, in as it were an off-hand manner, he spoke of one whom he called a cousin; but, in describing his garb, he left no doubt in my grandfather's bosom that it was regarding him he seemed at once both so negligent and so anxious. Most providential therefore it was, that my grandfather had altered his dress before leaving Edinburgh, for the marks which Winterton gave of him were chiefly drawn from his ordinary garb, and by them, their host in consequence said he had seen no such person.

When Winterton had finished his repast, and was getting his second stoup of wine heated, he asked where he was to sleep. To the which question the host replied, that he feared he would, like others, be obligated to make a bench by the fireside his couch, all the beds in the house being already bespoke or occupied. 'Every one of them is double,' said the man, 'save only one, the which is paid for by a young man that goes off at break of day, and who is already asleep.'

At this Winterton swore a dreadful oath, that he would not sleep by the fire after riding fifty miles, while there was half a bed in the house, and commanded the host to go and tell the young man that he must half blankets with him.

My grandfather knew that this could only refer to him; so, when their host came and opened the sliding doors of the bed, he feigned himself to be very fast asleep at the back of the bed, and only groaned in drowsiness when he was touched.

'O, let him alane,' cried Winterton, 'I ken what it is to be tired; so, as there's room enough at the stock, when I have drank my posset I'll e'en creep in beside him.'

My grandfather, weary as he was, lay panting with apprehension, not doubting that he should be speedily discovered; but when Winterton had finished his drink, and came swaggering and jocose to be his bedfellow, he kept himself with his face to the wall, and snored like one who was in haste to sleep more than enough, insomuch that Winterton, when he lay down, gave him a deg with his elbow, and swore at him to be quiet. His own fatigue, however, soon mastered the disturbance which my grandfather made, and he began himself to echo the noise in defenceless sincerity.

On hearing him thus fettered by sleep, my grandfather began to consider with himself what he ought to do, being both afraid and perplexed he knew not wherefore; and he was prompted by a Power that he durst not and could not reason with, to rise and escape from the jeopardy wherein he then was. But how could this be done? for the house was still open, and travellers and customers were continually going and coming. Truly his situation was one of great tribulation, and escape therefrom a thing seemingly past hope and the unaided wisdom of man.

After lying about the period of an hour in great perturbation, he began to grow more collected, and the din and resort of strangers in the house also subsided, by which he was enabled, with help from on High, to gather his scattered thoughts, and to bind them up into the sheaves of purpose and resolution. Accordingly, when all was still, and several young men, that were sitting by the fire on account of every bed being occupied, gave note, by their deep breathing, that sleep had descended upon them, and darkened their senses with her gracious and downy wings, he rose softly from the side of Winterton, and stepping over him, slipped to the door, which he unbarred, and the moon shining bright he went to the stable to take out his horse. It was not his intent to have done this, but to have gone up into the streets of the city, and walked the walls thereof till he thought his adversary was gone; but seeing the moon so fair and clear, he determined to take his horse and forthwith proceed on his journey; for the river was low and fordable, and trintled its waters with a silvery sheen in the stillness of the beautiful light.

Scarcely, however, had he pulled the latch of the stable door, – even as he was just entering in, when he heard Winterton coming from the house rousing the hostler, whom he profanely rated for allowing him to over-sleep himself. For, wakening just as his bedfellow rose, he thought the morning was come, and that his orders had been neglected.

In this extremity my grandfather saw no chance of evasion. If he went out into the moonshine he would to a surety be discovered, and in the stable he would to a certainty be caught. But what could he do, and the danger so pressing? He had hardly a choice; however, he went into the stable, shut the door, and running up to the horses that were farthest ben, mounted into the hack, and hid himself among the hay.

In that concealment he was scarcely well down, when Winterton, with an hostler that was half asleep, came with a lantern to the door, banning the poor knave as if he had been cursing him with bell, book, and candle; the other rubbing his eyes and declaring it was still far from morning, and saying he was sure the other traveller was not gone. To the which there was speedy evidence; for on going towards Winterton's horse the hostler saw my grandfather's in its stall, and told him so.

At that moment a glimpse of the lantern fell on the horse's legs, and its feet being white, – 'Oho!' cried Winterton, 'let us look here. – Kenneth Shelty's Lightfoot; – the very beast; – and hae I been in the same hole wi' the tod and no kent it. The de'il's black collie worry my soul, but this is a soople trick. I did nae think the sleekit sinner had art enough to play't; – nae doubt, he's gane to hide himsel in the town till I'm awa, for he has heard what I said yestreen. But I'll be up sides wi' him. The de'il a foot will I gang this morning till he comes back for his horse.' And with these words he turned out of the stable with the hostler, and went back to the house.

No sooner were they well gone than my grandfather came from his hiding-place, and twisting a wisp of straw round his horse's feet, that they might not dirl or make a din on the stones, he led it cannily out, and down to the river's brink, and there mounting took the ford, and was soon free on the Gorbals side. Riding up the gait at a brisk trot, he passed on for a short time along the road that he had been told led to Kilmarnock; but fearing he would be followed, he turned off at the first wynd he came to on the left; and a blessed thing it was that he did so, for it led to the Reformation-leavened town of Paisley, where he arrived an hour before daylight. Winterton, little jealousing what had happened, went again to bed, as my grandfather afterwards learnt, and had fallen asleep. In the morning when he awoke, and was told that both man and horse were flown, he flayed the hostler's back and legs in more than a score of places, believing he had connived at my grandfather's secret flight.

My grandfather had never before been in the town of Paisley, but he had often heard from Abercorn's serving-men that were wont to sorn about his father's smiddy, of a house of jovial entertainment by the water-side, about a stone-cast from the abbey-yett, the hostess whereof was a certain canty dame called Maggy Napier, then in great repute with the shavelings of the abbey. Thither he directed his course, the abbey towers serving him for her sign, and the moonlight and running river were guides to her door, at the which he was not blate in chapping. She was, however, long of giving entrance; for it happened that some nights before, the magistrates of the town had been at a carousal with the abbot and chapter, the papistical denomination for the seven heads and ten horns of a monastery, and when they had come away and were going home, one of them, Bailie Pollock, a gaucy widower, was instigated by the devil and the wine he had drank, to stravaig towards Maggy Napier's, – a most unseemly thing for a bailie to do, especially a bailie of Paisley, but it was then the days of popish sinfulness. And when Bailie Pollock went thither, the house was full of riotous swankies, who being the waur of drink themselves, had but little reverence for a magistrate in the same state; so they handled him to such a degree that he was obliged to keep his bed and put collops to his eyes for three days. The consequence of which was, that the house fell under the displeasure of the town-council, and Maggy was admonished to keep it more orderly and doucely, – though the fault came neither from her nor her customers, as she told my grandfather, for detaining him so long, it being requisite that she should see he was in a condition of sobriety before letting him in. But, when admitted, he was in no spirit to enjoy her jocosity concerning Bailie Pollock's spree, so he told her that he had come far, and had far to go, and that having heard sore tidings of a friend, he was fain to go to bed and try if he could compose himself with an hour or two of sleep.

Maggy accordingly refrained from her jocularity, and began to sooth and comfort him, for she was naturally of a winsome way, and prepared a bed for him with her best sheets, the which, she said, were gi'en her in gratus gift frae the Lord Abbot, so that he undressed himself, and enjoyed a pleasant interregnum of anxiety for more than five hours; and when he awoke and was up, he found a breakfast worthy of the abbot himself ready, and his hostess was most courtly and kind, praising the dainties, and pressing him to eat. Nor, when he proposed to reckon with her for the lawin, would she touch the money, but made him promise, when he came back, he would bide another night with her, hoping he would then be in better spirits, – for she was wae to see so braw a gallant sae casten down, doless, and dowie.

When they had settled their contest, and my grandfather had come out to mount his beast, which a stripling was holding ready for him at a louping-on-stane near the abbey-yett, as he was going thither, a young friar, who was taking a morning stroll along the pleasant banks of the Cart, approached towards him, and after looking hard at him for some time, called him by name, and took him by both the hands, which he pressed with a brotherly affection.

This friar was of Lithgow parentage, and called Dominick Callender, and when he and my grandfather were playing-bairns, they had spent many a merry day of their suspicionless young years together. As he grew up, being a lad of shrewd parts, and of a very staid and orderly deportment, the monks set their snares for him, and before he could well think for himself he was wiled into their traps, and becoming a novice, in due season professed himself a monk. But it was some time before my grandfather knew him again, for the ruddy of youth had fled his cheek, and he was pale and of a studious countenance; and when the first sparklings of his pleasure at the sight of his old play-marrow had gone off, his eyes saddened into thoughtfulness, and he appeared like one weighed down with care and heavy inward dule.

After Dominick Callender and my grandfather had conversed some time, with many interchanges of the kindly remembrances of past pleasures, the gentle friar began to bewail his sad estate in being a professed monk, and so mournfully to deplore the rashness with which inexperienced youth often takes upon itself a yoke it can never lay down, that the compassion of his friend was sorrowfully awakened, for he saw he was living a life of bitterness and grief. He heard him, however, without making any reply, or saying any thing concerning his own lot of hazard and adventure; for, considering Dominick to be leagued with the papistical orders, he did not think him safe to be trusted, notwithstanding the unchanged freshness of the loving-kindness which he still seemed to bear in his heart; nor even, had he not felt this jealousy, would he have thought himself free to speak of his errand, far less to have given to any stranger aught that might have been an inkling of his noble master's zealous, but secret stirrings, for the weal of Scotland, and the enfranchisement of the worshippers of the true God.

When my grandfather had arrived at his horse, and prepared to mount, Dominick Callender said to him, if he would ride slowly for a little way he would walk by his side, adding, 'for maybe I'll ne'er see you again – I'm a-weary of this way of life, and the signs of the times bode no good to the church. I hae a thought to go into some foreign land, where I may taste the air of a freeman, and I feel myself comforted before I quit our auld hard-favoured, but warm-hearted Scotland, in meeting wi' ane that reminds me how I had once sunny mornings and summer days.'

This was said so much in the sincerity of a confiding spirit, that my grandfather could not refrain from observing, in answer, that he feared his friar's cloak did not sit easy upon him; which led him on to acknowledge that it was so.

'I am speaking to you, Gilhaize,' said he, 'with the frank heart of auld langsyne, and I dinna scruple to confess to one that I hae often thought of, and weary't to see again, and wondered what had become of, that my conscience has revolted against the errors of the papacy, and that I am now upon the eve of fleeing my native land, and joining the Reformed at Geneva. And maybe I'm no ordain't to spend a' my life in exile; for no man can deny that the people of Scotland are not inwardly the warm adversaries of the church. That last and cruellest deed, the sacrifice of the feckless old man of fourscore and upward, has proven that the humanity of the world will no longer endure the laws and pretensions of the church; and there are few in Paisley whom the burning of auld Mill has not kindled with the spirit of resistance.'

The latter portion of these words was as joyous tidings to my grandfather, and he tightened his reins and entered into a more particular and inquisitive discourse with his companion, by which he gathered that the martyrdom of Master Mill had indeed caused great astonishment and wrath among the pious in and about Paisley, and not only among them, but had estranged the affections even of the more worldly from the priesthood, of whom it was openly said, that the sense of pity towards the commonalty of mankind was extinguished within them, and that they were all in all for themselves.

But as they were proceeding through the town and along the road, conversing in a familiar but earnest manner on these great concerns, Dominick Callender began to inveigh against the morals of his brethren, and to lament again, in a very piteous manner, that he was decreed, by his monastic profession, from the enjoyment of the dearest and tenderest pleasures of man. And before they separated, it came out that he had been for some time touched with the soft enchantments of love for a young maiden, the daughter of a gentleman of good account in Paisley, and that her chaste piety was as the precious gum wherewith the Egyptians of old preserved their dead in everlasting beauty, keeping from her presence all taint of impurity, and of thoughts sullying to innocence, insomuch, that, even were he inclined, as he said many of his brethren would have been, to have acted the part of a secret canker to that fair blossom, the gracious and holy embalmment of her virtues would have proved an incorruptible protection.

'But,' he exclaimed with a sorrowful voice, 'that which is her glory, and my admiration and praise, is converted, by the bondage of my unnatural vows, into a curse to us both. The felicity that we might have enjoyed together in wedded life is forbidden to us as a great crime. But the laws of God are above the canons of the church, the voice of Nature is louder than the fulminations of the Vatican, and I have resolved to obey the one, and give ear to the other, despite the horrors that await on apostacy. Can you, Gilhaize, in aught assist my resolution?'

There was so much vehemence and the passion of grief in these ejaculations, that my grandfather wist not well what to say. He told him, however, not to be rash in what he did, nor to disclose his intents, save only to those in whom he could confide; for the times were perilous to every one that slackened in reverence to the papacy, particularly to such as had pastured within the chosen folds of the church.

'Bide,' said he, 'till you see what issue is ordained to come from this dreadful deed which so shaketh all the land, making the abbey towers topple and tremble to their oldest and deepest foundations. Truth is awakened, and gone forth conquering and to conquer. It cannot be that ancient iniquities will be much longer endured; the arm of Wrath is raised against them; the sword of Revenge is drawn forth from its scabbard by Justice; and Nature has burst asunder the cords of the Roman harlot, and stands in her freedom, like Samson, when the spirit of the Lord was mightily poured upon him, as he awoke from the lap of Delilah.'

The gentle friar, as my grandfather often told, stood for some time astounded at this speech, and then he said—

'I dream't not, Gilhaize, that beneath a countenance so calm and comely, the zealous fires of a warrior's bravery could have been kindled to so vehement a heat. But I will vex you with no questions. Heaven is on your side, and may its redeeming promptings never allow its ministers to rest, till the fetters are broken and the slaves are set free.'

With these words he stepped forward to shake my grandfather by the hand, and to bid him farewell; but just as he came to the stirrup he halted and said—

'It is not for nothing that the remembrance of you has been preserved so much brighter and dearer to me than that of all my kin. There was aye something about you, in our heedless days, that often made me wonder, I could not tell wherefore; and now, when I behold you in the prime of manhood, it fills me with admiration and awe, and makes me do homage to you as a master.'

Much more he added to the same effect, which the modesty of my grandfather would not allow him to repeat; but when they had parted, and my grandfather had ridden forward some two or three miles, he recalled to mind what had passed between them, and he used to say that this discourse with his early friend first opened to him a view of the grievous captivity which nature suffered in the monasteries and convents, notwithstanding the loose lives imputed to their inmates; and he saw that the Reformation would be hailed by many that languished in the bondage of their vows, as a great and glorious deliverance. But still he was wont to say, even with such as these, it was overly mingled with temporal concernments, and that they longed for it less on account of its immortal issues, than for its sensual emancipations.

And as he was proceeding on his way in this frame of mind, and thinking on all that he had seen and learnt from the day in which he bade adieu to his father's house, he came to a place where the road forked off in two different airts, and not knowing which to take, he stopped his horse and waited till a man drew nigh, whom he observed coming towards him. By this man he was told, that the road leading leftward led to Kilmarnock and Ayr, and the other on the right to Kilwinning; so, without saying any thing, he turned his horse's head into the latter; the which he was moved to do by sundry causes and reasons. First, he had remarked that the chances in his journey had, in a very singular manner, led him to gain much of that sort of knowledge which the Lords of the Congregation thirsted for; and, second, he had no doubt that Winterton was in pursuit of him to Kilmarnock, for some purpose of frustration or circumvention, the which, though he was not able to divine, he could not but consider important, if it was, as he thought, the prime motive of that varlet's journey.

But he was chiefly disposed to prefer the Kilwinning road, though it was several miles more of bout-gait, on account of the rich abbacy in that town; hoping he might glean and gather some account how the clergy there stood affected, the meeting with Dominick Callender having afforded him a vista of friends and auxiliaries in the enemy's camp little thought of. Besides all this, he reflected, that as it was of consequence he should reach the Lord Boyd in secrecy, he would be more likely to do so by stopping at Kilwinning, and feeing some one there to guide him to the Dean Castle by moonlight. I have heard him say, however, the speakable motives of his deviation from the straight road were at the time far less effectual in moving him thereto, than a something which he could not tell, that with an invisible hand took his horse as it were by the bridle-rings, and constrained him to go into the Kilwinning track. In the whole of this journey there was indeed a very extraordinary manifestation of a special providence, not only in the protection vouchsafed towards himself, but in the remarkable accidents and occurrences, by which he was enabled to enrich himself with the knowledge so precious at that time to those who were chosen to work the great work of the Gospel in Scotland.

As my grandfather came in sight of Kilwinning, and beheld the abbey with its lofty horned towers and spiky pinnacles, and the sands of Cunningham between it and the sea, it seemed to him as if a huge leviathan had come up from the depths of the ocean and was devouring the green inland, having already consumed all the herbage of the wide waste that lay so bare and yellow for many a mile, desert and lonely in the silent sunshine, and he ejaculated to himself, that the frugal soil of poor Scotland could ne'er have been designed to pasture such enormities.

As he rode on, his path descended from the heights into pleasant tracks, along banks feathered with the fragrant plumage of the birch and hazel, and he forgot, in hearkening to the cheerful prattle of the Garnock waters, as they swirled among the pebbles by the road side, the pageantries of that mere bodily worship which had worked on the ignorance of the world to raise such costly monuments of the long-suffering patience of Heaven, while they showed how much the divine nature of the infinite God, and the humility of His eternal Son, had been forgotten in this land among professing Christians.

When he came nigh the town, he inquired for an hostel, and a stripling, the miller's son, who was throwing stones at a flock of geese belonging to the abbey, then taking their pleasures uninvited in his father's mill-dam, guided him to the house of Theophilus Lugton, the chief vintner, horse-setter, and stabler, in the town; where, on alighting, he was very kindly received; for the gudewife was of a stirring, household nature, and Theophilus himself, albeit douce and temperate for a publican, was a man obliging and hospitable, not only as became him in his trade, but from a disinterested good-will. He was indeed, as my

72

grandfather came afterwards to know, really a person holden in great respect and repute by the visitors and pilgrims who resorted to the abbey, and by none more than by the worthy wives of Irvine, the most regular of his customers. For they being then in the darkness of papistry, were as much given to the idolatry of holidays and masses, as, thanks be and praise! they are now to the hunting out of sound gospel preachers and sacramental occasions. Many a stoup of burnt wine and spiced ale they were wont, at Pace and Yule, and other papistical high times, to partake of together in the house of Theophilus Lugton, happy and well content when their possets were flavoured with the ghostly conversation of some gawsie monk, well versed in the mysteries of requiems and purgatory.

Having parted with his horse to be taken to the stable by Theophilus himself, my grandfather walked into the house, and Dame Lugton set for him an elbow-chair by the chimla lug, and while she was preparing something for a repast, they fell into conversation, in the course of which she informed him that a messenger had come to the abbey that forenoon from Edinburgh, and a rumour had been bruited about soon after his arrival, that there was great cause to dread a rising among the heretics; for, being ingrained with papistry, she so spoke of the Reformers.

This news troubled my grandfather not a little, and the more he inquired concerning the tidings, the more reason he got to be alarmed, and to suspect that the bearer was Winterton, who being still in the town, and then at the abbey – his horse was in Theophilus Lugton's stable – he could not but think, that, in coming to Kilwinning instead of going right on to Kilmarnock, he had run into the lion's mouth. But, seeing it was so, and could not be helped, he put his trust in the Lord, and resolved to swerve in no point from the straight line which he had laid down for himself.

While he was eating of Dame Lugton's fare, with the relishing sauce of a keen appetite, in a manner that no one who saw him could have supposed he was almost sick with a surfeit of anxieties, one James Coom, a smith, came in for a mutchkin-cap of ale, and he, seeing a traveller, said,

'Thir's sair news! The drouth of cauld iron will be slockened in men's blood ere we hear the end o't.'

"Deed,' replied my grandfather, 'it's very alarming; Lucky, here, has just been telling me that there's like to be a straemash amang the Reformers. Surely they'll ne'er daur to rebel.'

'If a' tales be true, that's no to do,' said the smith, blowing the froth from the cap in which Dame Lugton handed him the ale, and taking a right good-willy waught.

'But what's said?' inquired my grandfather, when the smith had fetched his breath.

'Naebody can weel tell,' was his response; 'a' that's come this length is but the sough afore the storm. Within twa hours there has been a great riding hither and yon, and a lad straight frae Embro' has come to bid my Lord Abbot repair to the court; and three chiels hae been at me frae Eglinton Castle, to get their beasts shod for a journey. My Lord there is hyte and fykie; there's a gale in his tail, said they, light where it may. Now, atween oursels, my Lord has na the heart of a true bairn to that aged and worthy grannie of the papistry, our leddy the Virgin Mary – here's her health, poor auld deaf and dumb creature – she has na, I doubt, the pith to warsle wi' the blast she ance in a day had.'

'Haud that heretical tongue o' thine, Jamie Coom,' exclaimed Dame Lugton. 'It's enough to gar a body's hair stand on end to hear o' your familiarities wi' the Holy Virgin. I won'er my Lord Abbot has na langsyne tethert thy tongue to the kirk door wi' a red-het nail, for sic blasphemy. But fools are privileged, and so's seen o' thee.'

'And wha made me familiar wi' her, Dame Lugton – tell me that?' replied James; 'was na it my Lord himsel, at last Marymas, when he sent for me to make a hoop to mend her leg that sklintered aff as they were dressing her for the show. Eh! little did I think that I was ever to hae the honour and glory of ca'ing a nail intil the timber hip o' the Virgin Mary! Ah, lucky, ye would na hae tholed the dirl o' the dints o' my hammer as she did. But she's a saint, and ye'll ne'er deny that ye're a sinner.'

To this Dame Lugton was unable to reply, and the smith, cunningly winking, dippet his head up to the lugs in the ale-cap.

'But,' said my grandfather, 'no to speak wi' disrespeck of things considered wi' reverence, it does na seem to me that there is ony cause to think the Reformers hae yet rebelled.'

'I'm sure,' replied the smith, 'if they hae na, they ought, or the de'il a spunk's amang them. Isna a' the monks, frae John o' Groat's to the Border, getting ready their spits and rackses, fryingpans and branders, to cook them like capons and doos for Horney's supper? I never hear my ain bellows snoring at a gaud o' iron in the fire, but I think o' fat Father Lickladle, the abbey's head kitchener, roasting me o'er the low like a laverock in his collop-tangs; for, as Dame Lugton there weel kens, I'm ane o' the Reformed. Heh! but it's a braw thing this Reformation. It used to cost me as muckle siller for the sin o' getting fu', no aboon three or four times in the year, as would hae kept ony honest man blithe and ree frae New'ersday to Hogmanae; but our worthy hostess has found to her profit, that I'm now ane of her best customers. What say ye, Lucky?'

'Truly,' said Dame Lugton, laughing, 'thou's no an ill swatch o' the Reformers; and naebody need be surprised at the growth o' heresy wha thinks o' the dreadfu' cost the professors o't used to be at for pardons. But maybe they'll soon find that the de'il's as hard a taxer as e'er the kirk was; for ever since thou has refraint frae paying penance, thy weekly calks ahint the door hae been on the increase, Jamie, and no ae plack has thou mair to spare. So muckle gude thy reforming has done thee.'

'Bide awee, lucky,' cried the smith, setting down the ale-cap, which he had just emptied, 'bide awee, and ye'll see a change. Surely it was to be expecket, considering the spark in my hass, that the first use I would mak o' the freedom o' the Reformation would be to quench it, which I never was allowed to do afore; and whenever that's done, ye'll see me a geizen't keg o' sobriety, – tak the word o' a drowthy smith for't.'

At this jink o' their controversy, who should come into

the house, ringing ben to the hearth-stane with his iron heels and the rattling rowels o' his spurs, but Winterton, without observing my grandfather, who was then sitting with his back to the window-light, in the arm-chair at the chimla lug; and when he had ordered Dame Lugton to spice him a drink of her best brewing, he began to joke and jibe with the blacksmith; the which allowing my grandfather time to compose his wits, which were in a degree startled; he saw that he could not but be discovered, so he thought it was best to bring himself out. Accordingly, in as quiet a manner as he was able to put on, he said to Winterton—

'I hae a notion that we twa hae forgathered no lang sincesyne.'

At the sound of these words Winterton gave a loup, as if he had tramped on something no canny, syne a whirring sort of triumphant whistle, and then a shout, crying, 'Ha, ha! tod lowrie! hae I yirded you at last?' But instanter he recollected himsel', and giving my grandfather a significant look, as if he wished him no to be particular, he said, 'I heard o' you, Gilhaize, on the road, and I was fain to hae come up wi' you, that we might hae travelled thegither. Howsever, I lost scent at Glasgow.' And then he continued to haver with him, in his loose and profligate manner, anent the Glasgow damsels, till the ale was ready, when he pressed my grandfather to taste, never letting wot how they had slept together in the same bed; and my grandfather, on his part, was no less circumspect, for he discerned that Winterton intended to come over him, and he was resolved to be on his guard.

When Winterton had finished his drink, which he did hastily, he proposed to my grandfather that they should take a stroll through the town; and my grandfather being eager to throw stour in his eyes, was readily consenting thereto.

'Weel,' said the knave, when he had warily led him into the abbey kirk-yard, 'I did na think ye would hae gane back to my Lord; but it's a' very weel, since he has looked o'er what's past, and gi'en you a new dark.'

'He's very indulgent,' replied my grandfather, 'and I would be loath to wrang so kind a master;' and he looked at Winterton; the varlet, however, never winced, but rejoined lightly,—

'But I wish ye had come back to Widow Rippet's, for ye would hae spar't me a hard ride. Scarcely had ye ta'en the road when my Lord mindit that he had neglekit to gie you the sign, by the which ye were to make yoursel and message kent to his friends, and I was sent after to tell you.'

'I'm glad o' that,' replied my grandfather, 'what is't?' Winterton was a thought molested by this thrust of a question, and for the space of about a minute said nothing, till he had considered with himself, when he rejoined—

'Three lads were sent off about the same time wi' you, and the Earl was nae quite sure, he said, whilk of you a' he had forgotten to gie the token whereby ye would be known as his men. But the sign for the Earl of Eglinton, to whom I guess ye hae been sent, by coming to Kilwinning, is no the same as for the Lord Boyd, to whom I thought ye had been missioned; for I hae been at the Dean Castle, and finding you not there, followed you hither.'

'I'll be plain wi' you', said my grandfather to this draughty speech, 'I'm bound to the Lord Boyd; but coming through

Paisley, when I reached the place where the twa roads branched, I took the ane that brought me here instead of the gate to Kilmarnock; so, as soon as my beast has eaten his corn, I mean to double back to the Dean Castle.'

'How, in the name of the saints and souls! did ye think, in going frae Glasgow to Kilmarnock, o' taking the road to Paisley?'

'Deed, an' ye were acquaint,' said my grandfather, 'wi' how little I knew o' the country, ye would nae speir that question; but since we hae fallen in thegither, and are baith, ye ken, in my Lord Glencairn's service, I hope ye'll no objek to ride back wi' me to the Lord Boyd's.'

'Then it's no you that was sent to the Earl of Eglinton?' exclaimed Winterton, pretending more surprise than he felt; 'and all my journey has been for naething. Howsoever, I'll go back wi' you to Kilmarnock, and the sooner we gang the better.'

Little farther discourse then passed, for they returned to the hostel, and ordering out their horses, were soon on the road; and as they trotted along, Winterton was overly outspoken against the papisticals, calling them all kinds of ill names, and no sparing the Queen Regent. But my grandfather kept a calm tongue, and made no reflections.

'Howsever,' said Winterton, pulling up his bridle, and walking his horse, as they were skirting the moor of Irvine, leaving the town about a mile off on the right, 'you and me, Gilhaize, that are but servants, need nae fash our heads wi' sic things, the wyte o' wars lies at the doors of kings, and the soldiers are free o' the sin o' them. But how will ye get into the presence and confidence of the Lord Boyd?'

'I thought,' replied my grandfather pawkily, 'that ye had gotten our master's token; and I maun trust to you.'

'O,' cried Winterton, 'I got but the ane for the lad sent to Eglinton Castle.'

'And hae ye been there?' said my grandfather.

Winterton didna let wot that he heard this, but stooping over on the off-side of his horse, pretended he was righting something about his stirrup-leather. My grandfather was, however, resolved to probe him to the quick; so, when he

was again sitting upright, he repeated the question, if he
had been to Eglinton Castle.

'O, ay,' cried the false loon; 'I was there, but the bird
was flown.'

'And how got he the ear of the Earl,' said my grandfather,
'not having the sign?'

In for a penny in for a pound, was Winterton's motto,
and ae lie with him was father to a race. 'Luckily for him,'
replied he, 'some of the serving-men kent him as being in
Glencairn's service, so they took him to their master.'

My grandfather had no doubt that there was some truth
in this, though he was sure Winterton knew little about
it; for it agreed with what James Coom, the smith, had
said about the lads from Eglinton that had been at his
smiddy to get the horses shod, and remembering the
leathern purses under the Earl his master's pillow, he was
persuaded that there had been a messenger sent to the head
of the Montgomeries, and likewise to other lords, friends
of the Congregation; but he saw that Winterton went by
guess, and lied at random. Still, though not affecting to
notice it, nor expressing any distrust, he could not help
saying to him, that he had come a long way, and after all
it looked like a gowk's errand.

The remark, however, only served to give Winterton
inward satisfaction, and he replied with a laugh, that it
made little odds to him where he was sent, and that
he'd as lief ride in Ayrshire as sorn about the causey of
Enbrough.

In this sort of talk and conference they rode on together,
the o'ercome every now and then of Winterton's discourse
being concerning the proof my grandfather carried with
him, whereby the Lord Boyd would know he was one of
Glencairn's men. But, notwithstanding all his wiles and
devices to howk the secret out of him, his drift being so
clearly discerned, my grandfather was enabled to play with
him till they were arrived at Kilmarnock, where Winterton
proposed to stop till he had delivered his message to the
Lord Boyd, at the Dean Castle.

'That surely cannot be,' replied my grandfather; 'for ye
ken, as there has been some mistak about the sign whereby

I am to make myself known, ye'll hae to come wi' me to expound, in case of need. In trooth, now that we hae forgatherit, and as I hae but this ae message to a' the shire of Ayr, I would fain hae your company till I see the upshot.'

Winterton could not very easily make a refusal to this, but he hesitated and swithered, till my grandfather urged him again; – when seeing no help for it, and his companion, as he thought, entertaining no suspicion of him, he put on a bold face and went forward.

When they had come to the Dean Castle, which stands in a pleasant green park about a mile aboon the town-head of Kilmarnock, on entering the gate, my grandfather hastily alighted, and giving his horse a sharp prick of his spur as he lap off, the beast ran capering out of his hand, round the court of the castle.

With the well-feigned voice of great anxiety, my grand-father cried to the servants to shut the gate and keep it in; and Winterton alighting, ran to catch it, giving his own horse to a stripling to hold. At the same moment, however, my grandfather sprung upon him, and seizing him by the throat, cried out for help to master a spy.

Winterton was so confounded that he gasped, and looked round like a man demented; and my grandfather ordered him to be taken by the serving-men to their master, before whom, when they were all come, he recounted the story of his adventures with the prisoner, telling his Lordship what his master, the Earl of Glencairn, suspected of him. To which, when Winterton was asked what he had to say, he replied bravely, that it was all true, and he was none ashamed to be so catched, when it was done by so clever a fellow.

He was then ordered by the Lord Boyd to be immured in the dungeon-room, the which may be seen to this day; and though his captivity was afterwards somewhat relaxed, he was kept a prisoner in the castle till after the death of the Queen Dowager, and the breaking up of her two-faced councils. This exploit won my grandfather great favour, and he scarcely needed to show the signet-ring when he told his message from the Lords of the Congregation.

By such devices and missions, as my grandfather was engaged in for the Earl Glencairn with the Lord Boyd, a thorough understanding was concerted among the Reformed throughout the kingdom; and, encouraged by their great strength and numbers, which far exceeded what was expected, the Lords of the Congregation set themselves roundly to work, and the protestant preachers openly published their doctrines.

Soon after my grandfather had returned from the shire of Ayr, there was a weighty consultation held at the Earl his patron's lodging in Edinburgh, whereat, among others present, was that pious youth, afterwards the good Regent Murray. He was by office and appointment then the head and lord of the priory of St Andrews; but his soul cleaving to the Reformation and the Gospel, he laid down the use of that title, and about this time began to be called the Lord James Stuart.

The Lords of the Congregation, feeling themselves strong in the goodness of their cause and the number of their adherents, resolved at this council, that they should proceed firmly but considerately to work, and seek redress as became true lieges, by representation and supplication. Accordingly a paper was drawn up, wherein they set forth how, for conscience sake, the Reformed had been long afflicted with banishment, confiscation of goods, and death in its cruellest forms. That continual fears darkened their lives, till, being no longer able to endure such calamities, they were compelled to beg a remedy against the oppressions and tyranny of the Estate Ecclesiastical, which had usurped an unlimited domination over the minds of men, – the faggot and the sword being the weapons which the prelates employed to enforce their mandates, – plain truths that were thus openly stated in order to show that the suppliants were sincere; and they concluded with a demand, that the original purity of the Christian religion should be restored, and the government so improved as to afford them security in their persons, opinions, and property.

Sir James Calder of Sandilands was the person chosen to present this memorial to the Queen Regent; and never, said my grandfather, was an agent more fitly chosen to uphold the dignity of his trust, or to preserve the respect which, as good subjects, the Reformed desired to maintain and manifest towards the authority regal. He was a man far advanced in life; but there was none of the infirmities of age under the venerable exterior with which time had clothed his appearance. Of great honour and a pure life, he was reverenced by all parties, and had acquired both renown and affection, through his services to the realm and his manifold virtues.

On a day appointed by the Queen Regent, the Lords and leaders of the Congregation attended Sandilands, each with a stately retinue, to Holyrood-house; my grandfather having leave from the Earl, his master, to wait on his person on that occasion.

It was a solemn day to the worshippers of the true God, who came in great multitudes to the town, many from distant parts, to be present, and to hear the issue of a conference that was to give liberty to the consciences of all devout Scotchmen. From the house in the Lawn-market, where the Lords assembled, down to the very yetts of the palace, the sight was as if the street had been paved with faces, and windows over windows, roofs and lum-heads, were clustered with women and children. All temporal cares and businesses were that day suspended: in the accents and voices of men there was an awful sobriety, few speaking, and what was said, sounded as if every one was affected with the sense of some high and everlasting interest at stake.

When the Lords went down into the street, there was, for a brief interval, a stir and a murmur in the multitude, which opened to the right and left as when the waves of the Red Sea were opened, and through the midst thereof prepared a miraculous road for the children of Israel. A deep silence succeeded, and Sandilands, with his hoary head uncovered, bearing in his hand the supplication and remonstrance, walked forward, and the Lords went after also all bare-headed, and every one with them followed in like manner, as reverentially as their masters. The people, as they passed along, slowly and devoutly, took off their caps and bonnets and bowed their heads as when the ark of the covenant of the Lord was of old brought back from the Philistines; and many wept, and others prayed aloud, and there was wonder, and awe, and dread, mingled with thoughts of unspeakable confidence and glory.

When Sandilands and those with him were conducted into the presence of the Queen-dowager, she was standing under a canopy of state, surrounded by many of the nobles and prelates, and by her maidens of honour. My grandfather had not seen her before, and having often heard her suspected of double-dealing, and of a superstitious zeal and affection for the papal abominations and cruelties, he had pictured to himself a lean and haggard woman, with a pale and fierce countenance, and was therefore greatly amazed when he beheld a lady of a most sweet and gracious aspect, with mild dark eyes beaming with a chaste dignity, and a high and fair forehead, bright and unwrinkled with any care, and lips formed to speak soft and gentle sentences. In her apparel she was less gay than her ladies, but nevertheless she was more queenly. Her dress and mantle were of the richest purple Genoese unadorned with embroidery, and round her neck she wore a ruff of fine ermine and a string of princely pearls: a small golden cross of curious graven gold dangled to her waist from a loup in the vale of her bosom.

Sandilands advanced several paces before the Lords by whom he was attended, and falling on his knees, read with a loud and firm voice the memorial of the Reformed; and when he had done so and was risen, the Queen received a paper that was given to her by her secretary, who stood behind her right shoulder, and also read an answer which had been prepared, and in which she was made to deliver many comfortable assurances, that at the time were received as a great boon with much thankfulness by all the Reformed, who had too soon reason to prove the insincerity of those courtly flatteries. For no steps were afterwards taken to give those indulgences by law that were promised; but the papists stirring themselves with great activity, and foreign matters and concerns coming in aid of their stratagems, long before a year passed the mind of the Queen and government was fomented into hostility against the protestants. She called into her favour and councils the Archbishop of St Andrews, with whom she had been at variance; and the devout said, when they heard thereof, that when our Saviour was condemned, on the same day Herod and Pilate were made friends, applying the text to this reconciliation; and boding therefrom woe to the true church. Moved by the hatred which his Grace bore to the Reformers, the Queen cited the protestant preachers to appear at Stirling to answer to the charges which might there be preferred against them.

My grandfather, when this perfidy came to a head, was at Finlayston-house, in the shire of Renfrew, with the Earl, his master, who, when he heard of such a breach of faith, smote the table, as he was then sitting at dinner, with his right hand, and said, 'Since the false woman has done this, there is nothing for us but the banner and the blade;' and starting from his seat he forthwith ordered horses, and, attended by my grandfather and ten armed servants, rode to Glasgow, where Sir Hugh Campbell of Loudon, then sheriff of Ayr, and other worthies of the time, were assembled on business before the Lords of Justiciary; and it was instanter agreed, that they should forthwith proceed to Stirling where the court was, and remonstrate with the Queen. So, leaving all temporal concerns, Sir Hugh took horse, and they arrived at Stirling about the time her Highness supped, and going straight to the castle, they stood in the ante-chamber, to speak if possible with her as she passed.

On entering the room to pass to her table she saw them, and looked somewhat surprised and displeased; but without saying any thing particular she desired the Earl to follow her, and Sir Hugh, unbidden, went also into the banquet-room. It was seldom that she used state in her household, and on this occasion, it being a popish fast, her table was frugally spread, and only herself sat at the board.

'Well, Glencairn,' said she, 'what has brought you hither from the west at this time? Is the realm to be for ever tossed like the sea by this tempest of heresies? The royal authority is not always to be insulted with impunity, and in spite of all their friends the protestant preachers shall be banished from Scotland, aye, though their doctrines were as sound as St Paul's.'

The Earl, as my grandfather heard him afterwards relate, replied, 'Your Majesty gave your royal promise that the Reformed should be protected, and they have done nothing since to cause the forfeiture of so gracious a boon: I implore your Majesty to call that sacred pledge to mind.'

'You lack reason, my Lord,' she cried, sharply; 'it becomes not subjects to burden their princes with promises which it may be inconvenient to keep.'

'If these, madam, are your sentiments,' replied the Earl, proudly, 'the Congregation can no longer acknowledge your authority, and must renounce their allegiance to your government.'

She had, at the moment, lifted the salt-celler to sprinkle her salad, – but she was so astonished at the boldness of this speech, that she dropt it from her hand, and the salt was spilt on the floor – an evil omen, which all present noted.

'My Lord Glencairn,' said she, thoughtfully, 'I would execute my great duties honestly, but your preachers trouble the waters, and I know not where the ford lies that I may safest ride. Go ye away and try to keep your friends quiet, and I will consider calmly what is best to be done for the weal of all.'

At these words the Earl and Sir Hugh Campbell bowed, and, retiring, went to the lodging of the Earl of Monteith, where they were mindet to pass the night; but, when they had consulted with that nobleman, my grandfather was ordered to provide himself with a fresh horse from Monteith's stable, and to set out for Edinburgh with letters for the Lord James Stuart.

'Gilhaize,' said his master, as he delivered them, 'I foresee we must buckle on our armour; but the cause of the Truth does not require that the first blow should come from our side. By this time John Knox, who has been long expected, may be hourly looked for; and as no man stands higher in the aversion of the papists than that brave honest man, we shall know, by the reception he meets with, what we ought to do.'

So my grandfather, putting the letters in his bosom, retired from the presence of the Earl, and by break of day reached the West-port, and went straight on to the Lord James Stuart's lodging in the Canongate. But, though the household were astir, it was some time before he got admittance; for their master was a young man of great method in all things, and his chaplain was at the time reading the first prayers of the morning, during which the doors were shut, and no one, however urgent his business, could gain admission into that house while the inmates were doing their homage to the King of kings.

As my grandfather, in the grey of the morning, was waiting in the Canongate till the worship was over in the house of the Lord James Stuart, he frequently rode up and down the street as far as the Luckenbooths and the Abbey's sanctuary siver, and his mind was at times smitten with the remorse of pity, when he saw, as the dawn advanced, the numbers of poor labouring men that came up out of the closes and gathered round the trone, abiding there to see who would come to hire them for the day. But his compassion was soon changed into a frame of thankfulness, at the boundless variety of mercies which are dealt out to the children of Adam, for he remarked, that, for the most part, these poor men, whose sustenance was as precarious as that of the wild birds of the air, were cheerful and jocund, many of them singing and whistling as blithely as the lark, that carries the sweet incense of her melodious songs in the censer of a sinless breast to the golden gates of the morning.

Hitherto he had never noted, or much considered, the complicated cares and trials wherewith the lot of man in every station is chequered and environed; and when he heard those bondmen of hard labour, jocund after sound slumbers and light suppers, laughing contemptuously as they beheld the humiliating sight, which divers gallants and youngsters, courtiers of the court, degraded with debauch, made of themselves as they stumbled homeward, he thought there was surely more bliss in the cup that was earned by the constancy of health and a willing mind, than in all the possets and malvesia that the hoards of ages could procure. So he composed his spirit, and inwardly made a vow to the Lord, that, as soon as the mighty work of the redemption of the Gospel from the perdition of papistry was accomplished, he would retire into the lea of some pleasant green holm, and take, for the purpose of his life, the attainment of that happy simplicity which seeks but the supply of the few wants with which man comes so rich from the hands of his Maker, that all changes in his natural condition of tilling the ground and herding the flocks only serve to make him poorer by increasing.

While he was thus ruminating in the street, he observed two strangers coming up the Canongate. One of them had the appearance of a servant, but he was of a staider and more thoughtful aspect than belongs to men of that degree, only he bore on his shoulder a willease, and had in his hand a small package wrapt in a woollen cover and buckled with a leathern strap. The other was the master; and my grandfather halted his horse to look at him as he passed, for he was evidently no common man nor mean personage, though in stature he was jimp the ordinary size. He was bent more with infirmities than the load of his years. His hair and long flowing beard were very grey and venerable, like those of the ancient patriarchs who enjoyed immediate communion with God. But though his appearance was thus aged, and though his complexion and countenance betokened a frail tenement, yet the brightness of youth shone in his eyes, and they were lighted up by a spirit over which time had no power.

In his steps and gait he was a little hasty and unsteady, and twice or thrice he was obliged to pause in the steep of the street to draw his breath; but even in this there was an affecting and great earnestness, a working of a living soul within, as if it panted to enter on the performance of some great and solemn hest.

He seemed to be eager and zealous, like the apostle Peter, in his temper, and as dauntless as the mighty and courageous Paul. Many in the street stopped, and looked after him with reverence and marvelling, as he proceeded with quick and desultory steps, followed by his sedate attendant. Nor was it surprising, for he was, indeed, one of those who, in their lives, are vast and wonderful, – special creations that are sent down from heaven, with authority attested by the glowing impress of the signet of God on their hearts, to avenge the wrongs done to His truths and laws in the blasphemies of the earth. – It was John Knox!

When he had passed, my grandfather rode back to the yett of the Lord James Stuart's lodgings, which by this time was opened, and instanter, on mentioning to the porter from whom he had come, was admitted to his master.

That great worthy was at the time sitting alone in a back chamber, which looked towards Salisbury Crags, and before him, but on the opposite side of the table, among divers letters and papers of business, lay a large Bible, with brass clasps thereon, in which, it would seem, some one had been expounding to him a portion of the Scriptures.

When my grandfather presented to him the letter from the Earl of Glencairn, he took it from him without much regarding him, and broke open the seal, and began to persue it to himself in that calm and methodical manner for which he was so famed and remarkable. Before, however, he had read above the half thereof, he gave as it were a sudden hitch, and turning round, looked my grandfather sharply in the face, and said,—

'Are you Gilhaize?'

But before any answer could be made, he waved his hand graciously, pointing to a chair, and desired him to sit down, resuming at the same time the perusal of the letter; and when he had finished it, he folded it up for a moment; but, as if recollecting himself, he soon runkled it up in his hand and put it into the fire.

'Your Lord informs me,' said he, 'that he has all confidence, not only in your honesty, Gilhaize, but in your discernment; and says, that in respect to the high question anent Christ's cause, you may be trusted to the uttermost. Truly, for so young a man, this is an exceeding renown. His letter has told me what passed last night with the Queen's Highness. I am grieved to hear it. She means well; but her feminine fears make her hearken to counsels that may cause the very evils whereof she is so afraid. But the sincerity of her favour to the Reformed will soon be tried, for last night John Knox arrived, and I was with him; and, strong in the assurances of his faith, he intends to lead on to the battle. This morning he was minded to depart for Fife. – 'Our Captain, Christ Jesus,' said he, 'and Satan, His adversary, are now at open defiance; their banners are displayed, and the trumpet is blown on both sides for assembling their armies.' As soon as it is known that he is within the kingdom, we shall learn what we may expect, and that presently too; for this very day the clergy meet in the monastery of the Greyfriars, and doubtless they will be advertised of his coming. You had as well try if you can gain admittance among the other auditors, to hear their deliberations; afterwards come again to me, and report what takes place; by that time I shall be advised whether to send you back to Glencairn or elsewhere.'

My grandfather, after this and some farther discourse, retired to the hall, and took breakfast with the household, where he was much edified with the douce deportment of all present, so unlike that of the lewd and graceless varlets who rioted in the houses of the other nobles. Verily, he used to say, the evidences of a reforming spirit were brightly seen there; and, to rule every one into a chaste sobriety of conversation, a pious clerk sate at the head of the board, and said grace before and after the meal, making it manifest how much all things about the Lord James Stuart were done in order.

Having taken breakfast, and reposed himself some time, for his long ride had made him very weary, he rose, and, changing his apparel, went to the Greyfriars church, where the clergy were assembling, and elbowing himself gently into the heart of the people waiting around for admission, he got in with the crowd when the doors were opened.

The matter that morning to be considered concerned the means to be taken, within the local jurisdictions of those there met, to enforce the process of the summons which had been issued against the reformed preachers to appear at Stirling.

But while they were busily conversing and contriving how best to aid and further that iniquitous aggression of perfidious tyranny, there came in one of the brethren of the monastery, with a frightened look, and cried aloud, that John Knox was come, and had been all night in the town. At the news the spectators, as if moved by one spirit, gave a triumphant shout, – the clergy were thunderstruck, – some started from their seats, unconscious of what they did, – others threw themselves back where they sat, – and all appeared as if a judgment had been pronounced upon them. In the same moment the church began to skail, – the session was adjourned, – and the people ran in all directions. The cry rose every where, 'John Knox is come!' All the town came rushing into the streets, – the old and the young, the lordly and the lowly, were seen mingling and marvelling together, – all tasks of duty, and servitude, and pleasure, were forsaken, – the sick-beds of the dying were deserted, – the priests abandoned their altars and masses, and stood pale and trembling at the doors of their churches, – mothers set down their infants on the floors, and ran to inquire what had come to pass, – funerals were suspended, and the impious and the guilty stood aghast, as if some dreadful apocalypse had been made; – travellers, with the bridles in their hands, lingering in profane discourse with their hosts, suddenly mounted, and speeded into the country with the tidings. At every cottage door and wayside bield, the inmates stood in clusters, silent and wondering, as horseman came following horseman, crying, 'John Knox is come!' Barks that had departed, when they heard the news, bore up to tell others that they saw afar at sea. The shepherds were called in from the hills; – the warders on the castle, when, at the sound of many quickened feet approaching, they challenged the comers, were answered, 'John Knox is come!' Studious men were roused from the spells of their books; – nuns, at their windows, looked out fearful and inquiring, – and priests and friars were seen standing by themselves, shunned like lepers. The whole land was stirred as with the inspiration of some new element, and the hearts of the persecutors were withered.

'No tongue,' often said my grandfather, 'could tell the sense of that great event through all the bounds of Scotland, and the papistical dominators shrunk as if they had suffered, in their powers and principalities, an awful and irremediable overthrow.'

When my grandfather left the Greyfriars, he went to the lodging of the Lord James Stuart, whom he found well instructed of all that had taken place, which he much marvelled at, having scarcely tarried by the way in going thither.

'Now, Gilhaize,' said my Lord, 'the tidings fly like wild-fire, and the Queen Regent, by the spirit that has descended into the hearts of the people, will be constrained to act one way or another. John Knox, as you perhaps know, stands under the ban of outlawry for conscience sake. In a little while we shall see whether he is still to be persecuted. If left free, the braird of the Lord, that begins to rise so green over all the land, will grow in peace to a plentiful harvest. But if he is to be hunted down, there will come such a cloud and storm as never raged before in Scotland. I speak to you thus freely, that you may report my frank sentiments to thir noble friends and trusty gentlemen, and say to them, that I am girded for the field, if need be.'

He then put a list of several well-known friends of the Reformation ayont the frith into my grandfather's hands, adding, 'I need not say that it is not fitting now to trust to paper, and therefore much will depend on yourself. The confidence that my friend the Earl, your master, has in you, makes me deal thus openly with you; and I may add, that if there is deceit in you, Gilhaize, I will never again believe the physiognomy of man – so go your ways; see all these, wheresoever they may be, – and take this purse for your charges.'

My grandfather accepted the paper and the purse; and reading over the paper, imprinted the names in it on his memory, and then said—

'My Lord, I need not risk the possession of this paper;

92

but it may be necessary to give me some token by which the lords and lairds therein mentioned may have assurance that I come from you.'

For some time the Lord James made no reply, but stood ruminating, with the forefinger of his left hand pressing his nether lip: then he observed—

'Your request is very needful;' and taking the paper, he mentioned divers things of each of the persons named in it, which he told my grandfather had passed between him and them severally when none other was present. 'By remembering them of these things,' said he, 'they will know that you are in verity sent from me.'

Being thus instructed, my grandfather left the Lord James, and proceeding forthwith to the pier of Leith, embarked in the Burntisland ferry-boat – and considering with himself, that the farthest away of those whom he was missioned to see ought to be the first informed, as the nearer had other ways and means of communion, he resolved to go forward to such of them as dwelt in Angus and Merns; by which resolution he reached Dundee shortly after the arrival there of the champion of the Reformation, John Knox.

This resolution proved most wise and fortunate; for, on landing in that town, he found a great concourse of the Reformed from the two shires assembled there, and among them many of those to whom he was specially sent. They had come to go with their ministers before the Queen Regent's counsel at Stirling, determined to avow their adherence to the doctrines of which those pious men were accused. And it being foreseen, that as they went forward others would join, my grandfather thought he could do no better in his mission than mingle with them, the more especially as John Knox was also to be of that great company.

On the day following, they accordingly all set forward towards Perth, – and they were a glorious army, mighty with the strength of their great ally the Lord of the hosts of heaven. No trumpet sounded in their march, nor was the courageous drum heard among them, – nor the shouts of earthly soldiery, – nor the neigh of the war-horse, – nor the voice of any captain. But they sang hymns of triumph, and psalms of the great things that Jehovah had of old done for his people; and though no banner was seen there, nor sword on the thighs of men of might, nor spears in the grasp of warriors, nor crested helmet, nor aught of the panoply of battle, yet the eye of faith beheld more than all these, for the hills and heights of Scotland were to its dazzled vision covered that day with the mustered armies of the dreadful God: – the angels of his wrath in their burning chariots; the archangels of his omnipotence, calm in their armour of storms and flaming fires, and the Rider on the white horse, were all there.

As the people with their ministers advanced, their course was like a river, which continually groweth in strength and spreadeth its waters as it rolls onward to the sea. On all sides came streams of new adherents to their holy cause, in so much that when they arrived at Perth it was thought best to halt there, lest the approach of so great a multitude, though without weapons, should alarm the Queen Regent's government. Accordingly they made a pause, and Erskine of Dun, one of the Lord James Stuart's friends, taking my grandfather with him, and only two other servants, rode forward to Stirling, to represent to her Highness the faith and the firmness of the people.

When they arrived, they found the town in consternation. Busy were the bailies, marshalling such of the burgesses as could be persuaded to take up arms; but all who joined them were feckless aged men, dealers and traffickers in commodities for the courtiers. Proud was the provost that day, and a type of the cause for which he was gathering his papistical remnants. At the sight of Dun and his three followers riding up the street to the castle, he was fain to draw out his sword and make a salutation; but it stuck sae dourly in, that he was obligated to gar ane of the town-officers hold the scabbard, while he pulled with such might and main at the hilt, that the blade suddenly broke off, and back he stumbled, and up flew his heels, so that even my grandfather was constrained, notwithstanding the solemnity of the occasion, to join in the shout of laughter that rose thereat from all present. But provosts and bailies, not being men of war, should not expose themselves to such adversities.

Nor was the fyke of impotent preparation within the walls of the castle better. The Queen had been in a manner lanerly with her ladies when the sough of the coming multitude reached her. The French guards had not come from Glasgow, and there was none of the warlike nobles of the papistical sect at that time at Stirling. She had therefore reason both for dread and panic, when the news arrived that all Angus and Merns had rebelled, for so it was at first reported.

On the arrival of Dun, he was on the instant admitted to her presence; for she was at the time in the tapestried chamber, surrounded by her priests and ladies, and many officers, all consulting her according to their fears. The sight, said my grandfather, for he also went into the presence, was a proof to him that the cause of the papacy was in the dead-thraws, the judgments of all present being so evidently in a state of discomfiture and desertion.

Dun going forward with the wonted reverences, the Queen said to him abruptly—

'Well, Erskine, what is this?'

Whereupon he represented to her, in a sedate manner, that the reformed ministers were not treated as they had been encouraged to hope; nevertheless, to show their submission to those in temporal authority over them, they were coming, in obedience to the citation, to stand trial.

'But their retinue – when have delinquents come to trial so attended?' she exclaimed eagerly.

'The people, please your Highness,' said Dun, with a steadfastness of manner that struck every one with respect for him, – 'the people hold the same opinions and believe the same doctrines as their preachers, and they feel that the offence, if it be offence, of which the ministers are accused, lies equally against them, and therefore they have resolved to make their case a common cause.'

'And do they mean to daunt us from doing justice against seditious schismatics?' cried her Highness somewhat in anger.

'They mean,' replied Dun, 'to let your Highness see

whether it be possible to bring so many to judgment. Their sentiment, with one voice, is, Cursed be they that seek the effusion of blood, or war, or dissension. Let us possess the evangile, and none within Scotland shall be more obedient subjects. In sooth, madam, they hold themselves as guilty of the crime charged as their ministers are, and they will suffer with them.'

'Suffer! call you rebellion suffering?' exclaimed the Queen.

'They have not yet rebelled,' said Dun, calmly; 'they come to remonstrate with your Highness first; for, as Christians, they are loth to draw the sword. They have no arms with them, to the end that no one may dare to accuse them of any treason.'

'It is a perilous thing when subjects,' said the Queen, much troubled, 'declare themselves so openly against the authority of their rulers.'

'It is a bold thing for rulers,' replied Dun, 'to meddle with the consciences of their subjects.'

'How!' exclaimed the Queen, startled and indignant.

'I will deal yet more plainly with your Highness,' said he firmly. 'This pretended offence, of which the Reformed are accused, is not against the royal authority. They are good and true subjects, and, by their walk and conversation, bear testimony to the excellence and purity of those doctrines for which they are resolved to sacrifice their lives rather than submit to any earthly dictation. Their controversies pertain to things of Christ's kingdom, – it is a spiritual warfare. But the papists, conscious of their weakness in the argument, would fain see your Highness abandon that impartial justice which you were called of Heaven to administer in your great office, and to act factiously on their side, as if the cause of the Gospel could be determined by the arm of flesh.'

'What has brought you here?' exclaimed the Queen, bursting into tears.

'To claim the fulfilment of your royal promises,' said Dun, making a lowly reverence, that by its humility took away all arrogance from the boldness of the demand.

'I will,' said she: 'I am ever willing to be just, but this

rising has shaken me with apprehensions; therefore, I pray you, Erskine, write to your brethren; bid them disperse; and tell them from me, that their ministers shall neither be tried nor molested.'

At these words, she took the arm of one of her ladies and hastily retired. Dun also withdrew, and the same hour sent my grandfather back to Perth with letters to the Congregation, to the effect of her request and assurance.

That same evening the multitude broke up and returned to their respective homes, rejoicing with an exceeding great joy at so blessed a termination of their weaponless Christian war. Dun, however, distrusting the influence of some of those who were of the Queen's council, and who had arrived at the castle soon after my grandfather's departure, did not return, as he had intended, next morning to Perth, but resolved to wait over the day of trial; or, at least, until the ministers were absolved from attendance on the summons, either by proclamation or other forms of law.

John Knox, among all the ministers who remained at Perth after the Congregation of the Reformed had dispersed, was the only one, my grandfather has been heard to say, that expressed no joy nor exultation at the assurances of the Queen Regent. 'We shall see, we shall see,' was all he said to those among them who gloried in the victory; adding, 'But if there is truth in the Word of God, it is not in the nature of the Beast to do otherwise than evil;' and his words of discernment and of wisdom were soon verified.

Erskine of Dun, while he remained at Stirling, had his eyes and ears open; and in their porches he placed, for sentinels, Distrust and Suspicion. He knew the fluctuating nature of woman; how every succeeding wave of feeling washes away the deepest traces that are traced on the quicksands of her unstable humours; and the danger having passed, he jealoused that the Queen Regent would forget her terrors, and give herself up to the headlong councils of the adversaries, whom, from her known adherence to the Romanish ritual, he justly feared she was inclined to favour. Nor was he left long in doubt.

On the evening before the day which had been appointed for the trial, no proclamation or other token was promulged to appease the anxieties of the cited preachers. He, there-fore, thought it needful to be prepared for the worst; so, accordingly, he ordered his two serving-men to have his horses in readiness forth the town in the morning, and there to abide his orders.

Without giving any other about him the slightest inkling of what he had conceited, he went up betimes to the castle, having learnt that the Queen Regent was that day to hold a council. And being a man held in great veneration by all parties, and well known to the household of the court, he obtained access to the ante-chamber after the council was met; and standing there, he was soon surprised by her Highness coming out, leaning on the arm of the Lord Wintoun, and seemingly much disturbed. On seeing him she was startled, and paused for a moment; but soon collecting all her pride, she dropped the Lord Wintoun's arm, and walked straight through the apartment without noticing any one, and holding herself aloft with an air of resolute dignity.

Dun augured no good from this; but following till the Lord Wintoun had attended her to the end of the long painted gallery, where she stopped at the door that opened to her private apartments, he there awaited that nobleman's return, and inquired of him if the process against the protestant ministers had been rescinded.

'No,' said Wintoun, peevishly; 'the summons have been called over, and they have not appeared, either in person or by agents.'

'Say you so, my Lord!' cried Dun; 'and what is the result?'

'Outlawry, for non-appearance, is pronounced against them,' replied Wintoun, haughtily, and went straight back into the council-chamber.

Dun thought it unnecessary to inquire farther; so, without making more ado, he instanter left the castle, and, going down the town, went to the spot where his horses stood ready, and, mounting, rode off with the tidings to Perth, grieving sorely at the gross perfidy and sad deceit which the Queen Regent had been so practised on, by the heads of the papist faction, to commit.

It happened on the same day, that John Knox, who remained at Perth, a wakeful warder on a post of peril, was moved by the spirit of God to preach a sermon, in which he exposed the idolatry of the mass and the depravity of image-worship. My grandfather was present, and he often said that preaching was an era and epoch worthy to be held in everlasting remembrance. It took place in the Greyfriars' church. There was an understanding among the people that it was to be there; but many fearing the monks might attempt to prevent it, a vast concourse, chiefly men, assembled at the ordinary mass hour, and remained in the church till the Reformer came, so that, had the friars tried to keep him out, they could not have shut the doors.

A lane was made through the midst of the crowd to admit the preacher to the pulpit; and when he was seen advancing, aged and feeble, and leaning on his staff, many were moved with compassion, and doubted if it could be the wonderful man of whom every tongue spoke. But when he had ascended and began, he seemed to undergo a great transfiguration. His abject mien and his sickly visage became majestic and glorious. His eyes lightened; his countenance shone as with the radiance of a spirit that blazed within; and his voice dirled to the heart like vehement thunder.

Sometimes he spoke to the understandings of those who heard him, of that insane doctrine which represented the mission of the Redeemer to consist of believing, in despite of sight, and smell, and touch, and taste, that wafers and wine were actually the flesh and blood of a man that was crucified, with nails driven through his feet and hands, many hundred years ago. Then, rising into the contemplation of the divinity of the Saviour, he trampled under the feet of his eloquence a belief so contrary to the instincts and senses with which Infinite Wisdom has gifted his creatures; and bursting into ecstasy at the thought of this idolatrous invention, he called on the people to look at the images and the effigies in the building around them, and believe, if they could, that such things, the handy works of carpenters and masons, were endowed with miraculous energies far above the faculties of man. Kindling into a still higher mood, he preached to those very images, and demanded of them, and those they represented, to show any proof that they were entitled to reverence. 'God forgive my idolatry,' he exclaimed, 'I forget myself – these things are but stocks and stones.'

Not one of all who heard him that day ever gave ear again to papistry.

When he had made an end, and had retired from the

church, many still lingered, discoursing of his marvellous lecture, and, among others, my grandfather.

An imprudent priest belonging to the convent, little aware of the great conversion which had been wrought, began to prepare for the celebration of the mass, and a callan who was standing near, encouraged by the contempt which some of those around expressed at this folly, jibed the priest, and he drove him away. The boy, however, returned, and levelling a stone at a crucifix on the altar, shattered it to pieces. In an instant, as if caught by a whirlwind, the whole papistical trumpery was torn down, and dashed into fragments. The cry of 'Down with the idols!' became universal: hundreds on hundreds came rushing to the spot. The magistrates and the ministers came flying to beseech order and to sooth the multitude; but a Divine ire was upon the people, who heard no voice but only the cry of 'Down with the idols!' and their answer was, 'Burn, burn, and destroy!'

The monasteries of the Black and the Grey Friars were sacked and rendered desolate, and the gorgeous edifice of the Carthusian monks levelled to the ground.

So dreadful a tumult had never before been heard of within the realm. Many of the best of the Reformed deplored the handle it would give to the blasphemies of their foes. Even my grandfather was smitten with consternation and grief; for he could not but think that such a terrible temporal outrage would be followed by a temporal revenge as ruthless and complete. Sober minds shuddered at the sudden and sacrilegious overthrow of such venerable structures; and many that stood on the threshold of the house of papistical bondage, and were on the point of leaving it, retired in again, and barred the doors against the light, and hugged their errors as blameless compared with such enormities. To no one did the event give pleasure but to John Knox. 'The work,' said he, 'has been done, it is true, by the rascal multitude; but when the nests are destroyed the rooks will fly away.'

The thing, however, most considered at that time, was the panic which this intemperance would cause to the Queen Regent; and my grandfather, seeing it had changed the complexion of his mission, resolved to return the same evening by the Queensferry to the Lord James Stuart at Edinburgh. For the people no sooner cooled, and came to a sense of reflection, than they discerned that they had committed a heinous offence against the laws, and, apprehending punishment, prepared to defend themselves.

Thus, by the irresolute and promise-breaking policy of the Queen, was the people maddened into grievous excesses, and many of those who submitted quietly in the faith of her assurances, and had returned to their respective homes, considered the trumpet as sounded, and began to gird themselves for battle.

It's far from my hand and intent, to write a history of the tribulations which ensued from the day of the uproar and first outbreaking of the wrath of the people against the images of the Romish idolatry; and therefore I shall proceed, with all expedient brevity, to relate what farther, in those sore times, fell under the eye of my grandfather, who, when he returned to Edinburgh, found the Lord James Stuart on the point of proceeding to the Queen Regent at Stirling, and he went with him thither.

On arriving at the castle, they found the French soldiery all collected in the town, and her Highness, like another fiery Bellona, vowing to avenge the calamities that had befallen the idols and images of Perth; and summoning and invoking the nobility, and every man of substance she could think of, to come with their vassals, that she might be enabled to chastise such sacrilegious rebellion.

The Lord James Stuart seeing her so bent on extremities, and knowing, by his secret intelligences, that strong powers were ready to start forward at a moment's warning, both in the West, and in Fife, Angus, and Merns, entreated her to listen to more moderate councils than those of revenge and resentment, and rather to think of pacification than of punishment. But she was fiery with passion, and a blinded instrument in the hands of Providence to work out the deliverance of the land, even by the crooked policy that her papistical counsellors hurried her into. So that the Lord James, seeing she was transported beyond reason, sent my grandfather and other secret emissaries to warn the Lords and leaders of the Congregation, and to tell them, that her Highness was minded to surprise Perth as soon as she had gathered a sufficient array.

The conduct of that great worthy was in this full of

wisdom, and foresight, and policy. By staying with the Queen he incurred the suspicion of the Reformed, to whom he was a devoted friend; but he gained a knowledge of the intents of their enemies, by which he was enabled to turn aside the edge of vengeance when it was meant to be most deadly. Accordingly, reckless of the opinions of men, he went forward with the Queen's army towards Perth; but before they had crossed the Water of Earn, word was brought to her Highness, that the Earl of Glencairn, at the head of two thousand five hundred of the Reformed, was advancing from the shire of Ayr.

Such were the fruits of my grandfather's mission to the Lord Boyd, and he heard likewise that the bold and free lairds of Angus and Merns, with all their followers, had formed themselves in battle-array to defend the town. Still, however, her Highness was resolute to go on; for she was instigated by her feminine anger, even as much as by the wicked councils of the papist lords by whom she was surrounded.

But when she reached the heights that overlooked the sweet valley of the Tay, whose green and gentle bosom was then sparkling with the glances of warlike steel, her heart was softened, and she called to her the Lord James Stuart and the young Earl of Argyle, – the old Lord, his father, had died some time prior, – and sent them to the army of the Congregation, that peace might still be preserved. They accordingly went into the town, and sending notice to the leaders of the Reformed to appoint two of their party to confer with them, John Knox and the Master Willocks were nominated. My grandfather, who attended the Lord James on this occasion, was directed by him to receive the two deputies at the door and to conduct them in; and when they came he was much troubled to observe the state of their minds; for Master Willocks was austere in his looks as if resolved on quarrel, and the Reformer was agitated and angry, muttering to himself as he ascended the stairs, making his staff often dirl on the steps. No sooner were they shown into the presence of the two lords, even before the door was shut, than John Knox began to upbraid the Lord

James for having broken the covenant and forsaken the Congregation.

Much to that effect, my grandfather afterwards learnt, passed; but the Lord James pacified him with the assurance that his heart and spirit were still true to the cause, and that he had come with Argyle to prevent, if possible, the shedding of blood; he likewise declared both for himself and the Earl, who had hitherto always abided by the Queen, that if she refused to listen to reasonable terms, or should break any treaty entered into, they would openly take part against her.

Upon these assurances a treaty was concluded, by which it was agreed, that both armies should retire peaceably to their respective habitations; that the town should be made accessible to the Queen Regent; that no molestation should be given to those who were then in arms for the Congregation, and no persecutions undertaken against the Reformed, – with other covenants calculated to sooth the Congregation and allay men's fears. But no sooner was this treaty ratified, the army of the Congregation dispersed, and her Highness in possession of the town, than it was manifest no vows nor obligations were binding towards the heretics, as the Reformed were called. The Queen's French guards, even when attending her into the town, fired into the house of a known zealous protestant and killed his son; the inhabitants were plundered and insulted with impunity, and the magistrates were dismissed to make way for men devoted to papistry.

The Earl of Argyle and the Lord James Stuart, filled with wrath and indignation at such open perfidy, went straight into her Highness' presence without asking audience, and reproached her with deceit and craftiness; and having so vented their minds, instanter quitted the court and the town, and, attended by my grandfather and a few other servants, departed for Fife, to which John Knox had also retired after the dispersion of the Congregation at Perth. The Lord James, in virtue of being Prior of St Andrews, went thither attended by the Earl, and sent my grandfather to Crail, where the Reformer was then preaching, to invite him to meet them and others of the Congregation with all convenient expedition.

My grandfather never having been before in Crail, and not knowing how the people there might stand affected, instead of inquiring for John Knox, bethought himself of his acquaintance with Bailie Kilspinnie, and so speired his way to his dwelling, little hoping, from the fearful nature of that honest man, he would find him within. But, contrary to his expectation, he was not only there, but he welcomed my grandfather as an old and very cordial friend, leading him into his house and making much of him, telling him, with a voice of cheerfulness, that the day of reckoning had at last overtaken the lascivious idolaters.

Then he caused to be brought in before my grandfather the five pretty babies that his wife had abandoned for her papistical paramour, the eldest of whom was but turned of nine years. The thoughts of their mother's shame overcame their father at that moment, and the tears coming into his eyes he sobbed aloud as he looked at them, and wept bitterly, while they flocked around, and wreathed him, as it were, with their caresses and innocent blandishments. So tender a scene melted my grandfather's spirit into sadness; and he could not remain master of himself, when the eldest, a mild and meek little maiden, said to him, as if to excuse her father's sorrow, 'A foul friar made my mother an ill-doer, and took her away ae night when she was just done wi' harkening our prayers.'

At this juncture, a blooming and modest-eyed damsel came into the room; but, seeing a stranger, she drew back and was going away, when the bailie, drying his eyes, said—

'Come ben, Elspa; this is the young man that ye hae heard me sae commend for his kind friendship to me, in that dotage-dauner that I made in my distraction to St Andrews. This,' he added, turning to my grandfather, 'is Elspa Ruet, the sister of that misfortunate woman; – to my helpless bairns she does their mother's duty.'

Elspa made a gentle beck as her brother-in-law was speaking, and turning round, dropt a tear on the neck of the youngest baby, as she leant down to take it up for a screen to hide her blushing face, that reddent with the thought at seeing one who had so witnessed her sister's shame.

From that hour her image had a dear place in my grandfather's bosom, and after the settlement of the Reformation throughout the realm, he courted her, and she became his wife, and in process of time my grandmother. But of her manifold excellencies I shall have occasion to speak more at large hereafter, for she was no ordinary woman, but a saint throughout life, returning in a good old age to her Maker, almost as blameless as she came from His pure hands; and nothing became her more in all her piety, than the part she acted towards her guilty sister.

Having taken away the children, she then brought in divers refreshments, and a flagon of posset; but she remained not with the bailie and my grandfather while they partook thereof; so that they were left free to converse as they listed, and my grandfather was glad to find, as I have already said, that the poor man had triumphed over his fond grief, and was reconciled to his misfortunes as well as any father could well be, with so many deserted babies, and three of them daughters.

He likewise learnt, with no less solace and satisfaction, that the Reformed were strong in Crail, and that the magistrates and beinest burgesses had been present on the day before at the preaching of John Knox, and had afterwards suffered the people to demolish the images and all the monuments of papistry, without molestation or hinderance; so that the town was cleansed of the pollution of idolatry, and the worship of humble and contrite hearts established there, instead of the pagan pageantry of masses and altars.

After the repast was finished, the bailie conducted my grandfather to the house where John Knox then lodged, to whom he communicated his message from the Lord James Stuart.

'Tell your master,' was the reply of the Reformer, 'that I will be with him, God willing; and God is willing, for this invitation, and the state of men's minds, maketh His will manifest. Yea, I was minded myself to go thither; for that same city of St Andrews is the Zion of Scotland. Of old, the glad tidings of salvation were first heard there, – there, amidst the damps and the darkness of ages, the ancient Culdees, men whose memory is still fragrant for piety and purity of faith and life, supplied the oil of the lamp of the living God for a period of four hundred years, independent of pope, prelate, or any human supremacy. There it was that a spark of their blessed embers was, in our own day, first blown into a flame, – and there, please God, where I, His unworthy instrument, was condemned as a criminal for His truth's sake, shall I, in His strength, be the herald of His triumph and great victory.'

When my grandfather had returned to the bailie's house after delivering his message to the Reformer, he spent an evening of douce but pleasant pastime with him and the modest Elspa Ruet, whose conversation was far above her degree, and seasoned with the sweet savour of holiness. But ever and anon, though all parties strove to eschew the subject, they began to speak of her erring sister, the bailie compassionating her continuance in sin as a man and a Christian should, but showing no wish nor will to mind her any more as kith or kin to him or his; a temper that my grandfather was well content to observe he had attained. Not so was that of Elspa; but her words were few and well-chosen, and they made a deep impression on my grandfather; for she seemed fain to hide what was passing in her heart.

Twice or thrice she spoke of the ties of nature, intimating that they were as a bond and obligation laid on by THE MAKER, whereby kindred were bound to stand by one another in weal or in wo, lest those who sinned should be utterly abandoned by all the world. The which tender and Christian sentiment, though it was melodious to my grandfather's spirit, pierced it with a keen pain; for he thought of the manner in which he had left his own parents, even though it was for the blessed sake of religion, and his bosom was at the moment filled with sorrow. But, when he said how much he regretted and was yet unrepentant of that step, Elspa cheered him with a consolation past utterance, by reminding him, that he had neither left them to want nor to sin; that, by quitting the shelter of their wing, he had but obeyed the promptings of nature, and that if, at any time hereafter, father or mother stood in need of his aid or exhortation, he could still do his duty.

Without well considering what he said, the bailie observed on this, that he was surprised to hear her say so, and yet allow her sister to remain so long unreproved in her offences.

Elspa Ruet to this made no immediate reply, – she was indeed unable; – and my grandfather sympathized with her, for the sting had plainly penetrated to the very marrow of her soul. At last, however, she said,—

'Your reproach is just, I hae been to blame baith to Heaven and man – but the thing has na been unthought, only I kent na how to gang about the task; and yet what gars me say sae but a woman's weakness, for the road's no sae lang to St Andrews, and surely iniquity does not there so abound, that no ane would help me to the donsie woman's bower.'

My grandfather, on hearing this, answered, that if she was indeed minded to try to rescue her sister, he was ready and willing to do all with her and for her that she could desire; but, bearing in mind the light woman's open shame, he added, 'I'm fearful it's yet owre soon to hope for her amendment: she'll hae to fin the evil upshot of her ungodly courses, I doubt, before she'll be wrought into a frame of sincere penitence.'

'Nevertheless,' replied Elspa Ruet, 'I will try; it's my duty, and my sisterly love bids me no to be slothful in the task.' At which words she burst into sore and sorrowful weeping, saying, 'Alas, alas! that she should have so fallen! – I loved her – oh! naebody can tell how dearly – even as I loved myself. When I first saw my ain face in a looking-glass I thought it was her, and kissed it for the likeness, in pity that it didna look sae fair as it was wont to be. But it's the Lord's pleasure, and in permitting her to sink so low HE has no doubt some great lesson to teach.'

Thus, from less to more, as they continued conversing, it was agreed that Elspa Ruet should ride on a pad ahint my grandfather next morning to St Andrews, in order to try if the thing could be to move her sister to the humiliation of contrition for her loose life. And some small preparations being needful, Elspa departed and left the bailie and my grandfather together.

'But,' said my grandfather to him, after she had been some time away, 'is't your design to take the unfortunate woman back amang your innocent lassie bairns?'

'No,' replied the bailie; 'that's no a thing to be now thought of; please Providence, she'll ne'er again darken my door; I'll no, however, allow her to want. Her mother, poor auld afflicted woman, that has ne'er refrain't from greeting since her flight, she'll tak her in; but atween her and me there's a divorce for ever.'

By daylight my grandfather had his horse at the door; and Elspa having borrowed the provost's lady's pad over night, it was buckled on, and they were soon after on the road.

It was a sunny morning in June, and all things were bright, and blithe, and blooming. The spirits of youth, joy, and enjoyment, were spread abroad on the earth. The butterflies, like floating lilies, sailed from blossom to blossom, and the gowans, the bright and beautiful eyes of the summer, shone with gladness, as Nature walked on bank and brae, in maiden pride, spreading and showing her new flowery mantle to the sun. The very airs that stirred the glittering trees were soft and genial as the breath of life; and the leaves of the aspine seemed to lap the sunshine like the tongues of young and happy creatures that delight in their food.

As my grandfather and Elspa Ruet rode along together, they partook of the universal benignity with which all things seemed that morning so graciously adorned, and their hearts were filled with the hope that their united endeavours to save her fallen sister would be blessed with success. But when they came in sight of the papal towers and gorgeous edifices of St Andrews, which then raised their proud heads, like Babel, so audaciously to the heavens, they both became silent.

My grandfather's thoughts ran on what might ensue if the Archbishop were to subject him to his dominion, and he resolved, as early as possible, to make known his arrival to the Lord James Stuart, who, in virtue of being head of the priory, was then resident there, and to claim his protection. Accordingly he determined to ride with Elspa Ruet to the house of the vintner in the Shoegate, of which I have already spoken, and to leave her under the care of Lucky Kilfauns, as the hostess was called, until he had done so. But fears and sorrows were busy with the fancy of his fair companion; and it was to her a bitter thing, as she afterwards told him, to think that the purpose of her errand was to entreat a beloved sister to leave a life of shame and sin, and sadly doubting if she would succeed.

Being thus occupied with their respective cogitations, they entered the city in silence, and reached the vintner's door without having exchanged a word for several miles. There Elspa alighted, and being commended to the care of Lucky Kilfauns, who, though of a free outspoken nature, was a most creditable matron, my grandfather left her, and rode up the gait to the priory yett, where, on his arrival, he made himself known to the porter, and was admitted to the Lord Prior, as the Lord James was there papistically called.

Having told his Lordship that he had delivered his message to John Knox, and that the Reformer would not fail to attend the call, he then related partly what had happened to himself in his former sojourn at St Andrews, and how and for what end he had brought Elspa Ruet there that day with him, entreating the Lord James to give him his livery and protection, for fear of the Archbishop; which, with many pleasing comments on his devout and prudent demeanour, that noble worthy most readily vouchsafed, and my grandfather returned to the vintner's.

When my grandfather had returned to the vintner's, he found that Elspa had conferred with Lucky Kilfauns concerning the afflicting end and intent of her journey to St Andrews; and that decent woman, sympathizing with her sorrow, telling her of many woful things of the same sort she had herself known, and how a cousin of her mother's, by the father's side, had been wiled away from her home by the abbot of Melrose, and never heard tell of for many a day, till she was discovered, in the condition of a disconsolate nun, in a convent, far away in Nithsdale. But the great difficulty was to get access to Marion Ruet's bower, for so, from that day, was Mrs Kilspinnie called again by her sister; and, after no little communing, it was proposed by Lucky Kilfauns, that Elspa should go with her to the house of a certain widow, Dingwall, and there for a time take up her abode, and that my grandfather, after putting on the Prior's livery, should look about him for the gilly, his former guide, and, through him, make a tryst to meet the dissolute madam at the widow's house. Accordingly the matter was so settled, and while Lucky Kilfauns, in a most motherly and pitiful manner, carried Elspa Ruet to the house of the Widow Dingwall, my grandfather went back to the priory to get the cloak and arms of the Lord James' livery.

When he was equipped, he then went fearless all about the town, and met with no molestation; only he saw at times divers of the Archbishop's men, who recollected him, and who, as he passed, stopped and looked after him, and whispered to one another and muttered fierce words. Much he desired to fall in with that humane Samaritan, Leonard Meldrum, the seneschal of the castle, and fain would he have gone thither to inquire for him; but, until he had served the turn of the mournful Elspa Ruet, he would not allow any wish of his own to lead him to aught wherein there was the hazard of any trouble that might balk her pious purpose.

After daunering from place to place, and seeing nothing of the stripling, he was obligated to give twalpennies to a stabler's lad to search for him, who soon brought him to the vintner's, where my grandfather, putting on the look of a losel and roister, gave him a groat, and bade him go to the madam's dwelling, and tell her that he would be, from the gloaming, all the night at the Widow Dingwall's, where he would rejoice exceedingly if she could come and spend an hour or two.

The stripling, so fee'd, was right glad, and made himself so familiar towards my grandfather, that Lucky Kilfauns observing it, the better to conceal their plot, feigned to be most obstreperous, flyting at him with all her pith and bir, and chiding my grandfather, as being as scant o' grace as a gaberlunzie, or a novice of the Dominicans. However, they worked so well together, that the gilly never misdoubted either her or my grandfather, and took the errand to his mistress, from whom he soon came with a light foot and a glaikit eye, saying she would na fail to keep the tryst.

That this new proof of the progress she was making in guilt and sin might be the more tenderly broken to her chaste and gentle sister, Lucky Kilfauns herself undertook to tell Elspa what had been covenanted to prepare her for the meeting. My grandfather would fain have had a milder mediatrix, for the vintner's worthy wife was wroth against the concubine, calling her offence redder than the crimson of schism, and blacker than the broth of the burning brimstone of heresy, with many other vehement terms of indignation, none worse than the wicked woman deserved, though harsh to be heard by a sister, that grieved for her unregenerate condition far more than if she had come from Crail to St Andrews only to lay her head in the coffin.

The paction between all parties being thus covenanted, and Lucky Kilfauns gone to prepare the fortitude of Elspa Ruet for the trial it was to undergo, my grandfather walked out alone to pass the time till the trysted hour. It was then late in the afternoon, and as he sauntered along he could

not but observe that something was busy with the minds
and imaginations of the people. Knots of the douce and
elderly shopkeepers were seen standing in the street, with
their heads laid together; and as he walked towards the
priory he met the provost between two of the bailies, with
the dean of guild, coming sedately, and with very great
solemnity in their countenances, down the crown of the
causey, heavily laden with magisterial fears. He stopped
to look at them, and he remarked that they said little to
one another, but what they did say seemed to be words of
weight; and when any of their friends and acquaintances
happened to pass, they gave them a nod that betokened
much sadness of heart.

The cause of all this anxiety was not, in its effects and
influence, meted only to the men and magistrates: the
women partook of them even to a greater degree. They
were seen passing from house to house, out at one door
and into the next, and their faces were full of strange
matters. One in particular, whom my grandfather noticed
coming along, was often addressed with brief questions,
and her responses were seemingly as awful as an oracle's.
She was an aged carlin, who, in her day, had been a
midwife, but having in course of time waxed old, and
being then somewhat slackened in the joints of the right
side by a paralytic, she eked out the weakly remainder of
her thread of life in visitations among the families that, in
her abler years, she had assisted to increase and multiply.
She was then returning home after spending the day, as my
grandfather afterwards heard from the Widow Dingwall,
with the provost's daughter, at whose birth she had been
the howdy, and who, being married some months, had sent
to consult her anent a might-be occasion.

As she came toddling along, with pitty-patty steps, in a
rose satin mantle that she got as a blithemeat gift when
she helped the young master of Elcho into the world,
drawn close over her head, and leaning on a staff with
her right hand, while in her left she carried a Flanders
pig of strong ale, with a clout o'er the mouth to keep
it from jawping, scarcely a door or entry mouth was
she allowed to pass, but she was obligated to stop and

speak, and what she said appeared to be tidings of no comfort.

All these things bred wonder and curiosity in the breast of my grandfather, who, not being acquaint with any body that he saw, did not like for some time to inquire; but at last his diffidence and modesty were overcome, by the appearance of a strong party of the Archbishop's armed retainers, followed by a mob of bairns and striplings, yelling, and scoffing at them with bitter taunts and many titles of derision; and on inquiring at a laddie, what had caused the consternation in the town, and the passage of so many soldiers from the castle, he was told that they expected John Knox the day following, and that he was mindet to preach, but the Archbishop has resolved no to let him. It was even so; for the Lord James Stuart, who possessed a deep and forecasting spirit, had, soon after my grandfather's arrival with the Reformer's answer, made the news known to try the temper of the inhabitants and burghers. But, saving this marvelling and preparation, nothing farther of a public nature took place that night; so that, a short time before the hour appointed, my grandfather went to the house of Widow Dingwall, where he found Elspa Ruet sitting very disconsolate in a chamber by herself, weeping bitterly at the woful account which Lucky Kilfauns had brought of her sister's loose life, and fearing greatly that all her kind endeavours and humble prayers would be but as water spilt on the ground.

As the time of appointment drew near, Elspa Ruet was enabled to call in her wandering and anxious thoughts, and, strengthened by her duty, the blessing of the tranquil mind was shed upon her. Her tears were dried up, and her countenance shone with a serene benignity. When she was an aged withered woman, my grandfather has been heard to say, that he never remembered her appearance without marvelling at the special effusion of holiness and beauty which beamed and brightened upon her in that trying hour, nor without thinking that he still beheld the glory of its twilight glowing through the dark and faded clouds of her old age.

They had not sat long when a tapping was heard at the widow's door, and my grandfather, starting up, retired into a distant corner of the room, behind a big napery-press, and sat down in the obscurity of its shadow. Elspa remained in her seat beside the table, on which a candle was burning, and, as it stood behind the door, she could not be seen by any coming in, till they had passed into the middle of the floor.

In little more than the course of a minute, the voice of her sister was heard, and light footsteps on the timber stair. The door was then opened, and Marion swirled in with an uncomely bravery. Elspa started from her seat. The guilty and convicted creature uttered a shriek; but in the same moment her pious sister clasped her with loving-kindness in her arms, and bursting into tears, wept bitterly, with sore sobs, for some time on her bosom, which was wantonly unkerchiefed.

After a short space of time, with confusion of face, and frowns of mortification, and glances of rage, the abandoned Marion disengaged herself from her sister's fond and sorrowful embraces, and, retreating to a chair, sat down, and seemed to muster all the evil passions of the guilty breast, – fierce anger, sharp hatred, and gnawing contempt; and a bad boldness of look that betokened a worse spirit than them all.

'It was na to see the like of you I cam' here,' said she, with a scornful toss of her head.

'I ken that, Marion,' replied Elspa, mournfully.

'And what business then hae ye to come to snool me?'

Elspa for a little while made no answer to this, but, drying her eyes, she went to her seat composedly, and then said,—

'Cause ye're my sister, and brought shame and disgrace on a' your family. – O Marion, I'm wae to say this! – but ye're owre brave in your sin.'

'Do ye think I'll e'er gae back to that havering, daunering cuif o' a creature, the Crail bailie?'

'He's a man o' mair worth and conduct, Marion,' replied her sister, firmly, 'than to put that in your power – even, woman, if ye were penitent, and besought him for charity.'

'Weel, weel, no to clishmaclaver about him, how's a' wi' the bairns?'

'Are ye no frighted, Marion, to speer sic a question, when ye think how ye left them, and what for ye did sae?'

'Am na I their mither, have na I a right to speer?'

'No,' said Elspa; 'when ye forgot that ye were their father's wife, they lost their mother.'

'Ye need na be sae snell wi' your taunts,' exclaimed Marion, evidently endeavouring to preserve the arrogance she had assumed; 'ye need na be sae snell; I'm far better off, and happier than e'er I was in James Kilspinnie's aught.'

'That's no possible,' said her sister. 'It would be an unco thing of Heaven to let wickedness be happier than honesty. But, Marion, dinna deceive yoursel', ye hae nae sure footing on the steading where ye stan'. The Bishop will nae mair, than your gudeman, thole your loose life to him. If he kent ye were here, I doubt he would let you bide, and what would become of you then?'

'He's no sic a fool as to be angry that I am wi' my sister.'

'That may be,' replied Elspa: 'I'm thinking, however, if in my place here he saw but that young man,' and she pointed to my grandfather, whom her sister had not till then observed, 'he would have some cause to consider.'

Marion attempted to laugh scornfully, but her heart gurged within her, and instead of laughter, her voice broke out into wild and horrid yells, and falling back in her chair, she grew stiff and ghastly to behold, in so much, that both Elspa and my grandfather were terrified, and had to work with her for some time before they were able to recover her; nor indeed did she come rightly to herself till she got relief by tears; but they were tears of rage, and not shed for any remorse on account of her foul fault. Indeed, no sooner was she come to herself, than she began to rail at her sister and my grandfather, calling them by all the terms of scorn that her tongue could vent. At last she said—

'But nae doubt ye're twa Reformers.'

'Ay,' replied Elspa, 'in a sense we are sae, for we would fain help to reform you.'

But after a long, faithful, and undaunted endeavour on the part of Elspa, in this manner, to reach the sore of her sinful conscience, she saw that all her ettling was of no avail, and her heart sank, and she began to weep, saying, – 'O Marion, Marion, ye were my dear sister ance, but frae this night, if ye leave me to gang again to your sins, I hope the Lord will erase the love I bear you utterly out of my heart, and leave me but the remembrance of what ye were when we were twa wee playing lassies, clapping our young hands, and singing for joy in the bonny spring mornings that will never, never come again.'

The guilty Marion was touched with her sorrow, and for a moment seemed to relent and melt, replying in a softened accent—

'But tell me, Eppie, for ye hae na telt me yet, how did ye leave my weans?'

'Would you like to see them?' said Elspa, eagerly.

'I would na like to gang to Crail,' replied her sister, thoughtfully; 'but if –, and she hesitated.

'Surely, Marion,' exclaimed Elspa, with indignation,

'ye're no sae lost to all shame as to wish your innocent dochters to see you in the midst of your iniquities?'

Marion reddened, and sat abashed and rebuked for a short time in silence, and then reverting to her children, she said, somewhat humbly—

'But tell me how they are – poor things!'

'They are as weel as can be hoped for,' replied Elspa, moved by her altered manner; 'but they'll lang miss the loss of their mother's care. O, Marion, how could ye quit them! The beasts that perish are kinder to their young, for they nourish and protect them till they can do for themselves; but your wee May can neither yet gang nor speak. – She's your very picture, Marion, – as like you as – God forbid that she ever be like you!'

The wretched mother was unable to resist the energy of her sister's appeal, and, bursting into tears, wept bitterly for some time.

Elspa, compassionating her contrition, rose, and, taking her kindly by the hand, said, – 'Come, Marion, we'll gang hame – let us leave this guilty city – let us tarry no longer within its walls – the curse of Heaven is darkening over it, and the storm of the hatred of its corruption is beginning to lighten: – let us flee from the wrath that is to come.'

'I'll no gang back to Crail – I dare na gang there – every one would haud out their fingers at me – I canna gang to Crail – Eppie, dinna bid me – I'll mak away wi' mysel' before I'll gang to Crail.'

'Dinna say that,' replied her sister: 'O, Marion, if ye felt within the humiliation of a true penitent, ye would na speak that way, but would come and hide your face in your poor mother's bosom; often, often, Marion, did she warn you no to be ta'en up wi' the pride and bravery of a fine outside.'

'Ye may gang hame yoursel',' exclaimed the impenitent woman, starting from her seat; 'I'll no gang wi' you to be looket down on by every one. If I should hae had a misfortune, nane's the sufferer but mysel'; and what would I hae to live on wi' my mother? She's pinched enough for her ain support. No; since I hae't in my power, I'll tak my pleasure o't. Ony body can repent when they like, and it's no convenient yet for me. Since I hae slippit the tether, I may as well tak a canter o'er the knowes. I won'er how I could be sae silly as to sit sae lang willy-waing wi' you about that blethering bodie, James Kilspinnie. He could talk o' naething but the town-council, the cost o' plaiding, and the price o' woo'. No, Eppie, I'll no gang wi' you, but I'll be glad if ye'll gang o'er the gait and tak your bed wi' me. I hae a braw bower – and, let me tell you, this is no a house of the best repute.'

'Is your's ony better,' replied Elspa, fervently. 'No, Marion; sooner would I enter the gates of death, than darken your guilty door. Shame upon you, shame! – But the sweet Heavens, in their gracious hour of mercy, will remember the hope that led me here, and some day work out a blessed change. The prayers of an afflicted parent, and the cries of your desolate babies, will assuredly bring down upon you the purifying fires of self-condemnation. Though a wicked pride at this time withholds you from submitting to the humiliation which is the just penalty of your offences, still the day is not far off, when you will come begging for a morsel of bread to those that weep for your fall, and implore you to eschew the evil of your way.'

To these words, which were spoken as with the vehemence of prophecy, the miserable woman made no answer, but plucked her hand sharply from her sister's earnest pressure, and quitted the room with a flash of anger. My grandfather then conveyed the mournful Elspa back to the house of Lucky Kilfauns, and returned to the priory.

The next day, Elspa Ruet, under the escorting of my grandfather, was minded to have gone home to Crail, but the news that John Knox was to preach on the morrow at St Andrews had spread far and wide; no man could tell by what wonderful reverberation the tidings had awakened the whole land. From all quarters droves of the Reformed and the Pious came pressing to the gates of the city, like sheep to the fold and doves to the windows. The Archbishop and the priests and friars were smitten with dread and consternation; the doom of their fortunes was evident in the distraction of their minds: but the Earl of Argyle and the Lord James Stuart, at the priory, remained calm and collected.

Foreseeing that the step they had taken would soon be visited by the wrath of the Queen Regent, they resolved to prepare for the worst, and my grandfather was ordered to hold himself in readiness for a journey. Thus was he prevented from going to Crail with Elspa Ruet, who, with a heavy heart, went back in the evening with the man and horses that brought the Reformer to the town. For John Knox, though under the ban of outlawry, was so encouraged with inward assurances from on High, that he came openly to the gate, and passed up the crown o' the causey on to the priory, in the presence of the Archbishop's guards, of all the people, and of the astonished and dismayed priesthood.

As soon as the Antichrist heard of his arrival, he gave orders for all his armed retainers, to the number of more than a hundred men at arms, to assemble in the cloisters of the monastery of the Blackfriars; for he was a man of a soldierly spirit, and though a loose and immoral churchman, would have made a valiant warrior; and going

thither himself, he thence sent word to the Lord James
Stuart at the priory, that if John Knox dared to preach in
the cathedral, as was threatened, he would order his guard
to fire on him in the pulpit.

My grandfather, with others of the retinue of the two
noblemen, had accompanied the Archbishop's messenger
into the Prior's chamber, where they were sitting with John
Knox when this bold challenge to the champion of Christ's
cause was delivered; and it was plain that both Argyle and
the Lord James were daunted by it, for they well knew
the fearlessness and the fierceness of their consecrated
adversary.

After the messenger had retired, and the Lord James,
in a particular manner, had tacitly signified to my grandfather to remain in the room, and had taken a slip of
paper, he began to write thereon, while Argyle said to the
Reformer,—

'Master Knox, this is what we could na' but expect; and
though it may seem like a misdooting of our cause now to
desist, I'm in a swither if ye should mak the attempt to
preach.'

The Reformer made no answer; and the Lord James,
laying down his pen, also said, 'My thoughts run wi'
Argyle's, – considering the weakness of our train, and
the Archbishop's preparations, with his own regardless
character, – I do think we should for a while rest in our
intent. The Queen Regent has come to Falkland wi' her
French force, and we are in no condition to oppose their
entrance into the town; besides, your appearance in the
pulpit may lead to the sacrifice of your own most precious
life, and the lives of many others who will no doubt stand
forth in your defence. Whether, therefore, you ought, in
such a predicament, to think of preaching, is a thing to be
well considered.'

'In the strength of the Lord,' exclaimed John Knox, with
the voice of an apostle, 'I will preach. God is my witness
that I never preached in contempt of any man, nor would
I willingly injure any creature; but I cannot delay my call
tomorrow if I am not hindered by violence. As for the fear
of danger that may come to me, let no man be solicitous;

for my life is in the custody of HIM whose glory I seek, and threats will not deter me from my duty when Heaven so offereth the occasion. I desire neither the hand nor the weapon of man to defend me; I only crave audience, which, if it be denied to me here at this time, I must seek where I may have it.'

The manner and confidence with which this was spoken silenced and rebuked the two temporal noblemen, and they offered no more remonstrance, but submitted as servants, to pave the way for this intent of his courageous piety. Accordingly, after remaining a short time, as if in expectation to hear what the Earl of Argyle might further have to say, the Lord James Stuart took up his pen again, and when he had completed his writing, he gave the paper to my grandfather, – (it was a list of some ten or twelve names,) – saying, 'Make haste, Gilhaize, and let these, our friends in Angus, know the state of peril in which we stand. Tell them what has chanced; how the gauntlet is thrown; and that our champion has taken it up, and is prepared for the onset.'

My grandfather forthwith departed on his errand, and spared not the spur till he had delivered his message to every one whose names were written in the paper; and their souls were kindled, and the spirit of the Lord quickened in their hearts.

The roads sparkled with the feet of summoning horse-men, and the towns rung with the sound of warlike preparations.

On the third day, towards the afternoon, my grandfather embarked at Dundee on his return, and was landed at the Fife water-side. There were many in the boat with him; and it was remarked by some among them, that, for several days, no one had been observed to smile, and that all men seemed in the expectation of some great event.

The weather being loun and very sultry, he travelled slowly with those who were bound for St Andrews, convers-ing with them on the troubles of the time, and the clouds that were gathering and darkening over poor Scotland; but every one spoke from the faith of his own bosom, that the terrors of the storm would not be of long duration, – so confident were those unlettered men of the goodness of Christ's cause in that epoch of tribulation.

While they were thus communing together, they came in sight of the city, with its coronal of golden spires, and Babylonian pride of idolatrous towers, and they halted for a moment to contemplate the gorgeous insolence with which Antichrist had there built up and invested the blood-stained throne of his blasphemous usurpation.

'The walls of Jericho,' said one of the travellers, 'fell at the sound but of rams' horns, and shall yon Babel withstand the preaching of John Knox?'

Scarcely had he said the words, when the glory of its magnificence was wrapt with a shroud of dust; a dreadful peal of thunder came rolling soon after, though not a spark of vapour was seen in all the ether of the blue sky; and the rumble of a dreadful destruction was then heard. My grandfather clapped spurs to his horse, and galloped on towards the town. The clouds rose thicker, and filled the whole air. Shouts and cries, as he drew near, were mingled with the crash of falling edifices. The earth trembled, and his horse stood still, regardless of the rowels, as if it had seen the angel of the Lord standing in his way. On all sides monks and nuns came flying from the town, wringing their hands as if the horrors of the last judgment had surprised them in their sins. The guards of the Archbishop were scattered among them like chaff in the swirl of the wind; then his Grace came himself on Sir David Hamilton's fleet mare, with Sir David and divers of his household fast following. The wrath of Heaven was behind them, and they rattled past my grandfather like the distempered phantoms that hurry through the dreams of dying men.

My grandfather's horse at last obeyed the spur, and he rode on and into the city, the gates of which were deserted. There he beheld on all sides, that the Lord had indeed put the besom of destruction into the hands of the Reformers; and that not one of all the buildings which had been polluted by the papistry, – no, not one had escaped the erasing fierceness of its ruinous sweep. The presence of the magistrates lent the grace of authority to the zeal of the people, and all things were done in order. The idols were torn down from the altars, and deliberately broken by the children with hammers into pieces. There was no speaking, – all was done in silence; the noise of the falling churches, the rending of the shrines, and the breaking of the images, were the only sounds heard. But for all that, the zeal of not a few was, even in the midst of their dread solemnity, alloyed with covetousness. My grandfather himself saw one of the town-council slip the bald head, in silver, of one of the twelve apostles into his pouch.

The triumph of the truth at St Andrews was followed by the victorious establishment, from that day thenceforward, of the Reformation in Scotland. The precautions taken by the deep forecasting mind of the Lord James Stuart, through the instrumentality of my grandfather and others, were of inexpressible benefit to the righteous cause. It was foreseen that the Queen Regent, who had come to Falkland, would be prompt to avenge the discomfiture of her sect, the papists; but the zealous friends of the Gospel, seconding the resolution of the Lords of the Congregation, enabled them to set all her power at defiance.

With an attendance of few more than a hundred horse, and about as many foot, the Earl of Argyle and the Lord James set out from St Andrews, to frustrate, as far as the means they had concerted might, the wrathful measures which they well knew her Highness would take. But this small force was by the next morning increased to full three thousand fighting men; and so ardently did the spirit of enmity and resistance against the papacy spread, that the Queen Regent, when she came with her French troops and her Scottish levies, under the command of the Duke of Chatelherault, to Cupar, found that she durst not encounter in battle the growing strength of the Congregation, so she consented to a truce, and, as usual in her dissimulating policy, promised many things which she never intended to perform. But the protestants, by this time knowing that the papists never meant to keep their pactions with them, discovering the policy of her Highness, silently moved onward. They proceeded to Perth, and having expelled the garrison, took the town, and fired the Abbey of Scone. But as my grandfather was not with them in those raids, being sent on the night of the great demolition at St

Andrews to apprise the Earl of Glencairn, his patron, of the
extremities to which matters had come there, it belongs not
to the scope of my story to tell what ensued, farther than
that from Perth the Congregation proceeded to Stirling,
where they demolished the monasteries; – then they went
to Lithgow, and herret the nests of the locust there; and
proceeding bravely on, purging the realm as they went
forward, they arrived at Edinburgh, and constrained the
Queen Regent, who was before them with her forces there,
to pack up her ends and her awls, and make what speed she
could with them to Dunbar. But foul as the capital then
was, and covered with the leprosy of idolatry, they were
not long in possession till they so medicated her with the
searching medicaments of the Reformation, that she was
soon scrapit of all the scurf and kell of her abominations.
There was not an idol or an image within her bounds that,
in less than three days, was not beheaded like a traitor and
trundled to the dogs, even with vehemence, as a thing that
could be sensible of contempt. But as all these things are set
forth at large in the chronicles of the kingdom, let suffice it
to say, that my grandfather continued for nearly two years
after this time a trusted emissary among the Lords of
the Congregation, in their many arduous labours and
perilous correspondences, till the Earl of Glencairn was
appointed to see idolatry banished and extirpated from
the West Country, – in which expedition, his Lordship,
being minded to reward my grandfather's services in the
cause of the Reformation, invited him to be of his force;
to which my grandfather, not jealousing the secularities
of his patron's intents, joyfully agreed, hoping to see the
corner-stone placed on the great edifice of the Reformation,
which all good and pious men began then to think near
completion.

Having joined the Earl's force at Glasgow, my grandfather went forward with it to Paisley. Before reaching that
town, however, they were met by a numerous multitude of
the people, halfway between it and the castle of Cruikstone,
and at their head my grandfather was blithened to see
his old friend, the gentle monk Dominick Callender,
in a soldier's garb, and with a ruddy and emboldened

countenance, and by his side, with a sword manfully girded on his thigh, the worthy Bailie Pollock, whose nocturnal revels at the abbey had brought such dule to the winsome Maggy Napier.

For some reason, which my grandfather never well understood, there was more lenity shown to the abbey here than usual; but the monks were rooted out – the images given over to destruction – and the old bones and miraculous crucifixes were either burnt or interred. Less damage, however, was done to the buildings than many expected, partly through the exhortation of the magistrates, who were desirous to preserve so noble a building for a protestant church, but chiefly out of some paction or covenant secretly entered into anent the distribution of the domains and property, wherein the house of Hamilton was concerned, the Duke of Chatelherault, the head thereof, notwithstanding the papistical nature of his blood and kin, having some time before gone over to the cause of the Congregation.

The work of the Reformation being thus abridged at Paisley, the Earl of Glencairn went forward to Kilwinnning, where he was less scrupulous; for having himself obtained a grant of the lands of the abbacy, he was fain to make a clean hand o't, though at the time my grandfather knew not of this.

As soon as the army reached the town, the soldiers went straight on to the abbey, and entering the great church, even while the monks were chanting their paternosters, they began to show the errand they had come on. Dreadful was the yell that ensued, when my grandfather, going up to the priest at the high altar, and pulling him by the scarlet and fine linen of his pageantry, bade him decamp, and flung the toys and trumpery of the mass after him as he fled away in fear.

This resolute act was the signal for the general demolition, and it began on all sides; my grandfather giving a leap, caught hold of a fine effigy of the Virgin Mary by the leg to pull it down; but it proved to be the one which James Coom the smith had mended, for the leg came off, and my grandfather fell backward, and was for a moment stunned by his fall. A band of the monks, who were standing trembling spectators, made an attempt, at seeing this, to raise a shout of a miracle; but my grandfather, in the same moment recovering himself, seized the Virgin's timber leg, and flung it with violence at them, and it happened to strike one of the fattest of the flock with such a bir that it was said the life was driven out of him. This, however, was not the case; for, although the monk was sorely hurt, he lived many a day after, and was obligated, in his auld years, when he was feckless, to be carried from door to door on a hand-barrow, begging his bread. The wives, I have heard tell, were kindly to him for he was a jocose carl; but the weans little respected his grey hairs, and used to jeer him as auld Father Paternoster, for even to the last he adhered to his beads. It was thought, however, by a certain pious protestant gentlewoman of Irvine, that before his death he got a cast of grace; for one day, when he had been carried over to beg in that town, she gave him a luggie of kail owre het, which he stirred with the end of the ebony crucifix at his girdle, thereby showing, as she said, a symptom that it held a lower place in his spiritual affections than if he had been as sincere in his errors as he let wot.

Although my grandfather had sustained a severe bruise by his fall, he was still enabled, after he got on his legs, to superintend the demolishment of the abbey till it was complete. But in the evening, when he took up his quarters in the house of Theophilus Lugton with Dominick Callender, who had brought on a party of the Paisley reformers, he was so stiff and sore, that he thought he would be incompetent to go over next day with the force that the Earl missioned to herry the Carmelyte convent at Irvine. Dominick Callender, had, however, among other things, learnt, in the abbey of Paisley, the salutary virtues of many herbs, and how to decoct from them their healing juices; and he instructed Dame Lugton to prepare an efficacious medicament, that not only mitigated the anguish of the pain, but so suppled the stiffness, that my grandfather was up by break of day, and ready for the march, a renewed man.

In speaking of this, he has been heard to say, it was a thing much to be lamented, that when the regular abolition of the monasteries was decreed, no care was taken to collect the curious knowledges and ancient traditionary skill preserved therein, especially in what pertained to the cure of maladies; for it was his opinion, and many were of the same mind, that among the friars were numbers of potent physicians, and an art in the preparation of salves and sirups, that has not been surpassed by the learning of the colleges. But it is not meet that I should detain the courteous reader with such irrelevancies; the change, however, which has taken place in the realm, in all things pertaining to life, laws, manners, and conduct, since the extirpation of the Roman idolatry, is, from the perfectest report, so wonderful, that the inhabitants can scarcely be said to be the same race of people; and, therefore, I have thought, that such occasional ancestral intimations might, though they proved neither edifying nor instructive, be yet deemed worthy of notation in the brief spaces which they happen herein to occupy. But now, returning from this digression, I will take up again the thread and clue of my story.

The Earl of Glencairn, after the abbey of Kilwinning was sacked, went and slept at Eglinton Castle, then a stalwart square tower, environed with a wall and moat, of a rude and unknown antiquity, standing on a gentle rising ground in the midst of a bleak and moorland domain. And his Lordship having ordered my grandfather to come to him betimes in the morning with twenty chosen men, the discreetest of the force, for a special service in which he meant to employ him, he went thither accordingly, taking with him Dominick Callender, and twelve godly lads from Paisley, with seven others, whom he had remarked in the march from Glasgow, as under the manifest guidance of a sedate and pious temper.

When my grandfather with his company arrived at the castle yett, and he was admitted to the Earl his patron, his Lordship said to him, more as a friend than a master,—

'I am in the hope, Gilhaize, that after this day, the toilsome and perilous errands on which, to the weal of Scotland and the true church, you have been so meritoriously missioned ever since you were retained in my service, will soon be brought to an end, and that you will enjoy in peace the reward you have earned so well, that I am better pleased in bestowing it than you can be in the receiving. But there is yet one task which I must put upon you. Hard by to this castle, less than a mile eastward, stands a small convent of nuns, who have been for time out of mind under the protection of the Lord Eglinton's family, and he, having got a grant of the lands belonging to their house, is desirous that they should be flitted in an amiable manner to a certain street in Irvine, called the Kirkgate, where a lodging is provided for them. To do this kindly I have bethought myself of you, for I know not in all my force any one so well qualified. Have you provided yourself with the twenty douce men that I ordered you to bring hither?'

My grandfather told his Lordship that he had done as he was ordered. 'Then,' resumed the Earl, 'take them with you, and this mandate to the superior, and one of Eglinton's men to show you the way; and when you have conveyed them to their lodging, come again to me.'

So my grandfather did as he was directed by the Earl, and marched eastward with his men till he came to the convent, which was a humble and orderly house, with a small chapel, and a tower, that in after times, when all the other buildings were erased, was called the Stane Castle, and is known by that name even unto this day. It stood within a high wall, and a little gate, with a stone cross over the same, led to the porch.

Compassionating the simple and silly sisterhood within, who, by their sequestration from the world, were become as innocent as birds in a cage, my grandfather halted his men at some distance from the yett, and going forward, rung the bell; to the sound of which an aged woman answered, who, on being told he had brought a letter to the superior, gave him admittance, and conducted him to a little chamber, on the one side of which was a grating, where the superior, a short corpulent matron, that seemed to bowl rather than to walk as she moved along, soon made her appearance within.

He told her in a meek manner, and with some gentle prefacing, the purpose of his visit, and showed her the Earl's mandate; to all which, for some time, she made no reply, but she was evidently much moved; at last she gave a wild skreigh, which brought the rest of the nuns, to the number of thirteen, all rushing into the room. Then ensued a dreadful tempest of all feminine passions and griefs, intermingled with supplications to many a saint; but the powers and prerogatives of their saints were abolished in Scotland, and they received no aid.

Though their lamentation, as my grandfather used to say, could not be recited without moving to mirth, it was yet so full of maidenly fears and simplicity at the time to him, that it seemed most tender, and he was disturbed at the thought of driving such fair and helpless creatures into the bad world; but it was his duty; – so, after soothing them as well as he could, and representing how unavailing their refusal to go would be, the superior composed her grief, and exhorting the nuns to be resigned to their cruel fate, which, she said, was not so grievous as that which many of the saints had in their day suffered, they all became calm and prepared for the removal.

My grandfather told them to take with them whatsoever they best liked in the house; and it was a moving sight to see their simplicity therein. One was content with a flower-pot; another took a cage in which she had a lintie; some of them half-finished patterns of embroidery. One aged sister, of a tall and spare form, brought away a flask of eye-water which she had herself distilled; but, saving the superior, none of them thought of any of the valuables of the chapel, till my grandfather reminded them, that they might find the value of silver and gold hereafter, even in the spiritual-minded town of Irvine.

There was one young and graceful maiden among them who seemed but little moved by the event; and my grandfather was melted to sympathy and sorrow by the solemn serenity of her deportment, and the little heed she took of any thing. Of all the nuns she was the only one who appeared to have nothing to care for; and when they were ready, and came forth to the gate, instead of joining in their piteous wailings as they bade their peaceful home a long and last farewell, she walked forward alone. No sooner, however, had she passed the yett, than, on seeing the armed company without, she stood still like a statue, and, uttering a shrill cry, fainted away, and fell to the ground. Every one ran to her assistance; but when her face was unveiled to give her air, Dominick Callender, who was standing by, caught her in his arms, and was enchanted by a fond and strange enthusiasm. She was indeed no other than the young maiden of Paisley, for whom he had found his monastic vows the heavy fetters of a bondage that made life scarcely worth possessing; and when she was recovered, an interchange of great tenderness took place between them, at which the superior of the convent waxed very wroth, and the other nuns were exceedingly scandalized. But Magdalene Sauchie, for so she was called, heeded them not; for, on learning that popery was put down in the land by law, she openly declared, that she renounced her vows; and during the walk to Irvine, which was jimp a mile, she leant upon the arm of her lover: and they were soon after married, Dominick settling in that town as a doctor of physic, whereby he afterwards earned both gold and reputation.

But to conclude the history of the convent, which my grandfather had in this gentle manner herret, the nuns, on reaching the foot of the Kirkgate, where the Countess of Eglinton had provided a house for them, began to weep anew with great vehemence, fearing that their holy life was at an end, and that they would be tempted of men to enter into the temporalities of the married state; but the superior, on hearing this mournful apprehension, mounted upon the steps of the tolbooth stair, and, in the midst of a great concourse of people, she lifted her hands on high, and exclaimed, as with the voice of a prophetess, 'Fear not, my chaste and pious dochters; for your sake, and for my sake, I have an assurance at this moment from the Virgin Mary herself, that the calamity of the marriage-yoke will never be known in the Kirkgate of Irvine, but that all maidens who hereafter may enter, or be born to dwell therein, shall live a life of single-blessedness – unasked and untempted of men.' Which delightful prediction the nuns were so happy to hear, that they dried their tears, and chanted their Ave Maria, joyfully proceeding towards their appointed habitation. It stood, as I have been told, on the same spot where King James the Sixth's school was afterwards erected, and endowed out of the spoils of the Carmelytes' monastery, which, on the same day, was, by another division of the Earl of Glencairn's power, sacked and burnt to the ground.

When my grandfather had, in the manner rehearsed, disposed of those sisters of simplicity in the Kirkgate of Irvine, he returned back in the afternoon to the Earl of Glencairn at Eglinton Castle to report what he had done; and his Lordship again, in a most laudatory manner, commended his prudence and singular mildness of nature, mentioning to the Earl and Countess of Eglinton, then present with him, divers of the missions wherein he had been employed, extolling his zeal, and above all his piety. And the Lady Eglinton, who was a household character, striving, with great frugality, to augment the substance of her Lord, by keeping her maidens from morning to night eydent at work, some at their broidering drums, and some at their distaffs, managing all within the castle that pertained to her feminine part in a way most exemplary to the ladies of her time and degree, indeed to ladies of all times and degrees, promised my grandfather that when he was married, she would give his wife something to help the plenishing of their house, for the meek manner in which he had comported himself toward her friend, the superior of the nuns. Then the Earl of Glencairn said,—

'Gilhaize, madam, is now his own master, and may choose a bride when it pleases himself; for I have covenanted with my friend, your Lord, to let him have the mailing of Quharist, in excambio for certain of the lands of late pertaining to the abbacy of Kilwinning, the which lie more within the vicinage of this castle; and, Gilhaize, here is my warrant to take possession.'

With which words the Earl rose and presented him with a charter for the lands, signed by Eglinton and himself, and he shook him heartily by the hand, saying, that few in all the kingdom had better earned the guerdon of their service than he had done.

Thus it was that our family came to be settled in the shire of Ayr; for after my grandfather had taken possession of his fee, and mindful of the vow he had made in the street of Edinburgh on that blessed morning when John Knox, the champion of the true church, arrived from Geneva, he went into the east country to espouse Elspa Ruet, if he found her thereunto inclined, which happily he soon did. For their spirits were in unison; and from the time they first met, they had felt toward one another as if they had been acquaint in loving-kindness before, which made him sometimes say, that it was to him a proof and testimony that the souls of mankind have, perhaps, a living knowledge of each other before they are born into this world.

At their marriage, it was agreed that they should take with them into the west Agnes Kilspinnie, one of the misfortunate bailie's daughters. As for her mother, from the day of the overthrow and destruction of the papistry at St Andrews, she had never been heard of; all the tidings her sister could gather concerning her were, that the same night she had been conveyed away by some of the Archbishop's servants, but whither no one could tell. So they came with Agnes Kilspinnie to Edinburgh; and, for a ploy to their sober wedding, they resolved to abide there till the coming of Queen Mary from France, that they might partake of the shows and pastimes then preparing for her reception. They, however, during the season of their sojourn, feasted far better than on royal fare, in the gospel banquet of John Knox's sermons, of which they enjoyed the inexpressible beatitude three several Sabbath-days before the Queen arrived.

Of the joyous preparations to greet Queen Mary withal, neither my grandfather nor grandmother were ever wont to discourse much at large, for they were holy-minded persons, little esteeming the pageantries of this world. But my aunt, for Agnes Kilspinnie being in progress of time married to my father's fourth brother, became sib to me in that degree, was wont to descant and enlarge on the theme with much wonderment and loquacity, describing

the marvellous fabrics that were to have been hung with
tapestry to hold the ladies, and the fountains that were
to have spouted wine, which nobody was to be allowed
to taste, the same being only for an ostentation, in order
that the fact thereof might be recorded in the chronicles
for after-times. And great things have I likewise heard
her tell of the paraphernalia which the magistrates and
town-council were getting ready. No sleep, in a sense,
she used to say, did Maccalzean of Cliftonhall, who was
then provost, get for more than a fortnight. From night
to morning the sagacious bailies sat in council, exercising
their sagacity to contrive devices to pleasure the Queen,
and to help the custom of their own and their neighbours'
shops. Busy and proud men they were, and no smaller were
the worshipful deacons of the crafts. It was just a surprise
and consternation to every body, to think how their weak
backs could bear such a burden of cares. No time had they
for their wonted jocosity. To those who would fain have
speered the news, they shook their heads in a Solomon-like
manner, and hastened by. And such a battle and tribulation
as they had with their vassals, the magistrates of Leith! who,
in the most contumacious manner, insisted that their chief
bailie should be the first to welcome the Sovereign on the
shore. This pretence was thought little short of rebellion;
and the provost and the bailies, and all the wise men that
sat in council with them, together with the help of their
learned assessors, continued deliberating anent the same
for hours together. It was a dreadful business that for the
town of Edinburgh. And the opinions of the judges of the
land, and the lords of the council, were taken, and many
a device tried to overcome the upsetting, as it was called,
of the Leith magistrates; but all was of no avail. And it
was thought there would have been a fight between the
bailies of Leith and the bailies of Edinburgh, and that
blood would have been shed before this weighty question,
so important to the dearest interests of the commonweal
of Scotland, could be determined. But, in the midst of
their contention, and before their preparations were half
finished, the Queen arrived in Leith Roads; and the news
came upon them like the cry to the foolish virgins of the

bridegroom in the street. Then they were seen flying to their respective places of abode, to dress themselves in their coats of black velvet, their doublets of crimson satin, and their hose of the same colour, which they had prepared for the occasion. Anon they met in the council-chamber – what confusion reigned there! Then how they flew down the street! Provost Maccalzean, with the silver keys in his hand, and the eldest bailie with the crimson-velvet cod, whereon they were to be delivered to her Majesty, following as fast as any member of a city corporation could be reasonably expected to do. But how the provost fell, and how the bailies and town-council tumbled over him, and how the crowd shouted at the sight, are things whereof to understand the greatness it is needful that the courteous reader should have heard my aunty Agnes herself rehearse the extraordinary particularities.

Meanwhile the Queen left her galley in a small boat, and the bailies of Leith had scarcely time to reach the pier before she was on shore. Alas! it was an ill-omened landing. Few were spectators, and none cheered the solitary lady, who, as she looked around and heard no loyal greeting, nor beheld any show of hospitable welcome, seemed to feel as if the spirit of the land was sullen at her approach, and grudged at her return to the dark abodes of her fierce ancestors. In all the way from Leith to Holyrood she never spoke, but the tear was in her eye and the sigh in her bosom; and though her people gathered, when it was known she had landed, and began at last to shout, it was owre late to prevent the mournful forebodings, which taught her to expect but disappointments and sorrows from subjects so torn with their own factions, as to lack even the courtesies due to their sovereign, a stranger, and the fairest lady of all her time.

Soon after Queen Mary's return from France, my grandfather, with his wife and Agnes Kilspinnie, came from Edinburgh and took up their residence on his own free mailing of Quharist, where the Lady Eglinton was as good as her word in presenting to them divers articles of fine napery, and sundry things of plenishing both for ornament and use; and there he would have spent his days in blameless tranquillity, serving the Lord, but for the new storm that began to gather over the church, whereof it is needful that I should now proceed to tell some of the circumstantials.

No sooner had that thoughtless Princess, if indeed one could be so called, who, though reckless of all consequences, was yet double beyond the imagination of man; no sooner, I say, had she found herself at home, than, with all the craft and blandishments of her winning airs and peerless beauty, she did set herself to seduce the Lords of the Congregation from the sternness wherewith they had thrown down, and were determined to resist the restoration of the Roman idolatry; and with some of them she succeeded so far, that the popish priests were heartened, and, knowing her avowed partiality for their sect, the Beast began to shoot out its horns again, and they dared to perform the abomination of the mass in different quarters of the kingdom.

It is no doubt true, that the Queen's council, by proclamation, feigned to discountenance that resuscitation of idolatry; but the words of their edict being backed by no demonstration of resolution, save in the case of a few worthy gentlemen in the shire of Ayr and in Galloway, who took up some of the offenders in their district and jurisdiction, the evil continued to strike its roots, and to bud and flourish in its pestiferous branches.

When my grandfather heard of these things, his spirit was exceedingly moved, and he got no rest in the night, with the warsling of troubled thoughts and pious fears. Some new call, he foresaw, would soon be made on the protestants, to stand forth again in the gap that the Queen's arts had sapped in the bulwarks of their religious liberty, and he resolved to be ready against the hour of danger. So, taking his wife and Agnes Kilspinnie with him, he went in the spring to Edinburgh, and hired a lodging for them; and on the same night he presented himself at the lodging of the Lord James Stuart, who had some time before been created Earl of Murray; but the Earl was gone with the Queen to Lochleven. Sir Alexander Douglas, however, the master of his Lordship's horse, was then on the eve of following him with John Knox, to whom the Queen had sent a peremptory message, requiring his attendance; and Sir Alexander invited my grandfather to come with them; the which invitation he very joyfully accepted, on account of the happy occasion of travelling in the sanctified company of that brave worthy.

In the journey, however, save in the boat when they crossed the ferry, he showed but little of his precious conversation; for the knight and the Reformer rode on together some short distance before their train, earnestly discoursing, and seemingly they wished not to be over-heard. But when they were all seated in the ferry-boat, the ardour of the preacher, which on no occasion would be reined in, led him to continue speaking, by which it would seem, that they had been conversing anent the Queen's prejudices in matters of religion and the royal authority.

'When I last spoke with her Highness,' said John Knox, 'she laid sore to my charge, that I had brought the people to receive a religion different from what their princes allowed, asking sharply, if this was not contrary to the Divine command, which enjoins that subjects should obey their rulers; so that I was obliged to contend plainly, that true religion derived its origin and authority, not from princes, but from God; that princes were often most ignorant respecting it, and that subjects never could be bound to frame their religious sentiments according to the pleasure of their rulers, else the Hebrews ought to have conformed to the idolatry of Pharaoh, and Daniel and his associates to that of Nebuchadnezzar, and the primitive Christians to that of the Roman emperors.'

'And what could her Highness answer to this?' said Sir Alexander.

'She lacketh not the gift of a shrewd and ready wit,' replied Master Knox; for she nimbly remarked, 'That though it was as I had said, yet none of those men raised the sword against their princes;' – which enforced me to be more subtle than I was minded to have been, and to say, 'that nevertheless, they did resist, for those who obey not the commandments given them, do in verity resist.' – 'Ay,' cried her Highness, 'but not with the sword,' which was a thrust not easy to be turned aside, so that I was constrained to speak out, saying, 'God, madam, had not given them the means and the power.' Then said she, still more eagerly, 'Think you that subjects, having the power, may resist their princes?' – And she looked with a triumphant smile, as if she had caught me in a trap; but I replied, "If princes exceed their bounds, no doubt they may be resisted, even by power. For no greater honour or greater obedience is to be given to kings and princes than God has commanded to be given to father and mother. But the father may be struck with a phrenzy, in which he would slay his children; in such a case, if the children arise, join together, apprehend the father, take the sword from him, bind his hands and keep him in prison till the phrenzy be over, think you, madam,' quo' I, 'that the children do any wrong? Even so is it with princes that would slay the children of God that are subject to them. Their blind zeal is nothing but phrenzy, and therefore to take the power from them till they be brought to a more sober mind, is no disobedience to princes, but a just accordance to the will of God. – So I doubt not,' continued the Reformer, 'I shall again have to sustain the keen encounter of her Highness' wit in some new controversy.'

This was the chief substance of what my grandfather heard pass in the boat; and when they were again mounted, the knight and preacher set forward as before, some twenty paces or so in advance of the retinue.

On reaching Kinross, Master Knox rode straight to the shore, and went off in the Queen's barge to the castle, that he might present himself to her Highness before supper, for by this time the sun was far down. In the meantime, my grandfather went to the house in Kinross where the Earl of Murray resided, and his Lordship, though albeit a grave and reserved man, received him with the familiar kindness of an old friend, and he was with him when the Reformer came back from the Queen, who had dealt very earnestly with him to persuade the gentlemen of the west country to desist from their interruption of the popish worship.

'But to this,' said the Reformer to the Earl, 'I was obligated, by conscience and the fear of God, to say, that if her Majesty would exert her authority in executing the laws of the land, I would undertake for the peaceable behaviour of the protestants; but if she thought to evade them, there were some who would not let the papists offend with impunity.'

'Will you allow,' exclaimed her Highness, 'that they shall take my sword in their hands?'

'The sword of justice is God's,' I replied, 'and is given to princes and rulers for an end, which if they transgress, sparing the wicked and oppressing the innocent, they who in the fear of God execute judgment where God has commanded, offend not God, although kings do it not. The gentlemen of the west, madam, are acting strictly according to law; for the act of parliament gave power to all judges within their jurisdiction to search for and punish those who transgress its enactments;' and I added, 'it shall be profitable to your Majesty to consider what is the thing your Grace's subjects look to receive of your Majesty, and what it is that ye ought to do unto them by mutual contract. They are bound to obey you, and that not but in God; ye are bound to keep laws to them – ye crave of them service, they crave of you protection and defence. Now, madam, if you shall deny your duty unto them (which especially craves that ye punish malefactors), can ye expect to receive full obedience of them? I fear, madam, ye shall not.'

'You have indeed been plain with her Highness,' said the Earl thoughtfully; 'and what reply made she?'

'None,' said the Reformer; 'her countenance changed; she turned her head abruptly from me, and, without the courtesy of a good night, signified with an angry waving of her hand, that she desired to be rid of my presence; whereupon I immediately retired, and, please God, I shall, betimes in the morning, return to my duties at Edinburgh. It is with a sad heart, my Lord, that I am compelled to think, and to say to you, who stand so near to her in kin and affection, that I doubt she is not only proud but crafty; not only wedded to the popish faith, but averse to instruction. She neither is nor will be of our opinion; and it is plain that the lessons of her uncle, the Cardinal, are so deeply printed in her heart, that the substance and quality will perish together. I would be glad to be deceived in this, but I fear I shall not; never have I espied such art in one so young; and it will need all the eyes of the Reformed to watch and ward that she circumvent not the strong hold in Christ, that has been but so lately restored and fortified in this misfortunate kingdom.'

Nothing farther passed that night; but the servants being called in, and the preacher having exhorted them in their duties, and prayed with even more than his wonted earnestness, each one retired to his chamber, and the Earl gave orders for horses to be ready early in the morning, to convey Master Knox back to Edinburgh. This, however, was not permitted; for by break of day a messenger came from the castle, desiring him not to depart until he had again spoken with her Majesty; adding, that as she meant to land by sunrise with her falconer, she would meet him on the fields where she intended to take her pastime – and talk with him there.

Volume II

CHAPTER ONE

In the morning, all those who were in the house with the Earl of Murray and John Knox were early a-foot, and after prayers had been said, they went out to meet the Queen at her place of landing from the castle, which stands on an islet at some distance from the shore; but, before they reached the spot, she was already mounted on her jennet and the hawks unhooded, so that they were obligated to follow her Highness to the ground, the Reformer leaning on the Earl, who proffered him his left arm as they walked up the steep bank together from the brim of the lake.

The Queen was on the upland when they drew near to the field, and on seeing them approach she came ambling towards them, moving in her beauty, as my grandfather often delighted to say, like a fair rose caressed by the soft gales of the summer. A smile was in her eye, and it brightened on her countenance like the beam of something more lovely than light; the glow, as it were, of a spirit conscious of its power, and which had graced itself with all its enchantments to conquer some stubborn heart. Even the Earl of Murray was struck with the unwonted splendour of her that was ever deemed so surpassing fair; and John Knox said, with a sigh, 'THE MAKER had indeed taken gracious pains with the goodly fashion of such perishable clay.'

When she had come within a few paces of where they were advancing uncovered, she suddenly checked her jennet, and made him dance proudly round till she was nigh to John Knox, where, seeming in alarm, she feigned as if she would have slipped from the saddle, laying her hand on his shoulder for support; and while he, with more gallantry than it was thought in him, helped her to recover her seat, she said, with a ravishing look, 'The Queen thanks you, Master Knox, for this upholding,' dwelling on the word this in a special manner; which my grandfather noticed the more, as he as well as others of the retinue observed, that she was playing as it were in dalliance.

She then inquired kindly for his health, grieving she had not given orders for him to bed in the castle; and turning to the Earl of Murray, she chided his Lordship with a gentleness that was more winning than praise, why he had not come to her with Master Knox, saying, 'We should then perhaps have not been so sharp in our controversy.' But, before the Earl had time to make answer, she noticed divers gentlemen by name, and taking off her glove, made a most sweet salutation with her lily hand to the general concourse of those who had by this time gathered around.

In that gracious gesture, it was plain, my grandfather said, that she was still scattering her feminine spells; for she kept her hand for some time bare, and though enjoying the pleasure which her beautiful presence diffused, like a delicious warmth into the air, she was evidently self-collected, and had something more in mind than only the triumph of her marvellous beauty.

Having turned her horse's head, she moved him a few paces, saying, 'Master Knox, I would speak with you.' At which he went towards her, and the rest of the spectators retired and stood aloof.

They appeared for some time to be in an easy and somewhat gay discourse on her part; but she grew more and more earnest, till Mr Knox made his reverence and was coming away, when she said to him aloud, 'Well, do as you will, but that man is a dangerous man.'

Their discourse was concerning the titular Bishop of Athens, a brother of the Earl of Huntly, who had been put in nomination for a superintendent of the church in the West Country, and of whose bad character her Highness, as it afterwards proved, had received a just account.

But scarcely had the Reformer retired two steps when she called him back, and holding out to him her hand, with which, when he approached to do his homage, she familiarly took hold of his and held it, playing with his fingers as if she had been placing on a ring, saying, loud enough to be heard by many on the field,—

'I have one of the greatest matters that have touched me since I came into this realm to open to you, and I must have your help in it.'

Then, still holding him earnestly by the hand, she entered into a long discourse concerning, as he afterwards told the Earl of Murray, a difference subsisting between the Earl and Countess of Argyle.

'Her Ladyship,' said the Queen, for my grandfather heard him repeat what passed, 'has not perhaps been so circumspect in every thing as one could have wished, but her lord has dealt harshly with her.'

Master Knox having once before reconciled the debates of that honourable couple, told her Highness he had done so, and that not having since heard any thing to the contrary, he had hoped all things went well with them.

'It is worse,' replied the Queen, 'than ye believe. But, kind sir, do this much for my sake, as once again to put them at amity, and if the Countess behave not herself as she ought to do, she shall find no favour of me; but in no wise let Argyle know that I have requested you in this matter.'

Then she returned to the subject of their contest the preceding evening, and said, with her sweetest looks and most musical accents, 'I promise to do as ye required: I shall order all offenders to be summoned, and you shall see that I shall minister justice.'

To which he replied, 'I am assured then, madam, that you shall please God, and enjoy rest and tranquillity within your realm, which to your Majesty is more profitable than all the Pope's power can be.' And having said this much he made his reverence, evidently in great pleasure with her Highness.

Afterwards, in speaking to the Earl of Murray, as they returned to Kinross, my grandfather noted that he employed many terms of soft courtliness, saying of her, that she was a lady who might, he thought, with a little pains, be won to grace and godliness, could she be preserved from the taint of evil counsellors; so much had the winning sorceries of her exceeding beauty and her blandishments worked even upon his stern honesty, and enchanted his jealousy asleep.

When Master Knox had, with the Earl, partaken of some repast, he requested that he might be conveyed back to Edinburgh, for that it suited not with his nature to remain sorning about the skirts of the court; and his Lordship bade my grandfather be of his company, and to bid Sir Alexander Douglas, the master of his horse, choose for him the gentlest steed in his stable.

But it happened before the Reformer was ready to depart, that Queen Mary had finished her morning pastime, and was returning to her barge to embark for the castle, which the Earl hearing, went down to the brim of the loch to assist at her embarkation. My grandfather, with others, also hastened to the spot.

On seeing his Lordship, she inquired for 'her friend,' as she then called John Knox, and signified her regret that he had been so list to leave her, expressing her surprise that one so infirm should think so soon of a second journey; whereby the good Earl being minded to cement their happy reconciliation, from which he augured a great increase of benefits both to the realm and the cause of religion, was led to speak of his concern thereat likewise, and of his sorrow that all his own horses at Kinross being for the chase and road, he had none well-fitting to carry a person so aged, and but little used to the toil of riding.

Her Highness smiled at the hidden counselling of this remark, for she was possessed of a sharp spirit; and she said, with a look which told the Earl and all about her that she discerned the pith of his Lordship's discourse, she would order one of her own palfreys to be forthwith prepared for him.

When the Earl returned from the shore and informed Master Knox of the Queen's gracious condescension, he made no reply, but bowed his head in token of his sense of her kindness; and soon after, when the palfrey was brought saddled with the other horses to the door, he said, in my grandfather's hearing, to his Lordship, 'It needs, you see, my Lord, must be so; for were I not to accept this grace, it might be thought I refused from a vain bravery of caring nothing for her Majesty's favour;' and he added, with a smile of jocularity, 'whereas I am right well content to receive the very smallest boon from so fair and blooming a lady.'

Nothing of any particularity occurred in the course of the journey; for the main part of which Master Knox was thoughtful and knit up in his own cogitations, and when from time to time he did enter into discourse with my grandfather, he spoke chiefly of certain usages and customs that he had observed in other lands, and of things of indifferent import; but nevertheless there was a flavour of holiness in all he said, and my grandfather treasured many of his sweet sentences as pearls of great price.

Before the occurrence of the things spoken of in the foregoing chapter, the great Earl of Glencairn, my grandfather's first and constant patron, had been dead some time; but his son and successor, who knew the estimation in which he had been held by his father, being then in Edinburgh, allowed him, in consideration thereof, the privilege of his hall. It suited not however with my grandfather's quiet and sanctified nature to mingle much with the brawlers that used to hover there; nevertheless, out of a respect to the Earl's hospitality, he did occasionally go thither, and where, if he heard little to edify the Christian heart, he learnt divers things anent the Queen and court that made his fears and anxieties wax stronger and stronger.

It seemed to him, as he often was heard to say, that there was a better knowledge of Queen Mary's true character and secret partialities among those loose varlets than among their masters; and her marriage being then in the parlance of the people, and much dread and fear rife with the protestants that she would choose a papist for her husband, he was surprised to hear many of the lewd knaves in Glencairn's hall speak lightly of the respect she would have to the faith or spirituality of the man she might prefer.

Among those wuddy worthies he fell in with his ancient adversary Winterton, who, instead of harbouring any resentment for the trick he played him in the Lord Boyd's castle, was rejoiced to see him again: he himself was then in the service of David Rizzio, the fiddler, whom the Queen some short time before had taken into her particular service.

This Rizzio was by birth an Italian of very low degree;

a man of crouched stature, and of an uncomely physiognomy, being yellow-skinned and black-haired, with a beak-nose, and little quick eyes of a free and familiar glance, but shrewd withal, and possessed of a pleasant way of winning facetiously on the ladies, to the which his singular skill in all manner of melodious music helped not a little; so that he had great sway with them, and was then winning himself fast into the Queen's favour, in which ambition, besides the natural instigations of his own vanity, he was spirited on by certain powerful personages of the papistical faction, who soon saw the great efficacy it would be of to their cause, to have one who owed his rise to them constantly about the Queen, and in the depths of all her personal correspondence with her great friends abroad. But the subtle Italian, though still true to his papal breeding, built upon the Queen's partiality more than on the favour of those proud nobles, and, about the time of which I am now speaking, he carried his head at court as bravely as the boldest baron amongst them. Still in this he had as yet done nothing greatly to offend. The protestant Lords, however, independent of their aversion to him on account of his religion, felt, in common with all the nobility, a vehement prejudice against an alien, one too of base blood, and they openly manifested their displeasure at seeing him so gorgeous and presuming even in the public presence of the Queen; but he regarded not their anger.

In this fey man's service Winterton then was, and my grandfather never doubted that it was for no good he came so often to the Earl of Glencairn's, who, though not a man of the same weight in the realm as the old Earl his father, was yet held in much esteem, as a sincere protestant and true nobleman, by all the friends of the Gospel cause; and, in the sequel, what my grandfather jealoused was soon very plainly seen. For Rizzio learning, through Winterton's espionage and that of other emissaries, how little the people of Scotland would relish a foreign prince to be set over them, had a hand in dissuading the Queen from accepting any of the matches then proposed for her; and the better to make his own power the more sicker, he afterwards laid snares in the water to bring about a marriage with

that weak young prince, the Lord Henry Darnley. But it
falls not within the scope of my narrative to enter into
any more particulars here concerning that Italian, and
the tragical doom which, with the Queen's imprudence,
he brought upon himself; for, after spending some weeks
in Edinburgh, and in visiting their friends at Crail, my
grandfather returned with his wife and Agnes Kilspinnie
to Quharist, where he continued to reside several years,
but not in tranquillity.

Hardly had they reached their home, when word came of
quarrels among the nobility; and though the same sprung
out of secular debates, they had much of the leaven
of religious faction in their causes, the which greatly
exasperated the enmity wherewith they were carried on.
But even in the good Earl of Murray's raid, there was
nothing which called on my grandfather to bear a part.
Nevertheless those quarrels disquieted his soul, and he
heard the sough of discontents rising afar off, like the roar
of the bars of Ayr when they betoken a coming tempest.

After the departure of the Earl of Murray to France,
there was a syncope in the land, and men's minds were
filled with wonder, and with apprehensions to which they
could give no name; neighbours distrusted one another;
the papists looked out from their secret places, and were
saluted with a fear that wore the semblance of reverence.
The Queen married Darnley, and discreet men marvelled
at the rashness with which the match was concluded, there
being seemingly no cause for such uncomely haste, nor for
the lavish favours that she heaped upon him. It was viewed
with awe, as a thing done under the impulses of fraud,
or fainness, or fatality. Nor was their wedding-cheer cold
when her eager love changed into aversion. Then the spirit
of the times, which had long hovered in willingness to be
pleased with her intentions, began to alter its breathings,
and to whisper darkly against her. At last the murder of
Rizzio, a deed which, though in the main satisfactory to
the nation, was yet so foul and cruel in the perpetration,
that the tidings of it came like a thunder-clap over all the
kingdom.

The birth of Prince James, which soon after followed,

gave no joy; for about the same time a low and terrible whispering began to be heard of some hideous and universal conspiracy against all the protestants throughout Europe. None ventured to say that Queen Mary was joined with the conspirators; but many preachers openly prayed that she might be preserved from their leagues in a way that showed what they feared; besides this suspicion, mournful things were told of her behaviour, and the immoralities of her courtiers and their trains rose to such a pitch, compared with the chastity and plain manners of her mother's court, that the whole land was vexed with angry thoughts, and echoed to the rumours with stern menaces.

No one was more disturbed by these things than my pious grandfather; and the apprehensions which they caused in him came to such a head at last, that his wife, becoming fearful of his health, advised him to take a journey to Edinburgh, in order that he might hear and see with his own ears and eyes; which he accordingly did, and on his arrival went straight to the Earl of Glencairn, and begged permission to take on again his livery, chiefly that he might pass unnoticed, and not be remarked as having neither calling nor vocation. That nobleman was surprised at his request; but, without asking any question, gave him leave, and again invited him to use the freedom of his hall; so he continued as one of his retainers, till the Earl of Murray's return from France. But, before speaking of what then ensued, there are some things concerning the murder of the Queen's protestant husband, – the blackest of the sins of that age, – of which, in so far as my grandfather participated, it is meet and proper I should previously speak.

While the cloud of troubles, whereof I have spoken in the foregoing chapter, was thickening and darkening over the land, the event of the King's dreadful death came to pass; the which, though in its birth most foul and monstrous, filling the hearts of all men with consternation and horror, was yet a mean in the hands of Providence, as shall hereafter appear, whereby the kingdom of THE LORD was established in Scotland.

Concerning that fearful treason my grandfather never spoke without taking off his bonnet, and praying inwardly with such solemnity of countenance, that none could behold him unmoved. Of all the remarkable passages of his long life it was indeed the most remarkable; and he has been heard to say, that he could not well acquit himself of the actual sin of disobedience, in not obeying an admonition of the spirit which was vouchsafed to him on that occasion.

For some time there had been a great variance between the King and Queen. He had given himself over to loose and low companions; and though she kept her state and pride, ill was said of her, if in her walk and conversation she was more sensible of her high dignity. All at once, however, when he was lying ill at Glasgow of a malady, which many scrupled not to say was engendered by a malignant medicine, there was a singular demonstration of returning affection on her part, the more remarkable and the more heeded of the commonalty, on account of its suddenness, and the events that ensued; for while he was at the worst she minded not his condition, but took her delights and pastimes in divers parts of the country. No sooner, however, had his strength overcome the disease, than she was seized with this fond sympathy, and came flying with her endearments, seemingly to foster his recovery with caresses and love. The which excessive affection was afterwards ascribed to a guilty hypocrisy; for, in the sequel, it came to light, that while she was practising all those winning blandishments, which few knew the art of better, and with which she regained his confidence, she was at the same time engaged in an unconjugal correspondence with the Earl of Bothwell. The King, however, was won by her kindness, and consented to be removed from among the friends of his family at Glasgow to Edinburgh, in order that he might there enjoy the benefits of her soft cares, and the salutary attendance of the physicians of the capital. The house of the provost of Kirk o' Field, which stood not far from the spot where the buildings of the college now stand, was accordingly prepared for his reception, on account of the advantages which it afforded for the free and open air of a rising ground; but it was also a solitary place, a fit haunt for midnight conspirators and the dark purposes of mysterious crime.

There, for some time, the Queen lavished upon him all the endearing gentleness of a true and loving wife, being seldom absent by day, and sleeping near his sick chamber at night. The land was blithened with such assurances of their reconciliation; and the King himself, with the frank ardour of flattered youth, was contrite for his faults, and promised her the fondest devotion of all his future days. In this sweet cordiality, on Sunday, the 9th of February, A.D. 1567, she parted from him to be present at a masking in the palace; for the Reformation had not then so penetrated into the habits and business of men as to hallow the Sabbath in the way it has since done amongst us. But before proceeding farther, it is proper to resume the thread of my grandfather's story.

He had passed that evening, as he was wont to tell, in pleasant gospel conversation with several acquaintances, in the house of one Raphael Doquet, a pious lawyer in the Canongate; for even many writers in those days were smitten with the love of godliness; and as he was returning to his dry lodgings in an entry now called Baron Grant's Close, he encountered Winterton, who, after an end had been put to David Rizzio, became a retainer in the riotous household of the Earl of Bothwell. This happened a short way aboon the Netherbow, and my grandfather stopped to speak with him; but there was a haste and confusion in his manner which made him rather eschew this civility. My grandfather, at the time, however, did not much remark it; but scarcely had they parted ten paces, when a sudden jealousy of some unknown guilt or danger, wherein Winterton was concerned, came into his mind like a flash of fire, and he felt as it were an invisible power constraining him to dog his steps, in so much, that he actually did turn back. But on reaching the Bow, he was obligated to stop, for the ward was changing; and observing that the soldiers then posting were of the Queen's French guard, his thoughts began to run on the rumour that was bruited of a league among the papist princes to cut off all the Reformed with one universal sweep of the scythe of persecution, and he felt himself moved and incited to go to some of the Lords and leaders of the Congregation, to warn them of what he feared; but, considering that he had only a vague and unaccountable suspicion for his thought, he wavered, and finally returned home. Thus, though manifestly and marvellously instructed of the fruition of some bloody business in hand that night, he was yet overruled by the wisdom which is of this world, to suppress and refuse obedience to the promptings of the inspiration.

On reaching his chamber he unbuckled his belt, as his custom was, and laid down his sword and began to undress, when again the same alarm from on high fell upon him, and the same warning spirit whispered to his mind's ear unspeakable intimations of dreadful things. Fear came upon him and trembling, which made all his bones to shake, and he lifted his sword and again buckled on his belt. But again the prudence of this world prevailed, and, heeding not the admonition to warn the Lords of the Congregation, he threw himself on his bed, without however unbuckling his sword, and in that condition fell asleep. But though his senses were shut his mind continued awake, and he had fearful visions of bloody hands and glimmering daggers glaming over him from behind his curtains, till in terror he started up, gasping like one that had struggled with a stronger than himself.

When he had in some degree composed his thoughts, he went to the window, and opened it, to see by the stars how far the night had passed. The window overlooked the North Loch and the swelling bank beyond, and the distant frith and the hills of Fife. The skies were calm and clear, and the air was tempered with a bright frost. The stars in their courses were reflected in the still waters of the North Loch, as if there had been an opening through the earth, showing the other concave of the spangled firmament. But the dark outline of the swelling bank on the northern side was like the awful corpse of some mighty thing prepared for interment.

As my grandfather stood in contemplation at the window, he heard the occasional churme of discourse from passengers still abroad, and now and then the braggart flourish of a trumpet resounded from the royal masquing at the palace, – breaking upon the holiness of the night with the harsh dissonance of a discord in some solemn harmony. – And as he was meditating on many things, and grieving in spirit at the dark fate of poor Scotland, and the woes with which the children of salvation were environed, he was startled by the apparition of a great blaze in the air, which for a moment lighted up all the land with a wild and fiery light, and he beheld in the glass of the North Loch, reflected from behind the shadow of the city, a tremendous erruption of burning beams and rafters burst into the sky, while a horrible crash, as if the chariots of destruction were themselves breaking down, shook the town like an earthquake.

He was for an instant astounded; but soon roused by the clangour of an alarm from the castle; and while a cry rose from all the city, as if the last trumpet itself was sounding, he rushed into the street, where the inhabitants, as they had flown from their beds, were running in consternation like the sheeted dead startled from their graves. Drums beat to arms; – the bells rang; – some cried the wild cry of fire, and there was wailing and weeping, and many stood dumb with horror, and could give no answer to the universal question,

– 'God of the heavens, what is this?' Presently a voice was heard crying, 'The King, the King!' and all, as if moved by one spirit, replied, 'The King, the King!' Then for a moment there was a silence stiller than the midnight hour, and drum, nor bell, nor voice was heard, but a rushing of the multitude towards St Mary's Port, which leads to the Kirk o' Field.

Among others, my grandfather hastened to the spot by Todrick's Wynd; and as he was running down towards the postern gate, he came with great violence against a man who was struggling up through the torrent of the people, without cap or cloak, and seemingly maddent with terrors. Urged by some strong instinct, my grandfather grasped him by the throat; for, by the glimpse of the lights that were then placing at every window, he saw it was Winterton. But a swirl of the crowd tore them asunder, and he had only time to cry, 'It's ane of Bothwell's men.'

The people caught the Earl's name; but instead of seizing the fugitive, they repeated, 'Bothwell, Bothwell, he's the traitor!' and pressed more eagerly on to the ruins of the house, which were still burning. The walls were rent, and in many places thrown down; the west gable was blown clean away, and the very ground, on the side where the King's chamber had been, was torn as with a hundred ploughshares. Certain trees that grew hard by were cleft and riven as with a thunderbolt, and stones were sticking in their timber like wedges and the shot of cannon.

It was thought, that in such a sudden blast of desolation, nothing in the house could have withstood the shock, but that all therein must have been shivered to atoms. When, however, the day began to dawn, it was seen that many things had escaped unblemished by the fire; and the King's body, with that of the servant who watched in his chamber, was found in a neighbouring garden, without having suffered any material change, – the which caused the greater marvelling; for it thereby appeared that they were the only sufferers in that dark treason, making the truth plain before the people, that the contrivance and firing thereof was concerted and brought to maturity by some in authority with the Queen, – and who that was the people answered by crying as the royal corpse was carried to the palace, 'Bothwell, Lord Bothwell, he is the traitor!'

All the next day, and for many days after, consternation reigned in the streets of the city, and horror sat shuddering in all her dwelling-places. Multitudes stood in amazement from morning to night around the palace; for the Earl of Bothwell was within, and still honoured with all the homages due to the greatest public trusts. Ever and anon a cry was heard, 'Bothwell is the murderer!' and the multitude shouted, 'Justice, justice!' But their cry was not heard.

Night after night the trembling citizens watched with candles at their casements, dreading some yet greater alarm; and in the stillness of the midnight hour a voice was heard crying, 'the Queen and Bothwell are the murderers!' and another voice replied, 'Vengeance, vengeance! Blood for blood!'

Every morning on the walls of the houses writings were seen, demanding the punishment of the regicides, – and the Queen's name, and the name of Bothwell, and the names of many more, with the Archbishop of St Andrews at their head, were emblazoned on all sides as the names of the regicides. But Bothwell, with the resolute bravery of guilt in the confidence of power, heeded not the cry that thus mounted continually against him to Heaven, and the Queen feigned a widow's sorrow.

The whole realm was as when the ark of the covenant of the Lord was removed from Israel and captive in the hands of the Philistines. The injured sought not the redress of their wrongs; even the guilty were afraid of one another, and by the very cowardice of their distrust were prevented from banding at a time when they might have rioted at will. What aggravated these portents of a kingdom falling asunder, was the mockery of law and justice which the court attempted. Those who were accused of the King's death ruled the royal councils, and were greatest in the Queen's favour. The Earl of Bothwell dictated the very proceedings by which he was himself to be brought to trial, – and when the day of trial arrived, he came with the pomp and retinue of a victorious conqueror – to be acquitted.

But acquitted, as the guilty ever needs must be whom no one dares to accuse, nor any witness hazards to appear against, his acquittal served but to prove his guilt, and the forms thereof the murderous participation of the Queen. Thus, though he was assoilzied in form of law, the libel against him was nevertheless found proven by the universal verdict of all men. Yet, in despite of the world, and even of the conviction recorded within their own bosoms, did the infatuated Mary and that dreadless traitor, in little more than three months from the era of their crime, rush into an adulterous marriage; but of the infamies concerning the same, and of the humiliated state to which poor Scotland sank in consequence, I must refer the courteous reader to the histories and chronicles of the time – while I return to the narrative of my grandfather.

When the Earl of Bothwell, as I have been told by those who heard him speak of these deplorable blots on the Scottish name, had been created Duke of Orkney, the people daily expected the marriage. But instead of the ordinary ceremonials used at the marriages of former kings and princes, the Queen and all about her, as if they had been smitten from on high with some manifest and strange frenzy, resolved, as it were in derision and blasphemy, notwithstanding her own and the notour popery of the Duke, to celebrate their union according to the strictest forms of the protestants; and John Knox being at the time in the West Country, his colleague, Master Craig, was ordered by the Queen in council to publish the bans three several Sabbaths in St Giles' kirk.

On the morning of the first appointed day my grand-father went thither; a vast concourse of the people were assembled, and the worthy minister, when he rose in the pulpit with the paper in his hand, trembled and was pale, and for some time unable to speak; at last he read the names and purpose of marriage aloud, and he paused when he had done so, and an awful solemnity froze the very spirits of the congregation. He then laid down the paper on the pulpit, and lifting his hands and raising his eyes, cried with a vehement sadness of voice, – 'Lord God of the pure heavens, and all ye of the earth that hear me, I protest, as a minister of the gospel, my abhorrence and detestation of this hideous and adulterous sin; and I call all the nobility and all of the Queen's council to remonstrate with her Majesty against a step that must cover her with infamy for ever and ruin past all remede.' Three days did he thus publish the bans, and thrice in that manner did he boldly proclaim his protestation; for which he was called before the privy council, where the guilty Bothwell was sitting; and being charged with having exceeded the bounds of his commission, he replied with an apostolic bravery—

'My commission is from the word of God, good laws, and natural reason, to all which this proposed marriage is obnoxious. The Earl of Bothwell, there where he sits, knows that he is an adulterer, – the divorce that he has procured from his wife has been by collusion, – and he knows likewise that he has murdered the King and guiltily possessed himself of the Queen's person.'

Yet, notwithstanding, Mr Craig was suffered to depart, even unmolested by the astonished and overawed Bothwell; but, as I have said, the marriage was still celebrated; and it was the last great crime of papistical device that the Lord suffered to see done within the bounds of Scotland. For the same night letters were sent to the Earl of Murray from divers of the nobility, entreating him to return forthwith; and my grandfather, at the incitement of the Earl of Argyle, was secretly sent by his patron Glencairn to beg the friends of the state and the lawful prince, the son whom the Queen had born to her murdered husband, to meet without delay at Stirling.

Accordingly, with the flower of their vassals and retainers, besides Argyle and Glencairn, came many of the nobles; and having protested their detestation of the conduct of the Queen, they entered into a Solemn League and Covenant, wherein they rehearsed, as causes for their confederating against the misrule with which the kingdom was so humbled, that the Scottish people were abhorred and vilipendit amongst all Christian nations; declaring that they would never desist till they had revenged the foul murder of the King, rescued the Queen from her thraldom to the Earl of Bothwell, and dissolved her ignominious marriage.

The Queen and her regicide, for he could not be called her husband, were panic-struck when they heard of this avenging paction. She issued a bold proclamation, calling on her insulted subjects to take arms in her defence, and she published manifestoes, all lies. She fled with Bothwell from Edinburgh to the castle of Borthwick; but scarcely were they within the gates when the sough of the rising storm obliged him to leave her, and the same night, in the disguise of man's apparel, the Queen of all Scotland was seen flying, friendless and bewildered, to her sentenced paramour.

The covenanting nobles in the meantime were mustering their clans and their vassals; and the Earls of Morton and Athol having brought the instrument of the League to Edinburgh, the magistrates and town-council signed the same, and, taking the oaths, issued instanter orders for the burghers to prepare themselves with arms and banners, and to man the city walls. The whole kingdom rung with the sound of warlike preparations, and the ancient valour of the Scottish heart was blithened with the hope of erasing the stains that a wicked government had brought upon the honour of the land.

Meanwhile the regicide and the Queen drew together what forces his power could command and her promises allure, and they advanced from Dunbar to Carberry-hill, where they encamped. The army of the Covenanters at the same time left Edinburgh to meet them. Mary appeared at the head of her troops; but they felt themselves engaged in a bad cause, and refused to fight. She exhorted them with all the pith of her eloquence; – she wept, – she implored, – she threatened, – and she reproached them with cowardice, – but still they stood sullen.

To retreat in the face of an enemy who had already

surrounded the hill on which she stood was impracticable. In this extremity she called with a voice of despair for Kirkcaldy of Grange, a brave man, whom she saw at the head of the cavalry by whom she was surrounded, and he having halted his horse and procured leave from his leaders, advanced toward her. Bothwell, with a few followers, during the interval, quitted the field; and, as soon as Kirkcaldy came up, she surrendered herself to him, and was conducted by him to the head-quarters of the Covenanters, by whom she was received with all the wonted testimonials of respect, and was assured, if she forsook Bothwell and governed her kingdom with honest councils, they would honour and obey her as their sovereign. But the common soldiers overwhelmed her with reproaches, and on the march back to Edinburgh poured upon her the most opprobrious names.

'Never was such a sight seen,' my grandfather often said, 'as the return of that abject Princess to her capital.' On the banner of the League was depicted the corpse of the murdered king her husband lying under a tree, with the young prince his son kneeling before it, and the motto was, 'Judge and revenge my cause, O Lord.' The standard-bearer rode with it immediately before the horse on which she sat weeping and wild, and covered with dust, and as often as she raised her distracted eye the apparition of the murder in the flag fluttered in her face. In vain she supplicated pity, – yells and howls were all the answers she received, and volleys of execrations came from the populace, with 'Burn her, burn her, bloody murdress! Let her not live!'

In that condition she was conducted to the provost's house, into which she was assisted to alight, more dead than alive, and next morning she was conveyed a prisoner to Lochleven castle, where she was soon after compelled to resign the crown to her son, and the regency to the Earl of Murray, by whose great wisdom the Reformation was established in truth and holiness throughout the kingdom, – though for a season it was again menaced when Mary effected her escape, and dared the cause of the Lord to battle at Langside. But of that great day of victory it becomes not me to speak, for it hath received the blazon of many an abler pen; it is enough to mention, that my grandfather was there, and after the battle that he returned with the army to Glasgow, and was present at the thanksgiving. The same night he paid his last respects to the Earl of Murray, who permitted him to take away, as a trophy and memorial, the gloves which his Lordship had worn that day in the field, and they have ever since been sacredly preserved at Quharist, where they may be still seen. They are of York buff; the palm of the one for the right hand is still blue with the mark of the sword's hilt, and the forefinger stool is stained with the ink of a letter which the Earl wrote on the field to Argyle, who had joined the Queen's faction; the which letter, it has been thought, caused the swithering of that nobleman in the hour of the onset, by which Providence gave the Regent the victory – a conquest which established the Gospel in his native land for ever.

After the battle of Langside many of the nobles and great personages of the realm grew jealous of the good Regent Murray; and, by their own demeanour, caused him to put on towards them a reserve and coldness of deportment, which they construed as their feelings and fancies led them, much to his disadvantage; for he was too proud to court the good-will that he thought was his due. But to all people of a lower degree, like those in my grandfather's station, he was ever the same punctual and gracious superior, making, by the urbanity of his manner, small courtesies recollected and spoken of as great favours, in so much, that being well-beloved of the whole commonalty, his memory, long after his fatal death, was held in great estimation among them, and his fame as the sweet odour of many blessings.

Few things, my grandfather often said, gave him a sorer pang than the base murder by the Hamiltons of that most eminent worthy; and in all the labours and business of his long life, nothing came ever more pleasant to his thoughts, than the remembrance of the part he had himself in the retribution with which their many bloody acts were in the end overtaken and punished. Indeed, as far as concerns their guiltiest instigator and kinsman, the adulterous Antichrist of St Andrews, never was a just vengeance and judgment more visibly manifested, as I shall now, with all expedient brevity, rehearse, it being the last exploit in which my grandfather bore arms for the commonweal.

Bailie Kilspinnie of Crail having dealings with certain Glasgow merchants, who sold plaiding to the Highlanders of Lennox and Cowal, finding them doure in payment, owing, as they said, to their customers lengthening their credit of their own accord, on account of the times, the west having been from the battle of Langside unwontedly

tranquil, he, in the spring of 1571, came in quest of his
monies, and my grandfather having notice thereof, took
on behind him on horseback, to see her father, Agnes
Kilspinnie, who had lived in his house from the time of
his marriage to her aunt, Elspa Ruet. And it happened that
Captain Crawford of Jordanhill, who was then meditating
his famous exploit against the castle of Dumbarton, met
my grandfather by chance in the Trongait, and knowing
some little of him, and of the great regard in which he
was held by many noblemen, for one of his birth, spoke to
him cordially, and asked him to be of his party, assigning,
among other things, as a motive, that the great adversary
of the Reformation, the Archbishop of St Andrews, had,
on account of the doom and outlawry pronounced upon
him, for being accessary both to the murder of King Henry,
the Queen's protestant husband, and of the good Regent
Murray, taken refuge in that redoubtable fortress.

Some concern for the state of his wife and young family
weighed with my grandfather while he was in communion
with Jordanhill; but after parting from him, and going
back to the Saracen's inn in the Gallowgait, where Bailie
Kilspinnie and his daughter were, he had an inward urging
of the spirit, moving him to be of the enterprise, on a
persuasion, as I have heard him tell himself, that without he
was there something would arise to balk the undertaking.
So he was in consequence troubled in thought, and held
himself aloof from the familiar talk of his friends all the
remainder of the day, wishing that he might be able to
overcome the thirst which Captain Crawford had bred
within him to join his company.

Bailie Kilspinnie seeing him in this perplexity of soul,
spoke to him as a friend, and searched to know what
had taken possession of him, and my grandfather, partly
moved by his entreaty, and partly by the thought of the
great palpable Antichrist of Scotland, who had done the
bailie's fireside such damage and detriment, being in a
manner exposed to their taking, told him what had been
propounded by Jordanhill.

'Say you so,' cried the bailie, remembering the offence
done to his family, 'say you so; and that he is in a girn

that wants but a manly hand to grip him. Body and soul o' me, if the thing's within the power of the arm of flesh, he shall be taken, and brought to the wuddy, if the Lord permits justice to be done within the realm of Scotland.'

The which bold and valorous breathing of the honest magistrate of Crail kindled the smoking yearnings of my grandfather into a bright and blazing flame, and he replied—

'Then, sir, if you be so minded, I cannot perforce abide behind, but will go forth with you to the battle, and swither not with the sword till we have effected some notable achievement.'

They accordingly went forthwith to Captain Crawford, and proffered to him their service; and he was gladdened that my grandfather had come to so warlike a purpose; but he looked sharply at the bailie, and twice smiled to my grandfather, as if in doubt of his soldiership, saying, 'But, Gilhaize, since you recommend him, he must be a good man and true.'

So the same night they set out at dusk, with a chosen troop and band of not more than two hundred men; a boat, provided with ladders, dropped down the river with the tide, to be before them.

By midnight the expedition reached the bottom of Dumbuck-hill; where, having ascertained that the boat was arrived, Jordanhill directed those aboard to keep her close in with the shore, and move with their march.

The evening when they left Glasgow was bright and calm, and the moon, in her first quarter, shed her beautiful glory on mountain, and tower, and tree, leading them as with the light of a heavenly torch; and when they reached the skirts of the river, it was soon manifest that their enterprise was favoured from on high. The moon was by that time set, and a thick mist came rolling from the Clyde and the Leven, and made the night air dim as well as dark, veiling their movements from all mortal eyes.

Jordanhill's guide led them to a part of the rock which was seldom guarded, and shewed them where to place their ladders. He had been in the service of the Lord Fleming, the governor, but on account of contumelious usage had quitted it, and had been the contriver of the scheme.

Scarcely was the first ladder placed when the impatience of the men brought it to the ground; but there was a noise in the ebbing waters of the Clyde, that drowned the accident of their fall, and prevented it from alarming the soldiers on the watch. This failure disconcerted Jordanhill for a moment; but the guide fastened the ladder to the roots of an ash-tree, which grew in a cleft of the rock, and to the first shelf of the precipice they all ascended in safety.

The first ladder was then drawn up, and placed against the upper story, as it might be called, of the rock, reaching to the gap where they could enter into the fortress, while another ladder was tied in its place below. Jordanhill then ascended, leading the way, followed by his men, the bailie of Crail being before my grandfather.

They were now at a fearful height from the ground; but the mist was thick, and no one saw the dizzy eminence to which he had attained. It happened, however, that just as Jordanhill reached the summit, and while my grandfather and the bailie were about half-way up the ladder, the mist below rolled away, and the stars above shone out, and the bailie, casting his eyes downward, was so amazed and terrified at the eagle-flight he had taken, that he began to quake and tremble, and could not mount a step farther.

At that juncture delay was death to success. It was impossible to pass him. To tumble him off the ladder, and let him be dashed to pieces, as some of the men both above and below roughly bade my grandfather do, was cruel. All were at a stand.

Governed, however, by a singular inspiration, my grandfather took off his own sword-belt, and also the bailie's, and fastened him with them to the ladder by the oxters and legs, and then turning round the ladder, leaving him so fastened pendent in the air on the lower side, the assailants ascended over his belly, and courageously mounted to their perilous duty.

Jordanhill shouted as they mustered on the summit. The officers and soldiers of the garrison rushed out naked, but sword in hand. The assailants seized the cannon. Lord

Fleming, the governor, leaped the wall into the boat that had brought the scaling ladders, and was rowed away. The garrison thus deserted surrendered, and the guilty prelate was among the prisoners.

As soon as order was in some degree restored, my grandfather went, with two other soldiers, to where the bailie had been left suspended, and having relieved him from his horror, which the breaking daylight increased by showing him the fearful height at which he hung, he brought him to Jordanhill, who, laughing at his disaster, ordered him to be one of the guard appointed to conduct the Archbishop to Stirling.

In that service the worthy magistrate proved more courageous, and upbraided the prisoner several times on the road for the ill he had done to him. But that traitorous high-priest heard his taunts in silence, for he was a valiant and proud man; such indeed was his gallant bearing in the march, that the soldiers were won by it to do him homage as a true knight: and had he been a warrior as he was but a priest, it was thought by many that, though both papist and traitor, they might have been worked upon to set him free. To Stirling, however, he was carried; and on the fourth day, from the time he was taken, he was executed on the gallows; where, notwithstanding his guilty life, he suffered with the bravery of a gentleman dying in a righteous cause, in so much, that the papists honoured his courage, as if it had been the virtue of a holy martyr; and Bailie Kilspinnie all his days never ceased to wonder how so wicked a man could die so well.

Having thus set forth the main passages in my grandfather's life, I should now quit the public highway of history, and turn for a time into the pleasant footpath of his domestic vineyard, the plants whereof, under his culture, and the pious waterings of Elspa Ruet, my excellent progenitrex, were beginning to spread their green tendrils and goodly branches, and to hang out their clusters to the gracious sunshine, as it were in demonstration to the heavens that the labourer was no sluggard, and as an assurance that in due season, under its benign favour, they would gratefully repay his care with sweet fruit. But there is yet one thing to be told, which, though it may not be regarded as germane to the mighty event of the Reformation, grew so plainly out of the signal catastrophe related in the foregoing chapter, that it were to neglect the instruction mercifully intended, were I not to describe all its circumstances and particularities as they came to pass.

Accordingly to proceed. In the winter after the storming of Dumbarton Castle, Widow Ruet, the mother of my grandmother, hearing nothing for a long time of her poor donsie daughter Marion, had, from the hanging of Archbishop Hamilton, the antichristian paramour of that misguided creature, fallen into a melancholy state of moaning and inward grief, in so much, that Bailie Kilspinnie wrote a letter, invoking my grandfather to come with his wife to Crail, that they might join together in comforting the aged woman; which work of duty and of charity they lost no time in undertaking, carrying with them Agnes Kilspinnie to see her kin.

Being minded, both in the going and the coming, to partake of the feast of the heavenly and apostolic eloquence of the fearless Reformer's life-giving truths, they went by the way of Edinburgh; and in going about while there, to show Agnes Kilspinnie the uncos of the town, it happened as they were coming down from the Castle-hill, in passing the Weigh-house, that she observed a beggar woman sitting on a stair seemingly in great distress, for her hands were fervently clasped, and she was swinging her body backwards and forwards like a bark without a rudder on a billowy sea, when the winds of an angry heaven are let loose upon't.

What made this forlorn wretch the more remarkable, was a seeming remnant of better days in something about herself, besides the silken rags of garments that had once been costly. For, as she from time to time lifted her delicate hands aloft in her despairing ecstasy, the scrap of blanket, which was all her mantle, fell back, and showed such lily and lady-like arms, that it was impossible to look upon her without compassion, and not also to wonder from what high and palmy estate she had fallen into such abject poverty.

My grandfather and his wife, with Agnes, stopped for a moment, and conferred together about what alms they would offer to a gentlewoman brought so low; when she, observing them, came wildly towards them, crying, 'For the Mother of God, to save a famishing outcast from death and perdition.'

Her frantic gesture, far more than her papistical exclamation, made their souls shudder; and before they had time to reply, she fell on her knees, and taking Elspa by the hand, repeated the same vehement prayer, adding, 'Do, do, even though I be the vilest and guiltiest of womankind.'

'Marion Ruet! – O, my sister! – O, my dear Marion!' as wildly and as wofully did my grandmother, in that instant, also cry aloud, falling on the beggar-woman's neck, and sobbing as if her heart would have burst; for it was indeed the bailie's wife, and the mother of Agnes, that supplicated for a morsel.

This sad sight brought many persons around, among others a decent elderly carlin that kept a huxtry shop close by, who pitifully invited them to come from the public causey into her house; and with some difficulty my grandfather removed the two sisters thither. Agnes Kilspinnie, poor thing, following like a demented creature, not even able to drop a tear at so meeting with her humiliated parent, who, from the moment that she was known, could only gaze like the effigy of some extraordinary consternation carved in alabaster stone.

When they had been some time in the house of old Ursie Firikins, as the kind carlin was called, Elspa Ruet all the while weeping like a constant fountain, and repeating 'Marion, Marion!' with a fond and sorrowful tenderness that would allow her to say no more, my grandfather having got a drink of meal and water prepared, gave it to the famished outcast, and she gradually recovered from her stupor.

For many minutes, however, she sat still and said nothing, and when she did speak, it was in a voice of such misery of soul, that my grandfather never liked to tell what terrible thoughts the remembrance of it ever gave him. I shall therefore not venture to repeat what she said, farther than to mention, that, having sunk down on her knees, she spread her hands aloft and exclaimed, – 'Ay, the time's come now, and the words of her prophecy, that never ceased to dirl in my soul, are fulfilled. I will go back to Crail – my penitence shall be seen in my shame; – I will go openly, that all may take warning – and before all, in the face of day, will I confess the wrongs I hae done to my gudeman and bairns.'

She then rose and said to her sister, 'Elspa, ye hae heard my vow, and this very hour I will begin my pilgrimage.'

Some farther conversation ensued, in which she told them, that she had run a woful course after the havock at St Andrews; but, though humbled to the dust, and almost perishing of hunger, pride had still warsled with penitence, and would not let her return to seek shelter from her mother. 'But at last,' said she, 'all has now come to pass, and it is meet I submit to what is so plainly required of me.' Then turning to her daughter, she looked at her for some time with a watery and inquiring eye, and would have spoken, but her heart filled full and she could only weep.

By way of consolation, my grandfather told her they were then on their way to Crail, and that, as soon as they had procured for her some fit apparel, they would take her with them. At these words she lifted the skirt of her ragged gown, and looking at it for a moment, smiled, as if in contempt of all things, saying—

'No; this is the livery of Him that I hae served so weel. It is fit that my friends should behold the coat of many colours, and the garment of praise wherewith He rewards all those that serve Him as I hae done.' And no admonition, nor any affectionate petition, could shake her sad purpose.

'But,' said she, 'I ought not to shame you on the road; and yet, Elspa, at least till the entrance of the town, let me travel with you; for when I hae dreed my penance, we must part never to meet again. Darkness and dule is my portion now in this world. I hae earnt them, and it is just that I should enjoy them. They are my ain conquest, bought wi' the price of every thing but my soul; and wha kens but for this meeting that it might hae been bartered away too.'

In nothing, however, of all that then passed, was there any thing which so moved the tranquil heart of my grandfather, as the looks which, from time to time, the desolate woman cast at her daughter. Fain she seemed to speak, and to catch her in her arms; but ever and anon the sense of her own condition came upon her, and she began to weep, crying, – 'No, no: I darena do that – I darena even mysel' to a parent's privilege after what I hae done.'

The poor lassie sat unable to make any answer; but at last, in a timid manner, she took her mother softly by the hand, and the fond and lowly penitent, for a few moments, allowed it to linger in her grip, willing to have left it there; but suddenly stung by her conscience she snatched it away, and again broke out into piercing lamentations and confessions of unworthiness.

Meanwhile the charitable Ursie Firikins had made ready a mess of porridge, and the mournful Magdalen being soothed and consoled, was persuaded to partake. And afterwards, when they had sat some time, and the crowd, which had gathered out of doors in the street, was dispersed, my grandfather went to his lodgings; and having paid his lawin, returned to the two sisters and Agnes Kilspinnie, and they all walked to the shore of Leith together, where they found a boat going to Kinghorn, into which they embarked; and having slept there, they hired a cart to take them to Crail next morning, every one who saw them wondering at the dejected and ruinous appearance of the penitent. The particulars, however, of their journey, and of her reception in her native place, will furnish matter for another chapter.

When they came within a mile of the town, where a small public stood, that wayfaring men were wont to stop and refresh themselves at, my grandfather urged the disconsolate Marion, who had come all the way from Kinghorn without speaking a single word, to alight from the cart, and remain there till the cloud of night, when she might go to her mother's unafflicted by the gaze of the pitiless multitude.

To this, at first, she made no answer; but leaping out of the cart, and standing still for a moment, she looked wistfully at her sister and daughter, and then began to weep, crying, 'Gang ye awa, and no mind me; ye canna thole, and oughtna to share what I maun bear; and I'll never break another vow: so, in the face o' day, and of a' people, I'm constrained to enter Crail, – first, to confess my guilt at the door of the honest man and his bairns that I hae sae disgraced; and syne to beg my mother to take in the limmer that was scofft frae door to door, till the blessed time when ye were sent to stop me laying desperate hands on mysel'.'

Elspa remonstrated with her for some time, but she was not to be entreated: 'My guilt and my shamelessness were public,' said she, 'and it is meet that the world should behold what hae been the wages I hae earnt, and the depth of the humiliation to which my vain and proud heart has been brought; so, go ye on wi' your gudeman and Agnes, and let me come by mysel'.'

'No, Marion,' replied her sister, 'that sha'na be; I'll no let you do that: if ye will make sic a pilgrimage, I'll bear you company; for I can ne'er be ashamed nor mortified in being wi' you, when ye are seeking again the path of righteousness that ye were sae beguil't to quit.'

'Say nae I was beguil't; say naething to gar me think less o' my fault than I should: there was nae beguiler but my ain vain and sinful nature.'

Her daughter, who had all this time stood silent with the tear in her e'e, then said, 'I'll gang wi' you, mother, too.'

'Mother! – O Agnes Kilspinnie, dinna sae wrang yoursel', and your honest father, as to ca' the like o' me mother. But did ye say ye would come wi' me?' – and she dropt vehemently on her knees, and, spreading her arms to the skies, cried out with a loud and wild voice—

'God, God! is thy goodness so great, that thou canst already vouchsafe to me a mercy like this?'

Seeing her so bent on going into the town in her miserable estate, and his wife and her daughter so mindit to go with her, my grandfather said it would be as well for him to run forward and prepare her mother for her coming; so he left them, and hastened into the town, thinking they would come in the cart; but when he was gone, Marion, still in the hope she might get her sister and daughter dissuaded from accompanying her, told them that she was resolved to go on her bare feet; which, however, made them in pity still adhere the more closely to their determination; and, having paid the Kinghorn man for his cart, the three set forward together, Elspa on the right hand and Agnes on the left hand of the lowly penitent.

In the meantime my grandfather hastened to the dwelling of Widow Ruet, his gudemother, to tell her who was coming, and to prepare her aged mind for the sore shock. For though she was a sectarian of the Roman seed, she was nevertheless a most devout character, and abided more in the errors of her religion, because she thought herself too old to learn a new faith, than from that obstinacy of spirit which in those days so abounded in the breasts of the papisticals.

The news were at first as glad tidings to the humane old woman; but every now and then she began to start, and to listen, – and a tear fell from her eye. When she heard the voice or any one talking in the street, or the sound of a foot passing, she hurried to the window and looked hastily out. The struggle within her was great, and it grew every minute stronger and stronger; and after walking very wofully divers times across the floor, she went and closed the shutters of her window, and sitting down gave full vent to her grief. In that state she had not been long, when the sough of a din gathering at a distance was heard.

'Mother of Christ!' she cried, starting up, clapping her hands, 'Mother of Jesus, thou hast seen the fruit of thy womb exposed to ignominy. By thine own agonies in that hour, I implore thy support. O blessed Mary, thy sorrow was light compared to my burden, for thy bairn was holy, and meek, and kind, and without sin. But thou hast known what it was to sit by thy baby sleeping in its innocence; thou hast known what it was to love it for the very troubles it then gave thee. By the remembrance of that sweet watching and care, O pity me, and help me to receive my erring bairn!'

My grandfather could not stand her lament and ejaculations, and hearing the sound drawing nearer and nearer, he went out of the house to see if his presence might be any protection; but the sight he saw was even more sorrowful than the aged mother's grief.

Instead of the cart in which he expected to see the women, he beheld them coming along, side by side, together, attended by a great multitude; doors and windows flew open as they came along, and old and young looked out. Many cried, 'She has been well serv't for her shame.' Some laughed; and the young turned aside their heads to hide their tears. Among others that ran from the causey-side to look in the face of Marion – still beautiful, though faded, but shining with something brighter than beauty – there was a little boy that went up close to her, and took her by the hand, without speaking, and led her along. He was her own son; but still she moved not her solemn heavenward eye, though a universal sobbing burst from all the multitude; and my grandfather, at the piteous pageantry, was no longer able to remain master of his feelings. Seeing, however, that the mournful actors therein were going on towards Bailie Kilspinnie's, and not intending to stop, as he expected they would, at Widow Ruet's door, he ran forward to warn his old friend; but in this he was too late; some one had been already there;

and he found the poor man, with his three other children, standing at the door, seemingly utterly at a loss to know what his duty should be; nor was my grandfather in any condition of mind to help him with advice.

At that juncutre the multitude came rushing on before the women, and halted in front of the bailie's house; for, seeing him and his bairns, they were taught, by some sense of gentle sympathy, to divide and retire to a distance, leaving an open and silent space for the penitent to go forward.

When Agnes Kilspinnie and her brother saw their father and brother and sisters at the door, they quitted their mother and joined them, as if instructed by an instinct, while she slowly approached.

Elspa Ruet, who had hitherto maintained a serene and resigned composure of countenance, was so moved at this sad spectacle, that my grandfather, seeing her distress, stepped out and caught her in his arms, and supported her from falling, she was so faint with anguish of heart.

In the same moment, with a look that struck awe and consternation into every one around, Marion stepped on towards her husband and children, and gazed at them, and was dropping on her knees, when the bailie caught her in his arms, as if he would have carried her into the house. But he faltered in his purpose; and, casting his eyes on the five weans whom she had so deserted, he unloosed his embrace, and, gathering them before him, went in and shut the door.

The multitude uttered a fearful sough; Elspa Ruet, roused by it, rushed from my grandfather towards her sister, and stooping, tried to raise her up. Poor Marion, still kneeling, looked around to the people, who stood all as still as mourners at an interment, and her dark ringlets falling loose, made her pale face appear of an unearthly fairness. She seemed as if she would have said something to her sister, who had clasped her by the hand, but litherly swinging backward, she laid her head down on her husband's threshold, and gave a heavy sigh, and died.

The burial of Marion Ruet was decently attended by Bailie Kilspinnie and all his family; and though he did not carry the head himself, he yet ordered their eldest son to do so, because, whatever her faults had been, she was still the youth's mother. And my grandfather, with his wife, having spent some time after with their friends at Crail, returned homeward by themselves, passing over to Edinburgh, that they might taste once more of the elixir of salvation as dispensed by John Knox, who had been for some time in a complaining way, and it was by many thought that the end of his preaching was drawing nigh.

It happened that the dreadful tidings of the murder of the protestants in France, by the command of 'the accursed king,' reached Edinburgh in the night before my grandfather and his wife returned thither; and he used to speak of the consternation that they found reigning in the city when they arrived there, as a thing very awful to think of. Every shop was shut, and every window closed; for it was the usage in those days, when death was in a house, to close all the windows, so that the appearance of the town was as if, for the obduracy of their idolatrous sovereign, the destroying angel had slain all the first-born, and that a dead body was then lying in every family.

There was also a terrifying solemnity in the streets; for, though they were as if all the people had come forth in panic and sad wonderment, many were clothed in black, and there was a funereal stillness, – a dismal sense of calamity that hushed the voices of men, and friends meeting one another, lifted their hands, and shuddering, passed by without speaking. My grandfather saw but one, between Leith Wynd and the door of the house in the Lawnmarket where he proposed to lodge, that wore a smile, and it was not of pleasure, but of avarice counting its gains.

The man was one Hans Berghen, an armourer, that had feathered his nest in the raids of the war with the Queen Regent. He was a Norman by birth, and had learnt the tempering of steel in Germany. In his youth he had been in the Imperator's service, and had likewise worked in the arsenal of Venetia. Some said he was perfected in his trade by the infidel at Constantinopolis; but, however this might be, no man of that time was more famous among roisters and moss-troopers for the edge and metal of his weapons, than that same blasphemous incomer, who thought of nothing but the greed of gain, whether by dule to protestant or papist; so that the sight of his hard-favoured visage, blithened with satisfaction, was to my grandfather, who knew him well by repute, as an omen of portentous aspect.

For two days the city continued in that dismal state, and on the third, which was Sabbath, the churches were so filled, that my grandmother, being then in a tender condition, did not venture to enter the High Kirk, where the Reformer was waited for by many thirsty and languishing souls from an early hour in the morning, who desired to hear what he would say concerning the dark deeds that had been done in France. She therefore returned to the Lawnmarket; but my grandfather worked his way into the heart of the crowd, where he had not long been, when a murmur announced that Master Knox was coming, and soon after he entered the kirk.

He had now the appearance of great age and weakness, and he walked with slow and tottering steps, wearing a virl of fur round his neck, and a staff in one hand; godlie Richie Ballanden, his man, holding him up by the oxter. And when he came to the foot of the pulpit, Richie, by the help of another servent that followed with THE BOOK, lifted him up the steps into it, where he was seemingly so exhausted, that he was obligated to rest for the space of several minutes. No man who had never seen him before, could have thought that one so frail would have had ability to have given out even the psalm; but when he began the spirit descended upon him, and he was so kindled, that at last his voice became as awful as the thunders of wrath, and his arm was strengthened as with the strength of a champion's. The kirk dirled to the foundations; the hearts of his hearers shook, till the earth of their sins was shaken clean from them; and he appeared in the whirlwind of inspiration, as if his spirit was mounting, like the prophet Elijah in a fiery chariot, immediately to the gates of heaven.

His discourse was of the children of Bethlehem slain by Herod, and he spoke of the dreadful sound of a bell and a trumpet heard suddenly in the midnight hour, when all were fast bound, and lying defenceless in the fetters of sleep. He described the dreadful knocking at the doors – the bursting in of men with drawn swords – how babies were harled by the arms from their mothers' beds and bosoms, and dashed to death upon the marble floors. He told of parents that stood in the porches of their houses, and made themselves the doors that the slayers were obliged to hew in pieces before they could enter in. He pictured the women flying along the street in the nakedness of the bedchamber, with their infants in their arms, and how the ruffians of the accursed king, knowing their prey by their cries, ran after them, caught the mother by the hair, and the bairn by the throat, and in one act flung the innocent to the stones and trampled out its life. Then he paused, and said, in a soft and thankful voice, that in the horrors of Bethlehem there was still much mercy; for the idolatrous dread of Herod prompted him to slay but young children, whose blameless lives were to their weeping parents an assurance of their acceptance into heaven.

'What then,' he cried, 'are we to think of that night, and of that king, and of that people, among whom, by whom, and with whom, the commissioned murderer twisted his grip in the fugitive old man's grey hairs, to draw back his head that the knife might the surer reach his heart? With what eyes, being already blinded with weeping, shall we turn to that city where the withered hands of the grandmother were deemed as weapons of war by the strong and black-a-vised slaughterer, whose sword was owre vehemently used for a' the feckless remnant of life it had to cut! But deaths like these were brief and blessed compared to other things – which, Heaven be praised, I have not the power to describe – and which, among this protestant congregation, I trust there is not one able to imagine – or who, trying to conceive, descries but in dark and misty vision, the pains of mangled mothers; babes, untimely and unquickened, cast on the dunghills and into the troughs of swine; of black-iron hooks fastened into the mouths, and riven through the cheeks of brave men, whose arms are tied with cords behind, as they are dragged into the rivers to drown, by those who durst not in fair battle endure the lightning of their eyes. – O Herod! – Herod of Judea – thy name is hereafter bright, for in thy bloody business thou wast thyself no where to be seen. In the vouts and abysses of thy unstained palace, thou hidst thyself from the eye of history, and perhaps humanely sat covering thine ears with thy hands to shut out the sound of the wail and woe around thee. – But this Herod – let me not call him by so humane a name. – No: let all the trumpets of justice sound his own to everlasting infamy – Charles the Ninth of France! And let his ambassador that is here aye yet, yet to this time audaciously in this Christian land, let him tell his master, that sentence has been pronounced against him in Scotland; that the Divine vengeance will never depart from him or his house until repentance has ensued, and atonement been made in their own race; that his name will remain a blot – a blot of blood, a stain never to be effaced – a thing to be pronounced with a curse by all posterity; and that none proceeding from his loins shall ever enjoy his kingdom in peace.'

The preacher, on saying these prophetic words, paused, and with his eyes fixed upwards, he stood some time silent, and then, clasping his hands together, exclaimed, with fear and trembling upon him, 'Lord, Lord, thy will be done!'

Many thought that he had then received some great apocalypse; for it was observed of all men, that he was never after like the man he had once been, but highly and holily elevated above earthly cares and considerations, saving those only of his ministry, and which he hastened to close: he was as one that no longer had trust, portion, or interest in this temporal world, which in less than two months after he bade farewell and was translated to a better. Yes; to a better, – for assuredly, if there is ought in this life that may be regarded as the symbols of infeftment to the inheritance of Heaven, the labours and ministration of John Knox were testimonies that he had verily received the yird and stane of an heritage on High.

CHAPTER NINE

Shortly after my grandfather had returned with his wife
to their quiet dwelling at Quharist on the Garnock side,
he began, in the course of the winter following, to suffer
an occasional pang in that part of his body which was
damaged by the fall he got in rugging down the Virgin
Mary out of her niche in the idolatrous abbey-kirk of
Kilwinning, and the anguish of his suffering grew to such
a head by Candlemas, that he was obligated to send for his
old acquaintance, Dominick Callender, who had, after his
marriage with the regenerate nun, settled as a doctor of
physic in the godly town of Irvine. But for many a day
all the skill and medicamenting of Doctor Callender did
him little good, till Nature had, of her own accord, worked
out the root of the evil in the shape of a sklinter of bone.
Still, though the wound then closed, it never was a sound
part, and he continued in consequence a lamiter for life.
Yet were his days greatly prolonged beyond the common
lot of man; for he lived till he was ninety-one years, seven
months, and four days old; and his end at last was but a
pleasant translation from the bodily to the spiritual life.

For some days before the close he was calm and cheerful,
rehearsing to the neighbours that came to speer for him,
many things like those of which I have spoken herein.
Towards the evening a serene drowsiness fell upon him, like
the snow that falleth in silence, and froze all his temporal
faculties in so gentle a manner, that it could not be said he
knew what it was to die; being, as it were, carried, in the
downy arms of sleep, to the portal door of Death, where
all the pains and terrors that guard the same were hushed,
and stood mute around, as he was softly received in.

No doubt there was something of a providential design
in the singular prolongation of such a pious and blameless

life; for through it the possessor became a blessed mean of sowing, in the hearts of his children and neighbours, the seeds of those sacred principles, which afterwards made them stand firm in their religious integrity when they were so grievously tried. For myself I was too young, being scant of eight years when he departed, to know the worth of those precious things which he had treasured in the garnel of his spirit for seed-corn unto the Lord; and, therefore, though I often heard him speak of the riddling wherewith that mighty husbandman of the Reformation, John Knox, riddled the truths of the gospel from the errors of papistry, I am bound to say, that his own exceeding venerable appearance, and the visions of past events, which the eloquence of his traditions called up to my young fancy, worked deeper and more thoroughly into my nature, than the reasons and motives which guided and governed many of his other disciples. But, before proceeding with my own story, it is meet that I should still tell the courteous reader some few things wherein my father bore a part, – a man of very austere character, and of a most godly, though, as some said, rather of a stubbornly affection for the forms of worship which had been established by John Knox and the pious worthies of his times, he was withal a single-minded Christian, albeit more ready for a raid than subtile in argument. He had, like all who knew the old people his parents, a by-common reverence for them; and spoke of the patriarchs with whom of old the Lord was wont to hold communion, as more favoured of Him than David or Solomon, or any other princes or kings.

When he was very young, not passing, as I have heard him often tell, more than six or seven years of age, he was taken, along with his brethren, by my grandfather, to see the signing, at Irvine, of the Covenant, with which, in the lowering time of the Spanish armada, King James, the son of Mary, together with all the Reformed, bound themselves in solemn compact to uphold the protestant religion. Afterwards, when he saw the country rise in arms, and heard of the ward and watch, and the beacons ready on the hills, his imagination was kindled with some dreadful conceit of the armada, and he thought it could be nothing less than some awful and horrible creature sent from the shores of perdition to devour the whole land. The image he had thus framed in his fears haunted him continually; and night after night he could not sleep for thinking of its talons of brass, and wings of thunder, and nostrils flaming fire, and the iron teeth with which it was to grind and gnash the bodies and bones of all protestants, in so much, that his parents were concerned for the health of his mind, and wist not what to do to appease the terrors of his visions.

At last, however, the great Judith of the protestant cause, Queen Elizabeth of England, being enabled to drive a nail into the head of that Holofernes of the idolaters, and many of the host of ships having been plunged, by the right arm of the tempest, into the depths of the seas, and scattered by the breath of the storm, like froth over the ocean, it happened that, one morning about the end of July, a cry arose, that a huge galley of the armada was driven on the rocks at Pencorse; and all the shire of Ayr hastened to the spot to behold and witness her shipwreck and overthrow. Among others my grandfather, with his three eldest sons, went, leaving my father at home; but his horrors grew to such a passion of fear, that his mother, the calm and pious Elspa Ruet, resolved to take him thither likewise, and to give him the evidence of his eyes, that the dreadful armada was but a navy of vessels like the ship which was cast upon the shore. By this prudent thought of her, when he arrived at the spot his apprehensions were soothed; but his mind had ever after a strange habitude of forming wild and wonderful images of every danger, whereof the scope and nature was not very clearly discerned, and which continued with him till the end of his days.

Soon after the death of my grandfather, he had occasion to go into Edinburgh anent some matter of legacy that had fallen to us, through the decease of an uncle of my mother, a bonnet-maker in the Canongate; and, on his arrival there, he found men's minds in a sore fever concerning the rash counsels wherewith King Charles the First, then reigning, was mindit to interfere with the pure worship of God, and to enact a part in the kirk of Scotland little short of the papistical domination of the Roman Antichrist. To all men this was startling tidings; but to my father it was as an enormity that fired his blood and spirit with the fierceness of a furnace. And it happened that he lodged with a friend of ours, one Janet Geddes, a most pious woman, who had suffered great molestation in her worldly substance, from certain endeavours for the restoration of the horns of the mitre, and the prelatic buskings with which that meddling and fantastical bodie, King James the Sixth, would fain have buskit and disguised the sober simplicity of gospel ordinances.

No two persons could be more heartily in unison upon any point of controversy, than was my worthy father and Janet Geddes, concerning the enormities that would of a necessity ensue from the papistical pretensions and unrighteous usurpation of King Charles; and they sat crooning and lamenting together, all the Saturday afternoon and night, about the woes of idolatry that were darkening again over Scotland.

No doubt there was both reason and piety in their fears; but in the method of their sorrow, from what I have known of my father's earnest and simple character, I redde there might be some lack of the decorum of wisdom. But be this as it may, they heated the zeal of one another to a pitch of great fervour, and next morning, the Sabbath, they went together to the high kirk of St Giles to see what the power of an infatuated government would dare to do.

The kirk was filled to its uttermost bunkers; my father, however, got for Janet Geddes, she being an aged woman, a stool near the skirts of the pulpit; but nothing happened to cause any disturbance, till the godly Mr Patrick Henderson had made an end of the morning prayer, when he said, with tears in his eyes, with reference to the liturgy, which was then to be promulgated, 'Adieu, good people, for I think this is the last time of my saying prayers in this kirk;' and the congregation being much moved thereat, many wept.

No sooner had Mr Henderson retired, than Master Ramsay, that horn of the beast, which was called the Dean of Edinburgh, appeared in the pulpit in the pomp of his abominations, and began to read the liturgy. At the first words of which Janet Geddes was so transported with indignation that, starting from her stool, she made it fly whirring at his head, as she cried – 'Villain, dost thou say the mass at my lug?' Then such an uproar began, as had not been witnessed since the destruction of the idols; the women screaming, and clapping their hands in terrification, as if the legions of the Evil One had been let loose upon them; and the men crying aloud, 'Antichrist, antichrist! down wi' the pope!' and all exhortation to quiet them was drowned in the din.

Such was the beginning of those troubles in the church and state, so wantonly provoked by the weak and wicked policy of the first King Charles, and which in the end brought himself to an ignominious death; and such the cause of that Solemn League and Covenant, to which, in my green years, my father, soon after his return home, took me to be a party, and to which I have been enabled to adhere, with unerring constancy, till the glorious purpose of it has all been fulfilled and accomplished.

When my father returned home, my mother and all the family were grieved to see his sad and altered looks. We gathered around him, and she thought he had failed to get the legacy, and comforted him, by saying they had hitherto fenn't without it, and so might they still do.

To her tender condolements he however made no answer; but, taking a leathern bag, with the money in it, out of his bosom, he flung it on the table, saying, 'What care I for this world's trash, when the ark of the Lord is taken from Israel?' which to hear daunted the hearts of all present. And then he told us, after some time, what was doing on the part of the King to bring in the worship of the Beast again; rehearsing, with many circumstances, the consternation and sorrow and rage and lamentations that he had witnessed in Edinburgh.

I, who was the ninth of his ten children, and then not passing nine years old, was thrilled with an unspeakable fear; and all the dreadful things, which I had heard my grandfather tell of the tribulations of his time, came upon my spirit like visions of the visible scene, and I began to weep with an exceeding sorrow, insomuch that my father was amazed, and caressed me, and thanked Heaven that one so young in his house felt as a protestant child should feel in an epoch of such calamity.

It was then late in the afternoon, towards the gloaming, and having partaken of some refreshment, my father took the big Bible from the press-head, and, after a prayer uttered in great heaviness of spirit, he read a portion of the Revelations, concerning the vials and the woes, expounding the same like a preacher; and we were all filled with anxieties and terrors: some of the younger members trembled with the thought that the last day was surely at hand.

Next morning a sough and rumour of that solemn venting of Christian indignation which had been manifested at Edinburgh, having reached our country-side, and the neighbours hearing of my father's return, many of them came at night to our house to hear the news; and it was a meeting that none present thereat could ever after forget: – well do I mind every thing as if it had happened but yestreen. I was sitting on a laigh stool at the fireside, between the chumley-lug and the gown-tail of old Nanse Snoddie, my mother's aunty, a godly woman, that in her eild we took care of; and as young and old came in, the salutation was in silence, as of guests coming to a burial.

The first was Ebenezer Muir, an aged man, whose grandson stood many a blast in the persecution of the latter days, both with the Blackcuffs and the bloody dragoons of the remorseless Graham of Claver. He was bent with the burden of time, and leaning on his staff, and his long white hair hung down from aneath his broad blue bonnet. He was one whom my grandfather held in great respect for the sincerity of his principles and the discretion of his judgment, and among all his neighbours, and nowhere more than in our house, was he considered a most patriarchal character.

'Come awa, Ebenezer,' said my father, 'I'm blithe and I'm sorrowful to see you. This night we may be spar't to speak in peace of the things that pertain unto salvation; but the day and the hour is not far off, when the flock of Christ shall be scattered and driven from the pastures of their Divine Master.'

To these words of affliction Ebenezer Muir made no response, but went straight to the fireside, facing Nanse Snoddie, and sat down without speaking; and my father, then observing John Fullarton of Dykedivots coming in, stretched out his hand, and took hold of his, and drew him to sit down by his side.

They had been in a manner brothers from their youth upward: an uncle of John Fullarton's, by whom he was brought up, had been owner, and he himself had heired, and was then possessor of, the mailing of Dykedivot, beside ours. He was the father of four brave sons, the youngest of whom, a stripling of some thirteen or fourteen years, was at his back: the other three came in afterwards. He was, moreover, a man of a stout and courageous nature, though of a much-enduring temper.

'I hope,' said he to my father, 'I hope, Sawners, a' this straemash and hobbleshow that fell out last Sabbath in Embro' has been seen wi' the glamoured een o' fear, and that the King and government canna be sae far left to themsels as to meddle wi' the ordinances of the Lord.'

'I doot, I doot, it's owre true, John,' replied my father in a very mournful manner; and while they were thus speaking, Nahum Chapelrig came ben. He was a young man, and his father being precentor and schoolmaster of the parish, he had more lair than commonly falls to the lot of country folk; over and aboon this, he was of a spirity disposition, and both eydent and eager in whatsoever he undertook, so that for his years he was greatly looked up to amang all his acquaintance, notwithstanding a small spicin of conceit that he was in with himself.

On seeing him coming in, worthy Ebenezer Muir made a sign for him to draw near and sit by him; and when he went forward, and drew in a stool, the old man took hold of him by the hand, and said, 'Ye're weel come, Nahum;' and my father added, 'Ay, Nahum Chapelrig, it's fast coming to pass, as ye hae been aye saying it would; the King hasna restit wi' putting the prelates upon us.'

'What's te prelates, Robin Fullarton?' said auld Nanse Snoddie, turning round to John's son, who was standing behind his father.

'They're the red dragons o' unrighteousness,' replied the sincere laddie with great vehemence.

'Gude guide us!' cried Nanse with the voice of terror; 'and has the King daur't to send sic accursed things to devour God's people?'

But my mother, who was sitting behind me, touched her on the shoulder, bidding her be quiet; for the poor woman, being then doited, when left to the freedom of her own will, was apt to expatiate without ceasing on whatsoever she happened to discourse anent; and Nahum Chapelrig said to my father—

"Deed, Sawners Gilhaize, we could look for nae better; prelacy is but the prelude o' papistry: but the papistry o' this prelude is a perilous papistry indeed; for its roots of rankness are in the midden-head of Arminianism, which, in a sense, is a greater Antichrist than Antichrist himself, even where he sits on his throne of thraldom in the Roman vaticano. But, nevertheless, I trust and hope, that though the virgin bride of protestantism be for a season thrown on her back, she shall not be overcome, but will so strive and warsle aneath the foul grips of that rampant Arminian, the English high-priest Laud, that he shall himself be cast into the mire, or choket wi' the stoure of his own bakiefu's of abominations, wherewith he would overwhelm and bury the Evangil. Yea, even though the shield of his mighty men is made red, and his valiant men are in scarlet, he shall recount his worthies, but they shall stumble in their walk.'

While Nahum was thus holding forth, the house filled even to the trance-door with the neighbours, old and young; and several from time to time spoke bitterly against the deadly sin and aggression which the King was committing in the rape that the reading of the liturgy was upon the consciences of his people. At last Ebenezer Muir, taking off his bonnet, and rising, laid it down on his seat behind him, and then resting with both his hands on his staff, looked up, – and every one was hushed. Truly it was an affecting sight to behold that very aged, time-bent, and venerable man so standing in the midst of all his dismayed and pious neighbours, – his grey hairs flowing from his haffets, – and the light of our lowly hearth shining upon his bald head and reverent countenance.

'Friens,' said he, 'I hae lived lang in the world; and in this house I hae often partaken the sweet repast of the conversations of that sanctified character, Michael Gilhaize, whom we a' revered as a parent, not more for his ain worth than for the great things to which he was a witness in the trials and troubles of the Reformation; and it seems to me, frae a' the experience I hae gatherit, that when ance kings and governments hae taken a step, let it be ne'er sae rash, there's a something in the nature of rule

and power that winna let them confess a fau't, though they
may afterwards be constrained to renounce the evil of their
ways. It was therefore wi' a sore heart that I heard this day
the doleful tidings frae Embro', and moreover, that I hae
listened to the outbreathings this night of the heaviness
wherewith the news hae oppressed you a'. Sure am I, that
frae the provocation given to the people of Scotland by the
King's miscounselled majesty, nothing but tears and woes
can ensue; for by the manner in which they hae already
rebutted the aggression, he will in return be stirred to
aggrieve them still farther. I'm now an auld man, and may
be removed before the woes come to pass; but it requires
not the e'e of prophecy to spae bloodshed, and suffering,
and many afflictions in your fortunes. Nevertheless, friens,
be of good cheer, for the Lord will prosper his own cause.
Neither king, nor priest, nor any human authority, has the
right to interfere between you and your God; and allegiance
ends where persecution begins. Never, therefore, in the
trials awaiting you, forget, that the right to resist in matters
of conscience is the foundation-stone of religious liberty;
O see, therefore, that you guard it weel!'

The voice and manner of the aged speaker melted every
heart. Many of the women sobbed aloud, and the children
were moved, as I was myself, and as I have often heard
them in their manhood tell, as if the spirit of faith and
fortitude had entered into the very bones and marrow
of their bodies; nor ever afterwards have I heard psalm
sung with such melodious energy of holiness as that pious
congregation of simple country folk sung the hundred and
fortieth Psalm before departing for their lowly dwellings on
that solemn evening.

It was on the Wednesday that my father came home from Edinburgh. On Friday the farmer lads and their fathers continued coming over to our house to hear the news, and all their discourse was concerning the manifest foretaste of papistry which was in the praying of the prayers, that an obdurate prince and an alien Arminian prelate were attempting to thrust into their mouths, and every one spoke of renewing the Solemn League and Covenant, which, in the times of the Reformation and the dangers of the Spanish Armada, had achieved such great things for THE TRUTH AND THE WORD.

On Saturday, Mr Sundrum, our minister, called for my father about twelve o'clock. He had heard the news, and also that my father had come back. I was doing something on the green, I forget now what it was, when I saw him coming towards the door, and I ran into the house to tell my father, who immediately came out to meet him.

Little passed in my hearing between them, for, after a short inquiry concerning how my father had fared in the journey, the minister took hold of him by the arm, and they walked together into the fields; where, when they were at some distance from the house, Mr Sundrum stopped, and began to discourse in a very earnest and lively manner, frequently touching the palm of his left hand with the fingers of his right, as he spoke to my father, and sometimes lifting both his hands as one in amaze, ejaculating to the heavens.

While they were thus reasoning together, worthy Ebenezer Muir came towards the house, but, observing where they were, he turned off and joined them, and they continued all three in vehement deliberation, in so much, that I was drawn by the thirst of curiosity to slip so near towards

them, that I could hear what passed; and my young heart
was pierced at the severe terms in which the minister was
condemning the ringleaders of the riot, as he called the
adversaries of popedom in Edinburgh, and in a manner
rebuking my honest father as a sower of sedition.

My father, however, said stiffly, for he was not a man to
controvert with a minister, that in all temporal things he
was a true and leil subject, and in what pertained to the
King as king, he would stand as stoutly up for as any man in
the three kingdoms. But against a usurpation of the Lord's
rights, his hand, his heart, and his father's sword, that had
been used in the Reformation, were all alike ready.

Old Ebenezer Muir tried to pacify him, and reasoned in
great gentleness with both, expressing his concern that a
presbyterian minister could think that the attempt to bring
in prelacy, and the reading of court-contrived prayers, was
not a meddling with things sacred and rights natural, which
neither prince nor potentate had authority to do. But Mr
Sundrum was one of those that longed for the flesh-pots
of Egypt, and the fat things of a lordly hierarchy; and the
pacific remonstrances of the pious old man made him wax
more and more wroth at what he hatefully pronounced their
rebellious inclinations; at which bitter words both my father
and Ebenezer Muir turned from him, and went together
to the house with sadness in their faces, leaving him to
return the way he had come alone, a thing which filled
me with consternation, he having ever before been treated
and reverenced as a pastor ought always to be.

What comment my father and the old man made on his
conduct, when they were by themselves, I know not; but
on the Sabbath morning the kirk was filled to overflowing,
and my father took me with him by the hand, and we sat
together on the same form with Ebenezer Muir, whom we
found in the church before us.

When Mr Sundrum mounted into the pulpit, and read
the psalm, and said the prayer, there was nothing particular; but when he prepared to preach, there was a rustle
of expectation among all present; for the text he chose
was from Romans, chap. xiii. and verse 1 and 2; from
which he made an endeavour to demonstrate, as I heard

afterwards, for I was then too young to discern the matter of it myself, the duty and advantages of passive obedience – and, growing warm with his ungospel rhetoric, he began to rail and to daud the pulpit, in condemnation of the spirit which had kithed in Edinburgh.

Ebenezer Muir and my father tholed with him for some time; but at last he so far forgot his place and office, that they both rose and moved towards the door. Many others did the same, and presently the whole congregation, with the exception of a very few, also began to move, so that the kirk skayled; and from that day, so long as Mr Sundrum continued in the parish, he was as a leper and an excommunicant.

Meanwhile the alarm was spreading far and wide, and a blessed thing it was for the shire of Ayr, though it caused its soil to be soakened with the blood of martyrs, that few of the ministers were like the time-serving Mr Sundrum, but trusty and valiant defenders of the green pastures whereon they had delighted, like kind shepherds, to lead their confiding flocks, and to cherish the young lambs thereof with the tender embraces of a holy ministry. Among the rest, that godly and great saint, Mr Swinton of Garnock, our neighbour-parish, stood courageously forward in the gap of the broken fence of the vineyard, announcing, after a most weighty discourse, on the same day on which Mr Sundrum preached the erroneous doctrine of passive obedience, that next Sabbath he would administer the sacrament of the Lord's Supper, not knowing how long it might be in the power of his people to partake of it. Every body around accordingly prepared to be present on that occasion, and there was a wonderful congregation. All the adjacent parishes in succession did the same thing Sabbath after Sabbath, and never was there seen, in the memory of living man, such a zealous devotion and strictness of life as then reigned throughout the whole West Country.

At last the news came, that it was resolved among the great and faithful at Edinburgh to renew the Solemn League and Covenant; and the ministers of our neighbourhood having conferred together concerning the same, it was agreed among them, that the people should be invited

to come forward on a day set apart for the purpose, and
that as the kirk of Irvine was the biggest in the vicinage,
the signatures both for the country and that town should
be received there. Mr Dickson the minister, than whom
no man of his day was more brave in the Lord's cause,
accordingly made the needful preparation, and appointed
the time.

In the meanwhile the young men began to gird themselves for war. The swords that had rested for many a day
were drawn from their idle places; and the women worked
together, that their brothers and their sons might be ready
for the field; but at their work, instead of the ancient lilts,
they sung psalms and godly ballads. However, as I mean
not to enter upon the particulars of that awakening epoch,
but only to show forth the pure and the holy earnestness
with which the minds of men were then actuated, I shall
here refer the courteous reader to the annals and chronicles
of the time, – albeit the truth in them has suffered from the
alloy of a base servility.

The sixteenth day of June, in the year of our Lord 1638, was appointed for the renewal, at Irvine, of the Solemn League and Covenant. On the night before, my five elder brothers, who were learning trades at Glasgow and Kilmarnock, came home that they might go up with their father to the house of God, in order to set down their names together; me and my four sisters, the rest of his ten children, were still biding with our mother and him at the mailing.

From my grandfather's time there had been a by-common respect among the neighbours for our family on his account; and that morning my brother Jacob, who happened to be the first that went, at break of day, to the door, was surprised to see many of the cotters and neighbouring farmer lads already assembled on the lone, waiting to walk with us to the town, as a token of their reverence for the principles and the memory of that departed worthy; and they were all belted and armed with swords like men ready for battle.

Seeing such a concourse of the neighbours, instead of making exercise in the house, my father, as the morning was bright and lown, bade me carry the Bible and a stool to the dykeside, that our friends might have room to join us in worship, – which I did accordingly, placing the stool under the ash-tree at the corner of the stack-yard, and by all those who were present on that occasion the spot was ever afterwards regarded as a hallowed place. Truly there was a scene and a sight there not likely to be soon forgotten; for the awful cause that had brought together that meeting was a thing which no man who had a part therein could ever in all his days forget.

My father chose the lxxvi. Psalm, and when it was sung, he opened the Scriptures in Second Kings, and read aloud, with a strong voice, the xxiii. chapter, and every one likened Josiah to the old King, and Jehoahaz to his son Charles, by whose disregard of the Covenant the spirit of the land was then in such tribulation; and at the conclusion, instead of kneeling to pray, as he was wont, my father stood up, and, as if all temporal things were then of no account, he only supplicated that the work they had in hand for that day might be approved and sanctified.

The worship being over, the family returned into the house, and having partaken of a repast of bread and milk, my father put on his father's sword, and my brothers, who had brought weapons of their own home with them, also belted themselves for the road. I was owre young to be yet trysted for war, so my father led me out by the hand, and walking forward, followed by my brothers, the neighbours, two and two, fell into the rear, and the women, in their plaids, came mournful and in tears at some short distance behind.

As we were thus proceeding towards the main road, we heard the sound of a drum and fife, and saw over the hedge of the lane that leads to the clachan, a white banner waving aloft, with the words 'SOLEMN LEAGUE AND COVENANT' painted thereon; at the sight of which my father was much disturbed, saying, – 'This is some silly device of Nahum Chapelrig, that, if we allow to proceed, may bring scoff and scorn upon the cause as we enter the town;' and with that, dropping my hand, he ran forward and stopped their vain bravery; for it was, as he had supposed, the work of Nahum, who was marching, like a man-of-war, at the head of his band. However, on my father's remonstrance, he consented to send away his sounding instruments and idle banner, and to walk composedly along with us.

As we reached the town-end port, we fell in with a vast number of other persons, from different parts of the country, going to sign the Covenant, and, on a cart, worthy Ebenezer Muir and three other aged men like himself, who, being all of our parish, it was agreed that they should alight and walk to the kirk at the head of those who had come with my father. While this was putting in order, other men and lads belonging to the parish came and joined us, so that, to the number of more than a hundred, we went up the town together.

When we arrived at the tolbooth, we were obligated, with others, to halt for some time, by reason of the great crowd at the Kirkgate-foot waiting to see if the magistrates, who were then sitting in council, would come forth and go to the kirk; and the different crafts and burgesses, with their deacons, were standing at the Cross in order to follow them, if they determined, in their public capacity, to sign the Covenant, according to the pious example which had been set to all in authority by the magistrates and town-council of Edinburgh three days before. We had not, however, occasion to be long detained; for it was resolved, with a unanimous heart, that the provost should sign in the name of the town, and that the bailies and counsellors should, in their own names, sign each for himself; so they came out, with the town-officers bearing their battle-axes before them, and the crafts, according to their privilege, followed them to the kirk.

The men of our parish went next; but on reaching the kirk-yard yett, it was manifest that, large as the ancient fabric was, it would not be able to receive a moité of the persons assembled. Godly Mr David Dickson, the minister, had, however, provided for this; and on one of the old tombs on the south side of the kirk, he had ordered a table and chair to be placed, where that effectual preacher, Mr Livingstone, delivered a great sermon, – around him the multitude from the country parishes were congregated; but my father being well acquainted with Deacon Auld of the wrights, was invited by him to come into his seat in the kirk, where he carried me in with him, and we heard Mr Dickson himself.

Of the strain and substance of his discourse I remember nothing, save only the earnestness of his manner; but well do I remember the awful sough and silence that was in the kirk when, at the conclusion of the sermon, he prepared to read the words of the Covenant.

'Now,' said he, when he had come to the end, and was rolling it up, 'as no man knoweth how long, after this day, he may be allowed to partake of the sacrament of the Supper, the elders will bring forward the elements; and it is hoped that sisters in Christ will not come to communion till the brethren are served, who, as they take their seats at the Lord's table, are invited to sign their names to this solemn charter of the religious rights and liberties of God's people in Scotland.'

He then came down from the pulpit with the parchment in his hand, and going to the head of the sacramental table, he opened it again, and laid it down over the elements of the bread and wine which the elders had just placed there; and a minister, whose name I do not well recollect, sitting at his right hand, holding an inkstand, presented him with a pen, which, when he had taken, he prayed in silence for the space of a minute, and then, bending forward, he signed his name; having done so, he raised himself erect and said, with a loud voice, holding up his right hand, 'Before God and these witnesses, in truth and holiness, I have sworn to keep this Covenant.' At that moment a solemn sound rose from all the congregation, and every one stood up to see the men, as they sat at the table, put down their names.

From the day on which the Covenant was signed, though I was owre young to remember the change myself, I have heard it often said, that a great alteration took place in the morals and manners of the Covenanters. The Sabbath was observed by them with far more than the solemnity of times past; and there was a strictness of walk and conversation among them, which showed how much in sincerity they were indeed regenerated Christians. The company of persons inclined to the prelatic sect was eschewed as contagious, and all light pastimes and gayety of heart were suppressed, both on account of their tendency to sinfulness, and because of the danger with which the Truth and the Word were threatened by the Arminian Antichrist of the King's government.

But the more immediate effect of the renewal of the Solemn League and Covenant was the preparation for defence and resistance, which the deceitful policy of that false monarch, King Charles the First, taught every one to know would be required. The men began to practise firing at butts and targets, and to provide themselves with arms and munitions of war; while, in order to maintain a life void of offence in all temporal concerns, they were by ordinare obedient and submissive to those in authority over them, whether holding jurisdiction from the King, or in virtue of baronies and feudalities.

In this there was great wisdom; for it left the sin of the provocation still on the heads of the King and his evil counsellors, in so much that even, when the General Assembly, holden at Glasgow, vindicated the independence and freedom of Christ's kingdom, by continuing to sit in despite of the dissolution pronounced by King Charles' commissioner, the Marquis Hamilton, and likewise by decreeing the abolition of prelacy as an abomination, there was no political blame wherewith the people, in their capacity of subjects to their earthly prince, could be wyted or brought by law to punishment.

In the meantime, the King, who was as fey as he was false, mustered his forces, and his rampant high-priest, Laud, was, with all the voices of his prelatic emissaries, inflaming the honest people of England to wage war against our religious freedom. The papistical Queen of Charles was no less busy with the priesthood of her crafty sect, and aids and powers, both of men and money, were raised wherever they could be had, in order to reinstall the discarded episcopacy of Scotland.

The Convenanters however were none daunted, for they had a great ally in the Lord of hosts; and, with Him for their captain, they neither sought nor wished for any alien assistance, though they sent letters to their brethren in foreign parts, exhorting them to unite in the Covenant, and to join them for the battle. General Lesley, in Gustavus Adolphus' army, was invited by his kinsman, the Lord Rothes, to come home, that, if need arose, he might take the temporal command of the Covenanters.

The King having at last, according to an ancient practice of the English monarchs, when war in old times was proclaimed against the Scots, summoned his nobles to attend him with their powers at York, the Covenanters girded their loins, and the whole country rung with the din of the gathering of an host for the field.

One Captain Bannerman, who had been with Lesley in the armies of Gustavus, was sent from Edinburgh to train the men in our part; and our house being central for the musters of the three adjacent parishes, he staid a night in the week with us at Quharist for the space of better than two months, and his military discourse greatly instructed our neighbours in the arts and sratagems of war.

He was an elderly man, of a sedate character, and had gone abroad with an uncle from Montrose when he was quite a youth. In his day he had seen many strange cities, and places of wonderful strength to withstand the force of sieges. But, though bred a soldier, and his home in the camp, he had been himself but seldom in the field of battle. In appearance he was tall and lofty, and very erect and formal; a man of few words, but they were well chosen; and he was patient and pains-taking; of a contented aspect, somewhat hard-favoured, and seldom given to smile. To little children he was, however, bland and courteous; taking a pleasure in setting those that were of my age in battle-array, for he had no pastime, being altogether an instructive soldier; or, as William, my third brother, used to say, who was a free out-spoken lad, Captain Bannerman was a real dominie o' war.

Besides him, in our country-side, there was another officer, by name Hepburn, who had also been bred with the great Gustavus, sent to train the Covenanters in Irvine; but he was of a more mettlesome humour, and lacked the needful douceness that became those who were banding themselves for a holy cause; so that when any of his disciples were not just so list and brisk as they might have been, which was sometimes the case, especially among the weavers, he thought no shame, even on the Golf-fields, before all the folk and onlookers, to curse and swear at them, as if he had been himself one of the King's cavaliers, and they no better than ne'erdoweels receiving the wages of sin against the Covenant. In sooth to say, he was a young man of a disorderly nature, and about seven months after he left the town twa misfortunate creatures gave him the wyte of their bairns.

Yet, for all the regardlessness of his ways and moral conduct, he was much beloved by the men he had the training of; and, on the night before he left the town, lies were told of a most respectit and pious officer of the town's power, if he did not find the causey owre wide when he was going home, after partaking of Captain Hepburn's pay-way supper. But how that may have been is little of my business at present to investigate; for I have only spoken of Hepburn, to notify what happened in consequence of a brag he had with Bannerman, anent the skill of their respective disciples, the which grew to such a controversy between them, that nothing less would satisfy Hepburn than to try the skill of the Irvine men against ours, and the two neighbouring

parishes of Garnock and Stoneyholm. Accordingly a day
was fixt for that purpose, and the Craiglands-croft was the
place appointed for this probation of soldiership.

On the morning of the appointed day the country folk
assembled far and near, and Nahum Chapelrig, at the head
of the lads of his clachan, was the first on the field. The sight
to my young eyes was as the greatest show of pageantry that
could be imagined; for Nahum had, from the time of the
covenanting, been gathering arms and armour from all
quarters, and had thereby not only obtained a glittering
breastplate for himself, but three other coats of mail for the
like number of his fellows; and when they were coming over
the croft, with their fife and drum, and the banner of the
Covenant waving aloft in the air, every one ran to behold
such splendour and pomp of war; many of the women,
that were witnesses among the multitude, wept at such an
apparition of battles dazzling our peaceful fields.

My father, with my five brothers, headed the Covenanters of our parish. There was no garnish among that
band. They came along with austere looks and douce steps,
and their belts were of tanned leather. The hilts of many
of their swords were rusty, for they had been the weapons
of their forefathers in the raids of the Reformation. As my
father led them to their station on the right flank of Nahum
Chapelrig's array, the crowd of onlookers fell back, and
stood in silence as they passed by.

Scarcely had they halted, when there was a rushing
among the onlookers, and presently the townsmen, with
Hepburn on horseback, were seen coming over the brow
of the Gowan-brae. They were scant the strength of the
country folk by more than a score; but there was a band
of sailor boys with them that made the number greater; so
that, when they were all drawn up together forenent the
countrymen, they were more than man for man.

It is not to be suppressed nor denied, that, in the first
show of the day, Hepburn got far more credit and honour
than old sedate Bannerman; for his lads were lighter in the
heel, glegger in the eye, and brisker in the manoeuvres of
war: moreover, they were all far more similar in their garb
and appearance, which gave them a seeming compactness

that the countrymen had nothing like. But when the sham contest began, it was not long till Bannerman's disciples showed the proofs of their master's better skill to such a mark, that Hepburn grew hot, and so kindled his men by reproaches, that there was like to have been fighting in true earnest; for the blood of the country folk was also rising. Their eyes grew fierce, and they muttered through their teeth.

Old Ebenezer Muir, who was among the multitude, observing that their blood was heating, stepped forward, and lifting up his hand, cried, 'Sirs, stop;' and both sides instanter made a pause. 'This maunna be,' said he. 'It may be sport to those who are by trade soldiers to try the mettle o' their men, but ye're a covenanted people, obligated by a grievous tyranny to quit your spades and your looms only for a season; therefore be counselled, and rush not to battle till need be, which may the Lord yet prevent.'

Hepburn uttered an angry ban, and would have turned the old man away by the shoulder; but the combatants saw they were in the peril of a quarrel, and many of them cried aloud, 'He's in the right, and we're playing the fool for the diversion o' our adversaries.' So the townsmen and the country folk shook hands; but instead of renewing the contest, Captain Bannerman proposed that they should all go through their discipline together, it being manifest that there were little odds in their skill, and none in their courage. The which prudent admonition pacified all parties, and the remainder of the day was spent in cordiality and brotherly love. Towards the conclusion of the exercises, worthy Mr Swinton came on the field; and when the business of the day was over, he stepped forward, and the trained men being formed around him, the onlookers standing on the outside, he exhorted them in prayer, and implored a blessing on their covenanted union, which had the effect of restoring all their hearts to a religious frame and a solemnity befitting the spirituality of their cause.

One night, about a month after the ploy whereof I have spoken in the foregoing chapter, just as my father had finished the worship, and the family were composing themselves round the fireside for supper, we were startled by the sound of a galloping horse coming to the door; and before any one had time to open it, there was a dreadful knocking with the heft of the rider's whip. It was Nahum Chapelrig, who being that day at Kilmarnock, had heard, as he was leaving the town, the cry get up there, that the Aggressor was coming from York with all the English power, and he had flown far and wide on his way home publishing the dismal tidings.

My father, in a sober manner, bade him alight and partake of our supper, questioning him sedately anent what he had heard; but Nahum was raised, and could give no satisfaction in his answers; he however leapt from his horse, and, drawing the bridle through the ring at the door-cheek, came ben to the fire where we had all so shortly before been harmoniously sitting. His eyes were wide and wild; his hair, with the heat he was in, was as if it had been pomated; his cheeks were white, his lips red, and he panted with haste and panic.

'They're coming,' he cried, 'in thousands o' thousands; never sic a force has crossed the border since the day o' Flodden Field. We'll a' either be put to the sword, man, woman, and child, or sent in slavery to the plantations.'

'No,' replied my father, 'things are no just come to that pass; we have our swords yet, and hearts and hands to use them.'

The consternation, however, of Nahum Chapelrig that night was far ayont all counsel; so, after trying to sooth and reason him into a more temperate frame, my father was obligated to tell him, that since the battle was coming so near our gates, it behoved the Covenanters to be in readiness for the field, advising Nahum to go home, and be over with him betimes in the morning.

While they were thus speaking, James Newbigging also came to the door with a rumour of the same substance, which his wife had brought from Eglinton Castle, where she had been with certain cocks and hens, a servitude of the Eglintons on their mailing; so that there was no longer any dubiety about the news, though matters were not in such a desperate condition as Nahum Chapelrig had terrified himself with the thought of. Nevertheless the tidings were very dreadful; and it was a judgement-like thing to hear that an anointed king was so far left to himself as to be coming with wrath, and banners, and trampling war-horses, to destroy his subjects for the sincerity of their religious allegiance to that Almighty Monarch, who has but permitted the princes of the earth to be set up as idols by the hands of men.

James Newbigging, as well as Nahum, having come ben to the fireside, my father called for the Books again, and gave out the eight first verses of the forty-fourth Psalm, which we all sung with hearts in holy unison and zealous voices.

When James Newbigging and Nahum Chapelrig were gone away home, my father sat for some time exhorting us, who were his youngest children, to be kind to one another, to cherish our mother, and no to let auld doited aunty want, if it was the Lord's will that he should never come back from the battle. The which to hear caused much sorrow and lamentation, especially from my mother, who, however, said nothing, but took hold of his hand and watered it with her tears. After this he walked out into the fields, where he remained some time alone; and during his absence, me and the three who were next to me were sent to our beds; but, young as we then were, we were old enough to know the danger that hung over us, and we lay long awake, wondering and woful with fear.

About two hours after midnight the house was again startled by another knocking, and on my father inquiring who was at the door, he was answered by my brother Jacob, who had come with Michael and Robin from Glasgow to Kilmarnock, on hearing the news, and had thence brought William and Alexander with them to go with their father to the war. For they had returned to their respective trades after the day of the covenanting, and had only been out at Hepburn's raid, as the ploy with the Irvinemen was called in jocularity, in order that the neighbours, who venerated their grandfather, might see them together as Covenanters.

The arrival of her sons, and the purpose they had come upon, awakened afresh the grief of our mother; but my father entreated us all to be quiet, and to compose ourselves to rest, that we might be the abler on the morn to prepare for what might then ensue. Yet, though there was no sound in the house, save only our mother's moaning, few closed their eyes; and long before the sun every one was up and stirring, and my father and my five brothers were armed and belted for the march.

Scarcely were they ready, when different neighbours in the like trim came to go with them; presently also Nahum Chapelrig, with his banner, and fife, and drum, at the head of some ten or twelve lads of his clachan, came over; and on this occasion no obstacle was made to that bravery, which was thought so uncomely on the day of the covenanting.

While the armed men were thus gathering before our door, with the intent of setting forward to Glasgow, as the men of the West had been some time before trysted to do, by orders from General Lesley, on the first alarm, that godly man and minister of righteousness, the Reverend Mr Swinton, made his appearance with his staff in his hand, and a satchel on his back, in which he carried the Bible.

'I am come, my frien's,' said he, 'to go with you. Where the ensigns of Christ's Covenant are displayed, it is meet that the very lowest of his vassals should be there;' and having exhorted the weeping women around to be of good cheer, he prayed for them and for their little children, whom the Aggressor was perhaps soon to make fatherless. Nahum Chapelrig then exalted his banner, and the drum and fife beginning to play, the venerable man stepped forward, and heading the array with his staff in his hand, they departed amidst the shouts of the boys, and the loud sorrow of many a wife and mother.

I followed them, with my companions, till they reached the high road, where, at the turn that led them to Glasgow, a great concourse of other women and children belonging to the neighbouring parishes were assembled, having there parted from their friends. They were all mourning and weeping, and mingling their lamentations, with bitter predictions against the King and his evil counsellors; but seeing Mr Swinton, they became more composed; and he having made a sign to the drum and fife to cease, he stopped, and earnestly entreated them to return home and employ themselves in the concerns of their families, which, the heads being for a season removed, stood the more in need of all their kindness and care.

This halt in the march of their friends brought the onlookers, who were assembled round our house, running to see what was the cause; and, among others, it gave time to the aged Ebenezer Muir to come up, whom Mr Swinton no sooner saw, than he called on him by name, and bade him comfort the women, and invite them away from the high road, where their presence could only increase the natural grief that every covenanted Christian, in passing to join the army, could not but suffer, on seeing so many left defenceless by the unprovoked anger of the Aggressor. He then bade the drum again beat, and the march being resumed, the band of our parish soon went out of sight.

While our men continued in view Ebenezer Muir said nothing; but as soon as they had disappeared behind the brow of the Gowan-brae, he spoke to the multitude in a gentle and paternal manner, and bade them come with him into the neighbouring field and join him in prayer; after which, he hoped they would see the wisdom of returning to their homes. They accordingly followed him, and he having given out the twenty-third Psalm all present joined him, till the lonely fields and silent woods echoed to the melody of their pious song.

As we were thus standing around the old man in worship and unison of spirit, the Irvine men came along the road;

and seeing us, they hushed their drums as they passed by, and bowed down their banners in reverence and solemnity. Such was the outset of the worthies of the renewed Covenant, in their war with the first Charles.

After my father and brothers, with our neighbours that went with them, had returned from the bloodless raid of Dunse Law, as the first expedition was called, a solemn thanksgiving was held in all the country-side; but the minds of men were none pacified by the treaty concluded with the King at Berwick. For it was manifest to the world, that coming in his ire, and with all the might of his power, to punish the Covenanters as rebels, he would never have consented to treat with them on any thing like equal terms, had he not been daunted by their strength and numbers; so that the spirit awakened by his Ahab-like domination continued as alive and as distrustful of his word and pactions as ever.

After the rumours of his plain juggling about the verbals of the stipulated conditions, and his arbitrary prorogation of the parliament at Edinburgh, a thing which the best and bravest of the Scottish monarchs had never before dared to do without the consent of the States then assembled, the thud and murmur of warlike preparation was renewed both on anvil and in hall. And when it was known that the King, fey and distempered with his own weak conceits and the instigations of cruel counsellors, had, as soon as he heard that the Covenanters were disbanded, renewed his purposes of punishment and oppression, a gurl of rage, like the first brush of the tempest on the waves, passed over the whole extent of Scotland, and those that had been in arms fiercely girded themselves again for battle.

As the King's powers came again towards the borders, the Covenanters, for the second time, mustered under Lesley at Dunse; but far different was this new departure of our men from the solemnity of their first expedition. Their spirits were now harsh and angry, and their drums sounded hoarsely on the breeze. Godly Mr Swinton, as he headed them again, struck the ground with his staff, and, instead of praying, said, 'It is the Lord's pleasure, and he will make the Aggressor fin' the weight of the arm of flesh. Honest folk are no ever to be thus obligated to leave their fields and families by the provocations of a prerogative that has so little regard for the people. In the name and strength of God, let us march.'

With six and twenty thousand horse and foot Lesley crossed the Tweed, and in the first onset the King's army was scattered like chaff before the wind. When the news of the victory arrived among us, every one was filled with awe and holy wonder; for it happened on the very day which was held as a universal fast throughout the land; on that day likewise, even in the time of worship, the castle of Dumbarton was won, and the covenanted Earl of Haddington repelled a wasteful irruption from the garrison of Berwick.

Such disasters smote the King with consternation; for the immediate fruit of the victory was the conquest of Newcastle, Tynemouth, Shields, and Durham.

Baffled and mortified, humbled but not penitent, the rash and vindictive Monarch, in a whirlwind of mutiny and desertion, was obligated to retreat to York, where he was constrained, by the few sound and sober-minded that yet hovered around him, to try the effect of another negotiation with his insulted and indignant subjects. But as all the things which thence ensued are mingled with the acts of perfidy and aggression by which, under the disastrous influence of the fortunes of his doomed and guilty race, he drew down the vengeance of his English subjects, it would lead me far from this household memorial to enter more at large on circumstances so notour, though they have been strangely palliated by the supple spirit of latter times, especially by the sordid courtliness of the crafty Clarendon. I shall therefore skip the main passages of public affairs, and hasten forward to the time when I became myself inlisted on the side of our national liberties, briefly however noticing, as I proceed, that after the peace which was concluded at Ripon my father and my five brothers came home. None of them received any hurt in battle; but in the course of the winter the old man was visited with a great income of pains and aches, in so much that, for the remainder of his days, he was little able to endure fatigue or hardship of any kind; my second brother, Robin, was therefore called from his trade in Glasgow to look after the mailing, for I was still owre young to be of any effectual service; Alexander continued a bonnet-maker at Kilmarnock; but Michael, William, and Jacob, joined and fought with the forces that won the mournful triumph of Marstonmoor, where fifty thousand subjects of the same King and laws contended with one another, and where the Lord, by showing himself on the side of the people, gave a dreadful admonition to the government to recant and conciliate while there was yet time.

Meanwhile the worthy Mr Swinton, having observed in me a curiosity towards books of history and piety, had taken great pains to instruct me in the rights and truths of religion, and to make it manifest alike to the ears and eyes of my understanding, that no human authority could, or ought to dictate in matters of faith, because it could not discern the secrets of the breast, neither know what was acceptable to Heaven in conduct or in worship. He likewise expounded to me in what manner the Covenant was not a temporal but a spiritual league, trenching in no respect upon the natural and contributed authority of the kingly office. But, owing to the infirm state of my father's health, neither my brother Robin nor I could be spared from the farm, in any of the different raids that germinated out of the King's controversy with the English parliament; so that in the whigamore expedition, as it was profanely nicknamed, from our shire, with the covenanted Earls of Cassilis and Eglinton, we had no personality, though our hearts went with those that were therein.

When, however, the hideous tidings came of the condemnation and execution of the King, there was a stop in the current of men's minds, and as the waters of Jordan when the ark was carried in, rushed back to their fountain-head, every true Scot on that occasion felt in his heart the ancient affections of his nature returning with a compassionate horror. Yet even in this they were true to the Covenant; for it was not to be hidden that the English parliament, in doing what it did in that tragical event, was guided by a speculative spirit of political innovation and change, different and distinct, both in principle and object, from the cause which made our Scottish Covenanters have recourse to arms. In truth, the act of bringing kings to public condign punishment was no such new thing in the chronicles of Scotland, as that brave historian, George Buchanan, plainly shows, to have filled us with such amazement and affright, had the offences of King Charles been proven as clearly personal, as the crimes for which the ancient tyrants of his pedigree suffered the death: – but his offences were shared with his counsellors, whose duty it was to have bridled his arbitrary pretensions. He was in consequence mourned as a victim, and his son, the second Charles, at once proclaimed and acknowledged King of Scotland. How he deported himself in that capacity, and what gratitude he and his brother showed the land for its faith and loyalty in the wreck and desperation of their royal fortunes, with a firm and a fearless pen I now purpose to show. But as the tale of their persecutions is ravelled with the sorrows and the sufferings of my friends and neighbours, and the darker tissue of my own woes, it is needful, before proceeding therein, that I should entreat the indulgence of the courteous reader to allow a few short passages of my private life now to be here recorded.

Some time before the news of King Charles' execution reached us in the West, the day had been set for my marriage with Sarah Lochrig; but the fear and consternation which the tidings bred in all minds, many dreading that the event would be followed by a total breaking up of the union and frame of society, made us consent to defer our happiness till we saw what was ordained to come to pass.

When, however, it was seen and felt that the dreadful beheading of an anointed monarch as a malefactor, had scarcely more effect upon the tides of the time than the death of a sparrow, – and that men were called as usual to their daily tasks and toils, – and that all things moved onward in their accustomed courses, – and that laws and jurisdictions, and all the wonted pacts and processes of community between man and man, suffered neither molestation nor hindrance, godly Mr Swinton bestowed his blessing on our marriage, and our friends their joyous countenance at the wedding feast.

My lot was then full of felicity, and I had no wish to wander beyond the green valley where we established our peaceful dwelling. It was in a lown holm of the Garnock, on the lands of Quharist, a portion of which my father gave me in tack; and Sarah's father likewise bestowed on us seven rigs, and a cow's grass of his own mailing, for her tocher, as the beginning of a plenishment to our young fortunes. Still, like all the neighbours, I was deeply concerned about what was going on in the far-off world of conflicts and negotiations; and this was not out of an idle thirst of curiosity, but from an interest mingled with sorrows and affections; for, after the campaign in England, my three brothers, Michael, William, and Alexander, never domiciled themselves at any civil calling. Having caught the roving spirit of camps, they remained in the skirts of the array which the covenanted Lords at Edinburgh continued to maintain; and here, poor lads! I may digress a little, to record the brief memorials of their several unhappy fates.

When King Charles the Second, after accepting and being sworn to abide by the Covenant, was brought home, and the crown of his ancient progenitors placed upon his head at Scoone, by the hands of the Marquis of Argyle, in the presence of the great and the godly Covenanters, my brothers went in the army that he took with him into England. Michael was slain at the battle of Worcester, by the side of Sir John Shaw of Greenock, who carried that day the royal banner. Alexander was wounded in the same fight, and left upon the field, where he was found next morning by the charitable inhabitants of the city, and carried to the house of a loyal gentlewoman, one Mrs Deerhurst, that treated him with much tenderness; but after languishing in agony, as she herself wrote to my father, he departed this life on the third day.

Of William I have sometimes wished that I had never heard more; for after the adversity of that day, it would seem he forgot the Covenant and his father's house. Ritchie Minigaff, an old servant of the Lord Eglinton's, when the Earl his master was Cromwell's prisoner in the Tower of London, saw him there among the guard, and some years after the Restoration he met him again among the King's yeomen at Westminster, about the time of the beginning of the persecution. But Willy then begged Ritchie, with the tear in his eye, no to tell his father; nor was ever the old man's heart pierced with the anguish which the thought of such backsliding would have caused, though he often wondered to us at home, with the anxiety of a parent's wonder, what could have become of blithe light-hearted Willy. No doubt he died in the servitude of the faithless tyrant; but the storm that fell among us, soon after Ritchie had told me of his unfortunate condition, left us neither time nor opportunity to inquire about any distant friend. But to return to my own story.

From my marriage till the persecution began, I took no part in the agitations of the times. It is true, after the discovery of Charles Stuart's perfidious policy, so like his father's, in corresponding with the Marquis of Montrose for the subjection of Scotland by the tyranny of the sword, at the very time he was covenanting with the commissioners sent from the Lords at Edinburgh with the offer of the throne of his ancestors, that with my father and my brother Robin, together with many of our neighbours, I did sign the Remonstrance against making a prince of such a treacherous and unprincipled nature king. But in that we only delivered reasons and opinions on a matter of temporal expediency; for it was an instrument that neither contained nor implied obligation to arm; indeed our deportment bore testimony to this explanation of the spirit in which it was conceived and understood. For when the prince had received the crown and accepted the Covenant, we submitted ourselves as good subjects. Fearing God, we were content to honour in all rights and prerogatives, not contrary to Scripture, him whom, by His grace in the mysteries of His wisdom, He had, for our manifold sins as a nation and a people, been pleased to ordain and set over us for king. And verily no better test of our sincerity could be, than the distrust with which our whole countryside was respected by Oliver Cromwell, when he thought it necessary to build that stronghold at Ayr, by which his Englishers were enabled to hold the men of Carrick, Kyle, and Cunningham in awe, – a race that, from the days of Sir William Wallace and King Robert the Bruce, have ever been found honest in principle, brave in affection, and dauntless and doure in battle. But it is not necessary to say more on this head; for full of griefs and grudges as were the hearts of all true Scots, with the thought of their country in southern thraldom, while Cromwell's Englishers held the upper hand amongst us, the season of their dominion was to me and my house as a lown and pleasant spring. All around me was bud, and blossom, and juvenility, and gladness, and hope. My lot was as the lot of the blessed man. I ate of the labour of my hands, I was happy, and it was well with me; my wife, as the fruitful vine that spreads its clusters on the wall, made my lowly dwelling more beautiful to the eye of the heart

than the golden palaces of crowned kings, and our pretty
bairns were like olive plants round about my table; – but
they are all gone. The flood and the flame have passed
over them; – yet be still, my heart; a little while endure
in silence; for I have not taken up the avenging pen of
history, and dipped it in the blood of martyrs, to record
only my own particular woes and wrongs.

It has been seen, by what I have told concerning the part my grandfather had in the great work of the Reformation, that the heads of the house of Argyle were among the foremost and the firmest friends of the resuscitated Evangil. The aged Earl of that time was in the very front of the controversy as one of the Lords of the Congregation; and though his son, the Lord of Lorn, hovered for a season, like other young men of his degree, in the purlieus and precincts of the Lady Regent's court, yet when her papistical counsels broke the paction with the protestants at Perth, I have rehearsed how he, being then possessed of the inheritance of his father's dignities, did, with the bravery becoming his blood and station, remonstrate with her Highness against such impolitic craft and perfidy, and, along with the Lord James Stuart, utterly eschew her presence and method of government.

After the return of Queen Mary from France, and while she manifested a respect for the rights of her covenanted people, that worthy Earl was among her best friends; and even after the dismal doings that led to her captivity in Lochleven Castle, and thence to the battle of Langside, he still acted the part of a true nobleman to a sovereign so fickle and so faithless. Whether he rued on the field that he had done so, or was smitten with an infirmity that prevented him from fighting against his old friend and covenanted brother, the good Regent Murray, belongs not to this history to inquire; but certain it is, that in him the protestant principles of his honourable house suffered no dilapidation; and in the person of his grandson, the first marquis of the name, they were stoutly asserted and maintained.

When the first Charles, and Laud, that ravenous Arminian

Antichrist, attempted to subvert and abrogate the presbyterian gospel worship, not only did the Marquis stand forth in the van of the Covenanters to stay the religious oppression then meditated against his native land, but laboured with all becoming earnestness to avert the pestilence of civil war. In that doubtless Argyle offended the false counsellors about the King; but when the English parliament, with a lawless arrogance, struck off the head of the miscounselled and bigoted monarch, faithful to his covenants and the loyalty of his race, the Marquis was among the foremost of the Scottish nobles to proclaim the Prince of Wales king. With his own hands he placed on Charles the Second's head the ancient diadem of Scotland. Surely it might therefore have been then supposed, that all previous offence against the royal family was forgotten and forgiven; yea, when it is considered that General Monk himself, the boldest in the cause of Cromwell's usurpation, was rewarded with a dukedom in England for doing no more for the King there than Argyle had done for him before in greater peril here, it could not have entered into the imagination of Christian men, that Argyle, for only submitting like a private subject to the same usurped authority when it had become supreme, would, after the Restoration, be brought to the block. But it was so; and though the machinations of political enemies converted that submission into treasons to excuse their own crime, yet there was not an honest man in all the realm that did not see in the doom of Argyle a dismal omen of the cloud and storm which so soon after burst upon our religious liberties.

Passing, however, by all those afflictions which took the colour of political animosities, I hasten to speak of the proceedings which, from the hour of the Restoration, were hatched for the revival of the prelatic oppression. The tyranny of the Stuarts is indeed of so fell a nature, that, having once tasted of blood in any cause, it will return again and again, however so often baffled, till it has either devoured its prey, or been itself mastered: and so it showed in this instance. For, regardless of those troubles which the attempt of the first Charles to exercise an authority in spiritual things beyond the rights of all earthly sovereignty caused to the realm and to himself, the second no sooner felt the sceptre in his grip, than he returned to the same enormities; and he found a fit instrument in James Sharp, who, in contempt of the wrath of God, sold himself to Antichrist for the prelacy of St Andrews.

But it was not among the ambitious and mercenary members of the clergy that the evidences of a backsliding generation were alone to be seen: many of the people, nobles, and magistrates, were infected with the sin of the same reprobation; and, in verity, it might have been said of the realm, that the restoration of King Charles the Second was hailed as an advent ordained to make men forget all vows, sobriety, and solemnities. It is, however, something to be said in commendation of the constancy of mind and principle of our West country folk, that the immorality of that drunken loyalty was less outrageous and offensive to God and man among them, and that although we did submit, and were commanded to commemorate the anniversary of the King's restoration, it was nevertheless done with humiliation and anxiety of spirit. But a vain thing it would be of me to attempt to tell the heartburning with which we heard of the manner that the Covenant, and all things which had been hallowed and honourable to religious Scotland, were treated in the town of Lithgow on that occasion, although all of my grandfather's stock knew, that from of old it was a seat and sink of sycophancy, alien to holiness, and prone to lick the dust aneath the feet of whomsoever ministered to the corruption abiding there.

Had the general inebriation of the kingdom been confined only to such mockers as the papistical progeny of the unregenerate town of Lithgow, we might perhaps have only grieved at the wantonness of the world; but they were soon followed by more palpable enormities. Middleton, the King's commissioner, coming on a progress to Glasgow, held a council of state there, at which was present the apostate Fairfoul, who had been shortly before nominated Archbishop of that city; and at his wicked incitement, Middleton, in a fit of actual intoxication from strong drink, let loose the blood-hounds of persecution, by that memorable act of council, which bears the date of the 1st of

October 1662, – an anniversary that ought ever to be held as a solemn fast in Scotland, if such things might be; for by it all the ministers that had received Gospel ordination from and after the year forty-nine, and who still refused to bend the knee to Baal, were banished, with their families, from their kirks and manses.

But to understand in what way that wicked act, and the blood-causing proclamation which ensued, came to take effect, it is needful, before proceeding to the recital, to bid the courteous reader remember the preaching of the doctrine of passive obedience by our time-serving pastor, Mr Sundrum, and how the kirk was deserted on that occasion; because, after his death, which happened in the forty-nine, godly Mr Swinton became our chosen pastor, and being placed and inducted according to the apostolic ordination of Presbytery, fell of course, like many of his Gospel brethren, under the ban of the aforesaid proclamation, of which some imperfect sough and rumour reached us on the Friday after it was framed.

At first the particulars were not known, for it was described as the muttering of unclean spirits against the purity of the Truth; but the tidings startled us like the growl of some unknown and dreadful thing, and I dreamt that night of my grandfather, with his white hair and the comely venerableness of his great age, appearing pale and sorrowful in a field before me, and pointing with a hand of streaming light to horsemen, and chariots, and armies with banners, warring together on the distant hills.

Saturday was then the market-day at Irvine, and though I had but little business there, I yet went in with my brother Robin, chiefly to hear the talk of the town. In this I but partook of the common sympathy of the whole country-side; for, on entering the town-end port, we found the concourse of people there assembled little short of the crowd at Marymas fair, and all eager to learn what the council held at Glasgow had done; but no one could tell. Only it was known, that the Earl of Eglinton, who had been present at the council, was returned home to the castle, and that he had sent for the provost that morning on very urgent business.

While we were thus all speaking and marvelling one with another, a cry got up that a band of soldiers was coming into the town from Ayr; the report of which, for the space of several minutes, struck every one with awe and apprehension. And scarcely had the sough of this passed over us, when it was told that the provost had privately returned from Eglinton Castle by the Gallows-knowes to the backsides, and that he had sent for the minister and the bailies, with others of the council, to meet him in the clerk's chamber.

No one wist what the meaning of such movements and mysteries could be; but all boded danger to the fold and flock, none doubting that the wolves of episcopalian covetousness were hungering and thirsting for the blood of the covenanted lambs. Nor were we long left to our guesses; for, soon after the magistrates and the minister had met, a copy of the proclamation of the council, held at Glasgow was put upon the tolbooth door, by which it was manifested to every eye that the fences of the vineyard were indeed broken down, and that the boar was let in, and wrathfully trampling down and laying waste.

CHAPTER EIGHTEEN

The proclamation was as a stunning blow on the forehead of the Covenanters; and for the next two Sabbaths
Mr Swinton was plainly in prayer a weighed down and
sorrowful-hearted man, but he said nothing in his dis-
courses that particularly affected the marrow of that sore
and solemn business. On the Friday night, however, before
the last Lord's day of that black October, he sent for my
brother, who was one of his elders, and told him that he had
received a mandatory for conformity to the proclamation,
and to acknowledge the prelatic reprobation that the King's
government had introduced into the church; but that it was
his intention, strengthened of the Lord, to adhere to his
vows and covenants, even to the uttermost, and not to quit
his flock, happen what would.

'The beild of the kirk and the manse,' said he, 'being
temporalities, are aneath the power and regulation of the
earthly monarch; but in the things that pertain to the
allegiance I owe to the King of kings, I will act, with His
heartening, the part of a true and loyal vassal.'

This determination being known throughout the parish,
and the first of November being the last day allowed
for conforming, on the Sabbath preceding we had a
throng kirk and a solemneezed congregation. According
to their wonted custom, the men, before the hour of
worship, assembled in the kirk-yard, and there was much
murmuring and marvelling among us, that nobody in
all the land would stand forth to renew the Covenant,
as was done in the year thirty-eight; and we looked
around and beheld the green graves of many friends
that had died since the great day of the covenanting,
and we were ashamed of ourselves and of our time,
and mourned for the loss of the brave spirits which,

in the darkness of his mysterious wisdom, the Lord had taken away.

The weather, for the season, was bright and dry; and the withered leaf still hung here and there on the tree, so that old and young, the infirm and the tender, could come abroad; and many that had been bed-rid were supported along by their relations to hear the word of Truth, for the last time, preached in the house of God.

Mr Swinton came, followed by his wife and family. He was, by this time, a man well stricken in years, but Mrs Swinton was of a younger generation; and they had seven children, – Martha, the eldest, a fine lassie, was not passing fourteen years of age. As they came slowly up the kirk-stile, we all remarked that the godly man never lifted his eyes from the ground, but came along perusing, as it were, the very earth for consolation.

The private door which, at that epoch, led to the minister's seat and the pulpit, was near to where the bell-rope hung on the outer wall, and as the family went towards it, one of the elders stepped from the plate at the main door to open it. But after Mrs Swinton and the children were gone in, the minister, who always stopped till they had done so, instead of then following, paused and looked up with a compassionate aspect, and laying his hand on the shoulder of old Willy Shackle, who was ringing the bell, he said—

'Stop, my auld frien', – they that in this parish need a bell this day to call them to the service of their Maker, winna come on the summons o' yours.'

He then walked in; and the old man, greatly affected, mounted the stool, and tied up the rope to the ring in the wall in his usual manner, that it might be out of the reach of the school weans. 'But,' said he, as he came down, 'I needna fash; for after this day little care I wha rings the bell: since it's to be consecrat to the wantonings o' prelacy, I wis the tongue were out o' its mouth and its head cracket, rather than that I should live to see't in the service of Baal and the hoor o' Babylon.'

After all the congregation had taken their seats, Mr Swinton rose and moved towards the front of the pulpit, and the silence in the church was as the silence at the martyrdom of some holy martyr. He then opened THE BOOK, and having given out the ninety-fourth Psalm, we sang it with weeping souls; and during the prayer that followed there was much sobbing and lamentations, and an universal sorrow. His discourse was from the fifth chapter of the Lamentations of Jeremiah, verse first, and first clause of the verse; and with the tongue of a prophet, and the voice of an apostle, he foretold, as things already written in the chronicles of the kingdom, many of those sufferings which afterwards came to pass. It was a sermon that settled into the bottom of the hearts of all that heard it, and prepared us for the woes of the vial that was then pouring out.

At the close of the discourse, when the precentor rose to read the remembering prayer, old Ebenezer Muir, then upwards of fourscore and thirteen, who had been brought into the church on a barrow by two of his grandsons, and was, for reason of his deafness, in the bench with the elders, gave him a paper, which, after rehearsing the names of those in distress and sickness, he read, and it was 'The persecuted kirk of SCOTLAND.'

'If I forget thee, O Jerusalem! let my right hand forget her cunning,' cried Mr Swinton at the words, with an inspiration that made every heart dirl; and surely never was such a prayer heard as that with which he followed up the divine words.

Then we sang the hundred and fortieth Psalm; at the conclusion of which the minister came again to the front of the pulpit, and with a calm voice, attuned to by ordinare solemnity, he pronounced the blessing; then, suddenly turning himself, he looked down to his family and said, 'The foxes have holes, and the birds of the air have nests; but the Son of man hath not where to lay his head.' And he covered his face with his hands, and sat down and wept.

Never shall I forget the sound which rose at that sight; it was not a cry of woe, neither was it the howl of despair, nor the sob of sorrow, nor the gurl of wrath, nor the moan of anguish, but a deep and dreadful rustling of hearts and spirits, as if the angel of desolation in passing by had shaken all his wings.

The kirk then began to skail; and when the minister and his family came out into the kirk-yard, all the heads of families present, moved by some sacred instinct from on high, followed them with one accord to the manse, like friends at a burial, where we told them, that whatever the Lord was pleased to allow to ourselves, a portion would be set apart for his servant. I was the spokesman on that occasion, and verily do I think, that as I said the words, a glorious light shone around me, and that I felt a fanning of the inward life, as if the young cherubims were present among us, and fluttering their wings with an exceeding great joy at the piety of our kind intents.

So passed that memorable Sabbath in our parish; and here I may relate, that we had the satisfaction and comfort to know, in a little time thereafter, that the same Christian faithfulness, with which Mr Swinton adhered to his gospel-trusts and character, was maintained on that day by more than three hundred other ministers, to the perpetual renown of our national worth and covenanted cause. And therefore, though it was an era of much sorrow and of many tears, it was thus, through the mysterious ways of Providence, converted into a ground of confidence in our religion, in so much, that it may be truly said, out of the ruins and the overthrow of the first presbyterian church the Lord built up among us a stronghold and sanctuary for his truth and law.

Nothing particular happened till the second week of November, when a citation came from Irvine, commanding the attendance of Mr Swinton on a suffragan of Fairfoul's, under the penalties of the proclamation. In the meantime we had been preparing for the event; and my father having been some time no more, and my brother with his family in a house of their own, it was settled between him and me, that I should take our mother into mine, in order that the beild of Quharist might be given up to the minister and his houseless little ones; which all our neighbours much commended; and there was no slackness on their part in making a provision to supply the want of his impounded stipend.

As all had foreseen, Mr Swinton, for not appearing to the citation, was pronounced a non-conformist; and the same night, after dusk, a party of the soldiers, that were marched from Ayr into Irvine on the day of the proclamation, came to drive him out of the manse.

There was surely in this a needless and exasperating severity, for the light of day might have served as well; but the men were not to blame, and the officer who came with them, having himself been tried in the battles of the Covenant, and being of a humane spirit, was as meek and compassionate in his tyrannical duty as could reasonably be hoped for. He allowed Mrs Swinton to take away her clothes, and the babies, that were asleep in their beds, time to be awakened and dressed; nor did he object to their old ploughman, Robin Harrow, taking sundry articles of provision for their next morning's repast; so that, compared with the lewd riots and rampageous insolence of the troopers in other places, we had great reason to be thankful for the tenderness with which our minister and his small family of seven children were treated on that memorable night.

It was about eight o'clock, when Martha, the eldest daughter, came flying to me like a demented creature, crying the persecutors were come, with naked swords and dreadful faces; and she wept and wrung her hands, thinking they were then murdering her parents and brothers and sisters. I did, however, all that was in my power to pacify her, saying, our lots were not yet laid in blood; and leaving her to the consolatory counsellings of my wife, I put on my bonnet, and hastened over to the manse.

The night was troubled and gusty. The moon was in her first quarter, and wading dim and low through the clouds on the Arran hills. Afar off, the bars of Ayr, in their roaring, boded a storm, and the stars were rushing through a swift and showery south-west carry. The wind, as it hissed over the stubble, sounded like the whisperings of desolation; and I was thrice startled in my walk by passing shapes and shadows, whereof I could not discern the form.

At a short distance from the manse door, I met the godly sufferer and his destitute family, with his second youngest child in his arms; Mrs Swinton had their baby at her bosom, and the other four poor terrified helpless creatures were hirpling at their sides, holding them by the skirts, and often looking round in terror, dreading the persecutors, by whom they were in that dismal and inclement night so cast upon the mercy of the elements. But He that tempers the wind to the shorn lamb was their protector.

'You see, Ringan Gilhaize,' said the minister, 'how it fares with them in this world whose principles are at variance with the pretensions of man. But we are mercifully dealt by – a rougher manner and a harder heart, in the agent of persecution that has driven us from house and home, I had laid my account for; therefore, even in this dispensation, I can see the gentle hand of a gracious Master, and I bow the head of thankfulness.'

While we were thus speaking, and walking towards Quharist, several of the neighbours, who had likewise heard the alarm of what had thus come to pass, joined us on the way; and I felt within myself, that it was a proud thing to be able to give refuge and asylum to an aged gospel minister and his family in such a time and on such a night.

We had not been long in the house, when a great concourse of his friends and people gathered around, and among others, Nahum Chapelrig, who had been some time his father's successor in the school. But all present were molested and angry with him, for he came in battle-array, with the sword and gun that he had carried in the raids of the civil war, and was bragging of valorous things then needful to be done.

'Nahum Chapelrig,' said the Worthy to him with severity, 'this is no conduct for the occasion. It would hae been a black day for Scotland had her children covenanted themselves for temporal things. No, Nahum; if the prelatic reprobation now attempted on the kirk gang nae farther than outing her ministers from their kirks and manses, it maun be tholet; so look to it, that ye give not the adversary cause to reproach us with longing for the flesh-pots of Egypt when we are free to taste of the heavenly manna. I redde ye, therefore, Nahum Chapelrig, before these witnesses, to unbuckle that belt of war, and lay down thae weapons of offence. The time of the shield and banner may come owre soon upon us. Let us not provoke the smiter, lest he draw his sword against us, and have law and reason on his side. Therefore, I say unto thee, Peter, put up thy sword.'

The zealous dominie, being thus timeously rebuked, unharnished himself, and the minister having returned thanks for the softness with which the oppression was let down upon him, and for the pious affection of his people, we returned home to our respective dwellings.

But though by this Christian submission the power of cruelty was at that time rendered innocent towards all those who did as Mr Swinton had done, we were, nevertheless, not allowed to remain long unvisited by another swirl of the rising storm. Before the year was out, Fairfoul, the Glasgow antichrist, sent upon us one of the getts that prelacy was then so fast adopting for her sons and heirs. A lang, thin, bare lad he was, that had gotten some spoonful or two of pagan philosophy at college, but never a solid meal of learning, nor, were we to judge by his greedy gaping, even a satisfactory meal of victuals. His name was Andrew Dornock; and, poor fellow, being eschewed among us on account of his spiritual leprosy, he drew up with divers loose characters, that were nae overly nice of their company.

This made us dislike him more and more, in so much, that, like others of his nature and calling, he made sore and secret complaints of his parishioners to his mitred master; representing, for aught I ken to the contrary, that, instead of believing the Gospel according to Charles Stuart, we preferred that of certain four persons, called Matthew, Mark, Luke, and John, of whom, it may be doubted, if he, poor man, knew more of than the names. But be that as it may, to a surety he did grievously yell and cry, because we preferred listening to the gospel melody of Mr Swinton under a tree to his feckless havers in the kirk; as if it was nae a more glorious thing to worship God in the freedom and presence of universal Nature, beneath the canopy of all the heavens, than to bow the head in the fetters of episcopal bondage below the stoury rafters of an auld bigging, such as our kirk was, a perfect howf of cloks and spiders. Indeed, for that matter, it was said, that the only sensible thing Andrew Dornock ever uttered from the pulpit was, when he first rose to speak therein, and which was caused by a spider, that just at the moment lowered itself down into his mouth: 'O Lord,' cried the curate, 'we're puzhened wi' speeders!'

It might have been thought, considering the poor hand which the prelatic curates made of it in their endeavours to preach, that they would have set themselves down content with the stipend, and allowed the flocks to follow their own shepherds in peace; but their hearts were filled with the bitterness of envy at the sight of the multitudes that went forth to gather the manna in the fields, and their malice was exasperated to a wonderful pitch of wickedness, by the derision and contempt with which they found themselves regarded. No one among them all, however, felt this envy and malice more stirring within him, than did the arch-apostate James Sharp; for the faithfulness of so many ministers was a terror and a reproach to his conscience and apostacy, and made him labour with an exceeding zeal and animosity to extirpate so many evidences of his own religious guilt. Accordingly, by his malignant counsellings, edicts and decrees came out against our tabernacle in the wilderness, and, under the opprobrious name of conventicles, our holy meetings were made prohibited offences, and our ministers subjected to pains and penalties, as sowers of sedition.

It is a marvellous thing to think of the madness with which the minds of those in authority at that time were kindled; first, to create causes of wrong to the consciences of the people, and afterwards to enact laws for the natural fruit of that frantic policy. The wanton imposition of the prelatic oppression begat our field-preachings, and the attempts to disperse us by the sword brought on resistance. But it belongs not to me and my story to treat of the folly of a race and government, upon whom a curse was so manifestly pronounced; I shall therefore return from this generality to those particulars wherein I was myself a witness or a sufferer.

During the greater part of the year after the banishment of Mr Swinton from the manse and kirk, we met with little molestation; but from time to time rumours came over us like the first breathings of the cold blasts in autumn, that forerun the storms of winter. All thoughts of innocent pastimes and pleasures passed away, like the yellow leaves that fall from the melancholy trees; and there was a heaviness in the tread, and a solemnity in the looks of every one, that showed how widely the shadows of coming woes were darkening the minds of men.

But though the Court of Commission, which the apostate James Sharp procured to be established for the cognizance of those who refused to acknowledge the prelatic usurpation, was, in its proceedings, guided by as little truth or principle as the Spanish inquisition, the violence and tyranny of its awards fell less on those of my degree than on the gentry; and it was not till the drunkard Turner was appointed general of the West country that our personal sufferings began.

The curates furnished him with lists of recusants; and power having been given unto him to torment men for many days, he was as remorseless as James Sharp's own Court in the fines which he levied, and in eating the people up, by sending his men to live upon then at free quarters, till the fines were paid.

In our neighbourhood we were for some time gently dealt with; for the colonel, who, at Ayr, had the command under Turner, was of a humane spirit, and for a season, though the rumour of the oppressions in Dumfriesshire and Galloway, where the drunkard himself reigned and ruled, dismayed and troubled us beyond utterance, we were still permitted to taste of the gospel pastures with our own faithful shepherd.

But this was a blessing too great in those days to be of a continuance to any flock. The mild and considerate gentleman, who had softened the rigour of the prelatic rage, was removed from his command, and in his place came certain cruel officers, who, like the serpents that were sent among the children of Israel in the desert, defiled our dwellings, and afflicted many of us even unto death. The change was the more bitterly felt, because it was sudden, and came upon us in an unexpected manner, of which I will here set down some of the circumstantials.

According to the usage among us, from the time when Mr Swinton was thrust from the ministry, the parish had assembled, on the third Lord's day of May, in the year 1665, under the big sycamore-tree at Zachariah Smylie's gable, and which has ever since been reverenced by the name of the Poopit Tree. A cart served him for the place of lecture and exhortation; and Zachariah Smylie's daughter, Rebecca Armour, a godly widow, who resided with him, had, as her custom was in fine weather, ordered and arranged all the stools and chairs in the house, with the milk and washing-boynes upside down, around the cart as seats for the aged. When the day was wet or bleak, the worship was held in the barn; but on this occasion the morning was lown and the lift clear, and the natural quietude of the Sabbath reigned over all the fields. We had sung a portion of the psalm, and the harmonious sound of voices and spirits in unison was spreading into the tranquil air, as the pleasant fragrancy of flowers diffuses itself around, and the tune, to which we sung the divine inspiration, was the sweet and solemn melody of the Martyrs.

Scarcely, however, had we proceeded through the second verse, when Mr Swinton, who was sitting on a stool in the cart, with his back to the house, started up, and said, 'Christians, dinna be disheartened, but I think I see yonder the glimmerin' of spears coming atween the hedges.'

At these words we all rose alarmed, and, on looking round, saw some eight or ten soldiers, in the path leading from the high-road, coming towards us. The children and several of the women moved to run away, but Mr Swinton rebuked their timerarious fear, and said—

'O! ye of little faith, wherefore are ye thus dismayed? Let us put our trust in Him, who is mightier than all the armies of all the kings of all the earth. We are here doing homage to Him, and He will protect His true vassals and faithful people. In his name, therefore, Christians, I charge you to continue His praises in the psalm; for in His strength I will, to the end of my intent, this day fulfil the word and the admonition; yea, even in the very flouting of the adversary's banner.'

The vehemence of Elijah was in his voice; we resumed our former postures; and he himself leading on the psalm, we began to sing anew in a louder strain, for we were fortified and encouraged by his holy intrepidity. No one moved as it were an eyelid; the very children were steadfast; and all looked towards the man of God as he sat in his humble seat, serene, and more awful than ever was Solomon on the royal throne of the golden lions, arrayed in all his glory.

The rough soldiers were struck for a time with amazement at the religious bravery with which the worshipping was continued, and they halted as they drew near, and whispered together, and some of them spoke as if the fear of the Lord had fallen upon them. During the whole time that we continued singing, they stood as if they durst not venture to disturb us; but when the psalm was finished, their sergeant, a lewd roister, swore at them, and called on them to do their duty.

The men then advanced, but with one accord we threw ourselves in between them and the cart, and cried to Mr Swinton to make his escape; he however rose calmly from his seat and said—

'Soldiers, shed no blood; let us finish our prayer, – the worst of men after condemnation are suffered to pray, – ye will, therefore, not surely refuse harmless Christians the boon that is alloo't to malefactors. At the conclusion I will go peaceably with you, for we are not rebels; we yield all bodily obedience to the powers that be, but the upright mind will not bend to any earthly ordinance. Our bodies are subject to the King's authority, and to you, as his servants, if ye demand them, we are ready to deliver them up.'

But the sergeant told him harshly to make haste and come down from the cart. Two of the men then went into the house, and brought out the churn and bread and cheese, and with much ribaldry began to eat and drink, and to speak profane jests to the young women. But my brother interposed, and advised all the women and children to return to their homes. In the meantime, Zachariah Smylie had gone to the stable and saddled his horse, and Rebecca Armour had made a small providing of provisions for Mr Swinton to take with him to the tolbooth of Irvine; for thither the soldiers were intending to carry him that night, in order that he might be sent to Glasgow next day with other sufferers. When, however, the horse was brought out, and the godly man was preparing to mount, the sergeant took him by the sleeve, and pulled him back, saying, 'The horse is for me.'

Verily at this insult I thought my heart would have leapt out; and every one present gurled and growled; but the soldiers laughed at seeing the sergeant on horseback. Mr Swinton, however, calmly advised us to make no obstacle: 'Good,' said he, 'will come of this, and though for a season we are ordained to tribulation, and to toil through the slough of despond, yet a firm footing and a fair and green path lies in a peaceful land beyond.'

The soldiers then took him away, the blasphemous sergeant riding, like a Merry Andrew, on Zachariah Smylie's horse before them, and almost the whole congregation following with mournful and heavy hearts.

The testimony of the regard and respect which we showed to Mr Swinton in following him to the prison-door, was wickedly reported against us as a tumult and riot, wearing the aspect of rebellion; and accordingly, on the second day after he was sent from Irvine to Glasgow, a gang of Turner's worst troopers came to live at heck and manger among us. None suffered more from those ruthless men than did my brother's house and mine; for our name was honoured among the true and faithful, and we had committed the unpardonable sin against the prelacy of harbouring our minister and his destitute family, when they were driven from their home in a wild and wintry night.

We were both together, with old Zachariah Smylie, fined each in a heavy sum.

Thinking that by paying the money down we should rid ourselves and our neighbours of the presence and burden of the devouring soldiery, our friends, to enable us, made a gathering among them, and brought us the means, for we had not a sufficiency of our own. But this, instead of mitigating the oppression, became a reason with the officer set over us to persecute us still more; for he pretended to see in that neighbourliness the evidences of a treasonous combination; so that he not only took the money, but made a pretext of the readiness with which it was paid to double his severity. Sixteen domineering camp-reprobates were quartered on four honest families, and five of them were on mine.

What an example their conduct and conversation was at my sober hearth I need not attempt to describe. For some days they rampaged as if we had been barbarians, and the best in the house was not good enough for their ravenous wastrie; – but I was resolved to keep a uniform and steady abstinence from all cause of offence. So seeing they were passing from insolence into a strain of familiarity towards my wife and her two servant-lasses, we gave up the house and made our abode in the barn.

This silent rebuke for some time was not without a wholesome effect; and in the end they were so far tamed into civility by our blameless and peaceful demeanour, that I could discern more than one of them beginning to be touched with the humanity of respect for our unmerited punishment. But their officer, Lieutenant Swaby, an Englisher by birth, and a sinner by education, was of an incorrigible depravity of heart. He happened to cast his eye on Martha Swinton, the minister's eldest daughter, then but in her sixteenth year, and notwithstanding the sore affliction that she was in, with her mother, on account of her godly father's uncertain fate, he spared no stratagem to lure her to his wicked will. She was, however, strengthened against his arts and machinations; but her fortitude, instead of repressing the rigour of his persecutions, only made him more audacious, in so much that she was terrified to trust herself unguarded out of the house, – and the ire of every man and woman was rising against the sensual Swaby, who was so destitute of grace and human charity. But out of this a mean was raised, that in the end made him fain to be removed from among us.

For all the immoral bravery of the rampant soldiery, and especially of their libertine commander, they had not been long among us till it was discerned that they were as much under the common fears and superstitions as the most credulous of our simple country folk, in so much that what with our family devotions and the tales of witches and warlocks with which every one, as if by concert, delighted to awe them, they were loth to stir out of their quarters after the gloaming. Swaby, however, though less under those influences than his men, nevertheless partook largely of them, and would not at the King's commands, it was thought, have crossed the kirk-stile at midnight.

But though he was thus infirm with the dread of evil spirits, he was not daunted thereby from ill purposes; and having one day fallen in with old Mysie Gilmour on the road, a pawkie carlin of a jocose nature, he entered into a blethering discourse with her anent divers things, and from less to more, propounded to honest Mysie that she should lend a cast of her skill to bring about a secret meeting between him and the bonny defenceless Martha Swinton.

Mysie Gilmour was a Christian woman, and her soul was troubled with the proposal to herself, and for the peril with which she saw her minister's daughter environed. But she put on the mask of a light hypocrisy, and said she would maybe do something if he fee'd her well, making a tryst with him for the day following; purposing in the meanwhile, instead of furthering his wicked ends, to devise, with the counselling of some of her acquaintances, in what manner she could take revenge upon the profligate prodigal for having thought so little of her principle, merely because she was a lanerly widow bent with age and poortith.

Among others that she conferred with was one Robin Finnie, a lad who, when a callan, had been drummer to the host that Nahum Chapelrig led in the times of the Civil war to the raid of Dunse-hill. He was sib to herself, had a spice of her pawkrie, and was moreover, though not without a leavening of religion, a fellow fain at any time for a spree; besides which he had, from the campaigns of his youth, brought home a heart-hatred and a derisive opinion of the cavaliers, taking all seasons and occasions to give vent to the same, and he never called Swaby by any other name than the cavalier.

Between Mysie and Robin, with some of his companions, a paction was made that she should keep her tryst with Swaby, and settle on a time and place for him to come, in the delusion of expecting to find Martha Swinton; Robin covenanting, that between him and his friends the cavalier should meet with a lemane worthy of his love. Accordingly, at the time appointed, when she met Swaby on the road where they had foregathered the day before, she trysted him to come to her house on Hallowe'en, which happened to be then at hand, and to be sure no to bring his sword, or any weapon that might breed mischief.

After parting from him, the cavalier going one way and the carlin the other, Robin Finnie threw himself in his way, and going up to him with a seeming respectful-ness, said—

'Ye were speaking, sir, to yon auld wife; I hope ye hae gi'en her nae offence.'

The look with which Robin looked at Swaby, as he said this, dismayed the gallant cavalier, who cried, gazing back at Mysie, who was hirpling homeward – 'The devil! is she one of that sort?'

'I'll no say what she is, nor what others say o' her,' replied Robin, with solemnity; 'but ye'll no fare the waur that ye stand weel in her liking.'

Swaby halted, and again looked towards the old woman, who was then nearly out of sight. Robin at the same time moved onward.

'Friend!' cried the cavalier, 'stop. I must have some talk with you about the old—'

'Whisht!' exclaimed Robin, 'she's deevilish gleg o' the hearing. I would na for twenty merks she jealoused that I had telt you to take tent o' her cantrips.'

'Do you mean to say that she's a witch?' said Swaby in a low and apprehensive voice.

'I would na say sic a thing o' her for the world,' replied Robin very seriously; 'I would ne'er expek to hae a prosperous hour in this world, were I to ca' honest Mysie Gilmour ony thing sae uncanny. She's a pious wife, sir, – deed is she. Me ca' her a witch! She would deserve to be hang'd if she was a witch, – an it could be proven upon her.'

But these assurances gave no heartening to the gallant cavalier; on the contrary, he looked like one that was perplexed, and said, 'Devil take her, I wish I had had nothing to do with her.'

'Do,' cried Robin; 'sir, she's an auld withered hag, would spean a foal. Surely she did na sae beglamour your senses as to appear like a winsome young lass? But I hae heard o' sic morphosings. I'll no say, howsever, that honest Mysie ever tried her art sae far; – and what I hae heard tell of was done in the cruelty of jealousy. But it's no possible, captain, that ye were making up to auld Mysie. For the love o' peace, an ye were sae deluded, say nothing about it; for either the parish will say that ye hae an unco taste, or that Mysie has cast her cantrips o'er your judgment, – the whilk would either make you a laughing-stock, or, gin ye could prove that she kithed afore you like a blooming damsel, bring her to the wuddy. So I redde ye, captain, to let this story gang nae farther. But mind what I hae been saying, keep weel wi' her, as ye respek yoursel.'

In saying these words, Robin turned hastily into the wynd that led to the clachan, laughing in his sleeve, leaving the brave cavalier in a sore state o' dread and wonderment.

It seems that shortly after Robin Finnie had departed from the gallant cavalier, a lad, called Sandy Macgill, who was colleagued with him in the plot, came towards the captain with looks cast to the earth, and so full of thought, that he seemingly noticed nothing. Going forward in this locked-up state of the outward sense, he came close upon Swaby, when, affecting to be startled out of his meditations, he stopped suddenly short, and looked in the lieutenant's broad face, with all the alarm he could put into his own features, till he saw he was frightened out of his judgment, when he said—

'Gude be about us, sir, ye hae gotten scaith; the blighting blink o' an ill e'e has lighted upon you. – O, sir! O, sir! tak tent o' yoursel!'

Sandy had prepared a deal more to say, but finding himself overcome with an inward inclination to risibility at the sight of Swaby's terrification, he was obligated to flee as fast as he could from the spot; the which wild-like action of his no doubt dismayed the cavalier fully as meikle as all he had said.

But it's the nature of man to desire to do whatever he is forbidden. Notwithstanding all their mystical admonitions, Swaby still persevered in his evil intents, and accordingly he was seen lurking, without his sword, about the heel of the evening, on Hallowe'en, near the skirts of the clachan where Mysie Gilmour lived. And, as it had been conspired among her friends, Mungo Affleck, her gude-brother, a man weel stricken in years, but of a youthy mind, and a perfect pen-gun at a crack, came across the cavalier in his path, and Swaby having before some slight acquaintance with his garb and canny observes, hovered for a little in discourse with Mungo.

'I counsel you, sir,' said the pawkie auld carl as they were separating, 'no to gang far afield this night, for this is a night that there is na the like o' in a' the year round. It's Hallowe'en, sir, so be counselled by me, and seek your hame betimes; for mony a ane has met with things on Hallowe'en that they never after forgot.'

Considering the exploit on which the cavalier was then bowne, it's no to be thought that this was very heartening music, but, for all that, he said blithely, as Mungo told me himself. 'Nay, not so fast, governor, tell us what you mean by Hallowe'en!'

'Hallowe'en!' cried Mungo Affleck, with a sound o' serious sincerity; 'Do ye no ken Hallowe'en? But I need na say that. Ye'll excuse me, captain – what can you Englishers, that are brought up in the darkness o' human ordinances in gospel things, and who live in the thraldom of episcopalian ignorance, ken of Hallowe'en, or o' any other solemn day set apart for an occasion. – O, sir, Hallowe'en among us is a dreadful night! witches and warlocks, and a' lang-nebbit things, hae a power and a dominion unspeakable on Hallowe'en. The de'il at other times gi'es, it's said, his agents a mutchkin o' mischief, but on this night it's thought they hae a chappin; and one thing most demonstrable is; – but, sir, the sun's down – the blessed light o' day is ayont the hill, and it's no safe to be subjek to the whisking o' the mildew frae the tails o' the benweed ponies that are saddled for you awfu' carnavaulings, where Cluty plays on the pipes! so I wis you, sir, gude night and weel hame. – O, sir, an ye could be persuaded! – Tak an auld man's advice, and rather read a chapter of THE BOOK, an it should even be the unedifying tenth of Nehemiah, than be seen at the gloaming in this gait, about the dyke-sides, like a wolf yearning for some tender lamb of a defenceless fold.'

Mungo having thus delivered himself, went away, leaving Swaby as it were in a swither; for, on looking back, the old man saw him standing half turned round as if he was minded to go home. The power of the sin was however strong upon him, and shortly after the dusk had closed in, when the angels had lighted their candles at their windows in the sky to watch over the world in the hours of sleep, Swaby, with stealthy steps, came to Mysie Gilmour's door, and softly tirling at the pin was admitted; for all within was ready for his reception.

Robin Finnie and Sandy Macgill having carried thither Zachariah Smylie's black ram, a condumacious and outstropolous beast, which they had laid in Mysie's bed, and keepit frae baaing with a gude fothering of kail-blades, and a cloute soaken in milk.

Mysie, on opening the door, said to the gallant cavalier—

'Just step in, ye'll fin a' ready,' and she blew out her crusie which she had in her hand, and letting the captain grope in by himself, hirpled as fast as she could to one of the neighbours; for, although she had covenanted with him to come without his sword, she was terrified with the fear of some dreadful upshot.

As soon as he was in, Robin Finnie and Sandy Macgill went and harkened at the window, where they heard the gay gallant stumbling in the floor, churming sweet and amorous words as he went groping his way towards the bed where the auld toop was breathing thickly, mumbling and crunching the kail-blades in a state of as great sensual delight and satisfaction as any beast could well be. But no sooner had the cavalier placed his hand on the horned head of the creature, than he uttered a yell of despair; in the same moment the toop, in little less fright, jumpit out of the bed against him and knocked him down over a stool with a lounder. Verily Providence might be said, with reverence, to have had a hand in the mirth of his punishment; for the ram recovering its senses before the cavalier, and being in dread of danger, returned to the charge, and began to butt him as if it would have been his death. The cries that ensued are not to be told; all the neighbours came running to the door to see what was the matter, some with lighted sticks in their hands, and some with burning coals in the tongs. Robin Finnie and Sandy Macgill were like to die of laughing; but fearing the wrathful ram might dunt out the bowels or the brains, if he had any, of the poor young cavalier, they opened the door, and so delivered him from its horns. He was, however, by this time, almost in a state of distraction, believing the beast was the real Evil One; so that he no sooner felt himself free and saw the lights, than he flew to his quarters as if he had been pursued by a legion.

Some of his own soldiers that were lying in the clachan, and who had come out with the rest of the folk, saw through the stratagem, and, forgetting all reverence for their afflicted commander, laughed louder and longer than any body. In short, the story was o'er the whole parish next day, and the very weans, wherever the cavalier appeared, used to cry ba at him, by which his very life was made a shame and a burden to him, in so much that he applied for leave to give up his commission, and returned home to his kindred in the south of England, and we never heard tell of him after.

But, although in the exploit of Mysie Gilmour, and Robin Finnie with his confederates, we had a tasting of mirth and merriment, to the effect of lessening the dread and fear in which our simple country-folk held his Majesty's ungracious fine-levers, the cavalier captains and soldiers, still there was a gradual ingrowth of the weight of the oppression, wherewith we were laden more as bondsmen and slaves than as subjects; and, in the meantime, the spirit of that patriarch, my apostolic grandfather, was gathering to heart and energy within the silent recesses of my afflicted bosom.

I heard the murmuring, deep and sad, of my neighbours, at the insult and the contumely which they were obligated to endure from the irresponsible licentiousness of military domination – but I said nothing; I was driven, with my pious wife and our simple babies, from my own hearth by the lewd conversation of the commissioned freebooters, and obligated to make our home in an out-house, that we might not be molested in our prayers by their wicked ribaldry, – but I said nothing; I saw my honest neighbours plundered – their sons insulted – and their daughters put to shame, – but I said nothing; I was a witness when our godly minister, after having been driven with his wife and family out to the mercy of the winter's wind, was seized in the very time while he was worshipping the Maker of us all, and taken like a malefactor to prison, – but I said nothing; and I was told the story of the machinations against his innocent virgin daughter, when she was left defenceless among us, – and still I said nothing. Like the icy winter, tyranny had so incrusted my soul, that my taciturnity seemed as hard, impenetrable, cold, and cruel, as the frozen river's surface, but the stream of my feelings ran stronger and fiercer beneath; and the time soon came when, in proportion to the still apathy that made my brother and my friends to wonder how I so quietly bore the events of so much, my inward struggles burst through all outward passive forms, and, like the hurling and the drifting ice, found no effectual obstacle to its irresistible and natural destination.

Mrs Swinton, the worthy lady of that saint, our pastor, on hearing what had been plotted against the chaste innocence of her fair and blooming child, came to me, and with tears, in a sense the tears of a widow, very earnestly entreated of me that I would take the gentle Martha to her cousin, the Laird of Garlin's, in Dumfries-shire, she having heard that some intromissions, arising out of pacts and covenants between my wife's cousin and the Laird of Barscob, obligated me to go thither. This was on the Monday after the battering that the cavalier got from Zachariah Smylie's black ram; and I reasonably thinking that there was judgment in the request, and that I might serve by my compliance, the helpless residue, and the objects of a persecuted Christian's affections, I consented to take the damsel with me as far as Garlins, in Galloway; the which I did.

When I had left Martha Swinton with her friends, who, being persons of pedigree and opulence, were better able to guard her, I went to the end of my own journey; and here, from what ensued, it is needful I should relate that, in this undertaking, I left my own house under the care of my brother, and that I was armed with my grandfather's sword.

It happened that, on Tuesday the 13th November 1666, as I was returning homeward from Barscob, I fell in with three godly country men about a mile south of the village of Dalry in Galloway, and we entered into a holy and most salutary conversation anent the sufferings and the fortitude of God's people in that time of trouble. Discoursing with great sobriety on that melancholious theme, we met a gang of Turner's black-cuffs, driving before them, like beasts to the slaughter, several miserable persons to thrash out the corn, that it might be sold, of one of my companions, who, being himself a persecuted man, and unable to pay the fine

forfeited by his piety, had some days before been forced to
flee his house.

On seeing the soldiers and their prey coming towards
us, the poor man would have run away; but we exhorted
him not be afraid, for he might pass unnoticed, and so
he did; for, although those whom the military rabiators
were driving to thrash his corn knew him well, they were
enabled to bear up, and were so endowed with the strength
of martyrdom, that each of them, only by a look, signified
that they were in the spirit of fellowship with him.

After they had gone by, his heart, however, was so
afflicted that so many worthy persons should be so harmed
for his sake, that he turned back, and, in despite of all our
entreaties, went to them, while we went forward to Dalry,
where we entered a small public, and having ordered some
refreshment, for we were all weary, we sat meditating on
what could be the upshot of such tyranny.

While we were so sitting, a cry got up, that our companion was seized by the soldiers, and that they were
tormenting him on a red-hot gridiron for not having paid
his fine.

My blood boiled at the news. I rose, and those who were
with me followed, and we ran to the house – his own house
– where the poor man was. I beseeched two of the soldiers,
who were at the door, to desist from their cruelty; but while
I was speaking, other two, that were within, came raging
out like curs from a kennel, and flew at me; and one of
them dared to strike me with his nieve in the mouth. My
grandfather's sword flew out at the blow, and the insulter
lay wounded and bleeding at my feet. My companions in
the same moment rushed on the other soldiers, dashed their
teeth down their throats, and twisting their firelocks from
their hands, set the prisoner free.

In this there was rashness, but there was also redemption
and glory. We could not stop at what we had done; – we
called on those who had been brought to thrash the corn
to join with us, and they joined; – we hastened to the next
farm; – the spirit of indignation was there before us, and
master and man, and father and son, there likewise found
that the hilts of their fathers' covenanted swords fitted their

avenging grasps. We had now fired the dry stubble of the land – the flame spread – we advanced, and grew stronger and stronger. The hills, as it were, clapped their hands, and the valleys shouted of freedom. From all sides men and horse came exulting towards us; the gentleman and the hind knew no distinction. The cry was, 'Down with tyranny – we are and we will make free!' The fields rejoiced with the multitude of our feet as we advanced towards Dumfries, where Turner lay. His black-cuffs flung down their arms and implored our mercy. We entered Dumfries, and the Oppressor was our prisoner.

Hitherto the rising at Dalry had been as a passion and a spreading fire. The strength of the soldiers was consumed before us, and their arms became our weapons; but when we had gained possession of Dumfries, and had set a ward over the house where we had seized Turner, I saw that we had waded owre far into the river to think of returning, and that to go on was safer than to come back. It was indeed manifest that we had been triumphant rather by our haste than by the achievements of victorious battle; and it could be hidden from no man's thought that the power and the vengeance both of the government and the prelacy would soon be set in array against us. I therefore bethought myself, in that peril of our lives and cause, of two things which seemed most needful; first, Not to falter in our enterprise until we had proved the utmost of the Lord's pleasure in our behalf; and, second, To use the means under Him which, in all human undertakings, are required to bring whatsoever is ordained to pass.

Whether in these things I did well, or wisely, I leave to the adjudication of the courteous reader; but I can lay my hand upon my heart, and say aloud, yea, even to the holy skies, 'I thought not of myself nor of mine, but only of the religious rights of my sorely-oppressed countrymen.'

From the moment in which I received the blow of the soldier up till the hour when Turner was taken, I had been the head and leader of the people. My sword was never out of my grip, and I marched as it were in a path of light, so wonderful was the immediate instinct with which I was directed to the accomplishment of that adventure, the success of which overwhelmed the fierce and cruel Antichrists at Edinburgh with unspeakable consternation and panic. But I lacked that knowledge of the art of war by which men are banded into companies and ruled, however manifold their diversities, to one end and effect, so that our numbers having by this time increased to a great multitude, I felt myself utterly unable to govern them. We were as a sea of billows, that move onward all in one way, obedient to the impulse and deep fetchings of the tempestuous breath of the awakened winds of heaven, but which often break into foam, and waste their force in a roar of ineffectual rage.

Seeing this, and dreading the consequences thereof, I conferred with some of those whom I had observed the most discreet and considerate in the course of the raid, and we came to a resolve to constitute and appoint Captain Learmont our chief commander, he having earned an experience of the art and strategems of war under the renowned Lesley. Had we abided by that determination, some have thought our expedition might have come to a happier issue; but no human helps and means could change what was evidently ordained otherwise. It happened, however, that Colonel Wallace, another officer of some repute, also joined us, and his name made him bright and resplendent to our enthusiasm. While we were deliberating whom to choose for our leader, Colonel Wallace was in the same breath, for his name's sake, proposed, and was united in the command with Learmont. This was a deadly error, and ought in all time coming to be a warning and an admonition to people and nations in their straits and difficulties, never to be guided, in the weighty shocks and controversies of disordered fortunes, by any prejudice or affection so unsubstantial as the echo of an honoured name. For this Wallace, though a man of questionless bravery, and a gentleman of good account among all who knew him, had not received any gift from Nature of that spirit of masterdom without which there can be no command; so that he was no sooner appointed to lead us on, with Learmont as his second, than his mind fell into a strange confusion, and he heightened disorder into anarchy by ordering over much. We could not however undo the evil, without violating the discipline that we were all conscious our forces so grievously lacked; but, from the very moment that I saw in what manner he took upon him the command, I augured of nothing but disaster.

Learmont was a collected and an urbane character, and did much to temper and turn aside the thriftless ordinances of his superior. He, seeing how much our prosperity was dependent on the speed with which we could reach Edinburgh, hastened forward every thing with such alacrity, that we were ready on the morrow by mid-day to set out from Dumfries. But the element of discord was now in our cause, and I was reproached by many for having abdicated my natural right to the command. It was in vain that I tried to redeem the fault by taking part with Learmont, under the determination, when the black hour of defeat or dismay should come upon us, to take my stand with him, and, regardless of Wallace, to consider him as the chief and champion of our covenanted liberties. But why do I dwell on these intents? Let me hasten to describe the upshot of our enterprise.

As soon as we had formed, in the manner herein related, something like a head and council for ourselves, we considered, before leaving Dumfries, what ought to be done with General Turner, and ordered him to be brought before us; for those who had suffered from his fell orders and licentious soldiery were clamorous for his blood. But when the man was brought in, he was so manifestly mastered by his wine, as his vice often made him, that we thought it would be as it were to ask a man mad, or possessed, to account for his actions, as at that time to put the frantic drunkard on his defence; so we heeded not his obstreperous menaces, but ordered him to be put into bed, and his papers to be searched for and laid before us.

In this moderation there was wisdom; for, by dealing so gently by one who had proved himself so ruthless an agent of the prelatic aggressions, we bespoke the good opinion even of many among our adversaries; and in the end it likewise proved a measure of justice as well as of mercy. For, on examining his papers, it appeared, that pitiless as his domineering had been, it was far short of the universal cruelty of his instructions from the apostate James Sharp, and those in the council with him, who had delivered themselves over as instruments to the arbitrary prerogatives and tyrannous pretensions of the court. We therefore resolved to proceed no farther against him, but to keep him as an hostage in our hands. Many, however, among the commonalty complained of our lenity; for they had endured in their persons, their gear, and their families, great severities; and they grudged that he was not obligated to taste the bitterness of the cup of which he had forced them to drink so deeply.

In the meantime all the country became alive with the news of our exploit. The Covenanters of the shire of Ayr, headed by several of their ejected ministers whom they had cherished in the solitary dens and hidings in the moors and hills, to which they had been forced to flee from the proclamation against the field-preachings, advanced to meet us on our march. Verily it was a sight that made the heart of man dinle at once with gladness and sorrow to behold, as the day dawned on our course, in crossing the wide and lonely wilderness of Cumnock-moor, those religious brethren coming towards us, moving in silence over the heath, like the shadows of the slowly-sailing clouds of the summer sky.

As we were toiling through the deep heather on the eastern skirts of the Mearns-moor, a mist hovered all the morning over the pad of Neilston, covering like a snowy fleece the sides of the hills down almost to the course of our route, in such a manner that we could see nothing on the left beyond it. We were then within less than fourteen miles of Glasgow, where General Dalziel lay with the King's forces, keeping in thraldom the godly of that pious city and its neighbourhood. Captain Learmont, well aware, from the eager character of the man, that he would be fain to intercept us, and fearful of being drawn into jeopardy by the mist, persuaded Wallace to halt us some time.

As November was far advanced, it was thought by the country-folk that the mist would clear away about noon. We accordingly made a pause, and sat down on the ground; for many were weary, having overfatigued themselves in their zeal to come up with the main body, and we all stood in need of rest.

Scarcely, however, had we cast ourselves in a desultory manner on the heather, when some one heard the thud of a distant drum in the mist, and gave the alarm; at which we all again suddenly started to our feet, and listening, were not long left in doubt of the sound. Orders were accordingly given to place ourselves in array for battle; and while we were obeying the command in the best manner our little skill allowed, the beating of the drum came louder and nearer, intermingled with the shrill war-note of the spirity fife.

Every one naturally thought of the King's forces; and the Reverend Mr Semple, seeing that we were in some measure prepared to meet them, stepped out in front with all his worthy brethren in the camp, and having solemneezed us for worship, gave out a psalm.

By the time we had sung the first three verses the drum and fife sounded so near, that I could discern they played the tune of 'John, come kiss me now,' which left me in no doubt that the soldiers in the mist were my own friends and neighbours; for it was the same tune which was played when the men of our parish went to the raid of Dunse-hill, and which, in memorial of that era, had been preserved as a sacred melody amongst us.

Being thus convinced, I stepped out from my place to the ministers, and said, 'They are friends that are coming.' The worship was in consequence for a short space suspended, and I presently after saw my brother at the head of our neighbours coming out of the cloud; whereupon I went forward to meet him, and we shook hands sorrowfully.

'This is an unco thing, Ringan,' were his first words; 'but it's the Lord's will, and HE is able to work out a great salvation.'

I made no answer; but inquiring for my family, of whom it was a cheering consolation to hear as blithe an account as could reasonably be hoped for, I walked with him to our captains, and made him known to them as my brother.

Saving the innocent alarm of the drum in the mist, our march to Lanerk was without hinderance or molestation; and when we arrived there, it was agreed and set forth, on the exhortation of the ministers who were with us, that the Solemn League and Covenant should be publicly renewed; and, to the end that no one might misreport the spirituality of our zeal and intents, a Protestation was likewise published, wherein we declared our adherence and allegiance to the King undiminished in all temporalities; that we had been driven to seek redress by the sword for oppressions so grievous, that they could be no longer endured; and that all we asked and sought for was, the re-establishment of the presbyterian liberty of worship, and the restoration of our godly pastors to their gospel-rights and privileges.

The morrow after was appointed for the covenanting, and to be held as a day of fasting and humiliation for our own sins, which had provoked the Lord to bring us into such state of peril and suffering; and it was a sacred consolation, as Mr Semple showed in his discourse on the occasion, that, in all our long and painful travels from Dumfries, we had been guided from the commission of any offence, even towards those whose hearts were not with us, and had been brought so far on our way as blameless as a peaceable congregation going in the lown of a Sabbath morning to worship their Maker in the house of prayer.

But neither the sobriety of our demeanour, nor the honest protestation of our cause, had any effect on the obdurate heart of the apostate James Sharp, who happened, by reason of the Lord Rothes going to London, to be then in the chief chair of the privy-council at Edinburgh. He knew the deserts of his own guilt, and he hated us, even unto death, for the woes he had made us suffer. The sough, therefore, of our approach was to the consternation of his conscience as the sound of the wheels of an avenging God, groaning heavily in their coming with the weight of the engines of wrath and doom. Some said that he sat in the midst of the counsellors like a demented man; and others, that he was seen flying to and fro, wringing his hands, and weeping, and wailing, and gnashing his teeth. But though all power of forethought and policy was taken from him, there were others of the council who, being less guilty, were more governed, and they took measures to defend the capital against us. They commanded the gates to be fenced with cannon, and working on the terrors of the inhabitants with fearful falsehoods of crimes that were never committed, thereby caused them to band themselves for the protection of their lives and property, while they interdicted them from all egress, in so much, that many who were friendly to us were frustrated in their desire to come with the aid of their helps and means.

The tidings of the preparations for the security of Edinburgh, with the unhappy divisions and continual controversies in our councils, between the captains and the ministers, anent the methods of conducting the raid, had, even before we left Lanerk, bred much sedition among us, and an ominous dubiety of success. Nevertheless our numbers continued to increase, and we went forward in such a commendable order of battle, that, had the Lord been pleased with our undertaking, there was no reason to think the human means insufficient for the end. But in the mysteries of the depths of His wisdom he had judged, and for the great purposes of his providence he saw, that it was meet we should yet suffer. Accordingly, even while we were issuing forth from the port of the town, the face of the heavens became overcast, and a swift carry and a rising wind were solemn intimations to my troubled spirit that the heartening of His countenance went no farther with us at that time.

Nor indeed could less than a miracle in our behalf have availed; for the year was old in November, the corn was stacked, the leaf fallen, and Nature, in outcast nakedness, sat, like the widows of the martyrs, forlorn on the hills: her head was bound with the cloud, and she mourned over the desolation that had sent sadness and silence into all her pleasant places.

As we advanced the skies lowered, and the blast raved in the leafless boughs; sometimes a passing shower, as it travelled in the storm, trailed its watery skirts over our disheartened host, quenching the zeal of many, – and ever and anon the angry riddlings of the cruel hail still more and more exasperated our discontent. I observed that the men began to turn their backs to the wind, and to look wistfully behind, and to mutter and murmur to one another. But still we all advanced gradually, however falling into separate bands and companies, like the ice of the river's stream breaking asunder in a thaw.

In the afternoon the fits of the wind became less vehement; the clouds were gathered more compactly together, and the hail had ceased, but the rain was lavished without measure. The roads became sloughs, – our feet were drawn heavily out of the clay, – the burns and brooks raged from bank to brae, – and the horses swithered at the fords, in so much, that towards the gloaming, when we were come to Bathgate, several of our broken legions were seen far behind; and when we halted for the night, scarcely more than half the number with whom we had that morning left Lanerk could be mustered, and few of those who had fallen behind came up. But still Captain Learmont thought, that as soon as the men had taken some repose after that toilsome march, we should advance outright to Edinburgh. Wallace, however, objected, and that night was spent between them and the ministers in thriftless debate; moreover, our hardships were increased; for, by the prohibition of the privy-council against the egress of the inhabitants of the city, we were, as I have said, disappointed of the provisions and succour we had trusted to receive from them, and there was no hope in our camp, but only bitterness of spirit and the breathings of despair.

Seeing, what no man could hide from his reason, our cause abandoned of the Lord, I retired from the main body of the host, and sat alone on a rock, musing with a sore heart on all that had come so rashly to pass. It was then the last hour of the gloaming, and every thing around was dismayed and dishevelled. The storm had abated, and the rain was over, but the darkness of the night was closing fast in, and we were environed with perils. A cloud, like the blackness of a mortcloth, hung over our camp; the stars withheld their light, and the windows of the castle shone with the candles of our enemies, who, safe in their strong-hold, were fresh in strength and ready for battle.

I thought of my home, of the partner of my anxieties and cares, of the children of our love, and of the dangers of their defencelessness, and I marvelled with a weeping spirit at the manner in which I had been snatched up, and brought, as it were in a whirlwind, to be an actor in a scene of such inevitable woe. Sometimes, in the passion of that grief, I was tempted to rise, and moved to seek my way back to the nest of my affections. But as often as the thought came over my heart, with its soft and fond enticements, some rustle in the camp of the weary men who had borne in the march all that I had borne, and many of them in the cause far more, yea, even to the martyrdom of dear friends, I bowed my head and prayed for constancy of purpose and fortitude of mind, if the arm of flesh was ordained to be the means of rescuing the gospel, and delivering poor Scotland from prelatic tyranny, and the thraldom of an antichristian usurpation in the kingly power.

While I was thus sitting in this sad and solitary state, none doubting, that before another night our covenanted army would be, as the hail that smote so sorely on our march, seen no more, and only known to have been by the track of its course on the fields over which we had passed, a light broke in upon the darkness of my soul, and amidst high and holy experiences of consolation, mingled with awe and solemn wonder, I beheld as it were a bright and shining hand draw aside the curtain of time, and disclose the blessings of truth and liberty that were ordained to rise from the fate of the oppressors, who, in the pride and panoply of arbitrary power, had so thrown down the temple of God, and laid waste His vineyard.

I saw, that from our hasty enterprise they would be

drawn to commit still more grievous aggressions, and thereby incur some fearful forfeiture of the honours and predominancy of which they had for so many years shown themselves so unworthy; and I had a foretaste in that hour of the fulfilment of my grandfather's prophecy concerning the tasks that were in store for myself in the deliverance of my native land. So that, although I rose from the rock whereon I was sitting, in the clear conviction that our array would be scattered like chaff before the wind, I yet had a blessed persuasion that the event would prove in the end a link in the chain, or a cog in the wheel, of the hidden enginery with which Providence works good out of evil.

In the course of the night, shortly after the third watch had been set, some of those who had tarried by the way came to the camp with the tidings that Dalziel and all the royal forces in Glasgow were coming upon us. This, though foreseen, caused a great panic, and a council of war, consisting, as usual, of ministers and officers, was held, to determine what should be done; but it was likewise, as usual, only a fruitless controversy. I, however, on this occasion, feeling myself sustained in spirit by the assurances I had received in my meditations on the rock, ventured to speak my mind freely; which was to the effect, that, taking our dejected condition, the desertion of our friends, and our disappointments from the city, into consideration, we could do no better thing than evade the swords of our adversaries by disbanding ourselves, that each might be free to seek safety for himself.

Many were inclined to this counsel; and I doubt not it would have been followed; but, while conferring together, an officer came from the privy-council to propose a cessation of arms till our demands could be considered. It was manifest that this was a wily stratagem to keep us in the snare till Dalziel had time to come up; and I did all in my power to make the council see it in the same light; but there was a blindness of mind among us, and the greater number thought it augured a speedy redress of the wrongs for which we had come to seek reparation. Nor did their obstinacy in this relax till next morning, when, instead of anything like their improbable hopes, came a proclamation ordering us to disperse, and containing neither promise of indemnity nor of pardon. But then it was too late. Dalziel was in sight. His army was coming like a stream along the foot of the Pentland-hills, – we saw his banners and the glittering of his arms, and the sound of his musicants came swelling on the breeze.

It was plain that his purpose was to drive us in towards the town; but had we dispersed we might even then have frustrated his intent. There happened, however, besides Learmont and Wallace, to be several officers among us who had stubborn notions of military honour, and they would not permit so unsoldier-like a flight; there were also divers heated and fanatical spirits, whom, because our undertaking had been for religious ends, nothing could persuade that Providence would not interfere in some signal manner for their deliverance, yea, even to the overthrow of the enemy; and Mr Whamle, a minister, one of these, getting upon the top of the rock where I had sat the night before, began to preach of the mighty things that the Lord did for the children of Israel in the valley of Aijalon, where he not only threw down great stones from the heavens, but enabled Joshua to command the sun and moon to stand still, – which to any composed mind was melancholious to hear.

In sequence to these divisions and contrarities which enchanted us to the spot, Dalziel, considering that we were minded to give him battle, brought on his force; and it is but due to the renown of the valour of those present to record, that, notwithstanding a fearful odds, our men, having the vantage ground, so stoutly maintained their station that we repulsed him thrice.

But the victory, as I have said, was not ordained for us. In the afternoon Dalziel was reinforced by several score of mounted gentlemen from the adjacent counties, and with their horse, about sunset, our phalanx was shattered, our ranks broken, – and then we began to quit the field. The number of our slain, and of those who fell into the hands of the enemy, did not in the whole exceed two hundred men. The dead might have been greater, but for the compassion of the gentlemen, who had respect to the cause which had provoked us to arms, and who, instead of doing as Dalziel's men did, without remorse or pity, cried to the fugitives to flee, and spared many in consideration of the common wrongs.

When I saw that our host was dashed into pieces, and the fragments scattered over the fields, I fled with the flying, and gained, with about some thirty other fugitives, the brow of a steep part of the Pentland-hills, where the mounted gentlemen, even had they been inclined, could not easily follow us. There, while we halted to rest a little, we heard a shout now and then rise startling from the field of battle below; but night coming on, all was soon silent, and we sat, in the holiness of our mountain-refuge, in silent rumination till the moon, rolling slowly from behind Arthur's Seat, looked from her window in the cloud, as if to admonish us to flee farther from the scene of danger.

The Reverend Mr Witherspoon being among us, was the first to feel the gracious admonition, and, rising from the ground, he said—

'Friends, we must not tarry here, the hunters are forth, and we are the prey they pursue. They will track us long, and the hounds are not of a nature to lose scent, especially when they have tested, as they have done this day, the rich blood of the faithful and the true. Therefore let us depart; but where, O where shall we find a home to receive us? – Where a place of rest for our weary limbs, or a safe stone for a pillow to our aching heads? But why do I doubt? Blameless as we are, even before man, of all offence, save that of seeking leave to worship God according to our conscience, it cannot be that we shall be left without succour. No, my friens! though our bed be the damp grass and our coverlet the cloudy sky, our food the haws of the hedge and our drink the drumly burn, we have made for our hearts the down-beds of religious faith, and have found a banquet for our spirits in the ambrosial truths of the gospel-luxuries that neither a James Sharp nor a Charles Stuart can ever enjoy, nor all the rents and revenues, fines and forfeitures, which princes may exact and prelates yearn to partake of, can buy.'

He then offered up a thanksgiving that we had been spared from the sword in the battle; after which we shook hands in silence together, and each pursued his own way.

Mr Witherspoon lingered by my side as we descended the hill, and I discerned that he was inclined to be my companion; so we continued together, stretching towards the north-west, in order to fall into the Lithgow Road, being mindet to pass along the skirts of Stirlingshire, thence into Lennox, in the hope of reaching Argyle's country, by the way of the ferry of Balloch. But we had owre soon a cruel cause to change the course of our flight.

In coming down towards the Amond-water, we saw a man running before us in the glimpse of the moonshine, and it was natural to conclude, from his gestures and the solitude of the place, that no one could be so far a-field at such a time, but some poor fellow-fugitive from Rullion-green, where the battle was fought; so we called to him to stop, and to fear no ill, for we were friends. Still, however, he fled on, and heeded not our entreaty, which made us both marvel and resolve to overtake him. We thought it was not safe to follow long an unknown person who was so evidently afraid, and flying, as we supposed, to his home. Accordingly we hastened our speed, and I, being the nimblest, reached him at a place where he was stopped by a cleft in the rocks on the river's woody brink.

'Why do you fly so fast from us?' said I, 'we're frae the Pentland-hills too.'

At these words he looked wildly round, and his face was as ghastly as a ghost's in the moonlight; but distorted as he was by his fears, I discovered in him my neighbour, Nahum Chapelrig, and I spoke to him by the name.

'O, Ringan Gilhaize!' said he, and he took hold of me with his right hand, while he raised his left and shook it in a fearful and frantic manner, 'I am a dead man, my hours are numbered, and the sand-glass of my days is amaist a' run out. I had been saved from the sword, spared from the spear, and, flying from the field, I went to a farm-house yonder; I sought admission and shelter for a forlorn Christian man; but the edicts of the persecutors are more obeyed here than the laws of God. The farmer opened his casement, and speering if I had been at the raid of the Covenanters, which, for the sake of truth and the glory of God, I couldna deny, he shot me dead on the spot; for his bullet gaed in at my breast, and is fast in my—'

He could say no more; for in that juncture he gave as it

were a gurgle in the throat, and swirling round, fell down a bleeding corpse on the ground where he stood, before Mr Witherspoon had time to come up.

We both looked at poor guiltless Nahum as he lay on the grass, and, after some sorrowful communion, we lifted the body, and carrying it down aneath the bank of the river, laid stones and turfs upon it by the moonlight, that the unclean birds might not be able to molest his martyred remains. We then consulted together; and having communed concerning the manner of Nahum's death, we resolved not to trust ourselves in the power of strangers in those parts of the country, where the submission to the prelatic enormity had been followed with such woful evidence of depravity of heart. So, instead of continuing our journey to the northward, we changed our course, and, for the remainder of the night, sought our way due west, by the skirts of the moors and other untrodden ways.

CHAPTER TWENTY-SEVEN

At break of day we found ourselves on a lonely brae-side, sorely weary, hungry and faint in spirit: a few whin-bushes were on the bank, and the birds in them were beginning to chirp, – we sat down and wist not what to do.

Mr Witherspoon prayed inwardly for support and resignation of heart in the trials he was ordained to undergo; but doure thoughts began to gather in my bosom. I yearned for my family, – I mourned to know what had become of my brother in the battle, – and I grudged and marvelled, wherefore it was that the royal and the great had so little respect for the religious honesty of harmless country folk.

It was now the nine-and-twentieth day of November, but the weather for the season was open and mild, and the morning rose around us as in the glory of her light and beauty. As the gay and goodly sun looked over the eastern hills, we cast our eyes on all sides, and beheld the scattered villages and the rising smoke of the farms, but saw not a dwelling we could venture to approach, nor a roof that our fears, and the woful end of poor Nahum Chapelrig, did not teach us to think covered a foe.

While we were sitting communing on these things, we discovered, at a little distance on the left, an aged woman hirpling aslant the route we intended to take. She had a porringer in the one hand, and a small kit tied in a cloute in the other, by which we discerned that she was probably some laborous man's wife conveying his breakfast to him in the field.

We both rose, and going towards her, Mr Witherspoon said, 'For the love of God have compassion on two famishing Christians.'

The old woman stopped, and, looking round, gazed at

us for a space of time, with a countenance of compassionate reverence.

'Heh, sirs!' she then said, 'and has it come to this, that a minister of the gospel is obligated to beg an almous frae Janet Armstrong?' And she set down the porringer on the ground, and began to untie the cloute in which she carried the kit, saying. 'Little did I think that sic an homage was in store for me, or that the merciful Heavens would e'er requite my sufferings, in this world, wi' the honour of placing it in my power to help a persecuted servant of the living God. Mr Witherspoon, I ken you weel; meikle sweet counselling I hae gotten frae you when ye preached for our minister at Camrachle in the time of the great covenanting. I was then as a lanerly widow, for my gudeman was at the raid of Dunse-hill, and my heart was often sorrowful and sinking wi' a sinful misdooting of Providence, for I had twa wee bairns and but a toom garnel.'

She then opened the kit, which contained a providing of victual that she was carrying, as we had thought, to her husband, a quarrier in a neighbouring quarry; and bidding us partake, she said—

'This will be a blithe morning to John Armstrong, to think that out of our basket and store we hae had, for ance in our day, the blessing of gi'eing a pick to ane o' God's greatest corbies; and he'll no fin his day's dark ae hue the dreigher for wanting his breakfast on account of sic a cause.'

So we sat down, and began to partake of the repast with a greedy appetite, and the worthy woman continued to talk.

'Aye,' said she, 'the country-side has been in a consternation ever since Dalziel left Glasgow; – we a' jealoused that the Lanerk Covenanters would na be able to withstand his power and the king's forces; for it was said ye hadna a right captain of war among you a'. – But, Mr Witherspoon, ye could ne'er be ane of the ministers that were said to meddle with the battering-rams o' battle. – No: weel I wat that yours is a holier wisdom – ye would be for peace; – blessed are the peace-makers.'

Seeing the honest woman thus inclined to prattle of

things too high for her to understand, Mr Witherspoon's hunger being somewhat abated, he calmly interposed, and turned the discourse into kind inquiries concerning the state of her poor soul and her straitened worldly circumstances; and he was well content to find that she had a pleasant vista of the truths of salvation, and a confidence in the unceasing care of Providence.

'The same gracious hand that feeds the ravens,' said she, 'will ne'er let twa auld folk want, that it has been at the trouble to provide for so long. It's true we had a better prospek in our younger days; but our auld son was slain at the battle of Worcester, when he gaed in to help to put the English crown on the head of that false Charlie Stuart, who has broken his oath and the Covenant; and my twa winsome lassies diet in their teens, before they were come to years o' discretion. But 'few and evil are the days of man that is born of a woman,' as I hae heard you preach, Mr Witherspoon, which is a blessed truth and consolation to those who have not in this world any continued city.'

We then inquired what was the religious frame of the people in that part of the country, in order that we might know how to comport ourselves; but she gave us little heartening. 'The strength and wealth o' the gentry,' said she, 'is just sooket awa' wi' ae fine after anither, and it's no in the power of nature that they can meikle langer stand out against the prelacy.'

'I hope,' replied Mr Witherspoon, 'that there's no symptom of a laxity of principle among them?'

'I doot, I doot, Mr Witherspoon,' said Janet Armstrong, 'we canna hae a great dependence either on principle or doctrine when folk are driven demented wi' oppression. Many that were ance godly among us can thole no more, and they begin to fash and turn awa' at the sight of their persecuted friends.'

Mr Witherspoon sighed with a heavy heart on hearing this, and mournfully shook his head. We then thanked Janet for her hospitable kindness, and rising, were moving to go away.

'I hope, Mr Witherspoon,' said she, 'that we're no to part in sic a knotless manner; bide here till I gang for John

Armstrong and the other twa men that howk wi' him in the quarry. They're bearing plants o' the vineyard, – tarry, I pray you, and water them wi' the water of the Word.'

And so saying, she hastened down the track she was going, and we continued on the spot to wait her return.

'Ringan,' said Mr Witherspoon to me, 'I fear there's owre meikle truth in what she says concerning the state of religion, not only here, but among all the commonalty of the land. The poor beast that's overladen may be stubborn, and refuse for a time to draw, but the whip will at last prevail, until, worn out and weary, it meekly lies down to die. In like manner the stoutness of the covenanted heart will be overcome.'

Just as he was uttering these words, a whiz in a whin-bush near to where we were standing, and the sound of a gun, startled us, and on looking round we saw five men, and one of the black-cuffs with his firelock still at his shoulder, looking towards us from behind a dyke that ran along the bottom of the brae. There was no time for consultation; we fled, cowering behind the whin-bushes till we got round a turn in the hill, which, protecting us from any immediate shot, enabled us to run in freedom till we reached a hazel-wood, which having entered, we halted to take breath.

'We must not trust ourselves long here, Mr Witherspoon,' said I; 'let us go forward, for assuredly the blood-hounds will follow us in.'

Accordingly we went on; but it is not to be told what we suffered in passing through that wood; for the boughs and branches scourged us in the face, and the ground beneath our feet was marshy and deep, and grievously overspread with brambles that tore away our very flesh.

After enduring several hours of unspeakable suffering beneath those wild and unfrequented trees, we came to a little glen, down which a burn ran, and having stopped to consult, we resolved to go up rather than down the stream, in order that we might not be seen by the pursuers, whom we supposed would naturally keep the hill. But by this time our strength was in a manner utterly gone with fatigue, in so much, that Mr Witherspoon said it would be as well to fall into the hands of the enemy as to die in the wood. I however, encouraged him to be of good cheer; and it so happened, in that very moment of despair, that I observed a little cavern nook aneath a rock that overhung the burn, and thither I proposed we should wade and rest ourselves in the cave, trusting that Providence would be pleased to guide our persecutors into some other path. So we passed the water, and laid ourselves down under the shelter of the rock, where we soon after fell asleep.

CHAPTER TWENTY-EIGHT

We were graciously protected for the space of four hours, which we lay asleep under the rock. Mr Witherspoon was the first who awoke, and he sat watching beside me for some time, in great anxiety of spirit, as he afterwards told me; for the day was far spent, and the weather, as is often the custom in our climate, in the wane of the year, when the morning rises bright, had become coarse and drumly, threatening a rough night.

At last I awoke, and according to what we had previously counselled together, we went up the course of the burn, and so got out of that afflicting wood, and came to an open and wide moorland, over which we held our journeying westward, guided by the sun, that with a sickly eye was then cowering through the mist to his chamber ayont the hill.

But though all around us was a pathless scene of brown heather, here and there patched with the deceitful green of some perilous well-e'e; though the skies were sullen, and the bleak wind gusty, and every now and then a straggling flake of snow, strewed in our way from the invisible hand of the cloud, was a token of a coming drift, still a joyous encouragement was shed into our bosoms, and we saw in the wildness of the waste, and the omens of the storm, the blessed means with which Providence, in that forlorn epoch, was manifestly deterring the pursuer and the persecutor from tracking our defenceless flight. So we journeyed onward, discoursing of many dear and tender cares, often looking round, and listening when startled by the wind whispering to the heath and the waving fern, till the shadows of evening began to fall, and the dangers of the night season to darken around us.

When the snow hung on the heather like its own bells, we wished, but we feared to seek a place of shelter. Fain would we have gone back to the home for the fugitive, which we had found under the rock, but we knew not how to turn ourselves; for the lights of the moon and stars were deeply concealed in the dark folds of the wintry mantle with which the heavens were wrapt up. Our hearts then grew weary, and more than once I felt as if I was very willing to die.

Still we struggled on; and when it had been dark about an hour, we came to the skirts of a field, where the strips of the stubble through the snow showed us that some house or clachan could not be far off. We then consulted together, and resolved rather to make our place of rest in the lea of a stack, or an outhouse, than to apply to the dwelling; for the thought of the untimely end of harmless Nahum Chapelrig lay like clay on our hearts, and we could not but sorrow that, among the other woes of the vial of the prelatic dispensation, the hearts of the people of Scotland should be so turned against one another.

Accordingly going down the rigs, with as little interchange of discourse as could well be, we descried, by the schimmer of the snow, and a ghastly streak of moonlight that passed over the fields, a farm-steading, with several trees and stacks around it, and thither we softly directed our steps. Greatly, however, were we surprised and touched with distress, when, as we drew near, we saw that there was no light in the house, nor the sign of fire within, nor inhabitant about the place.

On reaching the door we found it open, and on entering in, every thing seemed as if it had been suddenly abandoned; but by the help of a pistol, which I had taken in the raid from one of Turner's disarmed troopers, and putting our trust in the protection we had so far enjoyed, I struck a light and kindled the fire, over which there was still hanging, on the swee, a kail-pot, wherein the family at the time of their flight had been preparing their dinner; and we judged by this token, and by the visible desertion, that we were in the house of some of God's people who had been suddenly scattered. Accordingly we scrupled not to help ourselves from the aumrie, knowing how readily they would pardon the freedom of need in a gospel minister, and a covenanted brother dejected with want and much suffering.

Having finished our supper, instead of sitting by the fire, as we at first proposed to do, we thought it would be safer to take the blankets from the beds and make our lair in the barn; so we accordingly retired thither, and lay down among some unthreshed corn that was lying ready on the floor for the flail.

But we were not well down when we heard the breathings of two persons near us. As there was no light, and Mr Witherspoon guessing by what we had seen, and by this concealment, that they must be some of the family, he began to pray aloud, thereby, without letting wot they were discovered, making them to understand what sort of guests we were. At the conclusion an old woman spoke to us, telling us dreadful things which a gang of soldiers had committed that afternoon; and her sad story was often interrupted by the moans of her daughter, the farmer's wife, who had suffered from the soldiers an unspeakable wrong.

'But what has become of our men, or where the bairns had fled, we know not, – we were baith demented by the outrage, and hid oursels here after it was owre late,' said that aged person, in a voice of settled grief, that was more sorrowful to hear than any lamentation could have been; and all the sacred exhortations that Mr Witherspoon could employ softened not the obduracy of her inward sorrowing over her daughter, the dishonoured wife. He, however, persuaded them to return with us to the house; for the enemy having been there, we thought it not likely he would that night come again. As for me, during the dismal recital, I could not speak. The eye of my spirit was fixt on the treasure I had left at home. Every word I heard was like the sting of an adder. My horrors and fears rose to such a pitch, that I could no longer master them. I started up and rushed to the door, as if it had been possible to arrest the imagined guilt of the persecutors in my own unprotected dwelling.

Mr Witherspoon followed me, thinking I had gone by myself, and caught me by the arm and entreated me to be composed, and to return with him into the house. But while he was thus kindly remonstrating with me, something took his foot, and he stumbled and fell to the ground. The accident served to check the frenzy of my thoughts for a moment, and I stooped down to help him up; but in the same instant he uttered a wild howl that made me start from him; and he then added, awfully—

'In the name of Heaven, what is this?'

'What is it?' said I, filled with unutterable dread.

'Hush, hush,' he replied as he rose, 'lest the poor women hear us;' and he lifted in his arms the body of a child of some four or five years old. I could endure no more; I thought the voices of my own innocents cried to me for help, and in the frenzy of the moment I left the godly man, and fled like a demoniac, not knowing which way I went.

A keen frost had succeeded the snow, and the wind blew piercingly cold; but the gloom had passed away. The starry eyes of the heavens were all wakefully bright, and the moon was moving along the fleecy edge of a cloud, like a lonely bark that navigates amidst the foaming perils of some dark inhospitable shore. At the time, however, I was in no frame of thought to note these things, but I know that such was then the aspect of that night; for as often yet, as the freezing wind sweeps over the fields strewed with snow, and the stars are shining vigilantly, and the moon hastily travels on the skirts of the cloud, the passion of that hour, at the sight thereof, revives in my spirit; and the mourning women, and the perished child in the arms of Mr Witherspoon, appear like palpable imagery before the eyes of my remembrance.

The speed with which I ran soon exhausted my strength. – I began to reflect on the unavailing zeal with which I was then hastening to the succour of those for whom my soul was suffering more than the tongue of the eloquent orator can express. – I stopped to collect my reason and my thoughts, which, I may well say, were scattered, like the wrack that drifts in the tempestuous air. – I considered, that I knew not a footstep of the road, that dangers surrounded me on all sides, and that the precipitation of my haste might draw me into accidents, whereby the very object would be lost which I was so eager to gain; and the storm within me abated, and the distraction of my bosom, which had so well nigh shipwrekt my understanding, was moderated, like the billows of the ocean when the blasts are gone by; so that, after I was some four or five miles away from yon house of martyrdom and mourning, a gracious dispensation of composure was poured into my spirit, and

I was thereby enabled to go forward in my journey with the circumspection so needful in that woful time.

But in proportion as my haste slackened, and the fiery violence of the fears subsided wherewith I was hurried on, the icy tooth of the winter grew feller in the bite, and I became in a manner almost helpless. The mind within me was as if the faculty of its thinking had been frozen up, and about the dawn of morning I walked in a willess manner, the blood in my veins not more benumbed in its course than was the fluency of my spirit in its power of resolution.

I had now, from the time that our covenanted host was scattered on Rullion-green, travelled many miles; and though like a bark drifting rudderless on the ocean tides, as the stream flows and the blast blows, I had held no constant course, still my progress had been havenward, in so much that about sunrise I found myself, I cannot well tell how, on the heights to the south of Castlemilk, and the city of Glasgow, with her goodly array of many towers glittering in the morning beams, lay in sight some few miles off on the north. I knew it not; but a herd that I fell in with on the hill told me what town it was, and the names of divers clachans, and the houses of men of substance in the lowlands before me.

Among others he pointed out to me Nether Pollock in the midst of a skirting of trees, the seat and castle of that godly and much-persecuted Christian and true Covenanter, Sir George Maxwell, the savour of whose piety was spread far and wide; for he had suffered much, both from sore imprisonment and the heavy fine of four thousand pounds imposed upon him, shortly after that conclave of Satan, Middleton's sederunt of the privy-council at Glasgow, where prelatic cruelty was brought to bed of her first-born, in that edict against the ministers at the beginning of the Persecution, whereof I have described the promulgation as it took place at Irvine.

Being then hungered and very cold, after discoursing with the poor herd, who was a simple stripling in the ignorance of innocence, I resolved to bend my way toward Nether Pollock, in the confident faith that the master thereof, having suffered so much himself, would know how to compassionate a persecuted brother. And often since I have thought that there was something higher than reason in the instinct of this confidence; for indeed, had I reasoned from what was commonly said – and, alas! owre truly – that the covenanted spirit was bent, if not broken, I would have feared to seek the gates of Sir George Maxwell, lest the love he had once borne to our cause had been converted, by his own sufferings and apprehensions, into dread or aversion. But I was encouraged of the spirit to proceed.

Just, however, as I parted from the herd, he cried after me, and pointed to a man coming up the hill at some distance, with a gun in his hand, and a bird-bag at his side, and two dogs at his heel, saying, 'Yon'er's Sir George Maxwell himsel ganging to the moors. Eh! but he has had his ain luck to fill his pock sae weel already.'

Whereupon I turned my steps toward Sir George, and, on approaching him, beseeched him to have compassion on a poor famished fugitive from the Pentlands.

He stopped, and looked at me in a most pitiful manner, and shook his head, and said, with a tender grief in his voice, 'It was a hasty business, and the worst of it no yet either heard nor over; but let us lose no time, for you are in much danger if you tarry so near to Glasgow, where Colonel Drummond came yesterday with a detachment of soldiers, and has already spread them over the country.'

In saying these words the worthy gentleman opened his bag, which, instead of being filled with game as the marvelling stripling had supposed, contained a store of provisions.

'I came not for pastime to the moor this morning,' said he, presenting to me something to eat, 'but because last night I heard that many of the outcasts had been seen yesterday lurking about thae hills, and as I could not give them harbour, nor even let them have any among my tenants, I have come out with some of my men, as it were to the shooting, in order to succour them. But we must not remain long together. Take with you what you may require, and go away quickly; and I counsel you not to take the road to Paisley, but to cross with what speed you can to the western parts of the shire, where, as the people have not been concerned in the raid, there's the less likelihood of Drummond sending any of his force in that direction.'

Accordingly, being thus plentifully supplied by the providence of that Worthy, my strength was wonderfully recruited, and my heart cheered. With many thanks I then hastened from him, praying that his private charitable intents might bring him into no trouble. And surely it was a thing hallowing to the affections of the afflicted Scottish nation to meet with such Christian fellowship. For to the perpetual renown of many honourable West-country families be it spoken, both master and men were daily in the moors at that time succouring the persecuted, like the ravens that fed Elijah in the wilderness.

After parting from Sir George Maxwell I continued to bend my course straight westward, and having crossed the road from Glasgow to Paisley, I directed my steps to the hillier parts of the country, being minded, according to the suggestions of that excellent person, to find my way by the coast side into the shire of Ayr. But though my anxiety concerning my family was now sharpened as it were with the anguish of fire, I began to reason with myself on the jeopardy I might bring upon them, were I to return while the pursuit was so fierce; and in the end I came to the determination only to seek to know how it fared with them, and what had become of my brother in the battle, trusting that in due season the Lord would mitigate the ire, and the cruelty that was let loose on all those who had joined in the Protestation and renewed the Covenant at Lanerk.

Towards the afternoon I found myself among the solitudes of the Renfrewshire moors. Save at times the melancholious note of the peeseweep, neither the sound nor the voice of any living thing was heard there. Being then wearied in all my limbs, and willingly disposed to sleep, I laid myself down on a green hollow on the banks of the Gryffe, where the sun shone with a pleasing warmth for so late a period of the year. I was not, however, many minutes stretched on the grass when I heard a shrill whistle of some one nigh at hand, and presently also the barking of a dog. From the kindly experience I had received of Sir George Maxwell's care this occasioned at first no alarm; but on looking up I beheld at some distance three soldiers with a dog, on the other side of the river.

Near the spot where I lay there was a cloven rock overspread with brambles and slae-bushes. It seemed to me as if the cleft had been prepared on purpose by Providence for a hiding-place. I crept into it, and, forgetting Him by whom I was protected, I trembled with a base fear. But in that very moment He at once rebuked my infirmity, and gave me a singular assurance of His holy wardenship, by causing an adder to come towards me from the roots of the bushes, as if to force me to flee into the view of the pursuers. Just, however, as in my horror I was on the point of doing so, the reptile looked at me with its glittering eyes, and then suddenly leapt away into the brake; – at the same moment a hare was raised by the dog, and the soldiers following it with shouts and halloes, were soon carried, by the impetuosity of the natural incitement which man has for the chace, far from the spot, and out of sight.

This adventure had for a time the effect of rousing me from out the weariness with which I had been oppressed, and I rose and continued my course westward, over the hills, till I came in sight of the Shaws-water, – the stream of which I followed for more than a mile with a beating heart; for the valley through which it flows is bare and open, and had any of the persecutors been then on the neighbouring hills, I must have soon been seen; but gradually my thoughts became more composed, and the terrors of the poor hunted creature again became changed into confidence and hope.

In this renewed spirit I slackened my pace, and seeing, at a short distance down the stream, before me a tree laid across for a bridge, I was comforted with the persuasion that some farm-town could not be far off, so I resolved to linger about till the gloaming, and then to follow the path which led over the bridge. For, not knowing how the inhabitants in those parts stood inclined in their consciences, I was doubtful to trust myself in their power until I had made some espionage. Accordingly, as the sun was still above the hills, I kept the hollowest track by the river's brink, and went down its course for some little time, till I arrived where the hills come forward into the valley; then I climbed up a steep hazel bank, and sat down to rest myself on an open green plot on the brow, where a gentle west wind shook the boughs around me, as if the silent spirits of the solitude were slowly passing by.

In this place I had not been long when I heard, as it were not far off, a sullen roar of falling waters rising hoarsely with the breeze, and listening again, another sound came solemnly mingled with it, which I had soon the delight to discover was the holy harmony of worship, and to my ears it was as the first sound of the rushing water which Moses brought from the rock to those of the thirsty Israelites, and I for some time so ravished with joy that I could not move from the spot where I was sitting.

At last the sweet melody of the psalm died away, and I arose and went towards the airt from which it had come; but as I advanced, the noise of the roaring waters grew louder and deeper, till they were as the breaking of the summer waves along the Ardrossan shore, and presently I found myself on the brink of a cliff, over which the river

tumbled into a rugged chasm, where the rocks were skirted
with leafless brambles and hazel, and garmented with ivy.

On a green sloping bank, at a short distance below the
waterfall, screened by the rocks and trees on the one side,
and by the rising ground on the other, about thirty of the
Lord's flock, old and young, were seated around the feet
of an aged grey-haired man, who was preaching to them,
– his left hand resting on his staff, – his right was raised in
exhortation, – and a Bible lay on the ground beside him.

I stood for the space of a minute looking at the mournful
yet edifying sight, – mournful it was, to think how God's
people were so afflicted, that they durst not do their
Heavenly King homage but in secrecy, – and edifying,
that their constancy was of such an enduring nature that
persecution served but to test it, as fire does the purity
of gold.

As I was so standing on the rock above the linn, the
preacher happened to lift his eyes towards me, and the
hearers, who were looking at him, turned round, and hastily
rising, began to scatter and flee away. I attempted to cry
to them not to be afraid, but the sound of the cataract
drowned my voice. I then ran as swiftly as I could towards
the spot of worship, and reached the top of the sloping
bank just as a young man was assisting Mr Swinton to
mount a horse which stood ready saddled tied to a tree;
for the preacher was no other than that godly man; but
the courteous reader must from his own kind heart supply
what passed at our meeting.

Fain he was at that time to have gone no farther on
with the exercise, and to have asked many questions
of me concerning the expedition to the Pentlands; but
I importuned him to continue his blessed work, for I
longed to taste the sweet water of life once more from so
hallowed a fountain; and, moreover, there was a woman
with a baby at her bosom, which she had brought to be
baptized from a neighbouring farm, called the Killochenn,
– and a young couple of a composed and sober aspect, from
the Back-o'-the-world, waiting to be joined together, with
his blessing, in marriage.

When he had closed his sermon and done these things, I

went with him, walking at the side of his horse, discoursing of our many grievous anxieties; and he told me that, after being taken to Glasgow and confined in prison there like a malefactor for thirteen days, he had been examined by the Bishop's court, and through the mediation of one of the magistrates, a friend of his own, who had a soft word to say with the Bishop, he was set free with only a menace, and an admonishment not to go within twenty miles of his own parish, under pain of being dealt with according to the edict.

Conversing in this manner, and followed by divers of those who had been solaced with his preaching, for the most part pious folk belonging to the town of Inverkip, we came to a bridge over the river.

'Here, Ringan,' said he, 'we must part for the present, for it is not meet to create suspicion. There are many of the faithful, no doubt, in thir parts, but it's no to be denied that there are likewise goats among the sheep. The Lady of Dunrod, where I am now going, is, without question, a precious vessel free of crack or flaw, but the Laird is of a courtly compliancy, and their neighbour, Carswell, she tells me, is a man of the dourest idolatry, his mother having been a papistical woman, and his father, through all the time of the first King Charles, an eydent ettler for preferment.'

So we then parted, he going his way to Dunrod Castle, and one of the hearers, a farmer hard by, offering me shelter for the night, I went with him.

The decent, thoughtful, elderly man, who so kindly invited me to his house, was by name called Gideon Kemp; and as we were going towards it together, he told me of divers things that worthy Mr Swinton had not time to do; among the rest, that the preaching I had fallen in with at the linn, which should thenceforth be called the Covenanters' Linn, was the first taste of gospel-fother that the scattered sheep of those parts had tasted for more than eight months.

'What's to come out o' a' this oppression,' said he, 'is wonderful to think o'. It's no in the power of nature that ony government or earthly institution framed by the wit and will o' man can withstand a whole people. The prelates may persecute, and the King's power may back their iniquities, but the day and the hour cannot be far off when both the power and the persecutors will be set at naught, and the sense of what is needful and right, no what is fantastical and arbitrary, govern again in the councils of this realm. I say not this in the boast of prediction and prophecy, but as a thing that must come to pass; for no man can say, that the peaceful worshipping according to the Word is either a sin, a shame, or an offence against reason; but the extortioning of fines, and the desolation of families, for attending the same, is manifestly guilt of a dark dye, and the Judge of Righteousness will avenge it.'

As we were thus walking sedately towards his dwelling, I observed and pointed out to him a lassie coming running towards us. It was his daughter; and when she came near, panting and out of breath with her haste, she said—

'O, father, ye maunna gang hame; – twa of Carswell's men hae been speering for you, and they had swords and guns. They're o'er the hill to the linn, for wee Willie telt them ye were gane there to a preaching.'

'This comes,' said the afflicted Gideon, 'of speaking of secret things before bairns; wha could hae thought, that a creature no four years old would have been an instrument of discovery? – It'ill no be safe now for you to come hame wi' me, which I'm wae for, as ye're sae sorely weary't; but there's a frien o' ours that lives ayont the Holmstone-hill, aboon the auld kirk; I'll convey you thither, and she'll gi'e you a shelter for the night.'

So we turned back, and again crossed the bridge before spoken of, and held our course toward the house of Gideon Kemp's wife's stepmother. But it was not ordain't that I was yet to enjoy the protection of a raftered dwelling; for just as we came to the Daff-burn, down the glen of which my godly guide was mindet to conduct me, as being a less observable way than the open road, he saw one of Ardgowan's men coming towards us, and that family being of the progeny of the Stewarts, were inclined to the prelatic side.

'Hide yoursel,' said he, 'among the bushes.'

And I den't myself in a nook of the glen, where I overheard what passed.

'I thought, Gideon,' said the lad to him, 'that ye would hae been at the conventicle this afternoon. We hae heard o't a'; and Carswell has sworn that he'll hae baith doited Swinton and Dunrod's leddy at Glasgow afore the morn, or he'll mak a tawnle o' her tower.'

'Carswell shouldna crack sae croose,' replied Gideon Kemp; 'for though his castle stands proud in the green valley, the time may yet come when horses and carts will be driven through his ha', and the foul toad and the cauld snail be the only visitors around the unblest hearth o' Carswell.'

The way in which that gifted man said these words made my heart dinle; but I hae lived to hear that the spirit of prophecy was assuredly in them: for, since the Revolution, Carswell's family has gone all to drift, and his house become a wastege; – folk say, a new road that's talked o' between Inverkip and Greenock is to go through the very middle o't, and so mak it an awful monument of what awaits and will betide all those who have no mercy on their fellow-creatures, and would exalt themselves by abetting the strength of the godless and the wrath of the oppressors.

Ardgowan's man was daunted by the words of Gideon Kemp, and replied in a subdued manner, 'It's really a melancholious thing to think that folk should hae gane so wud about ministers and religion; – but tak care of yoursel, Gideon, for a party of soldiers hae come the day to Cartsdyke to take up ony of the Rullion-green rebels that hae fled to thir parts, and they catcht, I hear, in a public in the Stenners, three men, and have sent them to Glasgow to be hanged.'

I verily thought my heart would at this have leapt out of my bosom.

'Surely,' replied Gideon Kemp, 'the wrath of government is no so unquenchable, that a' the misguided folk concernt in the rising are doom't to die. But hae ye heard the names of the prisoners, or where they belong to?'

'They're o' the shire o' Ayr, somewhere frae the skirts o' Irvine or Kilwinning; and I was likewise told their names, but they're no of a familiarity easy to be remembered.'

The horror which fell upon me at hearing this made me forget my own peril, and I sprung out of the place of my concealment, and cried—

'Do you ken if any of them was of the name of Gilhaize?'

Ardgowan's man was astounded at seeing me standing before him in so instanter a manner, and before making any response, he looked at Gideon Kemp with a jealous and troubled eye.

'Nay,' said I, 'you shall deal honestly with me, and from this spot you shall not depart till you have promist to use nae scaith to this worthy man.' So I took hold of him by the skirts of his coat, and added, – 'Ye're in the hands of one that tribulation has made desperate. I, too, am a rebel, as ye say, from Rullion-green, and my life is forfeited to the ravenous desires of those who made the laws that have created our offence. But fear no wrong, if you have aught of Christian compassion in you. Was Gilhaize the name of any of the prisoners?'

'I'll no swear't,' was his answer; 'but I think it was

something like that; – one of them, I think, they called Finnie.'

'Robin Finnie!' cried I, dropping his coat, 'he was wi' my brother; – I canna doubt it;' and the thought of their fate flooded my heart, and the tears flowed from my eyes.

The better nature of Ardgowan's man was moved at the sight of my distress, and he said to Gideon Kemp—

'Ye needna be fear't, Gideon; I hope ye ken mair o' me than to think I would betray either friend or acquaintance. But gang na' to the toun, for a' yon 'er's in a state o' unco wi' the news o' what's been doing the day at Cartsdyke, and every body's in the hourly dread and fear o' some o' the black-cuffs coming to devour them.'

'That's spoken like yoursel', Johnnie Jamieson,' said Gideon Kemp; 'but this poor man,' meaning me, 'has had a day o' weary travel among the moors, and is greatly in need of refreshment and a place of rest. When the sword, Johnnie, is in the hand, it's an honourable thing to deal stoutly wi' the foe; but when forlorn and dejectit, and more houseless than the beasts of the field, he's no longer an adversary, but a man that we're bound by the laws of God and nature to help.'

Jamieson remained for a short space in a dubious manner, and looking mildly toward me, he said, 'Gang you your ways, Gideon Kemp, and I'll ne'er say I saw you; and let your friend den himsel in the glen, and trust me: naebody in a' Inverkip will jealouse that ony of our house would help or harbour a covenanted rebel; so I'll can bring him to some place o' succour in the gloaming, where he'll be safer than he could wi' you.'

Troubled and sorrowful as I was, I could not but observe the look of soul-searching scrutiny that Gideon Kemp cast at Jamieson, who himself was sensible of his mistrust, for he replied—

'Dinna misdoot me, Gideon Kemp; I would sooner put my right hand in the fire, and burn it to a cinder, than harm the hair of a man that was in my power.'

'And I'll believe you,' said I; 'so guide me wheresoever you will.'

'Ye'll never thrive, Johnnie Jamieson,' added honest Gideon, 'if ye're no sincere in this trust.'

So after some little further communing, the worthy farmer left us, and I followed Jamieson down the Daff-burn, till we came to a mill that stood in the hollow of the glen, the wheel whereof was happing in the water with a pleasant and peaceful din that sounded consolatory to my hearing after the solitudes, the storms, and the accidents I had met with.

'Bide you here,' said Jamieson; 'the gudeman's ane o' your folk, but his wife's a thought camstrarie at times, and before I tak you into the mill I maun look that she's no there.'

So he hastened forward, and going to the door, went in, leaving me standing at the sluice of the mill-lade, where, however, I had not occasion to wait long, for presently he came out, and beckoned to me with his hand to come quickly.

CHAPTER THIRTY-TWO

Sauners Paton, as the miller was called, received me in a kindly manner, saying to Jamieson—

'I aye thought, Johnnie, that some day ye would get a cast o' grace, and the Lord has been bountiful to you at last, in putting it in your power to be aiding in such a Samaritan work. But,' he added, turning to me, 'it's no just in my power to do for you what I could wis; for, to keep peace in the house, I'm at times, like many other married men, obligated to let the gudewife tak her ain way; for which reason, I doubt ye'll hae to mak your bed here in the mill.'

While he was thus speaking, we heard the tongue of Mrs Paton ringing like a bell.

'For Heaven's sake, Johnnie Jamieson,' cried the miller, 'gang out and stop her frae coming hither till I get the poor man hidden in the loft.'

Jamieson ran out, leaving us together, and the miller placing a ladder, I mounted up into the loft, where he spread sacks for a bed to me, and told me to lie quiet, and in the dusk he would bring me something to eat. But before he had well descended, and removed the ladder from the trap-door, in came his wife.

'Noo, Sauners Paton,' she exclaimed, 'ye see what I hae aye prophesied to you is fast coming to pass. The King's forces are at Cartsdyke, and they'll be here the morn, and what's to come o' you then, wi' your covenanted havers? But, Sauners Paton, I hae ae thing to tell ye, and that's no twa; ye'll this night flit your camp; ye'll tak to the hills, as I'm a living woman, and no bide to be hang't at your ain door, and to get your right hand chappit aff, and sent to Lanerk for a show, as they say is done and doing wi' a' the Covenanters.'

'Naebody, Kate, will meddle wi' me, dinna ye be fear't,' replied the miller; 'I hae done nae ill, but patiently follow't my calling at home, so what hae I to dread?'

'Did na ye sign the remonstrance to the laird against the curate's coming; ca' ye that naething? Ye'll to the caves this night, Sauners Paton, if the life bide in your body. What a sight it would be to me to see you put to death, and maybe to fin a sword of cauld iron running through my ain body, for being colleague wi' you; for ye ken that it's the law now to mak wives respondable for their gudemen.'

'Kate Warden,' replied the miller, with a sedate voice; 'in sma' things I hae ne'er set mysel vera obdoorately against you.'

'Na! if I e'er heard the like o' that!' exclaimed Mrs Paton: 'A crossgraint man, that has just been as a Covenant and Remonstrance to happiness, submitting himsel in no manner o' way, either to me or those in authority over us, to talk o' sma' things! Sauners Paton, ye're a born rebel to your King, and kintra, and wife. But this night I'll put it out of your power to rebel on me. Stop the mill, Sauners Paton, and come out, and tak the door on your back; I hae owre meikle regard for you to let you bide in jeopardy ony langer here.'

'Consider,' said Sauners, a little dourly, as if he meditated rebellion, 'that this is the season of December; and where would ye hae me to gang in sic a night?'

'A grave in the kirk-yard's caulder than a tramp on the hills. My jo, ye'll hae to conform; for, positeevely, Sauners Paton, I'm positive, and for this night, till the blast has blawn by, ye'll hae to seek a refuge out o' the reach of the troopers' spear. – Hae ye stoppit the mill?'

The mistress was of so propugnacious a temper, that the poor man saw no better for't than to yield obedience so far, as to pull the string that turned off the water of the mill-lade from the wheel.

'Noo,' said he, 'to pleasure you, Kate, I hae stoppit the mill, and to pleasure me, I hope ye'll consent to stop your tongue; for, to be plain wi' you, frae my ain house I'll no gang this night; and ye shall hae't since ye will hae't, I hae a reason of my ain for biding at hame, and at hame I will bide; – na, what's mair, Kate, it's a reason that I'll no tell to you.'

'Dear pity me, Sauners Paton!' cried his wife; 'ye're surely grown o' late an unco reasonable man. But Leddy Stuart's quadrooped bird they ca' a parrot, can come o'er and o'er again ony word as weel as you can do reason; but reason here or reason there, I'll ne'er consent to let you stay to be put to the sword before my een; so come out o' the mill and lock the door.'

To this the honest man made no immediate answer; but, after a short silence, he said—

'Kate, my queen, I'll no say that what ye say is far wrang; it may be as weel for me to tak a dauner to the top o' Dunrod; but some providing should be made for a sojourn a' night in the wilderness. The sun has been set a lucky hour, and ye may as weel get the supper ready, and a creel wi' some vivers prepared.'

'Noo, that's like yoursel, Sauners Paton,' replied his wife; 'and surely my endeavour shall not be wanting to mak you conforttable.'

At these words Jamieson came also into the mill, and said, 'I hope, miller, the wife has gotten you persuaded o' your danger, and that ye'll conform to her kind wishes.' By which I discernt, that he had purposely egget her on to urge her gudeman to take the moors for the advantage of me.

'O, aye,' replied the miller; 'I could na but be consenting, poor queen, to lighten her anxieties; and though for a season,' he added, in a way that I well understood, 'the eyes above may be closed in slumber, a watch will be set to gi'e the signal when it's time to be up and ready; therefore let us go into the house, and cause no further molestation here.'

The three then retired, and, comforted by the words of this friendly mystery, I confided myself to the care of the defenceless sleeper's ever-wakeful Sentinel, and for several hours enjoyed a refreshing oblivion from all my troubles and fears.

Considering the fatigue I had undergone for so many days and nights together, my slumber might have been prolonged perhaps till morning, but the worthy miller, who withstood the urgency of his terrified wife to depart till he thought I was rested, soon after the moon rose came into the mill and wakened me to make ready for the road. So I left my couch in the loft, and came down to him; and he conducted me a little way from the house, where, bidding me wait, he went back, and speedily returned with a small basket in his hand of the stores which the mistress had provided for himself.

Having put the handle into my hand, he led me down to a steep shoulder of a precipice nigh the sea-shore, where, telling me to follow the path along the bottom of the hills, he shook me with a brotherly affection by the hand, and bade me farewell, – saying, in a jocose manner, to lighten the heaviness with which he saw my spirit was oppressed, – that the gudewife would make baith him and Johnnie Jamieson suffer in the body for the fright she had gotten. 'For ye should ken,' said he, 'that the terror she was in was a' bred o' Johnnie's pawkerie. He knew that she was aye in a dread that I would be laid hands on ever since I signed the remonstrance to the laird; and Johnnie thought, that if he could get her to send me out provided for the hills, we would find a way to make the provision yours. So, gude be wi' you, and dinna be overly down-hearted, when ye see how wonderfully ye are ta'en care o'.'

Being thus cherished, cheered, and exhorted, by the worthy miller of Inverkip, I went on my way with a sense of renewed hope dawning upon my heart. The night was frosty, but clear, and the rippling of the sea glittered as with a sparkling of gladness in the beams of the moon, then walking in the fullness of her beauty over those fields of holiness whose perennial flowers are the everlasting stars. But though for a little while my soul partook of the blessed tranquillity of the night, I had not travelled far when the heaven of my thoughts was overcast. Grief for my brother in the hands of the oppressors, and anxiety for the treasures of my hearth, whose dangers were doubtless increased by the part I had taken in the raid, clouded my reason with many fearful auguries and doleful anticipations. All care for my own safety was lost in those overwhelming reflections, in so much, that when the morning air breathed upon me as I reached the brow of Kilbride Hill, had I been then questioned as to the manner I had come there, verily I could have given no account, for I saw not, neither did I hear, for many miles, aught, but only the dismal tragedies with which busy imagination rent my heart with affliction, and flooded my eyes with the gushing streams of a softer sorrow.

But though my journey was a continued experience of inward suffering. I met with no cause of dread, till I was within sight of Kilwinning. Having purposed not to go home until I should learn what had taken place in my absence, I turned aside to the house of an acquaintance, one William Brekenrig, a covenanted Christian, to inquire, and to rest myself till the evening. Scarcely, however, had I entered on the path that led to his door, when a misgiving of mind fell upon me, and I halted and looked to see if all about the mailing was in its wonted state. His cattle were on the stubble – the smoke stood over the lum-head in the lown of the morning – the plough lay unyoked on the croft, but it had been lately used, and the furrows of part of a rig were newly turned. Still there was a something that sent solemnity and coldness into my soul. I saw nobody about the farm, which at that time of the day was strange and unaccountable; nevertheless I hastened forward, and coming to a parkyett, I saw my old friend leaning over it with his head towards me. I called to him by name, but he heeded me not; I ran to him and touched him, but he was dead.

The ground around where he had rested himself and expired was covered with his blood; and it was plain he had not been shot long, for he was warm, and the stream still trickled from the wound in his side.

I have no words to tell what I felt at the sight of this woful murder; but I ran for help to the house; and just as I turned the corner of the barn, two soldiers met me, and I became their prisoner.

One of them was a ruthless reprobate, who wanted to put me to death; but the other beggit my life: at the moment, however, my spirit was as it were in the midst of thunders and a whirlwind.

They took from me my pistols and my grandfather's sword, and I could not speak; they tied my hands behind me with a cutting string, and I thought it was a dream. The air I breathed was as suffocating as sulphur; I gasped with the sandy thirst of the burning desert, and my throat was as the drowth of the parched earth in the wilderness of Kedar.

Soon after this other soldiers came from another farm, where they had been committing similar outrages, and they laughed and were merry as they rehearsed their exploits of guilt. They taunted me and plucked me by the lip; but their boasting of what they had done flashed more fiercely over my spirit than even these indignities, and I inwardly chided the slow anger of the mysterious Heavens for permitting the rage of those agents of the apostate James Sharp and his compeers, whom a mansworn king had so cruelly dressed with his authority.

But even in the midst of these repinings and bitter breathings, it was whispered into the ears of my understanding, as with the voice of a seraph, that the Lord in all things moveth according to his established laws; and I was comforted to think, that in the enormities whereof I was a witness and partaker, there was a tempering of the hearts of the people, that they might become as swords of steel, to work out the deliverance of the land from the bloody methods of prelatic and arbitrary domination; in so much, that when the soldiers prepared to return to their quarters in Irvine, I walked with them – their captive, it is true; but my steps were firm, and they marvelled to one another at the proudness of my tread.

There was at the time a general sorrowing throughout the country, at the avenging visitations wherewith all those who had been in the raid, or who had harboured the fugitives, were visited. Hundreds, that sympathized with the sufferings of their friends, flocked to the town to learn who had been taken, and who were put to death or reserved for punishment. The crowd came pressing around as I was conducted up the gait to the tolbooth; the women wept, but the men looked doure, and the children wondered whatfor an honest man should be brought to punishment. Some, who knew me, cheered me by name to keep a stout heart; and the soldiers grew fear't for a rescue, and gurled at the crowd for closing so closely upon us.

As I was ascending the tolbooth-stair, I heard a shriek; and I looked round and beheld Michael, my first-born, a stripling then only twelve years old, amidst the crowd, stretching out his hands and crying, 'O, my father, my father!'

I halted for a moment, and the soldiers seemed to thaw with compassion; but my hands were tied, – I was captive on the threshold of the dungeon, and I could only shut my eyes and bid the stern agents of the persecutors go on. Still the cry of my distracted child knelled in my ear, and my agony grew to such a pitch, that I flew forward up the steps, and, in the dismal vaults within, sought refuge from the misery of my child.

Volume III

I was conducted into a straight and dark chamber, and the cord wherewith my hands were bound was untied, and a shackle put upon my right wrist; the flesh of my left was so galled with the cord, that the jailor was softened at the sight, and from the humanity of his own nature, refrained from placing the iron on it, lest the rust should fester the quick wound.

Then I was left alone in the gloomy solitude of the prison-room, and the ponderous doors were shut upon me, and the harsh bolts driven with a horrid grating noise, that caused my very bones to dinle. But even in that dreadful hour an unspeakable consolation came with the freshness of a breathing of the airs of paradise to my soul. Methought a wonderful light shone around me, that I heard melodious voices bidding me be of good cheer, and that a vision of my saintly grandfather, in the glorious vestments of his heavenly attire, stood before me, and smiled upon me with that holy comeliness of countenance which has made his image in my remembrance ever that of the most venerable of men; so that, in the very depth of what I thought would have been the pit of despair, I had a delightful taste of those blessed experiences of divine aid, by which the holy martyrs were sustained in the hours of trial, and cheered amidst the torments in which they sealed the truth of their testimony.

After the favour of that sweet and celestial encouragement, I laid myself down on a pallet in the corner of the room, and a gracious sleep descended upon my eyelids, and steeped the sense and memory of my griefs in forgetfulness. When I awoke the day was far spent, and the light through the iron stainchers of the little window showed that the shadows of the twilight were darkening over the world. I raised myself on my elbow, and listened to the murmur of the multitude that I heard still lingering around the prison; and sometimes I thought that I discovered the voice of a friend.

In that situation, and thinking of all those dear cares which filled my heart with tenderness and fear, and of the agonizing grief of my little boy, the sound of whose cries still echoed in my bosom, I rose upon my knees and committed myself entirely to the custody of Him that can give the light of liberty to the captive even in the gloom of the dungeon. And when I had done so I again prepared to lay myself on the ground; but a rustle in the darkness of the room drew my attention, and in the same moment a kind hand was laid on mine.

'Sarah Lochrig,' said I, for I knew my wife's gentle pressure, – 'How is it that you are with me in this doleful place? How found you entrance, and I not hear you come in?'

But before she had time to make any answer, another's fond arms were round my neck, and my affectionate young Michael wept upon my shoulder.

Bear with me, courteous reader, when I think of those things, – that wife and that child, and all that I loved so fondly, are no more! But it is not meet that I should yet tell how my spirit was turned into iron and my heart into stone. Therefore will I still endeavour to relate, as with the equanimity of one that writes but of indifferent things, what further ensued during the thirteen days of my captivity.

Sarah Lochrig, with the mildness of her benign voice, when we had mingled a few tears, told me, that after I went to Galloway with Martha Swinton, she had been moved by our neighbours to come with our children into the town, as being safer for a lanerly woman and a family left without its head; and a providential thing it was that she had done so; for on the very night that my brother came off with the men of the parish to join us, as I have noted down in its proper place, a gang of dragoons plundered both his house and mine; and but that our treasures had been time-ously removed, his family having also gone that day into Kilmarnock, the outrages might have been unspeakable.

We then had some household discourse, anent what was to be done in the event of things coming to the worst with me; and it was an admiration to hear with what constancy of reason, and the gifts of a supported judgment, that gospel-hearted woman spoke of what she would do with her children, if it was the Lord's pleasure to honour me with the crown of martyrdom.

'But,' said she, 'I hae an assurance within that some great thing is yet in store for you, though the hope be clouded with a doubt that I'll no be spar't to see it, and therefore let us not despond at this time, but use the means that Providence may afford to effect your deliverance.'

While we were thus conversing together the doors of the prison-room were opened, and a man was let in who had a cruisie in the one hand and a basket in the other. He was lean and pale-faced, bordering on forty years, and of a melancholy complexion; his eye was quick, deep set, and a thought wild; his long hair was carefully combed smooth, and his apparel was singularly well composed for a person of his degree.

Having set down the lamp on the floor, he came in a very reverential manner towards where I was sitting, with my right hand fettered to the ground, between Sarah Lochrig and Michael our son, and he said, with a remarkable and gentle simplicity of voice, in the Highland accent, that he had been requested by a righteous woman, Provost Reid's wife, to bring me a bottle of cordial wine and some little matters, that I might require for bodily consolation.

'It's that godly creature, Willie Sutherland the hangman,' said my wife. 'Though Providence has dealt hardly with him, poor man, in this life, every body says he has gotten arles of a servitude in glory hereafter.'

When he had placed the basket at the knees of Michael, he retired to a corner of the room, and stood in the shadow, with his face turned towards the wall, saying, 'I'm concern't that it's no in my power to leave you to yoursels till Mungo Robeson come back, for he has lockit me in, but I'll no hearken to what you may say;' and there was a modesty of manner in the way that he said this, which made me think it not possible he could be of so base a vocation as

the public executioner, and I whispered my opinion of him
to Sarah Lochrig. It was, however, the case; and verily in
the life and conduct of that simple and pious man there was
a manifestation of the truth, that to him whom the Lord
favours it signifieth not whatsoever his earthly condition
may be.

After I had partaken with my wife and son of some
refreshment which they had brought with them, and tasted
of the wine that Provost Reid's lady had sent, we heard
the bolts of the door drawn, and the clanking of keys, at
which Willie Sutherland came forward from the corner
where he had stood during the whole time, and lifting
the lamp from the floor, and wetting his fore-finger with
spittle as he did so, he trimmed the wick, and said, 'The
time's come when a' persons not prisoners must depart
forth the tolbooth for the night; but, Master Gilhaize, be
none discomforted thereat, your wife and your little one
will come back in the morning, and your lot is a lot of
pleasure; for is it not written in the book of Ecclesiastes,
fourth and eighth, "There is one alone, and there is not a
second; yea, he hath neither child nor brother?" and such
an one am I.'

The inner door was thrown open, and Mungo Robeson,
looking in, said, 'I'm wae to molest you, but ye'll hae to
come out, Mrs Gilhaize.' So that night we were separated;
and when Sarah Lochrig was gone, I could not but offer
thanksgiving that my lines had fallen in so pleasant a
place, compared with the fate of my poor brother, suffering
among strangers in the doleful prison of Glasgow, under
the ravenous eyes of the prelate of that city, then scarcely
less hungry for the bodies of the faithful and the true, than
even the apostate James Sharp himself.

The deep sleep into which I had fallen when Sarah Lochrig and my son were admitted to see me, and during the season of which they had sat in silence beside me till revived nature again unsealed my eyes, was so refreshing, that after they were gone away I was enabled to consider my condition with a composed mind, and free from the heats of passion and anxiety wherewith I had previously been so greatly tossed. And calling to mind all that had taken place, and the ruthless revenge with which the cruel prelates were actuated, I saw, as it were written in a book, that for my part and conduct I was doomed to die. I felt not, however, the sense of guilt in my conscience; and I said to myself, that this sore thing ought not to be, and that, as an innocent man and the head of a family, I was obligated by all expedient ways to escape, if it were possible, from the grasps of the tyranny. So from that time, the first night of my imprisonment, I set myself to devise the means of working out my deliverance; and I was not long without an encouraging glimmer of hope.

It seemed to me, that in the piety and simplicity of Willie Sutherland, instruments were given by which I might break through the walls of my prison; and accordingly, when he next morning came in to see me, I failed not to try their edge. I entered into discourse with him, and told him of many things which I have recorded in this book, and so won upon his confidence and the singleness of his heart, that he shed tears of grief at the thought of so many blameless men being ordained to an untimely end.

'It has pleased God,' said he, 'to make me as it were a leper and an excommunicant in this world, by the constraints of a low estate, and without any fault of mine. But for this temporal ignominy, He will, in His own good

305

time, bestow an exceeding great reward; – and though I
may be called on to fulfil the work of the persecutors, it
shall yet be seen of me, that I will abide by the integrity
of my faith, and that, poor despised hangman as I am, I
have a conscience that will not brook a task of iniquity,
whatsoever the laws of man may determine, or the King's
judges decree.'

I was, as it were, rebuked by this proud religious
declaration, and I gently inquired how it was that he
came to fall into a condition so rejected of the world.

'Deed, sir,' said he, 'my tale is easy told. My parents
were very poor needful people in Strathnavar, and no able
to keep me; and it happened that, being cast on the world,
I became a herd, and year by year, having a desire to learn
the Lowland tongue, I got in that way as far as Paisley,
where I fell into extreme want and was almost famished;
for the master that I served there being in debt, ran away,
by which cause I lost my penny-fee, and was obligated to
beg my bread. At that time many worthy folk in the shire of
Renfrew having suffered great molestation from witchcraft,
divers malignant women, suspectit of that black art, were
brought to judgment, and one of them being found guilty,
was condemned to die. But no executioner being in the
town, I was engaged, by the scriptural counsel of some
honest men, who quoted to me the text, "Suffer not a
witch to live," to fulfil the sentence of the law. After that I
bought a Question-book, having a mind to learn to read,
that I might gain some knowledge of THE WORD. Finding,
however, the people of Paisley scorn at my company, so that
none would give me a lesson, I came about five years since
to Irvine, where the folk are more charitable; and here I act
the part of an executioner when there is any malefactor to
put to death. But my Bible has instructed me, that I ought
not to execute any save such as deserve to die; so that, if ye
should be condemned, as like is you will be, my conscience
will ne'er allow me to execute you, for I see you are a
Christian man.'

I was moved with a tender pity by the tale of the simple
creature; but a strong necessity was upon me, and it was
needful that I should make use of his honesty to help

me out of prison. So I spoke still more kindly to him, lamenting my sad estate, and that in the little time I had in all likelihood to live, the rigour of the jailor would allow but little intercourse with my family, wishing some compassionate Christian friend would intercede with him in order that my wife and children, if not permitted to bide all night, might be allowed to remain with me as long and as late as possible.

The pious creature said that he would do for me in that respect all in his power, and that, as Mungo Robeson was a sober man, and aye wanted to go home early to his family, he would bide in the tolbooth to let out my wife, though it should be till ten o'clock at night, – 'for,' said he piteously, 'I hae nae family to care about.'

Accordingly he so set himself, that Mungo Robeson consented to leave the keys of the tolbooth with him; and for several nights every thing was so managed that he had no reason to suspect what my wife and I were plotting; for he being of a modest and retiring nature, never spoke to her when she parted from me, save when she thanked him as he let her out; and that she did not do every night, lest it should grow into a habit of expectation with him, and cause him to remark when the civility was omitted.

In the meantime all things being concerted between us, through the mean of a friend a cart was got in readiness, loaded with seemingly a hogget of tobacco and grocery wares, but the hogget was empty and loose in the head.

This was all settled by the nineteenth of December; on the twenty-fourth of the month the Commissioners appointed to try the Covenanters in the prisons throughout the shire of Ayr were to open their court at Ayr, and I was, by all who knew of me, regarded in a manner as a dead man. On the night of the twentieth, however, shortly before ten o'clock, James Gottera, our friend, came with the cart in at the town-head port, and in going down the gait stopped, as had been agreed, to give his beast a drink at the trough of the cross-well, opposite the tolbooth-stair foot.

When the clock struck ten, the time appointed, I was ready dressed in my wife's apparel, having, in the course of the day, broken the chain of the shackle on my arm;

and the door being opened by Willie Sutherland in the usual manner, I came out, holding a napkin to my face, and weeping in sincerity very bitterly, with the thought of what might ensue to Sarah Lochrig, whom I left behind in my place.

In reverence to my grief the honest man said nothing, but walked by my side till he had let me out at the outer-stair head-door, where he parted from me, carrying the keys to Mungo Robeson's house, aneath the tolbooth, while I walked towards James Gottera's cart, and was presently in the inside of the hogget.

With great presence of mind and a soldierly self-possession, that venturous friend then drew the horse's head from the trough, and began to drive it down the street to the town-end port, striving as he did so to whistle, till he was rebuked for so doing, as I heard, by an old woman then going home, who said to him that it was a shame to hear such profanity in Irvine when a martyr doomed to die was lying in the tolbooth. To the which he replied scoffingly, 'that martyr was a new name for a sworn rebel to king and country,' – words which so kindled the worthy woman's ire, that she began to ban his prelatic ungodliness to such a degree that a crowd collected, which made me tremble. For the people sided with the zealous carlin, and spoke fiercely, threatening to gar James Gottera ride the stang for his sinfulness in so traducing persecuted Christians. What might have come to pass is hard to say, had not Providence been pleased, in that most critical and perilous time, to cause a foul lum in a thacket house in the Seagate to take fire, by which an alarm was spread that drew off the mob, and allowed James Gottera to pass without farther molestation out at the town-end port.

From the time of my evasion from the tolbooth, and during the controversy between James Gottera and the mob in the street, there was a whirlwind in my mind that made me incapable of reason. But when we had passed thorough the town-end port, and the cart had stopped at the minister's carse till I could throw off my female weeds and put on a sailor's garb, provided for the occasion, tongue nor pen cannot express the passion wherewith my yearning soul was then affected.

The thought of having left Sarah Lochrig within bolts and bars, a ready victim to the tyranny which so thirsted for blood, lightened within me as the lightnings of heaven in a storm. I threw myself on the ground, – I grasped the earth, – I gathered myself as it were into a knot, and howled with horror at my own selfish baseness. I sprung up, and cried, 'I will save her yet!' and I would have run instanter to the town; but the honest man who was with me laid his grip firmly upon my arm, and said in a solemn manner—

'This is no Christian conduct, Ringan Gilhaize; the Lord has not forgotten to be gracious.'

I glowered upon him, as he has often since told me, with a shudder, and cried, 'But I hae left Sarah Lochrig in their hands, and, like a coward, run away to save mysel.'

'Compose yoursel, Ringan, and let us reason together,' was his discreet reply. 'It's vera true ye hae come away and left your wife as it were an hostage in the prison, but the persecutors and oppressors will respek the courageous affection of a loving wife, and Providence will put it in their hearts to spare her.'

'And if they do not, what shall I then be? and what's to become of my babies? – Lord, Lord, thou hast tried me beyond my strength!'

And I again threw myself on the earth, and cried that it might open and swallow me; for, thinking but of myself, I was become unworthy to live.

The considerate man stood over me in compassionate silence for a season, and allowed me to rave in my frenzy till I had exhausted myself.

'Ringan,' said he at last, 'ye were aye respekit as a thoughtful and discreet character, and I'll no blame you for this sorrow; but I entreat you to collek yoursel, and think what's best to be done, for what avails in trouble the cry of alas, alas! or the shedding of many tears? Your wife is in prison, but for a fault that will wring compassion even frae the brazen heart of the remorseless James Sharp, and bring back the blood of humanity to the mansworn breast of Charles Stuart. But though it were not so, they daurna harm a hair of her head; for there are things, man, that the cruellest dread to do for fear o' the world, even when they hae lost the fear o' God. I count her far safer, Ringan, frae the rage of the persecutors, where she lies in prison aneath their bolts and bars, than were she free in her own house; for it obligates them to deal wi' her openly and afore mankind, whose good-will the worst of princes and prelates are, from an inward power, forced to respek; whereas, were she sitting lanerly and defenceless, wi' naebody near but only your four helpless wee birds, there's no saying what the gleds might do. Therefore be counselled, my frien', and dinna gi'e yoursel up utterly to despair; but, like a man, for whom the Lord has already done great things, mak use of the means which, in this jeopardy of a' that's sae dear to you, he has so graciously put in your power.'

I felt myself in a measure heartened by this exhortation, and rising from the ground completed the change I had begun in my apparel; but I was still unable to speak, – which he observing, said—

'Hae ye considered the airt ye ought now to take, for it canna be that ye'll think of biding in this neighbourhood?'

'No; not in this land,' I exclaimed; 'would that I might not even in this life!'

'Whisht! Ringan Gilhaize, that's a sinful wish for a Christian,' said a compassionate voice at my side, which made us both start; and on looking round we saw a man who, during the earnestest of our controversy, had approached close to us unobserved.

It was that gospel-teacher, my fellow-sufferer, Mr Witherspoon; and his sudden apparition at that time was a blessed accident, which did more to draw my thoughts from the anguish of my affections than any thing it was possible for James Gottera to have said.

He was then travelling in the cloud of night to the town, having, after I parted from him in Lanerkshire, endured many hardships and perils, and his intent was to pass to his friends, in order to raise a trifle of money to transport himself for a season into Ireland.

But James Gottera, on hearing this, interposed his opinion, and said, a rumour was abroad that in all ports and towns of embarkation orders were given to stay the departure of passengers, so that to a surety he would be taken if he attempted to quit the kingdom.

By this time my mind had returned into something like a state of sobriety; so I told him how it had been concerted between me and Sarah Lochrig, that I should pass over to the wee Cumbrae, there to wait till the destroyers had passed by; for it was thought not possible that such an inordinate thirst for blood, as had followed upon our discomfiture at Rullion-green, could be of a long continuance; and I beseeched him to come with me, telling him that I was provided with a small purse of money in case need should require it, but in the charitable hearts of the pious we might count on a richer store.

Accordingly we agreed to join our fortunes again; and having parted from James Gottera at Kilwinning, we went on our way together, and my heart was refreshed by the kind admonitions and sweet converse of my companion, though ever and anon the thought of my wife in prison, and our defenceless lambs, shot like a fiery arrow through my bosom. But man is by nature a sordid creature, and the piercing December blast, the threatening sky, and the frequent shower, soon knit up my thoughts with the care of my worthless self: maybe there was in that the tempering hand of a beneficent Providence; for when I have at divers times since considered how much the anguish of my inner sufferings exceeded the bodily molestation, I could not but confess, though it was with a humbled sense of my own selfishness, that it was well for me, in such a time, to be so respited from the upbraidings of my tortured affections.

But not to dwell on the specialties of my own feelings on that memorable night, let it suffice, that after walking some four or five miles towards Pencorse ferry, where we meant to pass to the island, I became less and less attentive to the edifying discourse of Mr Witherspoon, and his nature also yielding to the influences of the time, we travelled along the bleak and sandy shore between Ardrossan and Kilbride hill without the interchange of conversation. The wind came wild and gurly from the sea, – the waves broke heavily on the shore, – and the moon swiftly wading the cloud, threw over the dreary scene a wandering and ghastly light. Often to the blast we were obligated to turn our backs, and the rain being in our faces, we little heeded each other.

In that state, so like sullenness, we had journeyed onward, it might be better than a mile, when, happening to observe something lying on the shore as if it had been cast out by the sea, I cried under a sense of fear—

'Stop, Mr Witherspoon; what's that?'

In the same moment he uttered a dreadful sound of horror, and on looking round, I saw we were three in company.

'In the name of Heaven,' exclaimed Mr Witherspoon, 'who and what are you that walk with us?'

But instanter our fears and the mystery of the appearance were dispelled, for it was my brother.

CHAPTER FOUR

'Weel, Ringan,' said my brother, 'we have met again in this world; it's a blessing I never looked for;' and he held out his two hands to take hold of mine, but the broken links of the shackle still round my wrist made him cry out—

'What's this? – Whare hae ye come frae? but I needna inquire.'

'I have broken out of the tolbooth o' Irvine,' said I, 'and I am fleeing here with Mr Witherspoon.'

'I too,' replied my brother mournfully, 'hae escaped from the hands of the persecutors.'

We then entered into some conversation concerning what had happened to us respectively, from the fatal twenty-eighth of November, when our power and host were scattered on Rullion-green, wherein Mr Witherspoon, with me, rehearsed to him the accidents herein set forth, with the circumstantials of some things that befell the godly man after I left him with the corpse of the baby in his arms; but which being in some points less of an adventurous nature than had happened to myself, I shall be pardoned by the courteous reader for not enlarging upon it at greater length. I should however here note, that Mr Witherspoon was not so severely dealt with as I was; for though an outcast and a fugitive, yet he was not a prisoner; on the contrary, under the kindly cover of the Lady Auchterfardel, whose excellent and truly covenanted husband was a sore sufferer by the fines of the year 1662, he received great hospitality for the space of sixteen days, and was saved between two feather beds, on the top of which the laird's aged mother, a bedrid woman, was laid, when some of Drummond's men searched the house on an information against him.

But disconsolatory as it was to hear of such treatment of a gospel-minister, though lightened by the reflection of the saintly constancy that was yet to be found in the land, and among persons too of the Lady of Auchterfardel's degree, and severe as the trials were, both of body and mind, which I had myself undergone, yet were they all as nothing compared to the hardships of my brother, a man of a temperate sobriety of manner, bearing all changes with a serene countenance and a placable mind, while feeling them in the uttermost depths of his capacious affections.

'On the night of the battle,' said he, 'it would not be easy of me to tell which way I went, or what ensued, till I found myself with three destitute companions on the skirts of the town of Falkirk. By that time the morning was beginning to dawn, and we perceived not that we had approached so nigh unto any bigget land; as the day, however, broke, the steeple caught our eye, and we halted to consider what we ought to do. And as we were then standing in a field diffident to enter the town, a young woman came from a house that stands a little way off the road, close to Graham's dyke, driving a cow to grass with a long staff, which I the more remarked as such, because it was of the Indian cane, and virled with silver, and headed with ivory.

'"Sirs," said Menie Adams, for that was the damsel's name, 'I see what ye are, but I'll no speir; howsever, be ruled by me, and gang na near the town of Falkirk this morning, for atwish the hours of dark and dawn there has been a congregationing o' horses and men, and other sediments o' war, that I hae a notion there's owre meikle o' the King's power in the place for any Covenanter to enter in, save under the peril o' penalties. But come wi' me, and I'll go back wi' you, and in our hay-loft you may scog yoursels till the gloaming.'

'Who could have thought,' said my brother, 'that in such discourse from a young woman, not passing four and twenty years of age, and of a pleasant aspect, any guilty stratagem of blood was hidden!'

He and his friends never questioned her truth, but went with her, and she conducted them to her father's house, and lodged them in the hay-loft.

It seems that Menie Adams was, however, at the time betrothed to the prelatic curate that had been laid upon the parish, and that, in consequence, aneath her courtesy, she had concealed a very treacherous and wicked intent. For no sooner had she got my brother and his three companions into the hay-loft, than she hies herself away to the town, and, in the hope of pleasing her prelatic lover, informs the captain of the troop there of the birds she had ensnared.

As soon as the false woman had thus committed the sin of perfidy, she went to the curate to brag how she had done a service to his cause; but he, though of the prelatic germination, being yet a person who had some reverence for truth and the gentle mercies of humanity, was so disturbed by her unwomanly disposition, that he bade her depart from his presence for ever, and ran with all possible speed to waken the poor men whom she had so betrayed.

On his way to the house he saw a party of the soldiers, whom their officer, as in duty bound, was sending to seize the unsuspecting sleepers, and running on before them, he just got forward in time to give the alarm. My brother and one of them, Esau Wardrop, the wife's brother of James Gottera, who had been so instrumental in my evasion, were providentially enabled to get out and flee; but the other two were taken by the soldiers and carried to prison.

The base conduct of that Menie Adams, as we some years after heard, did not go long unvisited by the displeasure of Heaven; for some scent of her guilt taking wind, the whole town, in a sense, grew wud against her, and she was mobbet, and the wells pumped upon her by the enraged multitude; and she never recovered from the handling that she therein suffered.

My brother and Esau Wardrop, on getting into the open fields, made all the speed they could, like the panting hart when pursued by the hunter, and distrusting the people of that part of the country, they travelled all day, not venturing to approach any reeking house. Towards gloaming, however, being hungry and faint, the craving of nature overcame their fears, and they went up to a house where they saw a light burning.

As they approached the door they faltered a little in their resolution, for they heard the dissonance of riot and revelry within. Their need, however, was great, and the importunities of hunger would not be pacified; so they knocked, and the door was soon opened by a soldier, the party within being a horde of Dalziel's men, living at free quarters in the house of that excellent Christian and much-persecuted man, the Laird of Ringlewood.

The moment that the man who came to the door saw, by the glimpse of the light, that both my brother and Esau Wardrop had swords at their sides, he uttered a cry of alarm, thinking the house was surrounded; at which all the riotous soldiers within flew to their arms, while the man who opened the door seized my brother by the throat and harl't him in. The panic, however, was but of short duration; for my brother soon expounded that they were two perishing men who came to surrender themselves; so the door was again opened, and Esau Wardrop commanded to come in.

'It's but a justice to say of those rampageous troopers,' said my brother, 'that, considering us as prisoners of war, they were free and kind enough, though they mocked at our cause, and derided the equipage of our warfare. But it was a humiliating sight to see in what manner they deported themselves towards the unfortunate family.'

Ringlewood himself, who had remonstrated against their insolence to his aged leddy, they had tied in his arm-chair and placed at the head of his own table, round which they sat carousing, and singing the roister ribaldry of camp-songs. At first, when my brother was taken into this scene of military domination, he did not observe the laird; for in the uproar of the alarm the candles had been overset and broken, but new ones being sworn for and stuck into the necks of the bottles of the wine they were lavishly drinking, he discovered him lying as it were asleep where he sat, with his head averted, and his eyes shut on the iniquity of the scene of oppression with which he was oppressed.

Some touch of contrition had led one of the soldiers to take the aged matron under his care; and on his intercession she was not placed at the table, but allowed to sit in a corner, where she mourned in silence, with her hands clasped together, and her head bent down over them upon her breast. The laird's grandson and heir, a stripling of some fifteen years or so, was obligated to be page and butler, for all the rest of the house had taken to the hills at the approach of the troopers.

As the drinking continued the riot increased, and the rioters growing heated with their drink, they began to quarrel: fierce words brought angry answers, and threats were followed by blows. Then there was an interposition, and a shaking of hands, and a pledging of renewed friendship.

But still the demon of the drink continued to grow stronger and stronger in their kindling blood, and the tumult was made perfect by one of the men, in the capering of his inebriety, rising from his seat, and taking the old leddy by the toupie to raise her head as he rudely placed his foul cup to her lips. This called up the ire of the fellow who had sworn to protect her, and he, not less intoxicated than the insulter, came staggering to defend her; a scuffle ensued, the insulter was cast with a swing away, and falling against the laird, who still remained as it were asleep, with his head on his shoulder, and his eyes shut, he overthrew the chair in which the old gentleman sat fastened, and they both fell to the ground.

The soldier, frantic with wine and rage, was soon, like a tiger, on his adversary; the rest rose to separate them. Some took one side, some another; bottles were seized for weapons, and the table was overthrown in the hurricane. Their serjeant, who was as drunk as the worst of them, tried in vain to call them into order, but they heeded not his call; which so enraged him, that he swore they should shift their quarters, and with that seizing a burning brand from the chumla, he ran into a bedchamber that opened from the room where the riot was raging, and set fire to the curtains.

My brother seeing the flames rising, and that the infuriated war-wolves thought only of themsevles, ran to extricate Ringlewood from the cords with which he was tied; and calling to the leddy and her grandson to quit the burning house, every one was soon out of danger from the fire.

The sense of the soldiers was not so overborne by their drink as to prevent them from seeing the dreadful extent of their outrage; but instead of trying to extinguish the flames, they marched away to seek quarters in some other place, cursing the serjeant for having so unhoused them in such a night.

At first they thought of carrying my brother and Esau Wardrop with them as prisoners; but one of them said it would be as well to give the wyte of the burning, at headquarters, to the rebels; so they left them behind.

Esau Wardrop, with the young laird and my brother, seeing it was in vain to stop the progress of the fire, did all that in them lay to rescue some of the furniture, while poor old Ringlewood and his aged and gentle lady, being both too infirm to lend any help, stood on the green, and saw the devouring element pass from room to room, till their ancient dwelling was utterly destroyed. Fortunately, however, the air was calm, and the out-houses escaping the ruinous contagion of the flames, there was still a beild left in the barn to which they could retire.

In the meantime the light of the burning spread over the country; but the people knowing that soldiers were quartered on Ringlewood, stood aloof in the dread of fire-arms, thinking the conflagration might be caused by some contest of war; so that the mansion of a gentleman much beloved of all his neighbours was allowed to burn to the ground before their eyes, without any one venturing to come to help him, to so great a degree had distrust and the outrages of military riot at that epoch altered the hearts of men.

My brother and Esau Wardrop staid with Ringlewood till the morning, and had, for the space of three or four hours, a restoring sleep. Fain would they have remained longer there, but the threat of the soldiers to accuse them as the incendiaries made Ringlewood urge them to depart; saying, that maybe a time would come when it would be in his power to thank them for their help in that dreadful night. But he was not long exposed to many sufferings; for the leddy on the day following, as in after-time we heard,

was seized with her dead-ill, and departed this life in the
course of three days; and the laird also, in less than a
month, was laid in the kirk-yard, with his ancestors, by
her side.

CHAPTER SIX

After leaving Ringlewood, the two fugitives, by divers journeyings and sore passages through moss and moor, crossed the Balloch ferry, and coming down the north side of the Clyde frith to Ardmore, they boated across to Greenock, where, in little more than an hour after their arrival, they were taken in Euphan Blair's public in Cartsdyke, and the same night marched off to Glasgow; of all which I have already given intimation, in recording my own trials at Inverkip.

But in that march, as my brother and Esau Wardrop were passing with their guard at the Inchinnan ferry, the soldiers heedlessly laying their firelocks all in a heap in the boat, the thought came into my brother's head, that maybe it might be turned to an advantage if he was to spoil the powder in the firelocks; so, as they were sitting in the boat, he, with seeming innocence, drew his hand several times through the water, and in lifting it, took care to drop and sprinkle the powder-pans of the firelocks, in so much, that by the time they were ferried to the Renfrew side, they were spoiled for immediate use.

'Do as I do,' said he softly to Esau Wardrop, as they were stepping out, and with that he feigned some small expedient for tarrying in the boat, while the soldiers taking their arms, leapt on shore. The ferryman also was out before them; and my brother seeing this, took up an oar, seemingly to help him to step out; but pretending at the time to stumble, he caught hold of Esau's shoulder, and pushing with the oar, shoved off the boat in such a manner, that the rope was pulled out of the ferryman's hand, who was in a great consternation. The soldiers, however, laughed at seeing how the river's current was carrying away their prisoners; for my brother was in no

321

hurry to make use of the oar to pull the boat back; on the contrary, he pushed her farther and farther into the river, until one of the guards beginning to suspect some stratagem, levelled his firelock, and threatened to shoot. Whereupon my brother and Esau quickened their exertions, and soon reached the opposite side of the river, while the soldiers were banning and tearing with rage to be so outwitted, and their firelocks rendered useless for the time.

As soon as the fugitives were within wadeable reach of the bank, they jumpit out of the boat and ran, and were not long within the scope of their adversaries' fire.

By this time the sun was far in the west, and they knew little of the country about where they were; but, before embarking, the ferryman had pointed out to them the abbey towers of Paisley, and they knew that, for a long period, many of the humane inhabitants of that town had been among the faithfullest of Scottishmen to the cause of the Kirk and Covenant; and therefore, they thought that, under the distraction of their circumstances, maybe it would be their wisest course to direct their steps, in the dusk of the evening, towards the town, and they threw aside their arms, that they might pass as simple wayfaring men.

Accordingly, having loitered in the way thither, they reached Paisley about the heel of the twilight, and searching their way into the heart of the town, they found a respectable public near the Cross, into which they entered, and ordered some consideration of vivers for supper, just as if they had been on market business. In so doing nothing particular was remarked of them; and my brother, by way of an entertainment before bed-time, told his companion of my grandfather's adventure in Paisley, the circumstantials whereof are already written in this book; drawing out of what had come to pass with him, cheering aspirations of happier days for themselves.

While they were thus speaking, one of the town-council, Deacon Fulton, came in to have a cap and a crack with any stranger that might be in the house. – This deacon was a man who well represented and was a good swatch of the plain honesty and strict principles which have long governed within that ancient borough of regality. He seeing them, and being withal a man of shrewd discernment, eyed them very sharply, and maybe guessing what they were and where they had come from, entered into a discreet conversation with them anent the troubles of the time. In this he showed the pawkrie, that so well becomes those who sit in council, with a spicerie of that wholesome virtue and friendly sympathy of which all the poor fugitives from the Pentland raid stood in so great need. For, without pretending to jealouse any thing of what they were, he spoke of that business as the crack of the day, and told them of many of the afflicting things which had been perpetrated after the dispersion of the Covenanters, saying—

'It's a thing to be deplored in all time coming, that the poor misguided folk, concern't in that rash wark, didna rather take refuge in the towns, and among their brethren and fellow-subjects, than flee to the hills, where they are hunted down wi' dog and gun as beasts o' an ill kind. Really every body's wae for their folly; though to be sure, in a government sense, their fault's past pardon. It's no indeed a thing o' toleration, that subjects are to rise against rulers.'

'True,' said my brother, 'unless rulers fall against subjects.'

The worthy magistrate looked a thought seriously at him; no in reproof for what he had said, or might say, but in an admonitory manner, saying—

'Ye're owre douce a like man, I think, to hae been either art or part in this headstrong Reformation, unless ye had some great cause to provoke you; and I doubt na ye hae discretion enough no to contest without need points o' doctrine; at least for me, I'm laith to enter on ony sort o' polemtic, for it's a Gude's truth, I'm nae deacon at it.'

My brother discerning by his manner that he saw through them, would have refrain't at the time from further discourse; but Esau Wardrop was, though a man of few words, yet of such austerity of faith, that he could not abide to have it thought that he was in any time or place afraid for himself to bear his testimony, even when manifestly uncalled on to do; so he here broke in upon the considerate and worthy counsellor, and said—

'That a covenanted spirit was bound, at a' times, and in a' situations, conditions, and circumstances, to uphold the cause.'

'True, true, we are a' Covenanters,' replied the deacon, 'and Gude forbid that I should e'er forget the vows I took when I was in a manner a bairn; but there's an unco difference between the auld covenanting and this Lanerk New-light. In the auld times, our forebears and our fathers covenanted to show their power, that the king and government might consider what they were doing. And they betook not themselves to the sword, till the quiet warning of almost all the realm united in one league had proved ineffectual; and when at last there was nae help for't, and they were called by their conscience and dangers to gird themselves for battle, they went forth in the might and power of the arm of flesh, as weel as of a righteous cause. But, sirs, this donsie business of the Pentland raid was but a splurt, and the publishing of the Covenant, after the poor folk had made themselves rebels, was, to say the least o't, a weak conceit.'

'We were not rebels,' cried Esau Wardrop.

'Hoot toot, friend,' said the counsellor, 'ye're owre hasty, I did na ca' the poor folk rebels in the sense of a rebellion, where might takes the lead in a controversy wi' right, but because they had risen against the law.'

'There can be nae rebellion against a law that teaches things over which man can have no control, the thought and the conscience,' said Esau Wardrop.

'Aye, aye,' replied the counsellor, 'a' that's vera true; but if it please the wisdom of the king, by and with the advice of his privy counsellors, to prohibit certain actions – and surely actions are neither thoughts nor consciences, – do ye mean to say that the subject's no bound to obey such royal ordinances?'

'Aye, if the acts are in themselves harmless, and trench not upon any man's rights of property and person.'

'Weel, I'll no debate that wi' you,' replied the worthy

counsellor; 'but surely ye'll ne'er maintain that conventicles, and the desertion of the regular and appointed places
of worship, are harmless; nor can it be denied that sic things
do not tend to aggrieve and impair the clergy baith in their
minds and means?'

'I confess that,' said Esau; 'but think, that the conventicles and desertions, whereof ye speak, sprang out of
an arbitrary and uncalled-for disturbance of the peaceful
worship of God. Evil-counselling caused them, and evil-
counselling punishes them till the punishment can be no
longer endured.'

'Ye're a doure-headed man,' said Deacon Fulton, 'and
really ye hae gi'en me sic a cast o' your knowledge, that
I can do no less than make you a return; so tak this, and
bide nae langer in Paisley than your needs call.' With that
he laid his purse on the table and went away. But scarcely
had he departed the house, when who should enter but
the very soldiers from whom my brother and Esau had so
marvellously escaped.

The noise of taking up my brother and Esau Wardrop to the tolbooth by the soldiers bred a great wonderment in the town, and the magistrates came into the prison to see them. Then it was that they recognised their friendly adviser among those in authority. But he signified, by winking to them, that they should not know him; to which they comported themselves so, that it passed as he could have wished.

'Provost,' said he to the chief magistrate, who was then present with them, 'though thir honest men be concerned in a fret against the king's government, they're no just iniquitous malefactors, and therefore it behoves us, for the little time they are to bide here, to deal compassionately with them. This is a damp and cauld place. I'm sure we might gi'e them the use of the council-chamber, and direk a bit spunk o' fire to be kindl't. It's, ye ken, but for this night they are to be in our aught; and their crime, ye ken, provost, was mair o' the judgment than the heart, and therefore we should think how we are a' prone to do evil.'

By this sort of petitionary exhorting, that worthy man carried his point; and the provost consented that the prisoners should be removed to the council-chamber, where he directed a fire to be lighted for their solace.

'Noo, honest men,' said their friend the deacon, when he was taking leave of them, after seeing them in the council-room, 'I hope ye'll make yoursels as conforttable as men in your situation can reasonably be; and look ye,' said he to my brother, 'if the wind should rise, and the smoke no vent sae weel as ye could wis', which is sometimes the case in blowy weather when the door's shut, just open a wee bit jinkie o' this window,' and he gave him a squeeze on the arm – 'it looks into my yard. – Heh! but it's weel

mindet, the bar on my back-yett's in the want o' reparation
– I maun see til't the morn.'

There was no difficulty in reading the whumplet meaning of this couthiness anent the reeking o' the chamber; and
my brother and Esau, when the door was locket on them
for the night, soon found it expedient to open the window,
and next morning the kind counsellor had more occasion
than ever to get the bar o' his back-yett repaired; for it had
yielded to the grip of the prisoners, who, long afore day,
were far beyond the eye and jurisdiction of the magistrates
of Paisley.

They took the straight road to Kilmarnock, intending,
if possible, to hide themselves among some of my brother
Jacob's wife's friends in that town. He had himself been
dead some short time before; but in the course of their
journey, in eschewing the high-road as much as possible,
they found a good friend in a cotter who lived on the edge
of the Mearns moor, and with him they were persuaded to
bide till the day of that night when we met in so remarkable
a manner on the sands of Ardrossan; and the cause that
brought him there was one of the severest trials to which
he had yet been exposed, as I shall now rehearse.

James Greig, the kind cotter who sheltered them for the
better part of three weeks, was but a poor man, and two
additional inmates consumed the meal which he had laid
in for himself and his wife, so that he was obligated to
apply twice for the loan of some from a neighbour, which
caused a suspicion to arise in that neighbour's mind; and
he being loose-tongued, and a talking man, let out what
he thought in a public at Kilmarnock, in presence of some
one connected with the soldiers then quartered in the
Dean-castle. A party, in consequence, had that morning
been sent out to search for them; but the thoughtless
man who had done the ill was seized with a remorse of
conscience for his folly, and came in time to advise them
to flee; but not so much in time as to prevent them from
being seen by the soldiers, who no sooner discovered them
than they pursued them. What became of Esau Wardrop
was never known; he was no doubt shot in his flight; but
my brother was more fortunate, for he kept so far before

those who in particular pursued him, that, although they kept him in view, they could not overtake him.

Running in this way for life and liberty, he came to a house on the road-side, inhabited by a lanerly woman, and the door being open he darted in, passing thorough to the yard behind, where he found himself in an enclosed place, out of which he saw no other means of escape but through a ditch full of water. The depth of it at the time he did not think of, but plunging in, he found himself up to the chin; at that moment he heard the soldiers at hand; so the thought struck him to remain where he was, and to go under a bramble-bush that overhung the water. By this means he was so effectually concealed, that the soldiers, losing sight of him, wreaked their anger and disappointment on the poor woman, dragging her with them to the Dean-castle, where they threw her into the dungeon, in the darkness of which she perished, as was afterwards well known through all that country-side.

After escaping from the ditch, my brother turned his course more northerly, and had closed his day of suffering on Kilbride-hill, where, drawn by his affections to seek some knowledge of his wife and daughter, he had resolved to risk himself as near as possible to Quharist that night; and coming along with the shower on his back, which blew so strong in our faces, he saw us by the glimpses of the tempestuous moonlight as we were approaching, and had denned himself on the road-side till we should pass, being fearful we might prove enemies. Some accidental lament or complaint, uttered unconsciously by me, made him, however, think he knew the voice, and moved thereby, he started up, and had just joined us when he was discovered in so awakening a manner.

Thus came my brother and I to meet after the raid of Pentland; and having heard from me all that he could reasonably hope for, regarding the most valued casket of his affections, he came along with Mr Witherspoon; and we were next morning safely ferried over into the wee Cumrae, by James Plowter the ferryman, to whom we were both well known.

There was then only a herd's house on the island; but

there could be no truer or kinder Christians than the herd and his wife. We staid with them till far in the year, hearing often, through James Plowter, of our friends; and above all the joyous news, in little more than a week after our landing, of Sarah Lochrig having been permitted to leave the tolbooth of Irvine, without farther dule than a reproof from Provost Reid, that had more in it of commendation than reproach.

It is well set forth in all the various histories of this dismal epoch, that the cry of blood had gone so vehemently up to heaven from the graves of the martyred Covenanters, that the Lord moved the heart of Charles Stuart to more merciful measures, but only for a season. The apostate James Sharp and the other counsellors, whose weakness or wickedness fell in with his tyrannical proselytising purposes, were wised from the rule of power, and the Earls of Tweeddale and Kincardine, with that learned sage and philosopher Sir John Murray, men of more beneficent dispositions, were appointed to sit in their places in the Privy Council at Edinburgh; – so that all in our condition were heartened to return to their homes.

As soon as we heard that the ravenous soldiery were withdrawn from the shire of Ayr, my brother and I, with Mr Witherspoon, after an abode of more than seven months in yon solitary and rocky islet, returned to Quharist. But, O courteous reader, I dare not venture to tell of the joy of the meeting, and the fond intermingling of embraces, that was too great a reward for all our sufferings; – for now I approach the memorials of those things, by which the terrible Heavens have manifested that I was ordained from the beginning to launch the bolt that was chosen from the quiver in the armory of the Almighty avenger, to overthrow the oppressor and oppression of my native land. It is therefore enough to state, that upon my return home, where I expected to find my lands waste and my fences broken down, I found all things in better order than they maybe would have been had the eye of the master been over them; for our kind neighbours, out of a friendly consideration for my family, had in the spring tilled the ground and sown the seed, by day-and-day-about labour; and surely it was a pleasant thing, in the midst of such a general depravity of the human heart, so prevalent at that period, to hear of such constancy and christian-mindedness; for it was not towards my brother and me only that such things were done; the same was common throughout the country towards the lands and families of the persecuted.

But the lown of that time was as a pet day in winter. In the harvest, however, when the proposal came out that we should give bonds to keep the peace, I made no scruple of signing the same, and of getting my wife's father, who was not out in the raid, to be my cautioner. In the doing of this I did not renounce the Covenant, but, on the contrary, I considered that by the bonds the King was as much bound to preserve things in the state under which I granted the bond, as I was to remain in the quiet condition I was when I signed it.

After the bonds of peace came the indulgence, and the chief heritors of our parish having something to say with the Lord Tweeddale, leave was obtained for Mr Swinton to come back, and we had made a paction with Andrew Dornock, the prelatic curate and incumbent, to let him have his manse again. But although Mr Swinton did return, and his family were again gathered around him, he would not, as he said himself to me, so far bow the knee to Baal as to bring the church of Christ in any measure or way into Erastian dependence on the civil magistrate. So he neither would return to the manse nor enter the pulpit, but continued, for the space of several years, to reside at Quharist, and to preach on the summer Sundays from the window in the gable.

In the spring, however, of the year 1674, he, after a lingering illness, closed his life and ministry. For sometime he had felt himself going hence, and the tenour of his prayers and sermons had for several months been of a high and searching efficacy; and he never failed, Sabbath after Sabbath, just before pronouncing the blessing, to return public thanks that the Lord was drawing him so softly away from the world, and from the storms that were gathering in the black cloud of prelacy which still overhung and darkened the ministry of the Kirk of Scotland, – a method

of admonition that was awfully awakening to the souls of
his hearers, and treasured by them as a solemn breathing
of the inspiration of prophecy.

When he was laid in the earth, and Mr Witherspoon, by
some handling on my part, was invited to fill the void which
his removal had left among us, the wind again began to
fisle, and the signs of a tempest were seen in the changes of
the royal Councils. The gracious-hearted statesmen before
spoken of were removed from their benignant spheres
like falling stars from the firmament, and the Duke of
Lauderdale was endowed with the power to persecute and
domineer.

Scarcely was he seated in the Council when the edicts of
oppression were renewed. The prelates became clamorous
for his interference, and the penalties of the bonds of peace
presented the means of supplying the inordinate wants of
his rapacious wife. Steps were accordingly soon taken to
appease and pleasure both. The court-contrived crime of
hearing the Gospel preached in the fields, as it was by
John in the Wilderness and Jesus on the Mount, was
again prohibited with new rigour; and I for one soon felt
that, in the renewed persecution of those who attended
the conventicles, the King had again as much broken the
conditions under which I gave the bond of peace, as he
had before broken the vows of the Solemn League and
Covenant; so that when the guilty project was ripened
in his bloody councils, that the West Country should be
again exasperated into rebellion, that a reason might be
procured for keeping up a standing army, in order that
the three kingdoms might be ruled by prerogative instead
of parliament, I freely confess that I was one of those who
did refuse to sign the bonds that were devised to provoke
the rebellion, – bonds, the terms whereof sufficiently
manifested the purpose that governed the framers in
the framing. We were required by them, under severe
penalties, to undertake that neither our families, nor our
servants, nor our tenants, nor the servants of our tenants,
nor any others residing upon our lands, should withdraw
from the churches or adhere to conventicles, or succour
field-preachers, or persons who had incurred the penalties

attached to these prelate-devised offences. And because we refused to sign these bonds, and continued to worship God in the peacefulness of the Gospel, the whole country was treated by the Duke of Lauderdale as in a state of revolt.

The English forces came mustering against us on the borders, the Irish garrisons were drawn to the coast to invade us, and the lawless Highlanders were tempted, by their need and greed, and a royal promise of indemnity for whatsoever outrages they might commit, to come down upon us in all their fury. By these means ten thousand ruthless soldiers and unreclaimed barbarians were let loose upon us, while we were sitting in the sun listening, I may say truly, to those gracious counsellings which breathe nothing but peace and good-will. When, since the burning days of Dioclesian the Roman Emperor, – when, since the massacre of the protestants by orders of the French king, on the eve of St Bartholomew, was so black a crime ever perpetrated by a guilty government on its own subjects? But I was myself among the greatest of the sufferers; and it is needful that I should now clothe my thoughts with sobriety, and restrain the ire of the pen of grief and revenge. – Not revenge! No; let the word be here – justice.

The Highland host came on us in want, and, but for their license to destroy, in beggary. Yet when they returned to their wild homes among the distant hills, they were laden as with the household wealth of a realm, in so much that they were rendered defenceless by the weight of their spoil. At the bridge of Glasgow, the students of the College and the other brave youths of that town, looking on them with true Scottish hearts, and wrathful to see that the barbarians had been such robbers of their fellow-subjects, stopped above two thousand of them, and took from them their congregations of goods and wares, wearing apparel, pots, pans, and gridirons, and other furniture, wherewith they had burdened themselves like bearers at a flitting. My house was stript to a wastage, and every thing was taken away; what was too heavy to be easily transported was, after being carried some distance, left on the road. The very shoes were taken off my wife's feet, and 'ye'll no be a refuse to gi'e me that,' said a red-haired reprobate as he took hold of Sarah Lochrig's hand, and robbed her of her wedding-ring. I was present and saw the deed; I felt my hands clench; but in my spirit I discovered that it was then the hour of outrage, and that the Avenger's time was not yet come.

Rarely has it fallen to the lot of man to be so blessed with such children as mine; but surely I was unworthy of the blessing. And yet, though maybe unworthy, Lord, thou knowest by the nightly anthems of thankfulness that rose from my hearth, that the chief sentiment in my breast, in those moments of melody, was my inward acknowledgment to Thee for having made this world so bright to me, with an offspring so good and fair, and with Sarah Lochrig, their mother, she whose life was the sweetness in the cup of my felicity. Let me not, however, hurry on, nor forget that I am but an historian, and that it befits not the juridical pen of the character to dwell upon my own woes, when I have to tell of the sufferings of others.

The trials and the tribulations which I had heard so much of, and whereof I had witnessed so many, made on me in a sense but little liable to be moved when told of any new outrage. But the sight of that Highlander wrenching from Sarah Lochrig's finger our wedding-ring, did, in its effects and influences, cause a change in my nature as sudden, and as wonderful, as that which the rod of Moses underwent in being quickened into a serpent.

For some time I sat as I was sitting while the deed was doing; and when my wife, after the plunderers had departed, said to me, soothingly, that we had reason to be thankful for having endured no other loss than a little world's gear, she was surprised at the sedateness with which I responded to her pious condolements. Michael, our first-born, then in the prime beauty of his manhood, had been absent when the robbery was committed, and coming in, on hearing what had been done, flamed with the generous rage of youth, and marvelled that I had been so calm. My blithe and blooming Mary, joined her ingenuous

admiration to theirs, but my mild and sensible Margaret
fell upon my neck, and weeping cried, 'O! father, it's no
worth the doure thought that gars your brows sae gloom;'
while Joseph, the youngest of the flock, then in his twelfth
year, brought the Bible and laid it on my knees.

I opened the book, and would have read a portion, but
the passage which caught my eye was, the beginning of
the sixth chapter of Jeremiah, 'O ye children of Benjamin,
gather yourselves to flee out of the midst of Jerusalem, and
blow the trumpet in Tekoa, and set up a sign of fire in
Beth-haccerem: for evil appeareth out of the north, and
great destruction.' And I thought it was a voice calling
me to arm, and to raise the banner against the oppressor;
and thereupon I shut the book, and retiring to the fields,
communed with myself for some time.

Having returned into the house, and sent Michael to
my brother's to inquire how it had fared with him and
his family, I at the same time directed Joseph to go to
Irvine, and tell our friends there to help us with a supply
of blankets, for the Highlanders had taken away my horses
and driven off my cattle, and we had no means of bringing
any thing.

But Joseph was not long gone when Michael came flying
back from my brother's, and I saw by his looks that
something very dreadful had been committed, and said—

'Are they all in life?'

'Aye, in life!' and, the tears rushing into his eyes, he
exclaimed, 'But O! I wish that my cousin Bell had been
dead and buried!'

Bell Gilhaize, my brother's only daughter, was the
lightest-hearted maiden in all our parish. It had long
been a pleasure both to her father and me to observe a
mingling of affections between her and Michael, and the
year following had been fixt for their marriage.

'The time of weeping, Michael,' said I, 'is past, and the
time of warring will soon come. It is not in man to bear
always aggression, nor can it be required of him ever to
endure contumely.'

'What has befallen Bell?' said his mother to him; but
instead of making her any answer he uttered a dreadful

sound, like the howl of madness, and hastily quitted the house.

Sarah Lochrig, who was a woman of a serene reason, and mild and gracious in her nature, looked at me with a silent sadness, that told all the anguish with which the horror that she guessed had darted into her soul; and then, with an energy that I never saw in her before, folded her own two daughters to her bosom, as if she was in terror for them, and bathed their necks with tears.

While we were in this state my brother himself came in. He was now a man well stricken in years, but of a hale appearance, and usually of an open and manly countenance. Nor on this occasion did he appear greatly altered; but there was a fire in his eye, and a severity in his aspect, such as I had never seen before, yet withal a fortitude that showed how strong the self-possession was, which kept the tempest within him from breaking out in word or gesture.

'Ringan,' said he, 'we have met with a misfortune. It's the will of Providence, and we maun bear it. But surely in the anger that is caused by provocation, our Creator tells us to resent. From this hour, all obligation, obedience, allegiance, all whatsoever that as a subject I did owe to Charles Stuart is at an end. I am his foe; and the Lord put strength into my arm to revenge the ruin of my bairn!'

There was in the utterance of these words a solemnity at first terrifying to hear; but his voice in the last clause of the sentence faltered, and he took off his bonnet and held it over his face, and wept bitterly.

I could make him no answer for some time; but I took hold of his hand, and when he had a little mastered his grief, I said, 'Brother, we are children of the same parents, and the wrongs of one are the wrongs of both. But let us not be hasty.'

He took the bonnet from his face, and looked at me sternly for a little while, and then he said—

'Ringan Gilhaize, till you have felt what I feel, you ne'er can know that the speed o' lightning is slow to the wishes and the will of revenge.'

At that moment his daughter Bell was brought in, led by

my son Michael. Her father, at the sight of her, clasped his
hands wildly above his head, and rushed out of the house.
My wife went towards her, but stopped and fell back into
my arms at the sight of her demented look. My daughters
gazed, and held up their trembling hands.

'Speak to her,' said Michael to his sisters; 'she'll maybe
heed you;' and he added, 'Bell, it's Mary and Peggy,' and
dropping her hand, he went to lead Mary to her, while she
stood like a statue on the spot.

'Dear Bell,' said I, as I moved myself gently from the
arms of my afflicted wife, 'come wi' me to the open air;' and
I took her by the hand which poor Michael had dropped,
and led her out to the green, but still she looked the same
demented creature.

Her father, who had by this time again overcome his
distress, seeing us on the green, came towards us, while
my wife and daughters also came out; but Michael could
no longer endure the sight of the rifled rose that he had
cherished for the ornament of his bosom, and he remained
to hide his grief in the house.

'Her mind's gone, Ringan,' said my brother, 'and she'll
ne'er be better in this world!' Nor was she; but she lived
many months after, and in all the time never shed a tear,
nor breathed a sigh, nor spoke a word; where she was led,
she went; where she was left, she stood. At last she became
so weak that she could not stand; and one day, as I was
sitting at her bedside, I observed that she lay unusually
still, and touching her hand, found that all her sorrows
were over.

From the day of the desolation of his daughter, my brother seldom held any communion with me; but I observed that with Michael he had much business, and though I asked no questions, I needed not to be told that there was a judgment and a doom in what they did. I was therefore fearful that some rash step would be taken at the burial of Bell; for it was understood that all the neighbours far and near intended to be present to testify their pity for her fate. So I spoke to Mr Witherspoon concerning my fears, and by his exhortations the body was borne to the kirk-yard in a solemn and peaceable manner.

But just as the coffin was laid in the grave, and before a spadeful of earth was thrown, a boy came running, crying, 'Sharp's kill't! – the apostate's dead!' which made every one turn round and pause; and while we were thus standing, a horseman came riding by, who confirmed the tidings, that a band of men whom his persecutions had made desperate, had executed justice on the apostate as he was travelling in his carriage with his daughter on Magus-moor. While the stranger was telling the news, the corpse lay in the grave unburied; and, dreadful to tell! when he had made an end of his tale, there was a shout of joy and exultation set up by all present, except by Michael and my brother. They stood unmoved, and I thought – do I them any wrong? – that they looked disconsolate and disappointed.

But though the judgment on James Sharp was a cause of satisfaction to all covenanted hearts, many were not yet so torn by the persecution as entirely to applaud the deed. I shall not therefore enter upon the particulars of what was done anent those who dealt his doom, for they were not of our neighbourhood.

The crime, however, of listening peacefully in the fields

to the truths of the Gospel became, in the sight of the persecutors, every day more and more heinous, and they gave themselves up to the conscience-soothing tyranny of legal ordinances, as if the enactment and execution of bloody laws, contrary to those of God, and against the unoffending privileges of our nature, were not wickedness of as dark a stain as the murderer's use of his secret knife. Edict and proclamation against field-preachings and conventicles came following each other, and the latest was the fiercest and fellest of all which had preceded. But the cause of truth, and the right of communion with the Lord, was not to be given up: 'It is not for glory,' we said in the words of those brave Scottish barons that redeemed, with King Robert the Bruce, their native land from the thraldom of the English Edward, 'nor is it for riches, neither is it for honour, but it is for liberty alone we contend, which no true man will lose but with his life;' and therefore it was that we would not yield obedience to the tyranny, which was revived with new strength by the death of James Sharp, in revenge for his doom, but sought, in despite of decrees and statutes, to hear THE WORD where we believed it was best spoken.

The laws of God, which are above all human authority, require that we should worship him in truth and in holiness, and we resolved to do so to the uttermost, and prepared ourselves with arms to resist whoever might be sent to molest us in the performance of that the greatest duty. But in so exercising the divine right of resistance, we were not called upon to harm those whom we knew to be our adversaries. Belting ourselves for defence, not for war, we went singly to our places of secret meeting in the glens and on the moors, and when the holy exercise was done, we returned to our homes as peacefully as we went thither.

Many a time I have since thought, that surely in no other age or land was ever such a solemn celebration of the Sabbath as in those days. The very dangers with which we were environed exalted the devout heart; verily it was a grand sight to see the fearless religious man moving from his house in the grey of the morning, with the Bible in his hand and his sword for a staff, walking towards the hills for many a weary mile, hoping the preacher would be there, and praying as he went, that there might be no molestation.

Often and often on those occasions has the Lord been pleased to shelter his worshippers from their persecutors, by covering them with the mantle of his tempest; and many a time at the dead of night, when the winds were soughing around, and the moon was bowling through the clouds, we have stood on the heath of the hills, and the sound of our psalms has been mingled with the roaring of the gathering waters.

The calamities which drove us thus to worship in the wilderness, and amidst the storm, rose to their full tide on the back of the death of the archapostate James Sharp; for all the religious people in the realm were in a manner regarded by the government as participators in the method of his punishment. And Claverhouse, whom I have now to speak of, got that special commission on which he rode so wickedly, to put to the sword whomsoever he found with arms at any preaching in the fields; so that we had no choice in seeking to obtain the consolations of religion, which we then stood so much in need of, but to congregate in such numbers as would deter the soldiers from venturing to attack us. This it was which caused the second rising, and led to the fatal day of Bothwell-brigg, whereof it is needful that I should particularly speak, not only on account of the great stress that was thereon laid by the persecutors, in making out of it a method of fiery ordeal to afflict the covenanted, but also because it was the overflowing fountain-head of the deluge that made me desolate. And herein, courteous reader, should aught of a fiercer feeling than belongs to the sacred sternness of truth and justice escape from my historical pen, thou wilt surely pardon the same, if there be any of the gracious ruth of Christian gentleness in thy bosom; for now I have to tell of things that have made the annals of the land as red as crimson, and filled my house with the blackness of ashes and universal death.

For a long period there had been, from the causes and circumstances premised, sore difficulties in the assembling

of congregations, and the sacrament of the Supper had not
been dispensed in many parts of the shire of Ayr from the
time of the Highland host; so that there was a great longing
in the hearts of the covenanted to partake once again of that
holy refreshment; and shortly after the seed-time it began
to be concerted, that early in the summer a day should be
set apart, and a place fixt for the celebration of the same.
About the time of the interment of my brother's desolated
daughter, and the judgment of the death executed on James
Sharp, it was settled that the moors of Loudon-hill should
be the place of meeting, and that the first Sabbath of June
should be the day. But what ministers would be there was
not settled; for who could tell which, in those times, would
be spared from prison?

It was, however, forethought and foreseen, that the
assemblage of communicants would be very considerable;
for in order that there might be the less risk of molestation,
a wish that it should be so was put forth among us, to
the end that the king's forces might swither to disperse
us. Accordingly, with my disconsolate brother and son, I
went to be present at that congregation, and we carried
our arms with us, as we were then in the habit of doing
on all occasions of public testimony by worship.

In the meantime a rent had been made in the Covenant,
partly by the over-zeal of certain young preachers, who not
feeling, as we did, that the duty of presbyterians went no
farther than defence and resistance, strove, with all the
pith of an effectual eloquence, to exasperate the minds of
their hearers into hostility against those in authority; and
it happened that several of those who had executed the
judgment on James Sharp, seeing no hope of pardon for
what they had done, leagued themselves with this party, in
the hope of thereby making head against their pursuers.

I have been the more strict in setting down these
circumstantials, because in the bloody afterings of that
meeting they were altogether lost sight of; and also, because
the implacable rage with which Claverhouse persecuted
the Covenanters has been extenuated by some discreet
historians, on the plea of his being an honourable officer
deduced from his soldierly worth elsewhere; whereas the

truth is, that his cruelties in the shire of Ayr, and other of our western parts, were less the fruit of his instructions, wide and severe as they were, than of his own mortified vanity and malignant revenge.

It was in the cool of the evening, on Saturday the last day of May, when my brother came over to my house, where, with Michael, I had prepared myself to go with him to Loudon-hill. Our intent was to walk that night to Kilmarnock, and abide till the morning with our brother Jacob's widow, not having seen her for a long time.

We had in the course of that day heard something of the publication of 'The Declaration and Testimony,' which, through the vehemence of the preachers before spoken of, had been rashly counselled at Ruglen, the 29th of the month; but there was no particulars, and what we did hear was like, as all such things are, greatly magnified beyond the truth. We, however, were grieved by the tidings; for we feared some cause of tribulation would be thereby engendered detrimental to the religious purposes of our journey.

This sentiment pressing heavily on our hearts, we parted from my family with many misgivings, and the bodements of further sorrows. But the outward expression of what we all felt was the less remarkable, on account of what so lately had before happened in my brother's house. Nor indeed did I think at the time, that the foretaste of what was ordained so speedily to come to a head was at all so lively in his spirit, or that of my son, as it was in mine, till, in passing over the top of the Gowan-brae, he looked round on the lands of Quharist, and said—

'I care nae, Ringan, if I ne'er come back; for though we hae lang dwelt in affection together yon'er, thae that were most precious to me are now both aneath the sod,' – alluding to his wife who had been several years dead, – and poor Bell, that lovely rose which the ruthless spoiler had so trampled into the earth.

344

'I feel,' said Michael, 'as if I were going to a foreign land, there is sic a farewell sadness upon me.'

But we strove to overcome this, and walked leisurely on the high-road towards Kilmarnock, trying to discourse of indifferent things; and as the gloaming faded, and the Night began to look forth, from her watch-tower in the heavens, with all her eyes of beautiful light, we communed of the friends that we trusted were in glory, and marvelled if it could be that they saw us after death, or ever revisited the persons and the scenes that they loved in life. Rebellion or treason, or any sense of thoughts and things that were not holy, had no portion in our conversation: we were going to celebrate the redemption of fallen man; and we were mourning for friends no more; our discourse was of eternal things, and the mysteries of the stars and the lights of that world which is above the firmament.

When we reached Kilmarnock we found that Jacob's widow had, with several other godly women, set out towards the place of meeting, to sojourn with a relation that night, in order that they might be the abler to gather the manna of the word in the morning. We therefore resolved not to halt there, but to go forward to the appointed place, and rest upon the spot. This accordingly doing, we came to the eastern side of Loudon-hill, the trysted place, shortly after the first scad of the dawn.

Many were there before us, both men and women and little children, and horses intermingled, some slumbering, and some communing with one another; and as the morning brightened, it was a hallowed sight to behold from that rising ground the blameless persecuted coming with sedate steps to worship their Maker on the mountain.

The Reverend Mr Thomas Douglas, who was to open the action, arrived about the rising of the sun, with several other ministers, and behind them four aged men belonging to Strathaven bearing the elements.

A pious lady, whose name I never heard, owing to what ensued, spread with her own hands a damask tablecloth on the ground, and the bread and wine were placed upon it with more reverence than ever was in kirk.

Mr Douglas having mounted upon a rock nigh to where

this was done, was about to give out the psalm, when we observed several country lads, that were stationed as watchers afar off, coming with great haste in; and they brought word, that Claverhouse and his dragoons were coming to disperse us, bringing with them the Reverend Mr King, a preacher of the gospel at Hamilton, and others that they had made prisoners, tied with cords two and two.

The tidings for a moment caused panic and consternation; but as the men were armed, and resolved to resist, it was thought, in consideration of the women and children, that we ought to go forward, and prevent the adversaries from advancing. Accordingly, to the number of forty horsemen, and maybe near to two hundred foot, we drew ourselves apart from the congregation, and marched to meet Claverhouse, thinking, perhaps, on seeing us so numerous, that he would not come on, – while Mr Douglas proceeded with the worship, the piety of none with him being abated by this grievous visitation.

Mr William Clelland, with Mr Hamilton, who had come with Mr Douglas, were our leaders, and we met Claverhouse on the moor of Drumclog.

The dragoons were the first to halt, and Claverhouse, having ordered his prisoners to be drawn aside, was the first who gave the word to fire. This was without any parley or request to know whether we came with hostile intent or no. Clelland, on seeing the dragoons make ready, cried to us all to den ourselves among the heather; by which forethought the shot flew harmless. Then we started up, and every one, with the best aim he could, fired at the dragoons as they were loading their carabines. Several men and horses were killed, and many wounded. Claverhouse seeing this, commanded his men to charge upon us; but the ground was rough, the heather deep, and the moss broken where peats had been dug, and the horses floundered, and several threw their riders, and fell themselves.

We had now loaded again, and the second fire was more deadly than the first. Our horsemen also seeing how the dragoons were scattered, fell in the confusion as it were man for man upon them. Claverhouse raged and commanded, but no one now could or would obey. In that extremity his horse was killed, and, being thrown down, I ran forward to seize him, if I could, prisoner; but he still held his sword in his hand, and rising as I came up, used it manfully, and with one stroke almost hued my right arm from my shoulder. As he fled I attempted for a moment to follow, but staggered and fell. He looked back as he escaped, and I cried – 'Blood for blood;' and it has been so, as I shall hereafter in the sequel relate.

When the day was won, we found we numbered among the slain on the side of the vanquished nearly twenty of the dragoons: on our side we lost but one man, John Morton – a ripe saint; but several were wounded; and John Weir and William Daniel died of their wounds. Such was the day of Drumclog.

Being wounded, I was carried to a neighbouring farm, attended by my brother and son, and there put upon a cart and sent home to Quharist, as it was thought I would be best attended there. They then returned to the rest of the host, who, seeing themselves thus brought into open war, resolved forthwith to proceed to Glasgow, and to raise again the banner of the Covenant.

But Claverhouse had fled thither, burning with the thought of being so shorn in his military pride by raw and undisciplined countrymen, whom, if we had been bred soldiers, maybe he would have honoured, but being what we were, though our honour was the greater, he hated us with the deadly aversion that is begotten of vanity chastised; for that it was which incited him to ravage the West country with such remorselessness, and which, when our men were next day repulsed at Glasgow with the loss of lives, made him hinder the removal of the bodies from the streets, till it was said the butchers' dogs began to prey upon them.

But not to insist on matters of hearsay, nor to dwell at any greater length on those afflicting events, I must refer the courteous reader to the history of the times for what followed, it being enough for me to state here, that as soon as the news spread of the battle and the victory, the persecuted ran flocking in from all quarters, by which the rope of sand, that the Lord permitted Monmouth to break at Bothwell-brigg, was soon formed. My brother and my son were both there, and there my gallant Michael lies. My brother, then verging on threescore, being among the prisoners, was, after sore sufferings in the Greyfriars churchyard of Edinburgh, sent on board a vessel as a bondsman to the plantations in America. His wrongs, however, were happily soon over; for the ship in which he was embarked perished among the Orkney islands, and he, with two hundred other sufferers, received the crown of martyrdom from the waves.

O Charles Stuart, king of Scotland! and thou, James Sharp! – false and cruel men – But ye are called to your account; and what avails it now to the childless father to rail upon your memory?

Before proceeding farther at this present time with the doleful tale of my own sufferings, it is required of me, as an impartial historian, to note here a very singular example of the spirit of piety which reigned in the hearts of the Covenanters, especially as I shall have to show that such was the cruel and implacable nature of the Persecution, that time had not its wonted influence to soften in any degree its rigour. Thirteen years had passed from the time of the Pentland raid; and surely the manner in which the country had suffered for that rising might, in so long a course of years, have subdued the animosity with which we were pursued; especially, as during the Earl of Tweeddale's administration the bonds of peace had been accepted. But Lauderdale, now at the head of the councils, was rapacious for money; and therefore all offences, if I may employ that courtly term, by which our endeavours to taste of the truth were designated, – all old offences, as I was saying, were renewed against us as recent crimes, and an innocent charity to the remains of those who had suffered for the Pentland raid was made a reason, after the battle of Bothwell-brigg, to revive the persecution of those who had been out in that affair.

The matter particularly referred to arose out of the following circumstances:

The number of honest and pious men who were executed in different places, and who had their heads and their right hands with which they signed the Covenant at Lanerk cut off, and placed on the gates of towns and over the doors of tolbooths, had been very great. And it was very grievous, and a sore thing to the friends and acquaintances of those martyrs, when they went to Glasgow, or Kilmarnock, or Irvine, or Ayr, on their farm-business, to tryst or market, to see the remains of persons, whom they so loved and respected in life, bleaching in the winds and the rains of Heaven. It was indeed a matter of great heart-sadness, to behold such animosity carried beyond the grave; and few they were who could withstand the sight of the orphans that came thither, pointing out to one another their fathers' bones, and weeping as they did so, and vowing with an innocent indignation, that they would revenge their martyrdom.

Well do I remember the great sorrow that arose one market-day in Irvine, some five or six years after the Pentland raid, when Mrs M'Coul came, with her four weans and her aged gudemother, to look at the relics of her husband, who was martyred for his part in that rising. The bones were standing, with those of another martyr of that time, on a shelf which had been put up for the purpose, below the first wicket-hole in the steeple, just above the door. The two women were very decent in their apparel, rather more so than the common country wives. The gudemother, in particular, had a cast of gentility both in her look and garments; and I have heard the cause of it expounded, from her having been the daughter of one of the Reformation preachers in the gospel-spreading epoch of John Knox. She had a crimson satin plaid over her head, and she wore a black silk apron and a grey camlet gown. With the one hand she held the plaid close to her neck, and the youngest child, a lassie of seven years or so, had hold of her by the fore-finger of the other.

Mrs M'Coul was more of a robust fabric, and she was without any plaid, soberly dressed in the weeds of a widow, with a clean cambric handkerchief very snodly prined over her breast. The children were likewise beinly apparelled, and the two sons were buirdly and brave laddies, the one about nine, and the other maybe eleven years old.

It would seem that this had been the first of their pilgrimages of sorrow; for they stood some time in a row at the foot of the tolbooth stair, looking up at the remains, and wondering, with tears in their eyes, which were those they had come to see.

Their appearance drew around them many on-lookers,

both of the country-folk about the Cross and inhabitants of the town; but every one respected their sorrow, and none ventured to disturb them with any questions; for all saw that they were kith or kin to the godly men who had testified to the truth and the Covenant in death.

It happened, however, that I had occasion to pass by, and some of the town's folk who recollected me, said whisperingly to one another, but loud enough to be heard, that I was one of the persecuted; whereupon Mrs M'Coul turned round and said to me, with a constrained composure—

'Can ye tell me whilk o' yon's the head and hand o' John M'Coul, that was executed for the covenanting at Lanerk?'

I knew the remains well, for they had been pointed out to me, and I had seen them very often, but really the sight of the two women and the fatherless bairns so overcame me, that I was unable to answer.

'It's the head and the hand beside it, that has but twa fingers left, on the Kirkgate end o' the skelf!' replied a person in the crowd, whom I knew at once by his voice to be Willy Sutherland the hangman, although I had not seen him from the night of my evasion. And here let me not forget to set down the Christian worth and constancy of that simple and godly creature, who, rather than be instrumental in the guilty judgment by which John M'Coul and his fellow-sufferer were doomed to die, did himself almost endure martyrdom, and yet never swerved in his purpose, nor was abated in his integrity, in so much, that when questioned thereafter anent the same by the Earl of Eglinton, and his lordship, being moved by the simplicity of his piety, said, 'Poor man, you did well in not doing what they would have had you to do.'

'My Lord,' replied Willy, 'you are speaking treason! and yet you persecute to the uttermost, which shows that you go against the light of your conscience.'

'Do you say so to me, after I kept you from being hanged?' said his Lordship.

'Keep me from being drowned, and I will still tell you the verity.' The which honesty in that poor man begat for him a compassionate regard that the dignities of many great and many noble in that time could never command.

When the sorrowful M'Couls had indulged themselves in their melancholy contemplation, they went away, followed by the multitude with silence and sympathy, till they had mounted upon the cart which they had brought with them into the town. But from that time every one began to speak of the impiety of leaving the bones so wofully exposed; and after the skirmish at Drumclog, where Robin M'Coul, the eldest of the two striplings above spoken of, happened to be, when Mr John Welsh, with the Carrick men that went to Bothwell-brigg, was sent into Glasgow to bury the heads and hands of the martyrs there, Robin M'Coul came with a party of his friends to Irvine, to bury his father's bones. I was not myself present at the interment, being, as I have narrated, confined to my bed by reason of my wound. But I was told by the neighbours, that it was a very solemn and affecting scene. The grieved lad carried the relics of his father in a small box in his hands, covered with a white towel; and the godly inhabitants of the town, young and old, and of all denominations, to the number of several hundreds, followed him to the grave where the body was lying; and Willy Sutherland, moved by a simple sorrow, was the last of all; and he walked, as I was told, alone, behind, with his bonnet in his hand; for, from his calling, he counted himself not on an equality with other men. But it is time that I should return from this digression to the main account of my narrative.

Being wounded, as I have rehearsed, at Drumclog, and carried to my own house, Sarah Lochrig, while she grieved with a mother's grief for the loss of our first-born and the mournful fate of my honest brother, advanced my cure more by her loving ministrations to my aching mind, than by the medicaments that were applied to the bodily wound, in so much that something like a dawn of comfort was vouchsafed to me.

Our parish was singularly allowed to remain unmolested when, after the woful day of Bothwell-brigg, Claverhouse came to ravage the shire of Ayr, and to take revenge for the discomfiture which he had suffered, in his endeavour to disturb the worship and sacrament at Loudon-hill. Still, however, at times clouds overcame my spirit; and one night my daughter Margaret had a remarkable dream, which taught us to expect some particular visitation.

It was surely a mysterious reservation for the greater calamity which ensued, that while the vial of wrath was pouring out around us, my house should have been allowed to remain so unmolested. Often indeed, when in our nightly worship I returned thanks for a blessing so wonderful in that time of general wo, has a strange fear fallen upon me, and I have trembled in thought, as if the thing for which I sent up the incense of my thanks to Heaven, was a device of the Enemy of man, to make me think myself more deserving of favour than the thousands of covenanted brethren who then, in Scotland, were drinking of the bitterness of the suffering. But in proportion as I was then spared, the heavier afterwards was my trial.

Among the prisoners taken at Bothwell-brigg were many persons from our parish and neighbourhood, who, after their unheard-of sufferings among the tombs and graves of the Greyfriars church-yard at Edinburgh, were allowed to return home. Though in this there was a show of clemency, it was yet but a more subtle method of the tyranny to reach new victims. For those honest men were not long home till grievous circuit-courts were set agoing, to bring to trial not only all those who were at Bothwell, or approved of that rising, but likewise those who had been at the Pentland raid; and the better to ensure condemnation and punishment, sixteen persons were cited from every parish to bear witness as to who, among their neighbours, had been out at Bothwell, or had harboured any of those who were there. The wicked curates made themselves, in this grievous matter, engines of espionage, by giving in the names of those, their parishioners, whom they knew could bear the best testimony.

Thus it was, that many who had escaped from the slaughter – from the horrors of the Greyfriars church-yard – and from the drowning in the Orkneys, – and, like myself, had resumed their quiet country labour, were marked out for destruction. For the witnesses cited to Ayr against us were persons who had been released from the Greyfriars church-yard, as I have said, and who, being honest men, could not, when put to their oaths, but bear witness to the truth of the matters charged against us. And nothing surely could better show the devilish spirit with which those in authority were at that time actuated, nor the unchristian nature of the prelacy, than that the prisoners should thus have been set free to be made the accusers of their neighbours; and that the curates, men professing to be ministers of the gospel, should have been such fit instruments for such unheard-of machinations. But to hasten forward to the fate and issue of this self-consuming tyranny, I shall leave all generalities, and proceed with the events of my own case; and, in doing so, I shall endeavour what is in me to inscribe the particulars with a steady hand; for I dare no longer now trust myself with looking to the right or to the left of the field of my matter. I shall, however, try to narrate things just as they happened, leaving the courteous reader to judge what passed at the time in the suffocating throbs wherewith my heart was then affected.

It was the last day of February, of the year following Bothwell-brigg, that, in consequence of these subtle and wicked devices, I was taken up. I had, from my wound, been in an ailing state for many months, and could then do little in the field; but the weather for the season was mild, and I had walked out in the tranquillity of a sunny afternoon to give my son Joseph some instructions in the method of ploughing; for, though he was then but in his thirteenth year, he was a by-common stripling in capacity and sense. He was indeed a goodly plant; and I had hoped, in my old age, to have sat beneath the shelter of his branches; but the axe of the feller was untimely laid to the root, and it was too soon, with all the blossoms of the fairest promise, cast down into the dust. But my task now is of vengeance and justice, not of sorrowing, and I must more sternly grasp the iron pen.

A party of soldiers, who had been that afternoon sent out to bring in certain persons (among whom I was one) in a list malignantly transmitted to the Archbishop of Glasgow, by Andrew Dornock, the prelatic usurper of our minister's place, as I was leaving the field where my son was ploughing, saw me from the road, and ordered me to halt till they came up, or they would fire at me.

It would have been unavailing of me, in the state I then was, to have attempted to flee, so I halted; and, after some entreaty with the soldiers, got permission from them to have my horse and cart yoket, as I was not very well, and so to be carried to Ayr. And here I should note down that, although there was in general a coarse spirit among the King's forces, yet in these men there was a touch of common humanity. This was no doubt partly owing to their having been some months quartered in Irvine, where they became naturally softened by the friendly spirit of the place. It was not, however, ordained that men so merciful should be permitted to remain long there.

As it was an understood thing that the object of the trials to which the Covenanters were in this manner subjected, was chiefly to raise money and forfeitures for the rapacious Duke of Lauderdale, then in the rule and power of the council at Edinburgh, my being carried away prisoner to

Ayr awakened less grief and consternation in my family than might have been expected from the event. Through the humane permission of my guard, having a little time to confer with Sarah Lochrig before going away, it was settled between us that she should gather together what money she could procure, either by loan, or by selling our corn and cattle, in order to provide for the payment of the fine that we counted would be laid upon us. I was then taken to the tolbooth of Ayr, where many other covenanted brethren were lying to await the proceedings of the circuit-court, which was to be opened by the Lord Kelburne from Glasgow, on the second day after I had been carried thither.

Among the prisoners were several who knew me well, and who condoled as Christians with me for the loss I had sustained at Bothwell; so, but for the denial of the fresh and heavenly air, and the freedom of the fields, the time of our captivity might have been a season of much solace: for they were all devout men, and the tolbooth, instead of resounding with the imprecations of malefactors, became melodious with the voice of Psalms and of holy communion, and the sweet intercourse of spirits that delighted in one another for the constancy with which they had borne their testimony.

When the Lord Kelburne arrived, on the first day that the court opened, I was summoned to respond to the offences laid to my charge, if any charge of offence it may be called, wherein the purpose of the court was seemingly to search out opinions that might serve as matter to justify the infliction of the fines, – the whole end and intent of those circuits not being to award justice, but to find the means of extorting money. In some respects, however, I was more mercifully dealt by than many of my fellow-sufferers; but in order to show how, even in my case, the laws were perverted, I will here set down a brief record of my examination, or trial as it was called.

The council-room was full of people when I was taken thither, and the Lord Kelburne, who sat at the head of the table, was abetted in the proceedings by Murray, an advocate from Edinburgh. They were sitting at a wide round table, within a fence which prevented the spectators from pressing in upon them. There were many papers and letters folded up in bundles lying before them, and a candle burning, and wax for sigillation. Besides Lord Kelburne and his counsellor, there were divers gentlemen seated at the table, and two clerks to make notations.

Lord Kelburne, in his appearance, was a mild-looking man, and for his years his hair was very hoary; for though he was seemingly not passing fifty, it was in a manner quite blanched. In speech he was moderate, in disposition indulgent, and verily towards me he acted in his harsh duty with much gentleness.

But Murray had a doure aspect for his years, and there was a smile among his features not pleasant to behold, breeding rather distrust and dread, than winning confidence or affection, which are the natural fruit of a countenance rightly gladdened. He looked at me from aneath his brows as if I had been a malefactor, and turning to the Lord Kelburne, said—

'He has the true fanatical yellow look.'

This was a base observe; for naturally I was of a fresh complexion, but my long illness, and the close air of the prison, had made me pale.

After some more impertinencies of that sort, he then said—

'Ringan Gilhaize, you were at the battle of Bothwell-brigg.'

'I was not,' said I.

357

'You do not mean to say so, surely?'

'I have said it,' was my answer.

Whereupon one of the clerks whispered to him that there were three of the name in the list.

'O!' cried he, 'I crave your pardon, Ringan, there are several persons of your name; and though you were not at Bothwell yourself, maybe ye ken those of your name who were there, – Do you?'

'I did know two,' was my calm answer; 'one was my brother, and the other my son.'

All present remained very silent as I made this answer; and the Lord Kelburne bending forward, leant his cheek on his hand as he rested his elbow on the table, and looked very earnestly at me. Murray resumed—

'And pray now, Ringan, tell us what has become of the two rebels?'

'They were convenanted Christians,' said I; 'my son lies buried with those that were slain on that sore occasion.'

'But your brother; he was of course younger than you?'

'No; he was older.'

'Well, well, no matter as to that; but where is he?'

'I believe he is with his Maker; but his body lies among the rocks at the bottom of the Orkney seas.'

The steadiness of the Lord Kelburne's countenance saddened into the look of compassion, and he said to Murray—

'There is no use in asking him any more questions about them, proceed with the ordinary interrogatories.'

There was a murmur of satisfaction towards his Lordship at this; and Murray said—

'And so you say that those in the late rebellion at Bothwell were not rebels?'

'I said, sir, that my son and my brother were convenanted Christians.'

This I delivered with a firm voice, which seemed to produce some effect on the Lord Kelburne, who threw himself back in his chair, and crossing his arms over his breast, looked still more eagerly towards me.

'Do you mean then to deny,' said Murray, 'that the late rebellion was not a rebellion?'

'It would be hard, sir, to say what it was; for the causes thereto leading,' replied I, 'were provocations concerning things of God, and to those who were for that reason religiously there, I do not think, in a right sense, it can be called rebellion. Those who were there for carnal motives, and I doubt not there were many such, I fancy every honest man may say it was with them rebellion.'

'I must deal more closely with him,' said Murray to his Lordship; but his Lordship, before allowing him to put any more questions, said himself to me—

'But you know, to state the thing plainly, that the misguided people who were at Bothwell, had banded themselves against the laws of the realm, whether from religious or carnal motives is not the business we are here to sift, that point is necessarily remitted to God and their consciences.'

Murray added, 'It is most unreasonable to suppose, that every subject is free to determine of what is lawful to be obeyed. The thought is ridiculous. It would destroy the end of all laws which are for the advantage of communities, and which speak the sense of the generality touching the matter and things to which they refer.'

'My Lord,' said I, addressing myself to Lord Kelburne, 'it surely will ne'er be denied, that every subject is free to exercise his discretion with respek to his ain conduct; and your Lordship kens vera weel, that it is the duty of subjects to know the laws of the land; and your Lordship likewise knows, that God has given laws to all rulers as well as subjects, and both may and ought to know His laws. Now if I, knowing both the laws of God and the laws of the land, find the one contrary to the other, undoubtedly God's laws ought to hae the preference in my obedience.'

His Lordship looked somewhat satisfied with this answer; but Murray said to him—

'I will pose him with this question. If presbyterian government were established, as it was in the year 1648, and some ministers were not free to comply with it, and a law were made that none should hear them out o' doors, would you judge it reasonable that such ministers or their people should be at liberty to act in contempt of that law.'

And he looked mightily content with himself for this subtlety; but I said—

'Really, sir, I canna see a reason why hearkening to a preaching in the fields should be a greater guilt than doing the same thing in doors.'

'If I were of your principles,' said the advocate, 'and thought in my conscience that the laws of the land were contrary to the laws of God, and that I could not conform to them, I would judge it my duty rather to go out of the nation and live elsewhere, than disturb the peace of the land.'

'That were to suppose two things,' said I; 'first, that rulers may make laws contrary to the laws of God, and that when such laws are once made, they ought to be submitted to. But I think, sir, that rulers being under the law of God act wickedly, and in rebellion to him, when they make enactments contrary to his declared will; and surely it can ne'er be required that we should allow wickedness to be done.'

'I am not sure,' said Murray to his Lordship, 'that I do right in continuing this irrelevant conversation.'

'I am interested in the honest man's defence,' replied Lord Kelburne, 'and as 'tis in a matter of conscience, let us hear what makes it so.'

'Well then,' resumed the advocate, 'what can you say to the barbarous murder of Archbishop Sharp? – You will not contend that murder is not contrary to the law of God?'

'I ne'er contended,' said I, 'that any sin was permitted by the law of God – far less murder, which is expressly forbidden in the Ten Commands.'

'Then ye acknowledge the murder of the Archbishop to have been murder?'

'That's between those that did it and God.'

'Hooly, hooly, friend!' cried Murray; 'that, Ringan, winna do; was it or was it not murder?'

'Can I tell, who was not there?'

'Then, to satisfy your conscience on that score, Ringan, I would ask you, if a gang of ruffians slay a defenceless man, do or do they not commit murder?'

'I can easily answer that.'

Lord Kelburne again bent eagerly forward, and rested

his cheek again on his hand, placing his elbow on the table, while I continued—

'A gang of ruffians coming in wantonness, or for plunder, upon a defenceless man, and putting him to death, there can be no doubt is murder; but it has not yet been called murder to kill an enemy in battle; and therefore, if the captain of a host go to war without arms, and thereby be defenceless, it cannot be said, that those of the adverse party, who may happen to slay him, do any murder.'

'Do you mean to justify the manner of the death of the Archbishop?' exclaimed the advocate, starting back, and spreading out his arms in wonderment.

''Deed no, sir,' replied I, a little nettled at the construction he would put upon what I said; 'but I will say, even here, what Sir Davie Lindsay o' the Mount said on the similar event o' Cardinal Beaton's death,—

> 'As for this Cardinal, I grant
> He was the man we might well want;
> God will forgive it soon:
> But of a truth, the sooth to say,
> Although the loon be well away,
> The fact was foully done.'

There was a rustle of gratification among all in the court as I said the rhyme, and Lord Kelburne smiled; but Murray, somewhat out of humour, said—

'I fancy, my Lord, we must consider this as an admission that the killing of the Archbishop was murder?'

'I fear,' said his Lordship, 'that neither of the two questions have been so directly put as to justify me to pronounce any decision, though I am willing to put the most favourable construction on what has passed.' And then his Lordship, looking to me, added—

'Do you consider the late rebellion, being contrary to the King's authority, rebellion?'

'Contrary to the King's right authority,' replied I, 'it was not rebellion, but contrary to an authority, beyond the right, taken by him, despite the law of God, it was rebellion.'

'Wherefore, honest man,' rejoined his Lordship kindly,

'would you make a distinction that may bring harm on your own head? Is not the King's authority instituted by law and prerogative, and knowing that, cannot ye say, that those who rise in arms against it are rebels?'

'My Lord,' said I, 'you have my answer; for in truth and in conscience I can give none other.'

There was a pause for a short space, and one of the clerks looking to Lord Kelburne, his Lordship said, with a plain reluctance, 'It must even be so; write down that he is not clear the late rebellion should be called a rebellion;' and casting his eyes entreatingly towards me, he added – 'But I think you acknowledge that the assassination of Archbishop Sharp was a murder?'

'My Lord,' said I, 'your questions are propounded as tests, and therefore, as an honest man, I cannot suffer that my answers should be scant, lest I might be thought to waver in faith and was backward in my testimony. No, my Lord, I will not call the killing of Sharp murder; for, on my conscience, I do verily think he deserved the death: First, because of his apostacy; second, because of the laws of which he was the instigator, whereby the laws of God have been contravened; and, third, for the woes that those laws have brought upon the land, the which stirred the hearts of the people against him. Above all, I think his death was no murder, because he was so strong in his legalities, that he could not be brought to punishment by those to whom he had caused the greatest wrong;' and I thought, in saying these words, of my brother's desolated daughter – of his own sad death in the stormy seas of the Orkneys – and of my brave and gallant Michael, that was lying in his shroudless grave in the cold clay of Bothwell.

Lord Kelburne was troubled at my answer, and was about to remonstrate; but seeing the tear start into my eye as those things came into my mind, he said nothing, but nodding to the clerk, he bade him write down that I would not acknowledge the killing of the Archbishop a murder. He then rose and adjourned the court, remanding me to prison, saying, that he would send me word what would be the extent of my punishment.

The same night it was intimated to me that I was fined in five hundred marks, and that bonds were required to be given for the payment; upon the granting of which, in consideration of my ill health, the Lord Kelburne had consented I should be set free.

This was, in many respects, a more lenient sentence than I had expected; and in the hope that perhaps Sarah Lochrig might have been able to provide the money, so as to render the granting of the bonds and the procuring of cautioners unnecessary, I sent over a man on horseback to tell her the news; and the man in returning brought my son Joseph behind him, sent by his mother to urge me to give the bonds at once, as she had not been able to raise so much money; and the more to incite me, if there had been need for incitement, she had willed Joseph to tell me that a party of Claverhouse's dragoons had been quartered on the house that morning, to live there till the fine was paid.

Of the character of these freebooters I needed no certificate. They had filled every other place wherever they had been quartered with shame and never-ceasing sorrow, and therefore I was indeed roused to hear that my defenceless daughters were in their power. So I lost no time in sending my son to entreat two of his mother's relations, who were bein merchants in Ayr, to join me in the bond, – a thing which they did in the most compassionate manner; – and, the better to expedite the business, I got it to be permitted by the Lord Kelburne that the bonds should be sent the same day to Irvine, where I hoped to be able next morning to discharge them. All this was happily concerted and brought to a pleasant issue before sunset; – at which time I was discharged from the tolbooth, carrying with me many pious wishes from those who were there, and who had not been so gently dealt by.

It was my intent to have proceeded home the same night, but my son was very tired with the many errands he had run that day, and by his long ride in the morning; moreover, I was myself in need of repose, for my anxiety had brought on a disturbance in my blood, and my limbs shook, and I was altogether unable to undertake any journey. I was therefore too easily entreated of Archibald Lochrig, my wife's cousin, and one of my cautioners, to stop in his house that evening. But next morning, being much refreshed with a pleasant sleep and the fallacious cheering of happy dreams, I left Ayr, with my son, before the break of day, and we travelled with light feet, for our hearts were lifted up with hope.

Though my youth was long past, and many things had happened to sadden my spirit, I yet felt on that occasion an unaccountable sense of kindliness and joy. The flame of life was as it were renewed, and brightened in the pure and breezy air of the morning, and a bounding gladness rose in my bosom as my eye expatiated around in the freedom of the spacious fields. On the left-hand the living sea seemed as if the pulses of its moving waters were in unison with the throbbings of my spirit; and, like jocund maidens disporting themselves in the flowing tide, the gentle waves, lifting their heads, and spreading out their arms and raising their white bosoms to the rising sun, came as it were happily to the smooth sands of the sparkling shore. The grace of enjoyment brightened and blithened all things. There was a cheerfulness in the songs of the little birds that enchanted the young heart of my blooming boy to break forth into singing, and his carol was gayer than the melody of the lark. But that morning was the last time that either of us could ever after know pleasure any more in this world.

Eager to be home, and that I might share with Sarah Lochrig and our children the joy of thankfulness for my deliverance, I had resolved to call, in passing through Irvine, at the clerk's chamber, to inquire if the bonds had been sent from Ayr, that my cautioners might be as soon as possible discharged. But we had been so early a-foot that we reached the town while the inhabitants were yet all asleep, so that we thought it would be as well to go straight home; and accordingly we passed down the gait and through the town-end port without seeing any person in the street, save only the town-herd, as he was going with his horn to sound for the cows to be sent out to go with him to the moor.

The sight of a town in the peacefulness of the morning slumbers, and of a simple man going forth to lead the quiet cattle to pasture, filled my mind with softer thoughts than I had long known, and I said to my son—

'Surely those who would molest the peace of the poor hae ne'er rightly tasted the blessing of beholding the confidence with which they trust themselves in the watches of the night and amidst the perils of their barren lot.' And I felt my heart thaw again into charity with all men, and I was thankful for the delight.

As I was thus tasting again the luxury of gentle thoughts, a band of five dragoons came along the road, and Joseph said to me that they were the same who had been quartered in our house. I looked at them as they passed by, but they turned their heads aside.

'I wonder,' said my son, 'that they did na speak to me: I thought they had a black look.'

'No doubt, Joseph,' was my answer, 'the men are no lost to a' sense of shame. They canna but be rebuked at the sight of a man that, maybe against their will, poor fellows, they were sent to oppress.'

'I dinna like them the day, father, they're unco like ill-doers,' said the thoughtful and observing stripling.

But my spirit was at the time full of good-will towards all men, and I reasoned with him against giving way to unkind thoughts, expounding, to the best of my ability, the nature of gospel-charity, and the heavenlyness of good-will, saying to him—

'The nature of charity's like the light o' the sun, by which all things are cherished. It is the brightness of the soul, and the glorious quality which proves our celestial descent. Our other feelings are common to a' creatures, but the feeling of charity is divine. It's the only thing in which man partakes of the nature of God.'

Discoursing in this scriptual manner, we reached the Gowan-brae. My heart beat high with gladness. My son bounded forward to tell his mother and sisters of my coming. On gaining the brow of the hill he leapt from the ground with a frantic cry and clasped his hands. I ran towards him – but I remember no more, – though at times something crosses my mind, and I have wild visions of roofless walls, and a crowd of weeping women and silent men digging among ashes, and a beautiful body, all dropping wet, brought on a deal from the mill-dam, and of men, as it was carried by, seizing me by the arms and tying my hands, – and then I fancy myself in a house fastened to a chair; – and sometimes I think I was lifted out and placed to beek in the sun and to taste the fresh air. But what these things import I dare only guess, for no one has ever told me what became of my benign Sarah Lochrig and our two blooming daughters; – all is phantasma that I recollect of the day of my return home. I said my soul was iron, and my heart converted into stone. O that they were indeed so! But sorrowing is a vain thing, and my task must not stand still.

When I left Ayr the leaves were green, and the fields gay, and the waters glad; and when the yellow leaf rustled on the ground, and the waters were drumly, and the river roaring, I was somehow, I know not by what means, in the kirk-yard, and a film fell from the eyes of my reason, and I looked around, and my little boy had hold of me by the hand, and I said to him, 'Joseph, what's yon sae big and green in our lair?' and he gazed in my face, and the tears came into his eyes, and he replied—

'Father, they are a' in the same grave.' I took my hand out of his; – I walked slowly to the green tomb; – I knelt down, and I caused my son to kneel beside me, and I vowed enmity for ever against Charles Stuart and all of his line; and I prayed, in the words of the Psalmist, that when he was judged he might be condemned. Then we rose; but my son said to me—

'Father, I canna wish his condemnation; but I'll fight by your side till we have harlt him down from his bloody throne.'

And I felt that I had forgotten I was a Christian, and I again knelt down and prayed, but it was for the sin I had done in the vengeance of the latter clause. 'Nevertheless, Lord,' I then cried, 'as thou thyself didst take the sceptre from Saul, and gave the crown to David, make me an instrument to work out the purposes of thy dreadful justice, which in time will come to be.'

Then I rose again, and went towards the place where my home had been; but when I saw the ruins I ran back to the kirk-yard, and threw myself on the grave, and cried to the earth to open and receive me.

But the Lord had heard my prayer, and while I lay there he sent down his consoling angel, and the whirlwind of my spirit was calmed, and I remembered the promise of my son to fight by my side, and I rose to prepare myself for the warfare.

While I was lying on the ground several of the neighbours had heard my wild cries, and came into the kirk-yard; but by that time the course of the tempest had been staid, and they stood apart with my son, who told them I was come again to myself, and they thought they ought not to disturb me; when, however, they saw me rise, they drew near and spoke kindly to me, and Zachariah Smylie invited me to go back with him to his house; for it was with him that I had been sheltered during the phrenzy. But I said—

'No: I will neither taste meat nor drink, nor seek to rest myself, till I have again a sword.' And I entreated him to give me a little money, that, with my son, we might go into Irvine and provide ourselves with weapons.

The worthy man looked very sorrowful to hear me so speak, and some of the others, that were standing by, began to reason with me, and to represent the peril of any enterprise at that time. But I pointed to the grave, and said—

'Friens, do you ken what's in yon place, and do ye counsel me to peace?' At which words they turned aside and shook their heads; and Zachariah Smylie went and brought me a purse of money, which having put into my bosom, I took my son by the hand, and bidding them all farewell, we walked to the town silently together, and I thought of my brother's words in his grief, that the speed of lightning was slow to the wishes of revenge.

CHAPTER SIXTEEN

On arriving in Irvine, we went to the shop of Archibald
Macrusty, a dealer in iron implements, and I bought from
him two swords without hilts, which he sold, wrapt in
straw-rope, as scythe-blades, – a method of diguise that
the ironmongers were obligated to have recourse to at
that time, on account of the search now and then made
for weapons by the soldiers, ever from the time that
Claverhouse came to disarm the people; and when I
had bought the two blades we went to Bailie Girvan's
shop, which was a nest of a' things, and bought two
hilts, without any questions being asked; for the bailie
was a discreet man, with a warm heart to the Covenant,
and not selling whole swords, but only hilts and hefts, it
could not be imputed to him that he was guilty of selling
arms to suspected persons.

Being thus provided with two swords, we went into
James Glassop's public, where, having partaken of some
refreshment, we remained solemnly sitting by ourselves till
towards the gloaming, when, recollecting that it would be a
comfort to us in the halts of our undertaking, I sent out my
son to buy a Bible, and while he was absent I fell asleep.

On awaking from my slumber I felt greatly composed
and refreshed. I reflected on the events of the day, and
the terrible truths that had broken in upon me, and I
was not moved with the same stings of desperation that,
on my coming to myself, had shot like fire through my
brain; so I began to consider of the purpose whereon I
was bowne, and that I had formed no plan, nor settled
towards what airt I should direct my steps. But I was not
the less determined to proceed, and I said to my son, who
was sitting very thoughtful with THE BOOK lying on the
table before him—

'Open the Bible, and see what the Lord instructs us to do at this time.' And he opened it, and the first words he saw and read were those of the nineteenth verse of the forty-eighth chapter of the Prophet Jeremiah,—

'O inhabitant of Aroer, stand by the way and espy; ask him that fleeth, and her that escapeth, and say, What is done?'

So I rose, and bidding my son close the Book, and bring it with him, we went out, with our sword-hilts, and the blades still with the straw-rope about them, in our hands, into the street together, where we had not long been when a soldier on horseback passed us in great haste; and many persons spoke to him as he rode by, inquiring what news he had brought; but he was in trouble of mind, and heeded them not till he reached the door of the house where the captain of the soldiers then in Irvine was abiding.

When he had gone into the house and delivered his message, he returned to the street, where by that time a multitude, among which we were, had assembled, and he told to the many, who inquired as it were with one voice, – That Mr Cargill, and a numerous party of the Cameronians, had passed that afternoon through Galston, and it was thought they meditated some disturbance on the skirts of Kilmarnock, which made the commander of the King's forces in that town send for aid to the captain of those then in Irvine.

As soon as I heard the news, I resolved to go that night to Kilmarnock, and abide with my sister-in-law, the widow of my brother Jacob, by whose instrumentality I thought we might hear where the Cameronians then were. For, although I approved not of their separation from the general presbyterian kirk of Scotland, nor was altogether content with their declaration published at Sanquhar, there was yet one clause which, to my spirit, impoverished of all hope, was as food and raiment; and that there may be no perversion concerning the same in after times, I shall here set down the words of the clause, and the words are these:—

'Although we be for government and governors such as the Word of God and our Covenant allows, yet we for ourselves, and all that will adhere to us, do, by thir presents, disown Charles Stuart, that has been reigning (or rather tyrannizing as we may say) on the throne of Britain these years bygone, as having any right or title to, or interest in, the crown of Scotland for government, he having forfeited the same several years since by his perjury and breach of Covenant both to God and His Kirk;' and further, I did approve of those passages wherein it was declared, that he 'should have been denuded of being king, ruler, or magistrate, or having any power to act or to be obeyed as such:' as also, 'we being under the standard of our Lord Jesus Christ, Captain of Salvation, do declare a war with such a tyrant and usurper, and all the men of his practices, as enemies to our Lord.'

Accordingly, on hearing that the excommunicated and suffering society of the Cameronians were so near, I resolved, on receiving the soldier's information, and on account of that recited clause of the Sanquhar declaration, to league myself with them, and to fight in their avenging battles; for, like me, they had endured irremediable wrongs, injustice, and oppressions, from the persecutors, and for that cause had, like me, abjured the doomed and papistical race of the tyrannical Stuarts. With my son, therefore, I went toward Kilmarnock, in the hope and with the intent expressed; and though the road was five long miles, and though I had not spoken more to him all day, nor for days, and weeks, and months before, than I have set down herein, we yet continued to travel in silence.

The night was bleak, and the wind easterly, but the road was dry, and my thoughts were eager; and we hastened onward, and reached the widow's door, without the interchange of a word in all the way.

'Wha do ye want?' said my son, 'for naebody hae lived here since the death of aunty.'

I was smote upon the heart, by these few words, as it were with a stone; for it had not come into my mind to think of inquiring how long the eclipse of my reason had lasted, nor of what had happened among our friends in the interim. This shock, however, had a salutary effect in staying the haste which was still in my thoughts, and I conversed with my son more collectedly than I could have done before it, and he told me of many things very doleful to hear, but I was thankful to learn, that the end of my brother's widow had been in peace, and not caused by any of those grievous unchances which darkened the latter days of so many of the pious in that epoch of the great displeasure.

But the disappointment of finding that Death had barred her door against us, made it needful to seek a resting-place in some public, and as it was not prudent to carry our blades and hilts into any such place of promiscuous resort, we went up the town, and hid them by the star-light in a field at a dyke-side, and then returning as wayfarers, we entered a public, and bespoke a bed for the night.

While we were sitting in that house by the kitchen fire, I bethought me of the Bible which my son had in his hand, and told him that it would do us good if he would read a chapter; but just as he was beginning, the mistress said—

'Sirs, dinna expose yoursels; for wha kens but the enemy may come in upon you. It's an unco thing now-a-days to be seen reading the Bible in a change-house.'

So, being thus admonished, I bade my son put away the Book; and we retired from the fireside, and sat by oursels in the shadow of a corner: and well it was for us that we did so, and a providential thing that the worthy woman had been moved to give us the admonition; for we were not many minutes within the mirk and obscurity into which we had removed, when two dragoons, who had been skirring the country, like blood-hounds, in pursuit of Mr Cargill, came in and sat themselves down by the fire. Being sorely tired with their day's hard riding, they were wroth and blasphemous against all the Covenanters for the trouble they gave them; and I thought when I heard them venting their bitterness, that they spoke as with the voice of the persecutors that were the true cause of the grievances whereof they complained; for no doubt it was a hateful thing to persons dressed in authority not to get their own way, yet I could not but wonder how it never came into the minds of such persons, that if they had not trodden upon the worm it would never have turned. As for the Cameronians they were at war with the house of Stuart, and having disowned King Charles, it was a thing to be looked for, that all of his sect and side would be their consistent enemies. So I was none troubled by what the soldiers said of them, but my spirit was chafed into the quick to hear the remorselessness of their enmity against all the Covenanters and presbyterians, respecting whom they swore with the hoarseness of revenge, wishing in such a frightful manner the whole of us in the depths of perdition, that I could no longer hear them without rebuking their cruel hatred and most foul impiety.

'What gars you, young man' said I to the fiercest of the two dragoons, an Englisher, 'what gars you in that dreadful manner hate and blaspheme honest men, who would, if they were permitted, dwell in peace with all mankind?'

'Permitted!' cried he, turning round and placing his chair between me and the door, 'and who does not permit them? Let them seek the way to heaven according to law, and no one will trouble them.'

'The law, I'm thinking,' replied I very mildly, 'is mair likely to direct them to another place.'

'Here's a fellow,' cried the soldier, riotously laughing to his companion, 'that calls the King's proclamation the devil's fingerpost. I say, friend, come a little nearer the light. Is your name Cargill?'

'No,' replied I; and the light of the fire then happening to shine bright in his face, my son laid his trembling hand on mine, and whispered to me with a faltering tongue—

'O! it's one of the villains that burnt our house, and——'

What more he added I know not, for at the word I leapt from my seat, and rushed upon the soldier. His companion flew in between us, but the moment that the criminal saw my son, who also sprung forward, he uttered a fearful howl of horror, and darted out of the house.

The other soldier was surprised, but collected; and shutting the door, to prevent us from pursuing or escaping, said—

'What the devil's this?'

'That's my father,' said my son boldly, 'Ringan Gilhaize of Quharist.'

The dragoon looked at me for a moment, with concern in his countenance, and then replied, 'I have heard of your name, but I was not of the party. It was a damned black job. But sit down, Ecclesfield will not be back. He has ever since of a night been afraid of ghosts, and he's off as if he had seen one. So don't disturb yourself, but be cool.'

I made no answer, nor could I; but I returned and sat down in the corner where we had been sitting, and my son, at the same time, took his place beside me, laying his hand on mine: and I heard his heart beating, but he too said not a word.

It happened that none of the people belonging to the house were present at the uproar; but hearing the noise, the mistress and the gudeman came rushing ben. The soldier, who still stood calmly with his back to the door, nodded to them to come towards him, which they did, and he began to tell them something in a whisper. The landlord held up his hands and shook his head, and the mistress cried, with tears in her eyes, 'No wonder! no wonder!'

'Had ye no better gang out and see for Ecclesfield?' said the landlord, with a significant look to the soldier.

The young man cast his eyes down, and seemed thought-ful.

'I may be blamed,' said he.

'Gang but the house, gudewife, and bring the gardivine,' resumed the gudeman; and I saw him touch her on the arm, and she immediately went again into the room whence they had issued. 'Come into the fire, Jack Windsor, and sit down,' continued he; and the soldier, with some reluctance, quitted the door, and took his seat between me and it, where Ecclesfield had been sitting.

'Ye ken, Jack,' he resumed when they were seated, 'that unless there are two of you present, ye canna put any man to the test, so that every body who has not been tested is free to go wheresoever it pleasures himsel.'

The dragoon looked compassionately towards me; and the mistress coming in at the time with a case-bottle under her arm, and a green Dutch dram-glass in her hand, she filled it with brandy, and gave it to her husband.

'Here's to you, Jack Windsor,' said the landlord, as he put the glass to his lips, 'and I wish a' the English in England were as orderly and good-hearted as yoursel, Jack Windsor.'

He then held the glass to the mistress, and she made it a lippy.

'Hae, Jack,' said the landlord, 'I'm sure, after your hard travail the day, ye'll no be the waur of a dram.'

'Curse the liquor,' exclaimed the dragoon, 'I'm not to be bribed by a dram.'

'Nay,' cried the landlord, 'Gude forbid that I should be a briber,' still holding the glass towards the soldier, who sat in a thoughtful posture, plainly swithering.

'That fellow Ecclesfield,' said he, as it were to himself, 'the game's up with him in this world.'

'And in the next too, Jack Windsor, if he does na repent,' replied the landlord; and the dragoon put forth his hand, and taking the glass, drank off the brandy.

'It's a damned hard service this here in Scotland,' said Windsor, holding the empty glass in his hand.

''Deed is't, Jack,' said the landlord, 'and it canna be a pleasant thing to a warm-hearted lad like you, Jack Windsor, to be ravaging poor country folk, only because they hae gotten a bee in their bonnets about prelacy.'

'Damn prelacy, says I,' exclaimed the dragoon.

'Whisht, whisht, Jack,' said the landlord; 'but when a man's sae scomfisht as ye maun be the night after your skirring, a word o' vexation canna be a great faut. Gudewife, fill Jack's glass again. Ye'll be a' the better o't, Jack;' and he took the glass from the dragoon's hand and held it to his wife, who again filled it to the flowing eye.

'I should think,' said the dragoon, 'that Ecclesfield cannot be far off. He ought not to have run away till we had tested the strangers.'

'Ah! Jack Windsor,' replied the landlord, holding out the glass to him, 'that's easy for you, an honest lad wi' a clear conscience, to say, but think o' what Ecclesfield was art and part in. Ye may thank your stars, Jack, that ye hae ne'er been guilty o' the foul things that he's wyted wi'. Are your father and mother living, Jack Windsor?'

'I hope so,' said the dragoon, 'but the old man was a little so so when I last heard of 'em.'

'Aye, Jack', replied the landlord, 'auld folks are failing subjects. Ye hae some brothers and sisters nae doubt?

They maun be weel-looked an they're ony thing like you, Jack.'

'I have but one sister,' replied the dragoon, 'and there's not a gooder girl in England, nor a lady in it that has the bloom of Sally Windsor.'

'Ye're braw folk, you Englishers, and ye're happy folk, whilk is far better,' said the landlord, presenting the second glass, which Jack drank off at once, and returned to the mistress, signifying with his hand that he wanted no more; upon which she retired with the gardivine, while the landlord continued, 'it's weel for you in the south yonder, Jack, that your prelates do not harass honest folk.'

'We have no prelates in England, thank God,' said the dragoon; 'we wouldn't have 'em, our parsons are other sort o' things.'

'I thought ye had an host o' bishops, Jack,' said the landlord.

'True, and good fellows some on 'em are; but though prelates be bishops, bishops a'n't prelates, which makes a difference.'

'And a blessed difference it is; for how would ye like to hear of your father's house being burnt and him in prison, and your bonny innocent sister? – Eh! is nae that Ecclesfield's foot clampering wi' his spurs at the door?'

The dragoon listened again, and looked thoughtful for a little time, and turned his eyes hastily towards the corner where we were sitting.

The landlord eyed him anxiously.

'Yes,' cried the poor fellow, starting from his seat, and striking his closed right hand sharply into his left; 'yes, I ought and I will;' adding calmly to the landlord, 'confound Ecclesfield, where the devil is he gone? I'll go see;' and he instantly went out.

The moment he had left the kitchen, the landlord rose and said to us, 'Flee, flee, and quit this dangerous town!'

Whereupon we rose hastily, and my son lifting the Bible, which he had laid in the darkness of the corner, we instanter left the house, and, notwithstanding the speed that was in our steps as we hurried up the street, I had a glimpse of the compassionate soldier standing at the corner of the house when we ran by.

Thus, in a very extraordinary manner, was the dreadful wo that had befallen me and mine most wonderfully made a mean, through the conscience of Ecclesfield, to effectuate our escape.

CHAPTER EIGHTEEN

On leaving the public we went straight to the place where our blades and belts lay, and took them up, and proceeded in an easterly direction. But I soon found that I was no longer the man I had once been; suffering and the fever of my frenzy had impaired my strength, and the weight of four and fifty years was on my back; so that I began to weary for a place of rest for the night, and I looked often around to discover the star of any window; but all was dark, and the bleak easterly wind searched my very bones; even my son, whose sturdy health and youthy blood made him abler to thole the night-air, complained of the nipping cold.

Many a time yet, when I remember that night, do I think with wonder and reverence of our condition. An infirm grey-haired man, with a deranged head and a broken heart, going forth amidst the winter's wind, with a little boy, not passing thirteen years of age, to pull down from his throne the guarded King of three mighty kingdoms, – and we did it, – such was the doom of avenging justice, and such the pleasure of Heaven. But let me proceed to rehearse the trials I was required to undergo before the accomplishment of that high predestination.

Weary, as I have said, very cold and disconsolate, we walked hirpling together for some time; at last we heard the rumbling of wheels before us, and my son running forward came back and told me it was a carrier. I hastened on, and with a great satisfaction found it was Robin Brown, the Ayr and Kilmarnock carrier. I had known him well for many years, and surely it was a providential thing that we met him in our distress, for he was the brother of a godly man, on whose head, while his family were around him, Claverhouse, with his own bloody hands, placed the glorious diadem of martyrdom.

He had been told what had befallen me and mine, and was greatly amazed to hear my voice, and that I was again come to myself; and he helped both my son and me into the cart; and, as he walked by the wheel, he told me of many things which had happened during my eclipse, and of the dreadful executions at Edinburgh of the prisoners taken at Airsmoss, and how that papist James Stuart, Duke of York, the King's brother, was placed at the head of the Scottish councils, and was then rioting in the delights of cruelty, with the use of the torture and the thumbikins upon prisoners suspected, or accused of being honest to their vows and their religious profession. But my mind was unsettled, and his tale of calamity passed over it like the east wind that blew that night so freezingly, cruel to the sense at the time, but of which the morrow showed no memorial.

I said nothing to Robin Brown of what my intent was, but that I was on my way to join the Cameronians, if I knew where they might be found; and he informed me, that after the raid of Airsmoss they had scattered themselves into the South country, where, as Claverhouse had the chief command, the number of their friends was likely to be daily increased, by the natural issue of his cruelties, and that vindictive exasperation, which was a passion and an affection of his mind for the discomfiture he had met with at Drumclog.

'But,' said the worthy man, 'I hope, Ringan Gilhaize, ye'll yet consider the step before ye tak it. Ye're no at this time in a condition o' health to warsle wi' hardship, and your laddie there's owre young to be o' ony fek in the way o' war; for ye ken the Cameronians hae declar't war against the King, and, being few and far apart, they're hunted down in a' places.'

'If I canna fight wi' men,' replied my brave stripling, 'I can help my father; but I'm no fear't: David was but a herd laddie, maybe nae aulder nor bigger than me, when he fell't the muckle Philistine wi' a stane.'

I made no answer myself to Robin Brown's remonstrance, because my resolution was girded as it were with a gir of brass and adamant, and, therefore, to reason more or farther concerning aught but of the means to achieve my purpose, was a thing I could not abide. Only I said to him, that being weary, and not in my wonted health, I would try to compose myself to sleep, and he would waken me when he thought fit, for that I would not go with him to Glasgow, but shape our way towards the South country. So I stretched myself out, and my dear son laid himself at my back, and the worthy man happing us with his plaid, we soon fell asleep.

When the cart stopped at the Kingswell, where Robin was in the usage of halting half an hour, he awoke us; and there being no strangers in the house we alighted, and going in, warmed ourselves at the fire.

Out of a compassion for me the mistress warmed and spiced a pint of ale; but, instead of doing me any good, I had not long partaken of the same when I experienced a great coldness and a trembling in my limbs, in so much that I felt myself very ill, and prayed the kind woman to allow me to lie down in a bed; which she consented to do in a most charitable manner, causing her husband, who was a covenanted man, as I afterwards found, to rise out of his, and give me their own.

The cold and the tremblings were but the symptoms and beginnings of a sore malady, which soon rose to such a head that Robin Brown taiglet more than two hours for me; but still I grew worse and worse, and could not be removed for many days. On the fifth I was brought so nigh unto the gates of death that my son, who never left the bed-stock, thought at one time I had been released from my trouble. But I was reserved for the task that the Lord had in store for me, and from that time I began to recover; and nothing could exceed the tenderness wherewith I was treated by those Samaritan Christians, the landlord and his wife of the public at Kingswell. This distemper, however, left a great imbecility of body behind it; and I wondered whether it could be of providence to prevent me from going forward with my avenging purpose against Charles Stuart and his counsellors.

Being one day in this frame of dubiety, lying in the bed, and my son sitting at my pillow, I said to him, 'GET THE BOOK, and open and read;' which he accordingly did; and the first verse that he cast his eye upon was the twenty-fourth of the seventh chapter of Isaiah, 'With arrows and with bows shall men come.'

'Stop,' said I, 'and go to the window and see who are coming;' but when he went thither and looked out he could see no one far nor near. Yet still I heard the tramp of many feet, and I said to him, 'Assuredly, Joseph, there are many persons coming towards this house, and I think they are not men of war, for their steps are loose, and they march not in the order of battle.'

This I have thought was a wonderful sharpness of hearing with which I was for a season then gifted; for soon after a crowd of persons were discovered coming over the moor towards the house, and it proved to be Mr Cargill, with about some sixty of the Cameronians, who had been hunted from out their hiding-places in the south.

CHAPTER NINETEEN

It is surely a most strange matter, that whenever I come to think and to write of the events of that period, and of my sickness at Kingswell, my thoughts relapse into infirmity, and all which then passed moves, as it were, before me in mist, disorderly and fantastical. But wherefore need I thus descant of my own estate, when so many things of the highest concernment are pressing upon my tablets for registration? Be it therefore enough that I mention here how much I was refreshed by the prayers of Mr Cargill, who was brought into my sick-chamber, where he wrestled with great efficacy for my recovery; and that after he had made an end, I felt so much strengthened, that I caused myself to be raised from my bed and placed in a chair at the open window, that I might see the men who had been heartened from on high, by the sense of their sufferings, to proclaim war against the man-sworn King, our common foe.

They were scattered before the house, to the number of more than fifty, some sitting on stones, others stretched on the heather, and a few walking about by themselves, ruminating on mournful fancies. Their appearance was a thought wild and raised, – their beards had not been shaven for many a day, – their apparel was also much rent, and they had all endured great misfortunes in their families and substance. Their homes had been made desolate; some had seen their sons put to death, and not a few the ruin of their innocent daughters and the virtuous wives of their bosoms, – all by the fruit of laws and edicts which had issued from the councils of Charles Stuart, and were enforced by men drunken with the authority of his arbitrary will.

But though my spirit clove to theirs, and was in unison with their intent, I could not but doubt of so poor a handful of forlorn men, though it be written, that the race is not to the swift nor the battle to the strong, and I called to my son to bring me the Book, that I might be instructed from the Word what I ought at that time to do; and when he had done so I opened it, and the twenty-second chapter of Genesis met my eye, and I was awed and trembled, and my heart was melted with sadness and an agonizing grief. For the command to Abraham to sacrifice Isaac his only son, whom he so loved, on the mountains in the land of Moriah, required of me to part with my son, and to send him with the Cameronians; and I prayed with a weeping spirit and the imploring silence of a parent's heart, that the Lord would be pleased not to put my faith to so great a trial.

I took the Book again, and I opened it a second time, and the command of the sacred oracle was presented to me in the fifth verse of the fifth chapter of Ecclesiastes—

'Better is it that thou shouldest not vow, than that thou shouldest vow and not pay.'

But still the man and the father were powerful with my soul; and the weakness of disease was in me, and I called my son towards me, and I bowed my head upon his hands as he stood before me, and wept very bitterly, and pressed him to my bosom, and was loath to send him away.

He knew not what caused the struggle wherewith he saw me so moved, and he became touched with fear lest my reason was again going from me. But I dried my eyes, and told him it was not so, and that maybe I would be better if I could compose myself to read a chapter. So I again opened the volume, and the third command was in the twenty-sixth verse of the eighth chapter of St Matthew:

'Why are ye fearful, O ye of little faith?'

But still notwithstanding my rebellious heart would not consent; – and I cried, – 'I am a poor infirm, desolate, and destitute man, and he is all that is left me. O that mine eyes were closed in death, and that this head, which sorrow, and care, and much misery have made untimely grey, were laid on its cold pillow, and the green curtain of the still kirk-yard were drawn around me in my last long sleep.'

Then again the softness of a mother's fondness came upon my heart, and I grasped the wondering stripling's hands in mine, and shook them, saying, 'But it must be so, it is the Lord's will, – thrice has he commanded, and I dare not rebel thrice.'

'What has he commanded, father,' said the boy, 'what is his will, for ye ken it maun be done?'

'Read,' said I, 'the twenty-second chapter of Genesis.'

'I ken't, father; it's about Abraham and wee Isaac; but though ye tak me into the land of Moriah, and up to the top of the hill, maybe a ram will be catched by the horns in a whin-bush for the burnt-offering, and ye'll no hae ony need to kill me.'

At that moment Mr Cargill came again into the room to bid me farewell; but seeing my son standing with the tear of simplicity in his eye, and me in the weakness of my infirm estate weeping upon his hands, he stopped and inquired what then had so moved us; whereupon I looked towards him and said—

'When I was taken with the malady that has thus changed the man in me to more than the gentleness of woman, ye ken, as I have already told you, we were bowne to seek your folk out and to fight on your side. But when I beheld your dejected and much-persecuted host, a doubt came to me, that surely it could not be that the Lord intended through them to bring about the deliverance of the land; and under this doubt as to what I should now do, and my limbs being moreover still in the fetters of sickness, I consulted the oracle of God.'

'And what has been the answer?'

'It has instructed me to send my son with you. But O, it is a terrible probation.'

'You have done well, my friend,' replied the godly man, 'to seek advice from THE WORD; but apply again, and maybe – maybe, Ringan, ye'll no be put to so great a trial.'

To this I could only say, 'Alas! sir, twice have I again consulted the oracle, and twice has the answer been an exhortation and a reproach that I should be so loth to obey.'

'But what for, father,' interposed my son, 'need ye be sae fashed about it. I would ne'er refuse; – I'm ready to gang, if ye were na sae weakly; – and though the folk afore the house are but a wee waff-like, ye ken it is written in the Book, that the race is not to the swift nor the battle to the strong.'

Mr Cargill looked with admiration at the confidence of this young piety, and laying his hand on the boy's head, said, 'I have not found so great faith, no, not in Israel. The Lord is in this, Ringan, put your trust in Him.'

Whereupon I took my son's hand and I placed it in the martyr's hand, and I said, 'Take him, lead him wheresoever ye will. I have sinned almost to disobedience, but the confidence has been renewed within me.'

'Rejoice,' said Mr Cargill, in words that were as the gift of health to my enfeebled spirit, 'Rejoice, and be exceeding glad; for great is your reward in heaven; for so persecuted they the prophets which were before you.'

As he pronounced the latter clause I felt my thoughts flash with a wild remembrance of the desolation of my house; but he began to return thanks for the comfort that he himself enjoyed in his outcast condition, of beholding so many proofs of the unshaken constancy of faith still in the land, and prayed for me in words of such sweet eloquence, that even in the parting from my son, – my last, whom I loved so well, they cherished me with a joy passing all understanding.

At the conclusion of his inspired thanksgiving, I kissed my Joseph on the forehead, and bidding him remember what his father's house had been, bade him farewell.

His young heart was too full to reply; and Mr Cargill too was so deeply affected that he said nothing; so, after shaking me by the hand, he led him away.

And if I did sin when they were departed, in the complaint of my childless desolation, for no less could I account it, it was a sin that surely will not be heavily laid against me. 'O Absalom, my son, my son, – would I had died for thee,' cried the warlike King David, when Absalom was slain in rebellion against him, and he had still many children; but my innocent Absalom was all that I had left.

During the season that the malady continued upon me, through the unsuspected agency of Robin Brown, a paction was entered into with certain of my neighbours, to take the lands of Quharist on tack among them, and to pay me a secret stipend, by which, means were obtained to maintain me in a decency when I was able to be removed into Glasgow. And when my strength was so far restored that I could bear the journey, the same good man entered into a stipulation with Mrs Aird, the relict of a gospel minister, to receive me as a lodger, and he carried me in on his cart to her house at the foot of the Stockwell.

With that excellent person I continued several months unmolested, but without hearing any tidings of my son. Afflicting tales were however of frequent occurrence, concerning the rigour wherewith the Cameronians were hunted; so that what with anxiety, and the backwardness of nature to rally in ailments ayont fifty, I continued to languish, incapable of doing any thing in furtherance of the vow of vengeance that I had vowed. Nor should I suppress, that in my infirmity there was often a wildness about my thoughts, by which I was unfitted at times to hold communion with other men.

On these occasions I sat wondering if the things around me were not the substanceless imageries of a dream, and fancying that those terrible truths whereof I can yet only trust myself to hint, might be the fallacies of a diseased sleep. And I contested as it were with the reality of all that I saw, touched, and felt, and struggled like one oppressed with an incubus, that I might awake and find myself again at Quharist in the midst of my family.

At other times I felt all the loneliness of the solitude into which my lot was then cast, and it was in vain that

I tried to appease my craving affections with the thought, that in parting with my son I had given him to the Lord. I durst not say to myself there was aught of frenzy in that consecration; but when I heard of Cameronians shot on the hills or brought to the scaffold, I prayed that I might receive some token of an accepted offering in what I had done.

Sterner feelings too had their turns of predominance. I recalled the manifold calamities which withered my native land – the guilty provocations that the people had received – the merciless avarice and rapacious profligacy that had ruined so many worthies – the crimes that had scattered so many families – and the contempt with which all our wrongs and woes were regarded; and then I would remember my avenging vow, and supplicate for health.

At last, one day Mrs Aird, who had been out on some household cares, returned home in great distress of mind, telling me that the soldiers had got hold of Mr Cargill, and had brought him into the town.

This happened about the ninth or tenth of July, in the afternoon; and the day being very sultry, the heat had oppressed me with langour, and I was all day as one laden with sleep. But no sooner had Mrs Aird told me this, than I felt the langour depart from me, as if a cumbrous cloak had been taken away, and I rose up a recruited and re-animated man. It was so much the end of my debility of body and sorrowing of mind, that she was loquacious with her surprise when she saw me, as it were, with a miraculous restoration, prepare myself to go out in order to learn, if possible, some account of my son.

When, however, I went into the street, and saw a crowd gathered around the guard-house, my heart failed me a little, not for fear, but because the shouts of the multitude were like the yells and derisions of insult; and I thought they were poured upon the holy sufferer. It was not, however, so; the gospel-taught people of Glasgow were, notwithstanding their prelatic thraldom, moved far otherwise, and their shouts and scoffings were against a townsman of their own, who had reviled the man of God on seeing him a prisoner among the soldiers in the guard-house.

Not then knowing this I halted, dubious if I should go

forward; and while standing in a swither at the corner of the Stock well, a cart came up from the bridge, driven by a stripling. I saw that the cart and horse were Robin Brown's, and before I had time to look around, my son had me by the hand.

We said little, but rejoiced to see each other again. I observed, however, that his apparel was become old, and that his eyes were grown quick and eager like those of the hunted Cameronians whom I saw at Kingswell.

'We hae ta'en Robin Brown's cart frae him,' said he, 'that I might come wi't unjealoused into the town, to hear what's to be done wi' the minister; but I maun tak it back the night, and maybe we'll fa' in thegither again when I hae done my errand.'

With that he parted from me, and giving the horse a touch with his whip, drove it along towards the guard-house, whistling like a blithe country lad that had no care.

As soon as he had so left me, I went back to Mrs Aird, and providing myself with what money I had in the house, I went to a shop and bought certain articles of apparel, which having made up into a bundle, I requested, the better to disguise my intent, the merchant to carry it himself to Robin Brown the Ayr carrier's cart, and give it to the lad who was with it, to take to Joseph Gilhaize, – a thing easy to be done, both the horse and cart being well known in those days to the chief merchants then in Glasgow.

When I had done this I went to the bridge, and, leaning over it, looked into the peaceful flowing tide, and there waited for nearly an hour before I saw my son returning; and when at last he came, I could perceive, as he was approaching, that he did not wish I should speak to him, while at the same time he edged towards me, and in passing, said as it were to himself, 'The bundle's safe, and he's for Edinburgh;' by which I knew that the apparel I had bought for him was in his hands, and that he had learnt Mr Cargill was to be sent to Edinburgh.

This latter circumstance, however, opened to me a new light with respect to the Cameronians, and I guessed that they had friends in the town with whom they were in secret correspondence. But, alas! the espionage was not all on their part, as I very soon was taught to know by experience.

Though the interviews with Joseph, my son, passed, as I have herein narrated, they had not escaped observance. For some time before, though I was seen but as I was, an invalid man, somewhat unsettled in his mind, there were persons who marvelled wherefore it was that I dwelt in such sequestration with Mrs Aird; and their marvelling set the espial of the prelacy upon me. And it so fell out that some of those evil persons, who, for hire or malice, had made themselves the beagles of the persecutors, happened to notice the manner in which my son came up to me when he entered the city driving Robin Brown's cart, and they jealoused somewhat of the truth.

They followed him unsuspected, and saw in what manner he mingled with the crowd; and they traced him returning out of the town with seemingly no other cause for having come into it, than to receive the little store of apparel that I had provided for him. This was ground enough to justify any molestation against us, and accordingly the same night I was arrested, and carried next morning to Edinburgh. The cruel officers would have forced me to walk with the soldiers, but every one who beheld my pale face and emaciated frame, cried out against it, and a cart was allowed to me.

On reaching Edinburgh I was placed in the tolbooth, where many other sufferers for the cause of the Gospel were then lying. It was a foul and an unwholesome den: many of the guiltless inmates were so wasted, that they were rather like frightful effigies of death than living men. Their skins were yellow, and their hands were roped and warpt with veins and sinews in a manner very awful to see. Their eyes were vivid with a strange distemperature, and there was a charnel-house anatomy in the melancholy with which they welcomed a new brother in affliction, that made me feel when I entered among them, as if I had come into the dark abode of spectres, and manes, and dismal shadows.

The prison was crowded over-much, and though life was to many not worth the care of preservation, they yet esteemed it as the gift of their Maker, and as such considered it their duty to prolong for his sake. It was therefore a rule with them to stand in successive bands at the windows, in order that they might taste of the living air from without; and knowing from dismal experience, that those who came in the last suffered at first more than those who were before, it was a charitable self-denial among them to allow to such a longer period of the window, their only solace.

Thus it was that on the morning of the third day after I had been immured in that doleful place, I was standing with several others behind a party of those who were in possession of the enjoyment, in order that we might take their places when the hour expired; and while we were thus awaiting in patience the tedious elapse of the weary moments, a noise was heard in the streets as of the approach of a multitude.

There was something in the coming sound of that tumult unlike the noise of any other multitude; – ever and anon a feeble shouting, and then the roll of a drum; but the general sough was a murmur of horror followed by a rushing, as if the people were scared by some dreadful sight.

The noise grew louder and nearer, and hoarse bursts of aversion and anger, mingled with lamentations, were distinctly heard. Every one in the prison pressed to the window, wondering what hideous procession could occasion the expression of such contrarious feelings in the populace, and all eager to catch a glimpse of the dismal pageant, expecting that it was some devoted victim, who, according to the practice of the time, was treated as a sentenced criminal, even as he was conveyed to his trial.

'What do you see?' said I to one of the prisoners who clung to the bars of iron with which the window near where I stood was grated, and who thereby saw farther down the street.

'I can see but the crowd coming,' said he, 'and every one is looking as if he grewed at something not yet in sight.'

At that moment, and while he was speaking, there was a sudden silence in the street.

'What has happened?' said one of the sufferers near

me: my heart beat so wildly that I would not myself inquire.

'They have stopped,' was the answer; 'but now they come. I see the magistrates. Their guard is before them, – the provost is first – they are coming two and two – and they look very sorrowful.'

'Are there but the magistrates?' said I, making an effort to press in closer to the window.

'Aye, now it is at hand,' said the man who was clinging to the grating of the window. 'The soldiers are marching on each side – I see the prisoners; – their hands are tied behind, ilk loaded wi' a goad of iron – they are bareheaded – ane – twa – three – four – five – they are five fatherly-looking men.'

'They are Cameronians,' said I, somewhat released, I know not wherefore, unless it was because he spoke of no youth being among them.

'Hush!' said he, 'here is another – He is on horseback – I see the horse's head – Oh! the sufferer is an old grey-headed minister – his head is uncovered – he is placed with his face to the horse's tail – his hands are tied, and his feet are fastened with a rope beneath the horse's belly. – Hush! they are passing under the window.'

At that moment a shriek of horror rose from all then looking out, and every one recoiled from the window. In the same instant a bloody head on a halbert was held up to us. – I looked – I saw the ghastly features, and I would have kissed those lifeless lips; for, O! they were my son's.

I had laid that son, my only son, whom I so loved, on the altar of the Covenant, an offering unto the Lord; but still I did hope that maybe it would be according to the mercy of wisdom that He would provide a lamb in the bush for the sacrifice; and when the stripling had parted from me, I often felt as the mother feels when the milk of love is in her bosom, and her babe no longer there. I shall not, however, here relate how my soul was wounded at yon sight, nor ask the courteous reader to conceive with what agony I exclaimed, 'Wherefore was it, Lord, that I was commanded to do that unfruitful thing!' for in that very moment the cry of my failing faith was rebuked, and the mystery of the required sacrifice was brought into wonderful effect, manifesting that it was for no light purpose I had been so tried.

My fellow-sufferer, who hung by the bars of the prison-window, was, like the other witnesses, so shaken by the woful spectacle, that he suddenly jerked himself aside to avoid the sight, and by that action the weight of his body loosened the bar, so that when the pageantry of horrors had passed by, he felt it move in his grip, and he told us that surely Providence had an invisible hand in the bloody scene; for, by the loosening of that stancher, a mean was given whereby we might all escape. Accordingly it was agreed, that as soon as the night closed over the world, we should join our strengths together to bend the bar from its socket in the lintel.

And then it was I told them that what they had seen was the last relic of my martyred family; and we made ourselves wroth with the recital of our several wrongs; for all there had endured the scourge of the persecutors; and we took each other by the hand, and swore a dreadful oath, never to desist in our endeavours till we had wrenched the sceptre from the tyrannical grasp of the Stuarts, and broken it into pieces for ever; and we burst into a wild strain of complaint and clamour, calling on the blood of our murdered friends to mount, with our cries, to the gates of Heaven; and we sang, as it were with the voices of the angry waters and the winds, the hundred and ninth Psalm; and at the end of every verse we joined our hands, crying, 'Upon Charles and James Stuart, and all their guilty line, O Lord, let it be done;' and a vast multitude gathered around the prison, and the lamentations of many without was a chorus in unison with the dismal song of our vengeance and despair.

At last the shadows of the twilight began to darken in the town, and the lights of the windows were to us as the courses of the stars of that sky which, from our prison-chamber, could not be seen. We watched their progress, from the earliest yellow glimmering of the lamp in the darksome wynd, till the last little twinkling light in the dwelling of the widow that sits and sighs companionless with her distaff in the summits of the city. And we continued our vigil till they were all one by one extinguished, save only the candles at the bedsides of the dying. Then we twined a portion of our clothes into a rope, and, having fastened it to the iron bar, soon drew it from its place in the stone; but just as we were preparing to take it in, by some accident it fell into the street.

The panic which this caused prevented us from attempting any thing more at that time; for a sentinel walked his rounds on the outside of the tolbooth, and we could not but think he must have heard the noise. A sullen despair in consequence entered into many of our hearts, and we continued for the remainder of the night silent.

But though others were then shaken in their faith, mine was now confident. I saw, by what had happened in the moment of my remonstrance, that there was some great deliverance in reservation; so I sat apart by myself, and I spent the night in inward thanksgiving for what had been already done. Nor was this confidence long without its reward.

In the morning a brother of one of my fellow-sufferers coming to condole with him, it being generally reported that we were all doomed to die, he happened to see the bar lying on the street, and, taking it up, hid it till he had gone into a shop and provided himself with a cord. He then hastened to us, gave us the cord, and making what speed he could, brought the iron in his plaid; and, we having lowered the string from the window, he fastened the bar it to, and we drew it up undiscovered, and reset it in its place, by which the defect could not be seen by any one, not even from the street.

That morning, by the providence which was visible in this, became, in our prison, a season indeed of light and gratulation; and the day passed with us as a Sabbath to our spirits. The anvils of Fear were hushed, and the shuttles in the looms of Anxiety were at rest, while Hope again walked abroad in those sunny fields where, amidst vernal blossoms and shining dews, she expatiates on the delights of the flowing cluster and the ripened fruit.

The young man, who had been so guided to find the bar of iron, concerted with another friend of his to be in readiness at night on a signal from us, to master the sentinel. And at the time appointed they did so; and it happened that the soldier was the same humane Englisher, Jack Windsor, who had allowed me to escape at Kilmarnock, and he not only remained silent, but even when relieved from his post, said nothing; so that, to the number of more than twenty, we lowered ourselves into the street and escaped.

But the city gates at that hour being shut, there was no egress from the town, and many of us knew not where to hide ourselves till the morning. Such was my condition; and wandering up and down for some time, at last I turned into the Blackfriars-wynd, where I saw a light in a window: on looking around I beheld, by that light, engraven on the lintel of an opposite door, 'IN THE LORD IS MY HOPE.'

Heartened by the singular providence that was so manifest in that cheering text, I went to the door and knocked, and a maiden answered to the knocking.

I told her what I was, and whence I had come, and

entreated her to have compassion, and shelter me for the night.

'Alas!' said she, 'what can hae sent you here, for this is a bishop's house?'

I was astounded to hear that I had been so led into the lion's den; but I saw pity in the countenance of the damsel, and I told her that I was the father of the poor youth whose head had been carried by the executioner through the town the day before, and that I could not but believe Providence had sent me thither; for surely no one would ever think of searching for me in a bishop's house.

Greatly moved by what I said, she bade me softly follow her, and she led me to a solitary and ruinous chamber. She then retired, but presently returned with some refreshment, which having placed on an old chest, she bade God be with me, and went away.

With a spirit of inexpressible admiration and thanksgiving I partook of that repast, and then laying myself down on the bare floor, was blessed with the enjoyment of a downy sleep.

I slept in that ruinous room in the Bishop's house till far in the morning, when, on going to the window with the intent of dropping myself into the wynd, I saw that it was ordained and required of me to remain where I then was; for the inmates of the houses forent were all astir at their respective vocations; and at the foot of the wynd, looking straight up, was a change-house, into which there was, even at that early hour, a great resorting of bein elderly citizens for their dram and snap. Moreover, at the head of the wynd, an aged carlin, with a distaff in her arms and a whorl in her hand, sat on a doorstep tending a stand of apples and comfits; so that, to a surety, had I made any attempt to escape by the window, I must have been seen by some one, and laid hold of. I therefore retired back into the obscurity of the chamber, and sat down again on the old kist-lid, to abide the issues that were in reservation for me. I had not, however, been long there, till I heard the voices of persons entering into the next chamber behind where I was sitting, and I soon discerned by their courtesies of speech, that they were Lords of the Privy Council, who had come to walk with the Bishop to the palace, where a council was summoned in sudden haste that morning. The matter whereof they discoursed was not at first easily made out, for they were conversing on it when they entered; but I very soon gathered that it boded no good to the covenanted cause nor to the liberties of Scotland.

'What you remark, Aberdeen,' said one, 'is very just; man and wife are the same person; and although Queensberry has observed, that the revenue requires the penalties, and that husbands ought to pay for their wives, I look not on the question in that light; for it is not right, in my opinion, that the revenues of the crown should be in any degree

dependent on fines and forfeitures. But the presbyterians
are a sect whose main principle is rebellion, and it would
be happy for the kingdom were the whole race rooted out;
indeed I am quite of the Duke of York's opinion, that there
will be little peace among us till the Lowlands are made a
hunting-field, and therefore am I as earnest as Queensberry
that the fines should be enforced.'

'Certainly, my Lord Perth,' replied Aberdeen, 'it is not
to be denied, that, what with their Covenants, and Solemn
Leagues, and Gospel pretensions, the presbyterians are
dangerous and bad subjects; and though I shall not go so
far as to say, with the Duke, that the Lowlands should be
laid waste, I doubt if there be a loyal subject west the castle
of Edinburgh. Still the office which I have the honour to
hold does not allow me to put any interpretation on the law
different from the terms in which the sense is conceived.'

'Then,' said Perth, 'if there is any doubt about the terms,
the law must be altered; for, unless we can effectually crush
the presbyterians, the Duke will assuredly have a rough
accession. And it is better to strangle the lion in his nonage
than to encounter him in his full growth.'

'I fear, my Lord,' replied the Earl of Aberdeen, 'that
the presbyterians are stronger already than we are willing to let ourselves believe. The attempt to make them
accept the episcopalian establishment has now been made,
without intermission, for more than twenty years, and they
are even less submissive than they were at the beginning.'

'Yes, I confess,' said Lord Perth, 'that they are most
unreasonably stubborn. It is truly melancholy to see what
fools many sensible men make of themselves about the
forms of worship, especially about those of a religion so
ungentlemanly as the presbyterian, which has no respect
for the degrees of rank, neither out nor in the church.'

'I'm afraid, Perth,' replied Aberdeen laughing, 'that what
you say is applicable both to the King and his brother; for,
between ourselves, I do not think there are two persons
in the realm who attach so much importance to forms as
they do.'

'Not the King, my Lord, not the King!' cried Perth;

'Charles is too much a man of the world to trouble himself about any such trifles.'

'They are surely not trifles, for they overturned his father's throne, and are shaking his own,' replied Aberdeen emphatically. 'Pray, have you heard any thing of Argyle lately?'

'O yes,' exclaimed Perth merrily; 'a capital story. He has got in with a rich burgomaster's frow at Amsterdam; and she has guilders enew to indemnify him for the loss of half the Highlands.'

'Aye,' replied Aberdeen, 'I do not like that; for there has been of late a flocking of the presbyterian malcontents to Holland, and the Prince of Orange gives them a better reception than an honest man should do, standing as he does, both with respect to the crown and the Duke. This, take my word for it, Perth, is not a thing to be laughed at.'

'All that, Aberdeen, only shows the necessity of exterminating these cursed presbyterians. We shall have no peace in Scotland till they are swept clean away. It is not to be endured that a King shall not rule his own kingdom as he pleases. How would Argyle, and there was no man prouder in his jurisdictions, have liked had his tenants covenanted against him as the presbyterians have so insultingly done against his Majesty's government? Let every man bring the question home to his own business and bosom, and the answer will be a short one, *Down with the presbyterians!*'

While they were thus speaking, and I need not advert to what passed in my breast as I overheard them, Patterson the Bishop of Edinburgh came in; and with many interjections, mingled with wishes for a calm procedure, he told the Lords of our escape. He was indeed, to do him justice, a man of some repute for plausibility, and take him all in all for a prelate, he was, in truth, not void of the charities of human nature, compared with others of his sect.

'Your news,' said the Lord Perth to him, 'does not surprise me. The societies, as the Cameronians are called, have inserted their roots and feelers every where. Rely upon't, Bishop Patterson, that, unless we chop off the whole connexions of the conspiracy, you can hope neither for homage nor reverence in your appointments.'

'I could wish,' replied the Bishop, 'that some experiment were made of a gentler course than has hitherto been tried. It is now a long time since force was first employed: perhaps, were his Royal Highness to slacken the severities, conformity would lose some of its terrors in the eyes of the misguided presbyterians; at all events, a more lenient policy could do no harm; and if it did no good, it would at least be free from those imputed cruelties, which are supposed to justify the long-continued resistance that has brought the royal authority into such difficulties.'

At this juncture of their conversation a gentleman announced, that his master was ready to proceed with them to the palace, and they forthwith retired. Thus did I obtain a glimpse of the inner mind of the Privy Council, by which I clearly saw, that what with those members who satisfied their consciences as to iniquity, because it was made seemingly lawful by human statutes, and what with those who, like Lord Perth, considered the kingdom the King's estate, and the people his tenantry, not the subjects of laws by which he was bound as much as they; together with those others who, like the Bishop, considered mercy and justice as expedients of state policy, that there was no hope for the peace and religious liberties of the presbyterians, merely by resistance; and I, from that time, began to think it was only through the instrumentality of the Prince of Orange, then heir-presumptive to the crown, failing James Stuart, Duke of York, that my vow could be effectually brought to pass.

As soon as those of the Privy Council had, with their attendants, left the house, and proceeded to join the Duke of York in the palace, the charitable damsel came to me, and conveyed me, undiscovered, through the hall and into the Cowgate, where she had provided a man, a friend of her own, one Charles Brownlee, who had been himself in the hands of the Philistines, to conduct me out of the town; and by him I was guided in safety through the Cowgate, and put into a house just without the same, where his mother resided.

'Here,' said he, 'it will be as well for you to bide out the daylight, and being now forth the town-wall, ye'll can gang whare ye like unquestioned in the gloaming.' And so saying he went away, leaving me with his mother, an ancient matron, with something of the remnant of ladyness about her, yet was she not altogether an entire gentlewoman, though at the first glimpse she had the look of one of the very highest degree.

Notwithstanding, however, that apparition of finery which was about her, she was in truth and in heart a sincere woman, and had, in the better days of her younger years, been, as she rehearsed to me, gentlewoman to the Countess of Argyle's mother, and was on a footing of cordiality with divers ladies of the bedchamber of what she called the three nobilities, meaning those of Scotland, England, and Ireland; so that I saw there might by her be opened a mean of espial into the camp of the adversaries. So I told her of my long severe malady, and the shock I had suffered by what I had seen of my martyred son, and entreated that she would allow me to abide with her until my spirits were more composed.

Mrs Brownlee having the compassion of a Christian, and

the tenderness of her gentle sex, was moved by my story, and very readily consented. Instead therefore of going forth at random in the evening, as I was at one time mindet, I remained in her house; where indeed could I at that time flee in the hope of finding any place of refuge? But although this was adopted on the considerations of human reason, it was nevertheless a link in the chain of providential methods by which I was to achieve the fulfilment of my vow.

The house of Mrs Brownlee being, as I have intimated, nigh to the gate of the city, I saw from the window all that went into and came out therefrom; and the same afternoon I had visible evidence of the temper wherewith the Duke of York and his counsellors had been actuated that day at Holyrood, in consequence of the manner in which we had been delivered from prison; – for Jack Windsor, the poor sentinel who was on guard when we escaped by the window, was brought out, supported by two of his companions, his feet having been so crushed in the torturous boots before the Council, during his examination anent us, that he could scarcely mark them to the ground; his hands were also bound in cloths, through which the blood was still oozing, from the pressure of those dreadful thumbikins of iron that were so often used in those days to screw accusations out of honest men. A sympathizing crowd followed the destroyed sufferer, and the sight for a little while afflicted me with sore regret. But when I considered the compassion that the people showed for him, I was filled with a strange satisfaction, deducing therefrom encouraging persuasions, that every new sin of the persecutors removed a prop from their own power, making its overthrow more and more inevitable.

While I was peering from the window in these reflections, I saw Quintin Fullarton, the grandson of John Fullarton of Dykedivots, in the street, and knowing that from the time of Bothwell-brigg he had been joined with that zealous and martyred youth, Richard Cameron, and was, as Robin Brown told me, among other acquaintances at Airsmoss, I entreated Mrs Brownlee to go after him and bid him come to me, – which he readily did, and we had a mournful communing for some time.

He told me the particulars of my gallant Joseph's death, and that it was by the command of Claverhouse himself that the brave stripling's head was cut off and sent in ignominy to Edinburgh; where, by order of the Privy Council, it was placed on the Netherbow.

'What I hae suffered from that man,' said I, 'Heaven may pardon, but I can neither forget nor forgive.'

'The judgment time's coming,' replied Quintin Fullarton; 'and your part in it, Ringan Gilhaize, assuredly will not be forgotten, for in the heavens there is a Doer of justice and an Avenger of wrongs.'

And then he proceeded to tell me, that on the following afternoon there was to be a meeting of the heads of the Cameronian societies, with Mr Renwick, in a dell of the Esk, about half a mile above Laswade, to consult what ought to be done, the pursuit and persecution being so hot against them, that life was become a burden, and their minds desperate.

'We hae many friens,' said he, 'in Edinburgh, and I am intrusted to warn them to the meeting, which is the end of my coming to the town; and maybe, Ringan Gilhaize, ye'll no objek yoursel to be there?'

'I will be there, Quintin Fullarton,' said I; 'and in the strength of the Lord I will come armed, with a weapon of more might than the sword, and more terrible than the ball that flieth unseen.'

'What mean you, Ringan?' said he, compassionately; for he knew of my infirmity, and thought that I was still fevered in the mind. But I told him, that, for some time, feeling myself unable for warlike enterprises, I had meditated on a way to perplex our guilty adversaries, the which was to menace them with retaliation, for resistance alone was no longer enough.

'We have disowned Charles Stuart as our king,' said I, 'and we must wage war accordingly. But go your ways, and execute your purposes; and by the time you return this way, I shall have a paper ready, the sending forth of which will strike terror into the brazen hearts of our foes.'

I perceived that he was still dubious of me; but nevertheless he promised to call as he came back; and having gone away, I set myself down and drew up that declaration, wherein, after again calmly disowning the royal authority of Charles Stuart, we admonished our sanguinary persecutors, that, for self-preservation, we would retaliate according to our power, and the degree of guilt on such privy counsellors, lords of justiciary, officers, and soldiers, their abettors and informers, whose hands should continue to be imbrued in our blood. And on the return of Quintin Fullarton, I gave the paper to him, that it might be seen and considered by Mr Renwick and others, previous to offering it to the consideration of the meeting.

He read it over very sedately, and folded it up, and put it in the crown of his bonnet without saying a word; but several times, while he was reading, he cast his eyes towards me; and when he rose to go away, he said, – 'Ringan Gilhaize, you have endured much, but verily if this thing can be brought to pass, your own and all our sufferings will soon be richly revenged.'

'Not revenged,' said I; 'revenge, Quintin Fullarton, becomes not Christian men; but we shall be the executioners of the just judgments of Him whose ministers are flaming fires, and pestilence, and war, and storms, and perjured kings.'

With these words we parted; and next morning, by break of day, I rose, after the enjoyment of a solacing sleep, such as I had not known for many days, and searched my way across the fields toward Laswade. I did not, however, enter the clachan, but lingered among the woods till the afternoon, when, descending towards the river, I walked leisurely up the banks, where I soon fell in with others of the associated friends.

The place where we met was a deep glen, the scroggy sides whereof were as if rocks, and trees and brambles, with here and there a yellow primrose and a blue hyacinth between, had been thrown by some wild architect into many a difficult and fantastical form. Over a ledge of rock fell the bright waters of the Esk, and in the clear linn the trouts shuttled from stone and crevice, dreading the persecutions of the angler, who, in the luxury of his pastime, heedeth not what they may in their cool element suffer.

It was then the skirt of the afternoon, about the time when the sweet breathing of flowers and boughs first begins to freshen to the gentle senses, and the shadows deepen in the cliffs of the rocks, and darken among the bushes. The yellow sunbeams were still bright on the flickering leaves of a few trees, which here and there raised their tufty heads above the glen; but in the hollow of the chasm the evening had commenced, and the sobriety of the fragrant twilight was coming on.

As we assembled one by one, we said little to each other. Some indeed said nothing, nor even shook hands, but went and seated themselves on the rocks, round which the limpid waters were swirling with a soft and pleasant din, as if they solicited tranquillity. For myself, I had come with the sternest intents, and I neither noticed nor spoke to any one; but going to the brink of the linn, I sat myself down in a gloomy nook, and was sullen, that the scene was not better troubled into unison with the resentful mood of my spirit.

At last Mr Renwick came, and when he had descended into the dell, where we were gathered together, after speaking a few words of courtesy to certain of his acquaintance, he went to a place on the shelvy side of the glen, and took his station between two birch trees.

'I will be short with you, friends,' said he; 'for here we are too nigh unto the adversaries to hazard ourselves in any long debate; and therefore I will tell you, as a man speaking the honesty that is within him, I neither can nor do approve of the paper that I understand some among you desire we should send forth. I have, however, according to what was exhibited to me in private, brought here a proclamation, such as those who are most vehement among us wish to propound; but I still leave it with yourselves to determine whether or not it should be adopted – entering, as I here do, my caveat as an individual against it. This paper will cut off all hope of reconciliation – we have already disowned King Charles, it is true; but this implies, that we are also resolved to avenge, even unto blood and death, whatsoever injury we may in our own persons and friends be subjected to suffer. It pledges us to a war of revenge and extermination; and we have to consider, before we wage the same, the strength of our adversary – the craft of his counsellors – and the malice with which their fears and their hatred will inspire them. For my own part, fellow-sufferers, I do doubt if there be any warrandice in the Scriptures for such a defiance as this paper contains, and I would fain entreat you to reflect, whether it be not better to keep the door of reconciliation open, than to shut it for ever, as the promulgation of this retaliatory edict will assuredly do.'

The earnest manner in which Mr Renwick thus delivered himself had a powerful effect, and many thought as he did, and several rose and said that it was not Christian to bar the door on peace, and to shut out even the chance of contrition on the part of the King and his ministers.

I heard what they said – I listened to what they argued – and I allowed them to tell that they were willing to agree to more moderate councils; but I could abide no more.

'Moderation! – You, Mr Renwick,' said I, 'counsel moderation – you recommend the door of peace to be still kept open – you doubt if the Scriptures warrant us to undertake revenge; and you hope that our forbearance may work to repentance among our enemies. Mr Renwick, you have hitherto been a preacher, not a sufferer; with you the resistance to Charles Stuart's government has been a

thing of doctrine – of no more than doctrine, Mr Renwick
– with us it is a consideration of facts. Judge ye therefore
between yourself and us, – I say between yourself and us;
for I ask no other judge to decide, whether we are not, by
all the laws of God and man, justified in avowing, that we
mean to do as we are done by.

'And, Mr Renwick, you will call to mind, that in this
sore controversy, the cause of debate came not from us.
We were peaceable Christians, enjoying the shade of the
vine and fig-tree of the Gospel, planted by the care and
cherished by the blood of our forefathers, protected by the
laws, and gladdened in our protection by the oaths and the
covenants which the King had sworn to maintain. The
presbyterian freedom of worship was our property, – we
were in possession and enjoyment, no man could call our
right to it in question, – the King had vowed, as a condition
before he was allowed to receive the crown, that he would
preserve it. Yet, for more than twenty years, there has
been a most cruel, fraudulent, and outrageous endeavour
instituted, and carried on, to deprive us of that freedom and
birthright. We were asking no new thing from Government,
we were taking no step to disturb Government, we were in
peace with all men, when Government, with the principles
of a robber and the cruelty of a tyrant, demanded of us
to surrender those immunities of conscience which our
fathers had earned and defended; to deny the Gospel as it
is written in the Evangelists, and to accept the commentary
of Charles Stuart, a man who has had no respect to the
most solemn oaths, and of James Sharp, the apostate of St
Andrews, whose crimes provoked a deed, that but for their
crimson hue, no man could have doubted to call a most foul
murder. The King and his crew, Mr Renwick, are, to the
indubitable judgment of all just men, the causers and the
aggressors in the existing difference between his subjects
and him. In so far, therefore, if blame there be, it lieth not
with us nor in our cause.

'But, sir, not content with attempting to wrest from
us our inherited freedom of religious worship, Charles
Stuart and his abettors have pursued the courageous
constancy with which we have defended the same, with

more animosity than they ever did any crime. I speak not to you, Mr Renwick, of your own outcast condition, – perhaps you delight in the perils of martyrdom; I speak not to those around us, who, in their persons, their substance, and their families, have endured the torture, poverty, and irremediable dishonour, – they may be meek and hallowed men, willing to endure. But I call to mind what I am and was myself. I think of my quiet home, – it is all ashes. I remember my brave firstborn, – he was slain at Bothwell-brigg. Why need I speak of my honest brother; the waves of the ocean, commissioned by our persecutors, have triumphed over him in the cold seas of the Orkneys; and as for my wife, what was she to you? Ye cannot be greatly disturbed that she is in her grave. No, ye are quiet, calm, and prudent persons; it would be a most indiscreet thing of you, you who have suffered no wrong yourselves, to stir on her account; and then how unreasonable I should be, were I to speak of two fair and innocent maidens. – It is weak of me to weep, though they were my daughters. O men and Christians, brothers, fathers! but ye are content to bear with such wrongs, and I alone of all here may go to the gates of the cities, and try to discover which of the martyred heads mouldering there belongs to a son or a friend. Nor is it of any account whether the bones of those who were so dear to us, be exposed with the remains of malefactors, or laid in the sacred grave. To the dead all places are alike; and to the slave what signifies who is master. Let us therefore forget the past, – let us keep open the door of reconciliation, – smother all the wrongs we have endured, and kiss the proud foot of the trampler. We have our lives; we have been spared; the merciless bloodhounds have not yet reached us. Let us therefore be humble and thankful, and cry to Charles Stuart, O King, live for ever! – for he has but cast us into a fiery furnace and a lion's den.

'In truth, friends, Mr Renwick is quite right. This feeling of indignation against our oppressors is a most imprudent thing. If we desire to enjoy our own contempt, and to deserve the derision of men, and to merit the abhorrence of Heaven, let us yield ourselves to all that Charles Stuart and his sect require. We can do nothing better, nothing so

meritorious, nothing by which we can so reasonably hope
for punishment here and condemnation hereafter. But if
there is one man at this meeting, – I am speaking not of
shapes and forms, but of feelings, – if there is one here
that feels as men were wont to feel, he will draw his sword,
and say with me, Wo to the house of Stuart! Wo to the
oppressors! Blood for blood! Judge and avenge our cause,
O Lord!'

The meeting, with one accord, agreed that the declaration should go forth; and certain of those who were ready writers, being provided with implements, retired apart to make copies, while Mr Renwick, with the remainder, joined together in prayer.

By the time he had made an end, the task of the writers was finished, and then lots were cast to see whom the Lord would appoint to affix the declaration on the trones and kirk doors of the towns where the rage of the persecutors burnt the fiercest, and He being pleased to choose me for one to do the duty at Edinburgh, I returned in the gloaming back to the house of Mrs Brownlee, to abide the convenient season which I knew in the fit time would be prepared. Nor was it long till the same was brought to pass, as I shall now briefly proceed to set down.

Heron Brownlee, who, as I have narrated, brought me to his mother's house, was by trade a tailor, and kept his cloth-shop in the Canongate, some six doors lower down than St Mary's Wynd, just after passing the fleshers' stocks below the Netherbow; for in those days, when the court was at Holyrood, that part of the town was a place of great resort to the gallants, and all such as affected a courtly carriage. And it happened that, on the morning after the meeting, a proclamation was sent forth, describing the persons and clothing of the prisoners who had escaped from the tolbooth with me, threatening grievous penalties to all who dared to harbour them. This Heron Brownlee seeing affixed on the cheek of the Netherbow, came and told me; whereupon, after conferring with him, it was agreed that he should provide for me a suit of town-like clothes, and at the second-hand, that they might not cause observance by any novelty. This was in another respect needful; for my health being in a frail state, I stood in want of the halesome cordial of fresh air, whereof I could not venture to taste but in the dusk of the evening.

He accordingly provided the apparel, and when clothed therewith, I made bold to go out in the broad daylight, and even ventured to mingle with the multitude in the garden of the palace, who went daily there in the afternoon to see the nobles and ladies of the court walking with their pageantries, while the Duke's musicants solaced them with melodious airs and the delights of sonorous harmony. And it happened on the third time I went thither, that a cry rose of the Duke coming from the garden to the palace, and all the onlookers pressed to see him.

As he advanced, I saw several persons presenting petitions into his hands, which he gave, without then looking at, to the Lord Perth, whom I knew again by his voice; and I was directed, as by a thought of inspiration, to present, in like manner, a copy of our declaration, which I always carried about with me; so placing myself among a crowd of petitioners, onlookers, and servants, that formed an avenue across the road leading from the Canongate to the Abbey kirk-yard, and between the garden yett and the yett that opened into the front court of the palace. As the Duke returned out of the garden, I gave him the paper; but instead of handing it to the Lord Perth, as I had hoped he would do, he held it in his own hand, by which I perceived that if he had noticed by whom it was presented, and looked at it before he went into the palace, I would speedily be seized on the spot, unless I could accomplish my escape.

But how to effect that was no easy thing; for the multitude around was very great, and but three narrow yetts allowed of egress from the enclosure – one leading into the garden – one to the palace – and the other into the Canongate. I therefore calmly put my trust in Him who alone could save me, and remained, as it were, an indifferent spectator, following the Duke with an anxious eye.

Having passed from the garden into the court, the multitude followed him with great eagerness, and I also went in with them, and walked very deliberately across the front of the palace to the south-east corner, where there was a postern door that opened into the road leading to the King's park from the Cowgate-port, along the outside of the town wall. I then mended my pace, but not to any remarkable degree, and so returned to the house of Mrs Brownlee.

Scarcely was I well in, when Heron, her son, came flying to her with a report that a man was seized in the palace garden who had threatened the Duke's life, and he was fearful lest it had been me; and I was much grieved by these tidings, in case any honest man should be put to the torture on my account; but the Lord had mercifully ordained it otherwise.

In the course of the night, Heron Brownlee, after closing his shop, came again and told me that no one had been taken, but that some person in the multitude had given the Duke a dreadful paper, which had caused great consternation and panic; and that a council was sitting at that late hour with the Duke, expresses having arrived with accounts of the same paper having been seen on the doors of many churches both in Nithsdale and the shire of Ayr. The alarm indeed raged to such a degree among all those who knew in their consciences how they merited the doom we had pronounced, that it was said the very looks of many were withered as with a pestilent vapour.

Yet, though terrified at the vengeance declared against their guilt, neither the Duke nor the Privy Council were to be deterred from their malignant work. The curse of infatuation was upon them, and instead of changing the rule which had caused the desperation that they dreaded, they heated the furnace of persecution seven-fold; and voted, That whosoever owned or refused to disown the declaration, should be put to death in the presence of two witnesses, though unarmed when taken; and the soldiers were not only ordered to enforce the test, but were instructed to put such as adhered to the declaration at once to the sword, and to slay those who refused to disown it; and women were ordered to be drowned. But my pen sickens with the recital of horrors, and I shall pass by the dreadful things that ensued, with only remarking, that these bloody instructions consummated the doom of the Stuarts; for scarcely were they well published, when the Duke hastened to London, and soon after his mansworn brother Charles, the great author of all our woes, was cut off by poison, as it was most currently believed, and the Duke proclaimed King in his stead. What change we obtained by the calamity of his accession will not require many sentences to unfold.

As soon as it was known abroad that Charles the Second was dead, the Covenanters, who had taken refuge in Holland from the Persecution, assembled to consult what ought then to be done. For the papist, James Stuart, on the death of his brother, had caused himself to be proclaimed King of Scotland, without taking those oaths by which alone he could be entitled to assume the Scottish crown.

At the head of this congregation was the Earl of Argyle, who, some years before, had incurred the aversion of the tyrant to such a degree, that, by certain of those fit tools for any crime, then in dismal abundance about the court of Holyrood, he had procured his condemnation as a traitor, and would have brought him to the scaffold, had the Earl not fortunately effected his escape. And it was resolved by that congregation, that the principal personages then present should form themselves into a Council, to concert the requisite measures for the deliverance of their native land; the immediate issue of which was, that a descent should be made by Argyle among his vassals, in order to draw together a sufficient host to enable them to wage war against the Usurper, for so they lawfully and rightly denominated James Stuart.

The first hint that I gleaned of this design was through the means of Mrs Brownlee. She was invited one afternoon by the gentlewoman of the Lady Sophia Lindsay, the Earl's daughter-in-law, to view certain articles of female bravery which had been sent from Holland by his Lordship to her mistress; and, as her custom was, she, on her return home, descanted at large of all that she had seen and heard.

The receipt, at that juncture, of such gear from the Earl of Argyle, by such a Judith of courage and wisdom as the Lady Sophia Lindsay, seemed to me very remarkable, and I could not but jealouse that there was something about it like the occultation of a graver correspondence. I therefore began to question Mrs Brownlee how the paraphernalia had come, and what the Earl, according to the last accounts, was doing; which led her to expatiate on many things, though vague and desultory, that were yet in concordance with what I had overheard the Lord Perth say to the Earl of Aberdeen in the Bishop's house: in the end, I gathered that the presents were brought over by the skipper of a sloop, one Roderick Macfarlane, whom I forthwith determined to see, in order to pick from him what intelligence I could, without being at the time well aware in what manner the same would prove useful. I felt myself, however, stirred from within to do so; and I had hitherto, in all that concerned my avenging vow, obeyed every instinctive impulse.

Accordingly, next morning, I went early to the shore of Leith, and soon found the vessel and Roderick Macfarlane, to whom I addressed myself, inquiring, as if I intended to go thither, when he was likely to depart again for Amsterdam.

While I was speaking to him, I observed something in his mien above his condition; and that his hands were fair and delicate, unlike those of men inured to maritime labour. He perceived that I was particular in my inspection, and his countenance became troubled, and he looked as if he wist not what to do.

'Fear no ill,' said I to him; 'I am one in the jaws of jeopardy; in sooth, I have no intent to pass into Holland, but only to learn whether there be any hope that the Earl of Argyle and those with him will try to help their covenanted brethren at home.'

On hearing me speak so openly the countenance of the man brightened, and after eyeing me with a sharp scrutiny, he invited me to come down into the body of the bark, where we had some frank communion, his confidence being won by the plain tale of who I was and what I had endured. The Lord indeed was pleased, throughout that period of fears and tribulation, marvellously to endow the persecuted with a singular and sympathetic instinct, whereby they were enabled at once to discern their friends; for the dangers and difficulties, to which we were subject in our intercourse, afforded no time for those testimonies and experiences that in ordinary occasions are required to open the hearts of men to one another.

After some general discourse, Roderick Macfarlane told me, that his vessel, though seemingly only for traffic, had been hired by a certain Madam Smith in Amsterdam, and was manned by Highlanders of a degree above the common, for the purpose of opening a correspondence between Argyle and his friends in Scotland. Whereupon I proffered myself to assist in establishing a communication with the heads and leaders of the Covenanters in the West Country, and particularly with Mr Renwick and his associates, the Cameronians, who, though grievously scattered and hunted, were yet able to do great things in the way of conveying letters, or of intercepting the emissaries and agents of the Privy Council that might be employed to contravene the Earl's projects.

Thus it was that I came to be concerned in Argyle's unfortunate expedition – if that can be called unfortunate, which, though in itself a failure, yet ministered to make the scattered children of the Covenant again co-operate for the achievement of their common freedom. Doubtless the expedition was undertaken before the persecuted were sufficiently ripened to be of any effective service. The Earl counted overmuch on the spirit which the Persecution had raised; he thought that the weight of the tyranny had compressed us all into one body. But, alas! it had been so great, that it had not only bruised, but broken us asunder into many pieces; and time, and care, and much persuasion, were all requisite to solder the fragments together.

As the spring advanced, being, in the manner related, engaged in furthering the purposes of the exiled Covenanters, I prepared, through the instrumentality of divers friends, many in the West Country to be in readiness to join the Earl's standard of deliverance. It is not however to be disguised, that the work went on but slowly, and that the people heard of the intended descent with something like an actionless wonderment, in consequence of those by whom it had been planned not sending forth any declaration of their views and intents. And this indisposition, especially among the Cameronians, became a settled reluctance, when, after the Earl had reached Campbelton, he published that purposeless proclamation, wherein, though the wrongs and woes of the kingdom were pithily recited, the nature of the redress proposed was in no manner manifest. It was plain indeed, by many signs, that the Lord's time was not yet come for the work to thrive.

The divisions in Argyle's councils were greater even than those among the different orders into which the Covenanters had been long split – the very Cameronians might have been sooner persuaded to refrain from insisting on points of doctrine and opinion, at least till the adversary was overthrown, than those who were with the ill-fated Earl to act with union among themselves. In a word, all about the expedition was confusion and perplexity, and the omens and auguries of ruin, showed how much it wanted the favour that is better than the strength of numbers, or the wisdom of mighty men. But to proceed.

Sir John Cochrane, one of those who were with Argyle, had, by some espial of his own, a correspondence with divers of the Covenanters in the shire of Ayr; and he was so heartened by their representations of the spirit among them, that he urged, and overcame the Earl, to let him make a trial on that coast before waiting till the Highlanders were roused. Accordingly, with the three ships and the men they had brought from Holland, he went toward Largs, famed in old time for a great battle fought there; but, on arriving opposite to the shore, he found it guarded by the powers and forces of the government, in so much, that he was fain to direct his course farther up the river; and weighing anchor sailed for Greenock.

It happened at this juncture, after conferring with several of weight among the Cameronians, that I went to Greenock for the purpose of taking shipping for any place where I was likely to find Argyle, in order to represent to him, that, unless there was a clear account of what he and others with him proposed to do, he could expect no co-operation from the societies; and I reached the town just as the three ships were coming in sight.

I had not well alighted from my horse at Dugal M'Vicar the smith's public, – the best house it is in the town, and slated. It stands beside an oak tree on the open shore, below the Mansion-house-brae, above the place where the mariners boil their tar-pots. As I was saying, I had not well alighted there, when a squadron of certain time-serving and prelatic-inclined heritors of the shire of Renfrew, under the command of Houston of that ilk, came galloping to the town as if they would have devoured Argyle, host and ships and all; and they rode straight to the minister's glebe, where, behind the kirk-yard dyke, they set themselves in

418

battle array with drawn swords, the vessels having in the meanwhile come to anchor forenent the kirk.

Like the men of the town I went to be an onlooker, at a distance, of what might ensue; and a sore heart it was to me, to see and to hear that the Greenock folk stood so much in dread of their superior, Sir John Shaw, that they durst not, for fear of his black-hole, venture to say that day whether they were papists, prelates, or presbyterians, he himself not being in the way to direct them.

Shortly after the ships had cast anchor, Major Fullarton, with a party of some ten or twelve men, landed at the burn-foot, near the kirk, and having shown a signal for parley, Houston and his men went to him, and began to chafe and chide him for invading the country.

'We are no invaders,' said the Major, 'we have come to our native land to preserve the protestant religion; and I am grieved that such brave gentlemen, as ye appear to be, should be seen in the cause of a papist tyrant and usurper.'

'Ye lee,' cried Houston, and fired his pistol at the Major, the like did his men; but they were so well and quickly answered in the same language, that they soon were obligated to flee like drift to the brow of a hill, called Kilblain-brae, where they again showed face.

Those on board the ships seeing what was thus doing on the land, pointed their great guns to the airt where the cavaliers had rallied, and fired them with such effect, that the stoure and stones brattled about the lugs of the heritors, which so terrified them all that they scampered off; and, it is said, some drew not bridle till they were in Paisley with whole skins, though at some cost of leather.

When these tyrant tools were thus discomfited, Sir John Cochrane came on shore, and tried in vain to prevail on the inhabitants to join in defence of religion and liberty. So he sent for the baron-bailie, who was the ruling power of the town in the absence of their great Sir John, and ordered him to provide forthwith two hundred bolls of meal for the ships. But the bailie, a shrewd and gausie man, made so many difficulties in the gathering of the meal, to waste time till help would come, that the knight was glad to content himself with little more than a fifth part of his demand.

Meanwhile I had made my errand known to Sir John Cochrane, and when he went off with the meal-sacks to the ships I went with him, and we sailed the same night to the castle of Allengreg, where Argyle himself then was.

Whatever doubts and fears I had of the success of the expedition, were all wofully confirmed, when I saw how things were about that unfortunate nobleman. The controversies in our councils at the Pentland raid were more than renewed among those who were around Argyle; and it was plain to me that the sense of ruin was upon his spirit; for, after I had told him the purport of my mission, he said to me in a mournful manner—

'I can discern no party in this country that desire to be relieved; there are some hidden ones no doubt, but only my poor friends here in Argyle seem willing to be free. God hath so ordered it, and it must be for the best. I submit myself to his will.'

I felt the truth of what he said, that the tyranny had indeed bred distrust among us, and that the patience of men was so worn out that very many were inclined to submit from mere weariness of spirit; – but I added, to hearten him, if one of my condition may say so proud a thing of so great a person, That were the distinct ends of his intents made more clearly manifest, maybe the dispersed hearts of the Covenanters would yet be knit together. 'Some think, my Lord, ye're for the Duke of Monmouth to be king, but that will ne'er do, – the rightful heirs canna be set aside. James Stuart may be, and should be, put down; but, according to the customs registered, as I hae read in the ancient chronicles of this realm, when our nation in olden times cut off a king for his misdeeds, the next lawful heir was ay raised to the throne.'

To this the Earl made no answer, but continued some time thoughtful, and then said—

'It rests not all with me, – those who are with me, as you may well note, take over much upon them, and will not be controlled. They are like the waves, raised and driven wheresoever any blast of rumour wiseth them to go. I gave a letter of trust to one of their emissaries, and, like the raven, he has never returned. If, however, I could get to Inverary, I doubt not yet that something might be done; for I should then be in the midst of some that would reverence Argyle.'

But why need I dwell on these melancholious incidents? Next day the Earl resolved to make the attempt to reach Inverary, and I went with him; but after the castle of Arkinglass, in the way thither, had been taken, he was obligated, by the appearance of two English frigates which had been sent in pursuit of the expedition, to return to Allengreg; for the main stores and ammunition brought from Holland were lodged in that castle; the ships also were lying there; all which in a manner were at stake, and no garrison adequate to defend the same from so great a power.

On returning to Allengreg, Argyle saw it would be a golden achievement, if in that juncture he could master the frigates; so he ordered his force, which amounted to about a thousand men, to man the ships and four prizes which he had, together with about thirty cowan boats belonging to his vassals, and to attack the frigates. But in this also he was disappointed, for those who were with him, and wedded to the purpose of going to the Lowlands, mutinied against the scheme as too hazardous, and obliged him to give up the attempt, and to leave the castle with a weak and incapable garrison.

Accordingly, reluctant, but yielding to these blind councils, after quitting Allengreg, we marched for the Lowlands, and at the head of the Gareloch, where we halted, the garrison which had been left at Allengreg joined us with the disastrous intelligence, that, finding themselves unable to withstand the frigates, they had abandoned all.

I was near to Argyle when the news of this was brought to him, and I observed that he said nothing, but his cheek faded, and he hastily wrung his hands.

Having crossed the river Leven a short way above Dumbarton, without suffering any material molestation, we halted for the night. But as we were setting our watches a party of the government force appeared, so that, instead of getting any rest after our heavy march, we were obligated to think of again moving.

The Earl would fain have fought with that force, his numbers being superior, but he was again over-ruled; so that all we could do was, during the night, leaving our camp-fires burning for a delusion, to make what haste we could toward Glasgow.

In this the uncountenanced fortunes of the expedition were again seen. Our guides in the dark misled us; so that, instead of being taken to Glasgow, we were, after grievous traversing in the moors, landed on the banks of the Clyde near Kilpatrick, where the whole force broke up, Sir John Cochrane, being fey for the West Country, persuading many to go with him over the water, in order to make for the shire of Ayr.

The Earl seeing himself thus deserted, and but few besides those of his own kin left with him, rode about a mile on towards Glasgow, with the intent of taking some rest in the house of one who had been his servant; but on reaching the door it was shut in his face, and barred, and admission peremptorily refused. He said nothing, but turned round to us with a smile of such resigned sadness that it brought tears into every eye.

Seeing that his fate was come to such extremity, I proposed to exchange clothes with him, that he might the better escape, and to conduct him to the West Country, where, if any chance were yet left, it was to be found there, as Sir John Cochrane had represented. Whereupon he sent his kinsmen to make the best of their way back to the Highlands, to try what could be done among his clan; and having accepted a portion of my apparel, he went to the ferry-boat with Major Fullarton, and we crossed the water together.

On landing on the Renfrew side the Earl went forward alone, a little before the Major and me; but on reaching the ford at Inchinnan he was stopped by two soldiers, who laid hands upon him, one on each side, and in the grappling one of them the Earl fell to the ground. In a moment, however, his Lordship started up, and got rid of them by presenting his pistols. But five others at the same instant came in sight, and fired and ran in at him, and knocked him down with their swords. 'Alas! unfortunate Argyle,' I heard him cry as he fell; and the soldiers were so astonished at having so rudely treated so great a man, that they stood still with awe and dropped their swords, and some of them shed tears of sorrow for his fate.

Seeing what had thus happened, Major Fullarton and I fled and hid ourselves behind a hedge, for we saw another party of troopers coming towards the spot, – we heard afterwards that it was Sir John Shaw of Greenock, with some of the Renfrewshire heritors, by whom the Earl was conducted a prisoner to Glasgow. But of the dismal indignities, and the degradations to which he was subjected, and of his doleful martyrdom, the courteous reader may well spare me the sad recital, as they are recorded in all true British histories, and he will accept for the same those sweet but mournful lines which Argyle indited in the dungeon:

Thou, passenger, that shalt have so much time
To view my grave, and ask what was my crime;
No stain of error, no black vice's brand,
Was that which chased me from my native land.
Love to my country – twice sentenced to die—
Constrain'd my hands forgotten arms to try.
More by friends' fraud my fall proceeded hath
Than foes, though now they thrice decreed my death.
On my attempt though Providence did frown,
His oppress'd people God at length shall own;
Another hand, by more successful speed,
Shall raise the remnant, bruise the serpent's head.
Though my head fall, that is no tragic story,
Since, going hence, I enter endless glory.

The news of the fall of Argyle was as gladdening wine to the cruel spirit of James Stuart. It was treated by him as victory was of old among the conquering Romans, and he ordained medals of brass and of silver to be made, to commemorate, as a glorious triumph, the deed that was a crime. But he was not content with such harmless monuments of insensate exultation; he considered the blow as final to the presbyterian cause, and openly set himself to effect the re-establishment of the idolatrous abominations of the mass and monkrie.

The Lord Perth and his brother, the Lord Melford, and a black catalogue of others, whose names, for the fame of Scotland, I would fain expunge with the waters of oblivion, considering Religion as a thing of royal regulation, professed themselves papists, and got, as the price of their apostasy and perdition, certain places of profit in the government. Clouds of the papistical locust were then allured into the land, to eat it up leaf and blade again. Schools to teach children the deceits, and the frauds, and the sins of the jesuits, were established even in the palace of Holyrood-house; and the chapel, which had been cleansed in the time of Queen Mary, was again defiled with the pageantries of idolatry.

But the godly people of Edinburgh called to mind the pious bravery of their forefathers, and all that they had done in the Reformation; and they rose, as it were with one accord, and demolished the schools, and purified the chapel, even to desolation, and forced the papist priest to abjure his own idols. The old abhorrence of the abominations was revived; for now it was clearly seen what King Charles and his brother had been seeking, in the relentless persecution which they had so long sanctioned;

and many in consequence, who had supported and obeyed the prelatic apostacy as a thing but of innocent forms, trembled at the share which they had taken in the guilt of that aggression, and their dismay was unspeakable.

The tyrant, however, soon saw that he had over-counted the degree of the humiliation of the land; and being disturbed by the union which his open papistry was causing among all denominations of protestants, he changed his mood, and from force resorted to fraud, publishing a general toleration, – a device of policy which greatly disheartened the prelatic faction; for they saw that they had only laboured to strengthen a prerogative, the first effectual exercise of which was directed against themselves, every one discerning that the indulgence was framed to give head-rope to the papists. But the Covenanters made use of it to advance the cause of the gospel, as I shall now proceed to rehearse, as well as how through it I was enabled to perform my avenging vow.

Among the exiled Covenanters who returned with Argyle, and with whom I became acquainted while with him, was Thomas Ardmillan, whom, after my escape at the time when the Earl was taken, I fell in again with at Kirkintilloch, as I was making the best of my way into the East country, and we went together to Arbroath, where he embarked for Holland.

Being then minded to return back to Edinburgh, and to abide again with Mrs Brownlee, in whose house I had found a safe asylum, and a convenient place of espial, after seeing him on board the vessel, I also took shipping, and returned to Leith under an assurance that I should hear of him from time to time. It was not, however, until the indulgence was proclaimed that I heard from him, about which era he wrote to me a most scriptural letter, by the reverend Mr Patrick Warner, who had received a call from the magistrates and inhabitants of the covenanted town of Irvine, to take upon him the ministry of their parish.

Mr Warner having accepted the call, on arriving at Leith sent to Mrs Brownlee's this letter, with a request that, if I was alive and there, he would be glad to see me in his lodging before departing to the West country.

As the fragrance of Mr Warner's sufferings was sweet among all the true and faithful, I was much regaled with this invitation, and went forthwith to Leith, where I found him in a house that is clad with oystershells, in the Tod's-hole Close. He was sitting in a fair chamber therein, with that worthy bailie that afterwards was next year, at the time of the Revolution, Mr Cornelius Neilsone, and his no less excellent compeer on the same great occasion, Mr George Samsone, both persons of godly repute. Mr Cheyne, the town-clerk, was likewise present, a most discreet character; but being a lawyer by trade, and come of an episcopal stock, he was rather a thought, it was said, inclined to the prelatic sect. Divers others, douce and religious characters, were also there, especially Mr Jaddua Fyfe, a merchant of women's gear, then in much renown for his suavity. Mr Warner was relating to them many consolatory things of the worth and piety of the Prince and Princess of Orange, to whom the eyes of all the protestants, especially of the presbyterians, were at that time directed.

'Aye, aye,' said Mr Jaddua Fyfe, 'nae doot, nae doot, but the Prince is a man of a sweet-smelling odour, – that's in the way of character; – and the Princess; aye, aye, it is well known, that she's a pure snowdrop, and a lily o' the valley in the Lord's garden, – that's in the way of piety.'

'They're the heirs presumptive to the crown,' subjoined Mr Cheyne.

'They're weel entitled to the reverence and respect of us a',' added Mr Cornelius Neilsone.

'When I first got the call from Irvine,' resumed Mr Warner, 'that excellent lady, and precious vessel of god-liness, the Countess of Sutherland, being then at the Hague, sought my allowance to let the Princess know of my acceptance of the call, and to inquire if her Highness had any commands for Scotland; and the Princess in a most gracious manner signified to her that the best thing I, and those who were like me, could do for her, was to be earnest in praying that she might be kept firm and faithful in the reformed religion, adding many tender things of her sincere sympathy for the poor persecuted people of Scotland, and recommending that I should wait on the

Prince before taking my departure. I was not, however, forward to thrust myself into such honour; but at last yielding to the exhortations of my friends, I went to the house of Mynheer Bentinck, and gave him my name for an audience; and one morning, about eight of the clock, his servant called for me and took me to his house, and he himself conveyed me into the presence of the Prince, where, leaving me with him, we had a most weighty and edifying conversation.'

'Aye, aye,' interposed Mr Jaddua Fyfe, 'it was a great thing to converse wi' a prince; and how did he behave himsel, – that's in the way o' manners?'

'Ye need na debate, Mr Fyfe, about that,' replied Mr Samsone, 'the Prince kens what it's to be civil, especially to his friends;' and I thought, in saying these words, that Mr Samsone looked particular towards me.

'And what passed?' said the town-clerk, in a way as if he pawkily jealoused something. Mr Warner, however, in his placid and minister-like manner, responded—

'I told his Highness how I had received the call from Irvine, and thought it my duty to inquire if there was any thing wherein I could serve him in Scotland.

To this the Prince replied in a benign manner—'

'Aye, aye,' ejaculated Mr Jaddua Fyfe, 'nae doubt it was in a benignant manner, and in a cordial manner. Aye, aye, he had nae his ellwand to seek when a customer's afore the counter, – that's in the way o' business.'

'"I understand," said his Highness,' continued Mr Warner, '"you are called home upon the toleration lately granted; but I can assure you, that toleration is not granted for any kindness to your party, but to favour the papists, and to divide you among yourselves; yet I think you may be so wise as to take good of it, and prevent the evil designed, and, instead of dividing, come to a better harmony among yourselves when you have liberty to see and meet more freely." '

'To which,' said Mr Warner, 'I answered, that I heartily wished it might prove so, and that nothing would be wanting on my part to make it so; and I added, the presbyterians in Scotland, Great Sir, are looked upon as a very despicable party; but those who do so, measure them by the appearance at Pentland and Bothwell, as if the whole power of the presbyterians had been drawn out there; but I can assure your Highness that such are greatly mistaken; for many firm presbyterians were not satisfied as to the grounds and manner of those risings, and did not join; and others were borne down by the Persecution. In verity I am persuaded, that if Scotland were left free, of three parts of the people two would be found presbyterians. We are indeed a poor persecuted party, and have none under God to look to for our help and relief but your Highness, on account of that relation you and the Princess have to the crown.'

'That was going a great length, Mr Warner,' said Mr Cheyne, the town-clerk.

'No a bit, no a bit,' cried I; and Mr Jaddua Fyfe gave me an approving gloom, while Mr Warner quietly continued—

'I then urged many things, hoping that the Lord would incline his Highness' heart to espouse His interest in Scotland, and befriend the persecuted presbyterians. To which the Prince replied—

'Aye, aye, I like to hear what his Highness said, that's in the way of counselling,' said Mr Jaddua Fyfe.

'The Prince,' replied Mr Warner, 'then spoke to me earnestly, saying—

"I have been educated a presbyterian, and I hope so to continue; and I assure you, if ever it be in my power, I shall make the presbyterian church-government the established church-government of Scotland, and of this you may assure your friends, as in prudence you find it convenient." '

Discerning the weight and intimation that were in these words, I said, when Mr Warner had made an end, that it was a great thing to know the sentiment of the Prince; for by all signs the time could not be far off when we would maybe require to put his assurance and promise to the test. At which words of mine there were many exchanges of gathered brows and significant nods, and Mr Jaddua Fyfe, to whom I was sitting next, slyly pinched me in the elbow; all which spoke plainer than elocution, that those present were accorded with me in opinion; and I gave inward thanks that such a braird of renewed courage and zeal was beginning to kithe among us.

Besides Mr Warner, many other ministers, who had taken refuge in foreign countries, were called home, and it began openly to be talked, that King James would to a surety be set aside, on account of his malversations in the kingly office in England, and the even-down course he was pursuing there, as in Scotland, to abolish all property that the subjects had in the ancient laws and charters of the realm. But the thing came to no definite head, till that jesuit-contrived device for cutting out the protestant heirs to the crown was brought to maturity, by palming a man-child upon the nation as the lawful son of the Tyrant and his papistical wife.

In the meantime I had not been idle in disseminating throughout the land, by the means of the Cameronians, a faithful account of what Mr Warner had related of the pious character and presbyterian dispositions of the Prince of Orange; and through a correspondence that I opened with Thomas Ardmillan, Mynheer Bentinck was kept so informed of the growing affection for his master in Scotland, as soon emboldened the Prince, with what he heard of the inclinations of the English people, to prepare a great host and navy for the deliverance of the kingdoms. In the midst of these human means and stratagems, the bright right-hand of Providence was shiningly visible; for by the news of the Prince's preparations It smote the councils of King James with confusion and a fatal distraction.

Though he had so alienated the Scottish lieges, that none but the basest of men among us acknowledged his authority, yet he summoned all his forces into England, leaving his power to be upheld here by those only who were vile enough to wish for the continuance of slavery. Thus was the way cleared for the advent of the deliverer; and the faithful nobles and gentry of Scotland, as the army

was removed, came flocking into Edinburgh, and the Privy
Council, which had been so little slack in any crime, durst
not molest them, though the purpose of their being there
was a treason which the members could not but all well
know. Every thing, in a word, was now moving onward
to a great event; all in the land was as when the thaw
comes, and the ice is breaking, and the snows melting,
and the waters flowing, and the rivers are bursting their
frozen fetters, and the sceptre of winter is broken, and the
wreck of his domination is drifting and perishing away.

To keep the Privy Council in the confusion of the
darkness of ignorance, I concerted with many of the
Cameronians that they should spread themselves along
the highways, and intercept the government expresses
and emissaries, to the end that neither the King's faction
in England nor in Scotland might know aught of the
undertakings of each other; and when Thomas Ardmillan
sent me, from Mynheer Bentinck, the Prince's declaration
for Scotland, I hastened into the West Country, that I
might exhort the covenanted there to be in readiness, and
from the tolbooth stair of Irvine, yea on the very step where
my heart was so pierced by the cries of my son, I was the
first in Scotland to publish that glorious pledge of our
deliverance. On the same day, at the same hour, the like
was done by others of our friends at Glasgow and at Ayr;
and there was shouting, and joy, and thanksgiving, and
the magnificent voice of freedom resounded throughout
the land, and ennobled all hearts again with bravery.

When the news of the Prince's landing at Torbay arrived,
we felt that liberty was come; but long oppression had
made many distrustful, and from day to day rumours were
spread by the despairing members of the prelatic sect, the
breathings of their wishes, that made us doubt whether
we ought to band ourselves into any array for warfare.
In this state of swithering and incertitude we continued
for some time, till I began to grow fearful lest the zeal
which had been so rekindled would sink and go out if not
stirred again in some effectual manner. So I conferred with
Quintin Fullarton, who in all these providences had been
art and part with me, from the day of the meeting with Mr

Renwick near Laswade; and as the Privy Council, when it was known the Prince had been invited over, had directed beacons to be raised on the tops of many mountains, to be fired as signals of alarum for the King's party when the Dutch fleet should be seen approaching the coast, we devised, as a mean for calling forth the strength and spirit of the Covenanters, that we should avail ourselves of their preparations.

Accordingly we instructed four alert young men, of the Cameronian societies, severally and unknown to each other, to be in attendance on the night of the tenth of December at the beacons on the hills of Knockdolian, Lowthers, Blacklarg, and Bencairn, that they might fire the same if need or signal should so require, Quintin Fullarton having undertaken to kindle the one on Mistylaw himself.

The night was dark, but it was ordained that the air should be moist and heavy, and in that state when the light of flame spreads farthest. Meanwhile fearful reports from Ireland of papistical intents to maintain the cause of King James made the fancies of men awake and full of anxieties. The prelatic curates were also so heartened by those rumours and tidings, that they began to recover from the dismay with which the news of the Prince's landing had overwhelmed them, and to shoot out again the horns of antichristian arrogance. But when, about three hours after sunset, the beacon on the Mistylaw was fired, and when hill after hill was lighted up, the whole country was filled with such consternation and panic, that I was myself smitten with the dread of some terrible consequence. Horsemen passed furiously in all directions – bells were rung, and drums beat – mothers were seen flying with their children they knew not whither – cries and lamentations echoed on every side. The skies were kindled with a red glare, and none could tell where the signal was first shown. Some said the Irish had landed and were burning the towns in the south, and no one knew where to flee from the unknown and invisible enemy.

In the meantime, our Covenanters of the West assembled at their trysting-place, to the number of more than six thousand armed men, ready and girded for battle; and this appearance was an assurance that no power was then in all the Lowlands able to gainsay such a force; and next day, when it was discovered that the alarm had no real cause, it was determined that the prelatic priests should be openly discarded from their parishes. Our vengeance, however, was not meted upon them by the measure of our sufferings, but by the treatment which our own pastors had borne; and, considering how many of them had acted as spies and accusers against us, it is surprising, that of two hundred, who were banished from the parishes, few received any cause of complaint; even the poor feckless thing Andrew Dornock was decently expelled from the manse of Quharist, on promising he would never return.

This riddance of the malignants was the first fruit of the expulsion of James Stuart from the throne; but it was not long till we were menaced with new and even greater sufferings than we had yet endured. For though the tyrant had fled, he had left Claverhouse, under the title of Viscount Dundee, behind him; and in the fearless activity of that proud and cruel warrior, there was an engine sufficient to have restored him to his absolute throne, as I shall now proceed to rehearse.

The true and faithful of the West, by the event recorded in the foregoing chapter, being so instructed with respect to their own power and numbers, stood in no reverence of any force that the remnants of the Tyrant's sect and faction could afford to send against them. I therefore resolved to return to Edinburgh; for the longing of my grandfather's spirit to see the current and course of public events flowing from their fountain-head, was upon me, and I had not yet so satisfied the yearnings of justice as to be able to look again on the ashes of my house and the tomb of Sarah Lochrig and her daughters. Accordingly, soon after the turn of the year I went thither, where I found all things in uncertainty and commotion.

Claverhouse, or, as he was now titled, Lord Dundee, with that scorn of public opinion and defect of all principle, save only a canine fidelity, a dog's love, to his papistical master, domineered with his dragoons, as if he himself had been regnant monarch of Scotland; and it was plain and probable, that unless he was soon bridled, he would speedily act upon the wider stage of the kingdom the same Mahound-like part that he had played in the prenticeship of his cruelties of the shire of Ayr. The peril, indeed, from his courage and activity, was made to me very evident, by a conversation that I had with one David Middleton, who had come from England on some business of the Jacobites there, in connexion with Dundee.

Providence led me to fall in with this person one morning, as we were standing among a crowd of other onlookers, seeing Claverhouse reviewing his men in the front court of Holyrood-house. I happened to remark, for in sooth it must be so owned, that the Viscount had a brave though a proud look, and that his voice had the manliness of one ordained to command.

'Yes,' replied David Middleton, 'he's a born soldier, and if the King is to be restored, he is the man that will do it. When his Majesty was at Rochester, before going to France, I was there with my master, and being called in to mend the fire, I heard Dundee and my Lord, then with the King, discoursing concerning the royal affairs.

' "The question," said Lord Dundee to his Majesty, "is, whether you shall stay in England or go to France? My opinion, sir, is, that you should stay in England, make your stand here, and summon your subjects to your allegiance. 'Tis true, you have disbanded your army, but give me leave, and I will undertake to get ten thousand men of it together, and march through all England with your standard at their head, and drive the Dutch before you;" and,' added David Middleton, 'let him have time, and I doubt not, that, even without the King's leave, he will do as much.'

Whether the man in this did brag of a knowledge that he had not, the story seemed so likely, that it could scarcely be questioned; so I consulted with my faithful friend and companion, Quintin Fullarton, and other men of weight among the Cameronians; and we agreed, that those of the societies who were scattered along the borders to intercept the correspondence between the English and Scottish Jacobites, should be called into Edinburgh to daunt the rampageous insolence of Claverhouse.

This was done accordingly; and from the day that they began to appear in the streets, the bravery of those who were with him seemed to slacken. But still he carried himself as boldly as ever, and persuaded the Duke of Gordon, then governor of the castle, not to surrender, nor obey any mandate from the Convention of the States, by whom, in that interregnum, the rule of the kingdom was exercised. Still, however, the Cameronians were coming in, and their numbers became so manifest, that the dragoons were backward to show themselves. But their commander affected not to value us, till one day a singular thing took place, which, in its issues, ended the over-awing influence of his presence in Edinburgh.

I happened to be standing with Quintin Fullarton, and some four or five other Cameronians, at an entry-mouth forenent the Canongate-cross, when Claverhouse, and that tool of tyranny, Sir George Mackenzie the advocate, were coming up from the palace; and as they passed, the Viscount looked hard at me, and said to Sir George,

'I have somewhere seen that doure cur before.'

Sir George turned round also to look, and I said—

'It's true, Claverhouse, – we met at Drumclog;' and I touched my arm that he had wounded there, adding, 'and the blood shed that day has not yet been paid for.'

At these words he made a rush upon me with his sword, but my friends were nimbler with theirs; and Sir George Mackenzie interposing, drew him off, and they went away together.

The affair, however, ended not here. Sir George, with the subtlety of a lawyer, tried to turn it to some account, and making a great ado of it, as a design to assassinate Lord Dundee and himself, tried to get the Convention to order all strangers to remove from the town. This, however, was refused; so that Claverhouse, seeing how the spirit of the times was going among the members, and the boldness with which the Presbyterians and the Covenanters were daily bearding his arrogance, withdrew with his dragoons from the city, and made for Stirling.

In this retreat from Edinburgh he blew the trumpet of civil war; but in less than two hours from the signal, a regiment of eight hundred Cameronians was arrayed in the High-street. The son of Argyle, who had taken his seat in the Convention as a peer, soon after gathered three hundred of the Campbells, and the safety of Scotland now seemed to be secured by the arrival of Mackay with three Scotch regiments, then in the Dutch service, and which the Prince of Orange had brought with him to Torbay.

By the retreat of Claverhouse the Jacobite party in Edinburgh were so disheartened, and any endeavour which they afterwards made to rally was so crazed with consternation, that it was plain the sceptre had departed from their master. The capacity as well as the power for any effectual action was indeed evidently taken from them, and the ploughshare was driven over the ruins of their cause on the ever-memorable eleventh day of April, when William and Mary were proclaimed King and Queen.

But though thus the oppressor was cast down from his throne, and though thus, in Scotland, the chief agents in the work of deliverance were the outlawed Cameronians, as instructed by me, the victory could not be complete, nor the trophies hung up in the hall, while the Tyrant possessed an instrument of such edge and temper as Claverhouse. As for myself, I felt that while the homicide lived the debt of justice and of blood due to my martyred family could never be satisfied; and I heard of his passing from Stirling into the Highlands, and the wonders he was working for the Jacobite cause there, as if nothing had yet been achieved toward the fulfilment of my avenging vow.

When Claverhouse left Stirling, he had but sixty horse. In little more than a month he was at the head of seventeen hundred men. He obtained reinforcements from Ireland. The Macdonalds, and the Camerons, and the Gordons, were all his. A vassal of the Marquis of Athol had declared for him even in the castle of Blair, and defended it against the clan of his master. An event still more strange was produced by the spell of his presence, – the clansmen of Athol deserted their chief, and joined his standard. He kindled the hills in his cause, and all the life of the North was gathering around him.

Mackay, with the Covenanters, the regiments from Holland, and the Cameronians, went from Perth to oppose his entrance into the Lowlands. The minds of men were suspended. Should he defeat Mackay, it was plain that the crown would soon be restored to James Stuart, and the woes of Scotland come again.

In that dismal juncture I was alone; for Quintin Fullarton, with all the Cameronians, was with Mackay.

I was an old man, verging on threescore.

I went to and fro in the streets of Edinburgh all day long, inquiring of every stranger the news; and every answer that I got was some new triumph of Dundee.

No sleep came to my burning pillow, or if indeed my eyelids for very weariness fell down, it was only that I might suffer the stings of anxiety in some sharper form; for my dreams were of flames kindling around me, through which I saw behind the proud and exulting visage of Dundee.

Sometimes in the depths of the night I rushed into the street, and I listened with greedy ears, thinking I heard the trampling of dragoons and the heavy wheels of cannon; and often in the day, when I saw three or four persons speaking together, I ran towards them, and broke in upon their discourse with some wild interrogation, that made them answer me with pity.

But the haste and frenzy of this alarm suddenly changed: I felt that I was a chosen instrument; I thought that the ruin which had fallen on me and mine was assuredly some great mystery of Providence: I remembered the prophecy of my grandfather, that a task was in store for me, though I knew not what it was; I forgot my old age and my infirmities; I hastened to my chamber; I put money in my purse; I spoke to no one; I bought a carabine; and I set out alone to reinforce Mackay.

As I passed down the street, and out at the West Port, I saw the people stop and look at me with silence and wonder. As I went along the road, several that were passing inquired where I was going so fast? but I waived my hand and hurried by.

I reached the Queensferry without as it were drawing breath. I embarked; and when the boat arrived at the northern side I had fallen asleep; and the ferryman, in compassion, allowed me to slumber unmolested. When I awoke I felt myself refreshed. I leapt on shore, and went again impatiently on.

But my mind was then somewhat calmer; and when I reached Kinross I bought a little bread, and retiring to the brink of the lake dipt it in the water, and it was a savoury repast.

As I approached the Brigg of Earn I felt age in my limbs, and though the spirit was willing the body could not; and I sat down, and I mourned that I was so frail and so feeble. But a marvellous vigour was soon again given to me, and I rose refreshed from my resting-place on the wall of the bridge, and the same night I reached Perth. I stopped in a stabler's till the morning. At break of day, having hired a horse from him, I hastened forward to Dunkeld, where he told me Mackay had encamped the day before, on his way to defend the pass of Killicrankie.

The road was thronged with women and children flocking into Perth in terror of the Highlanders, but I heeded them not. I had but one thought, and that was to reach the scene of war and Claverhouse.

On arriving at the ferry of Inver, the field in front of the Bishop of Dunkeld's house, where the army had been encamped, was empty. Mackay had marched towards Blair-Athol, to drive Dundee and the Highlanders, if possible, back into the glens and mosses of the North; for he had learnt that his own force greatly exceeded his adversary's.

On hearing this, and my horse being in need of bating, I halted at the ferry-house before crossing the Tay, assured by the boatman that I should be able to overtake the army long before it could reach the meeting of the Tummel and the Gary. And so it proved; for as I came to that turn of the road where the Tummel pours its roaring waters into the Tay, I heard the echoing of a trumpet among the mountains, and soon after saw the army winding its toilsome course along the river's brink, slowly and heavily, as the chariots of Pharoah laboured through the sands of the Desert; and the appearance of the long array was as the many-coloured woods that skirt the rivers in autumn.

On the right hand, hills, and rocks, and trees, rose like the ruins of the ramparts of some ancient world; and I thought of the epochs when the days of the children of men were a thousand years, and when giants were on the earth, and all were swept away by the flood; and I felt as if I beheld the hand of the Lord in the cloud weighing the things of time in His scales, to see if the sins of the world were indeed become again so great, as that the cause of Claverhouse should be suffered to prevail. For my spirit was as a flame that blazeth in the wind, and my thoughts as the sparks that shoot and soar for a moment towards the skies with a glorious splendour, and drop down upon the earth in ashes.

General Mackay halted the host on a spacious green plain which lies at the meeting of the Tummel and the Gary, and which the Highlanders call Fascali, because, as the name in their tongue signifies, no trees are growing thereon. This place is the threshold of the Pass of Killicrankie, through the dark and woody chasms of which the impatient waters of the Gary come with hoarse and wrathful mutterings and murmurs. The hills and mountains around are built up in more olden and antic forms than those of our Lowland parts, and a wild and strange solemnity is mingled there with much fantastical beauty, as if, according to the ministrelsy of ancient times, sullen wizards and gamesome fairies had joined their arts and spells to make a common dwelling-place.

As the soldiers spread themselves over the green bosom of Fascali, and piled their arms and furled their banners, and laid their drums on the ground, and led their horses to the river, the General sent forward a scout through the Pass, to discover the movements of Claverhouse, having heard that he was coming from the castle of Blair-Athol, to prevent his entrance into the Highlands.

The officer sent to make the espial, had not been gone above half an hour, when he came back in great haste to tell that the Highlanders were on the brow of a hill above the house of Rinrorie, and that unless the Pass was immediately taken possession of, it would be mastered by Claverhouse that night.

Mackay, at this news, ordered the trumpets to sound, and as the echoes multiplied and repeated the alarum, it was as if all the spirits of the hills called the men to arms. The soldiers looked around as they formed their ranks, listening with delight and wonder at the universal bravery;

and I thought of the sight, which Elisha the prophet gave to the young man at Dothan, of the mountains covered with horses and chariots of fire, for his defence against the host of the King of Syria; and I went forward with the confidence of assured victory.

As we issued forth from the Pass into the wide country, extending towards Lude and Blair-Athol, we saw, as the officer had reported, the Highland hosts of Claverhouse arrayed along the lofty brow of the mountain, above the house of Rinrorie, their plaids waving in the breeze on the hill, and their arms glittering to the sun.

Mackay directed the troops, at crossing a raging brook called the Girnaig, to keep along a flat of land above the house of Rinrorie, and to form, in order of battle, on the field beyond the garden, and under the hill where the Highlanders were posted; the baggage and camp equipages, he at the same time ordered down into a plain that lies between the bank on the crown of which the house stands and the river Gary. An ancient monumental stone in the middle of the lower plain shows, that in some elder age a battle had been fought there, and that some warrior of might and fame had fallen.

In taking his ground on that elevated shelf of land, Mackay was minded to stretch his left wing to intercept the return of the Highlanders towards Blair, and, if possible, oblige them to enter the Pass of Killicrankie, by which he would have cut them off from their resources in the North, and so perhaps mastered them without any great slaughter.

But Claverhouse discerned the intent of his movement, and before our covenanted host had formed their array, it was evident that he was preparing to descend; and as a foretaste of the vehemence wherewith the Highlanders were coming, we saw them rolling large stones to the brow of the hill.

In the meantime the house of Rinrorie having been deserted by the family, the lady, with her children and maidens, had fled to Lude or Struan, Mackay ordered a party to take possession of it, and to post themselves at the windows which look up the hill. I was among those who went into the house, and my station was at the eastermost window, in a small chamber which is entered by two doors, – the one opening from the stair-head, and the other from the drawing-room. In this situation we could see but little of the distribution of the army or the positions that Mackay was taking, for our view was confined to the face of the hill whereon the Highlanders were busily preparing for their descent. But I saw Claverhouse on horseback riding to and fro, and plainly inflaming their valour with many a courageous gesture; and as he turned and winded his prancing war-horse, his breastplate blazed to the setting sun like a beacon on the hill.

When he had seemingly concluded his exhortation, the Highlanders stooped forward, and hurled down the rocks which they had gathered for their forerunners; and while the stones came leaping and bounding with a noise like thunder, the men followed in thick and separate bands, and Mackay gave the signal to commence firing.

We saw from the windows many of the Highlanders, at the first volley, stagger and fall, but the others came furiously down; and before the soldiers had time to stick their bayonets into their guns, the broad swords of the Clansmen hewed hundreds to the ground.

Within a few minutes the battle was general between the two armies; but the smoke of the firing involved all the field, and we could see nothing from the windows. The echoes of the mountains raged with the din, and the sounds were multiplied by them in so many different places, that we could not tell where the fight was hottest. The whole country around resounded as with the uproar of a universal battle.

I felt the passion of my spirit return; I could no longer restrain myself, nor remain where I was. Snatching up my carabine, I left my actionless post at the window, and hurried down stairs, and out of the house. I saw by the flashes through the smoke, that the firing was spreading down into the plain where the baggage was stationed, and by this I knew that there was some movement in the battle; but whether the Highlanders or the Covenanters were shifting their ground, I could not discover, for the valley was filled with smoke, and it was only at times that a sword, like a glance of lightning, could be seen in the cloud wherein the thunders and tempest of the conflict were raging.

CHAPTER THIRTY-THREE

As I stood on the brow of the bank in front of Rinrorie-house, a gentle breathing of the evening air turned the smoke like the travelling mist of the hills, and opening it here and there, I had glimpses of the fighting. Sometimes I saw the Highlanders driving the Covenanters down the steep, and sometimes I beheld them in their turn on the ground endeavouring to protect their unbonnetted heads with their targets, but to whom the victory was to be given I could discern no sign; and I said to myself, the prize at hazard is the liberty of the land and the Lord; surely it shall not be permitted to the champion of bondage to prevail.

A stronger breathing of the gale came rushing along, and the skirts of the smoke where the baggage stood were blown aside, and I beheld many of the Highlanders among the waggons plundering and tearing. Then I heard a great shouting on the right, and looking that way, I saw the children of the Covenant fleeing in remnants across the lower plain, and making toward the river. Presently I also saw Mackay with two regiments, all that kept the order of discipline, also in the plain. He had lost the battle. Claverhouse had won; and the scattered firing, which was continued by a few, was to my ears as the rivetting of the shackles on the arms of poor Scotland for ever. My grief was unspeakable.

I ran to and fro on the brow of the hill – and I stampt with my feet – and I beat my breast – and I rubbed my hands with the frenzy of despair – and I threw myself on the ground – and all the sufferings of which I have written returned upon me – and I started up and I cried aloud the blasphemy of the fool, 'There is no God.'

But scarcely had the dreadful words escaped my profane lips, when I heard, as it were, thunders in the heavens, and the voice of an oracle crying in the ears of my soul, 'The victory of this day is given into thy hands!' and strange wonder and awe fell upon me, and a mighty spirit entered into mine, and I felt as if I was in that moment clothed with the armour of divine might.

I took up my carabine, which in these transports had fallen from my hand, and I went round the gable of the house into the garden – and I saw Claverhouse with several of his officers coming along the ground by which our hosts had marched to their position – and ever and anon turning round and exhorting his men to follow him. It was evident he was making for the Pass to intercept our scattered fugitives from escaping that way.

The garden in which I then stood was surrounded by a low wall. A small goose-pool lay on the outside, between which and the garden I perceived that Claverhouse would pass.

I prepared my flint and examined my firelock, and I walked towards the top of the garden with a firm step. The ground was buoyant to my tread, and the vigour of youth was renewed in my aged limbs: I thought that those for whom I had so mourned walked before me – that they smiled and beckoned me to come on, and that a glorious light shone around me.

Claverhouse was coming forward – several officers were near him, but his men were still a little behind, and seemed inclined to go down the hill, and he chided at their reluctance. I rested my carabine on the garden-wall. I bent my knee and knelt upon the ground. I aimed and fired, – but when the smoke cleared away I beheld the oppressor still proudly on his war-horse.

I loaded again, again I knelt, and again rested my carabine upon the wall, and fired a second time, and again was disappointed.

Then I remembered that I had not implored the help of Heaven, and I prepared for the third time, and when all was ready, and Claverhouse was coming forward, I took off my bonnet, and kneeling with the gun in my hand, cried, 'Lord, remember David and all his afflictions;' and having so prayed, I took aim as I knelt, and Claverhouse raising his arm in command, I fired. In the same moment I looked up, and there was a vision in the air as if all the angels of brightness, and the martyrs in their vestments of glory, were assembled on the walls and battlements of heaven to witness the event, – and I started up and cried, 'I have delivered my native land!' But in the same instant I remembered to whom the glory was due, and falling again on my knees, I raised my hands and bowed my head as I said, 'Not mine, O Lord, but thine is the victory!'

When the smoke rolled away I beheld Claverhouse in the arms of his officers, sinking from his horse, and the blood flowing from a wound between the breast-plate and the arm-pit. The same night he was summoned to the audit of his crimes.

It was not observed by the officers from what quarter the summoning bolt of justice came, but thinking it was from the house, every window was instantly attacked, while I deliberately retired from the spot, – and, till the protection of the darkness enabled me to make my escape across the Gary, and over the hills in the direction I saw Mackay and the remnants of the flock taking, I concealed myself among the bushes and rocks that overhung the violent stream of the Girnaig.

Thus was my avenging vow fulfilled, – and thus was my native land delivered from bondage. For a time yet there may be rumours and bloodshed, but they will prove as the wreck which the waves roll to the shore after a tempest. The fortunes of the papistical Stuarts are foundered forever. Never again in this land shall any king, of his own caprice and prerogative, dare to violate the conscience of the people.

Quharist, 5th November 1696 .

It does not seem to be, as yet, very generally understood by the critics in the South, that, independently of phraseology, there is such an idiomatic difference in the structure of the national dialects of England and Scotland, that very good Scotch might be couched in the purest English terms, and without the employment of a single Scottish word.

In reviewing the Memoirs of that worshipful personage, Provost Pawkie, some objection has been made to the style, as being neither Scotch nor English, – not Scotch, because the words are English, – and not English, because the forms of speech are Scottish. What has been thus regarded as a fault by some, others acquainted with the peculiarities of the language may be led to consider as a beauty.

But however proper the Scottish dialect may have been in a composition so local as 'THE PROVOST,' it may be urged, that, in a work like the present, where something of a historical character is attempted, the English language would have been a more dignified vehicle. Why it should be so is not very obvious; at all events, the Author thinks the style he has adopted, in expressing sentiments and feelings entirely Scottish, ought not to be objected to in point of good taste. Should the objection, however, be made, he has an answer in the words of the celebrated Titian:—

It happened one day, says Antonio Perez in his Memoirs, that Francisco de Vargas, ambassador from Charles V to the Republic of Venice, remonstrated with the painter against his broad and coarse pencilling, so unlike the delicate touches of the great artists of that time: – 'Señor,' replied Titian, 'yo desconfiè de llegar à la delicadeza y primor del pinzel de Michael Angelo, Urbino, Corregio, y Parmisano, y que quando bien llegasse, serià estimado tras ellos, ò tenido por imitador dellos; y la ambič,ion natural,

448

no menos à mì Arte que à las otras, me hizo echar por camino nuevo, que me hiziesse çelebre en algo, como los otros lo fueron por el que signieron.'

Another misconception also prevails in the South, with respect to the Scottish political character. From the time of the North Briton of the unprincipled Wilkes, a notion has been entertained that the moral spine in Scotland is more flexible than in England. The truth however is, that an elementary difference exists in the public feelings of the two nations quite as great as in the idioms of their respective dialects. The English are a justice-loving people, according to charter and statute; the Scotch are a wrong-resenting race, according to right and feeling: and the character of liberty among them takes its aspect from that peculiarity.

Colonel Stewart, in his curious and complete work on the Highlands, has shown, that even the clans, among whom the doctrines and affections of hereditary right are still cherished more than ever they were in England at any period, hold themselves free to change their chieftains. It is so with the nation in general. Monarchy is an indestructible principle in our notions of civil government; and though we anciently exercised the right of changing our kings pretty freely, Cromwell found it necessary to overrun the kingdom with an army to obtain the grudged acquiescence which was yielded to the Anglo-Republican phantasy of his time. But in our *natural* attachment to monarchy and its various gradations, and in the homages which we in consequence freely perform, it does not follow that there should be any unmanly humility. On the contrary, servile loyalty is comparatively rare among us, and it was in England that the Stuarts first DARED to broach the doctrine of the divine right of kings.

The two most important public documents extant show the difference between the national character of the Scotch and of the English people in a very striking light. In dictating Magna Charta to the tyrant John, the English barons implied, that if he observed the conditions, they would obey him in all things else. But the Scottish nobles, in their Remonstrance to the Pope, declared, that they considered even their great and glorious Robert Bruce to be on his good behaviour.

The Remonstrance not being generally known, a translation is subjoined, of the time of Ringan Gilhaize – the sacred original is in the Register Office.

To our most holy Father in Christ, and our Lord, John, by the divine providence, Chief Bishop of the most Holy Roman and Universal Church, your humble and devoted sons, Duncan Earl of Fyfe, Thomas Randolph Earl of Murray, Lord Mannia and Annandale, Patrick de Dumbar Earl of March, Malisius Earl of Strathern, Malcolm Earl of Lennox, William Earl of Ross, Magnus Earl of Caithness and Orkney, William Earl of Sutherland, Walter Steward of Scotland, William de Soules Buttelarius of Scotland, James Lord Douglas, Roger de Mowbray, David Lord Brechin, David de Grahame, Ingleramus de Umfraville, John de Monteith Warder of the county of Monteith, Alexander Frazer, Gilbert de Hay Constable of Scotland, Robert de Keith Marishal of Scotland, Henry de Sancto Claro, John de Graham, David de Lyndsay, William Oliphant, Patrick de Graham, John de Fenton, William de Abernethie, David de Weyms, William de Monto fixo, Fergus de Ardrossan, Eustachius de Maxwel, William de Ramsay, William de Monte-alto, Allan de Murray, Donald Campbel, John Camburn, Reginald le Chene, Alexander de Seton, Andrew de Lescelyne, and Alexander Straton, and the rest of the Barons and Freeholders, and whole Community, or Commons of the kingdom of Scotland, send all manner of Filial Reverence, with devout kisses of your blessed and happy feet.

Most holy Father and Lord, we know and gather from ancient Acts and Records, that in every famous nation, this of Scotland hath been celebrat with many praises: this nation having come from Scythia the greater, through the Tuscan Sea, and by Hercules Pillars, and having for many ages taken its residence in Spain in the midst of a most fierce people, could never be brought in subjection by any people, how barbarous soever: And having removed from those parts, above 1200 years after the coming of the Israelites out of Egypt, did by many victories and much toil, obtain the parts in the West, which they still possess, having expelled the Britons, and intirely rooted out the Picts, notwithstanding of the frequent assaults and invasions they met with from the Norwegians, Danes, and English; and these parts and possessions they have always retained free from all manner of servitude, and subjection, as ancient histories do witness.

This kingdom hath been govern'd by an uninterrupted succession of 113 kings, all of our own native and royal stock, without the intervening of any stranger.

The true nobility and merits of these our princes and people are very remarkable, from this one consideration, (tho' there were no other evidence for it,) that the King of kings, the Lord Jesus Christ, after his passion and resurrection, honored them as it were the first (though living in the utmost ends of the earth,) with a call to his most holy Faith: neither would our Saviour have them confirmed in the Christian Faith, by any other instrument than his own first Apostle (tho' in order the second or third,) St Andrew, the most worthy brother of the blessed Peter, whom he would always have to be over us, as our patron or protector.

Upon the weighty consideration of these things, the most holy Fathers your predecessors did, with many great and singular favours and privileges, fence and secure this kingdom and people, as being the peculiar charge and care of the brother of St Peter; so that our nation hath hitherto lived in freedom and quietness under their protection, till the magnificent King Edward, father to the present king of England, did under the colour of friendship, and allyance, or confederacie, with innumerable oppressions, infest us who minded no fraud or deceit, at a time when we were without a king or head, and when the people were unacquainted with wars and invasions. It is impossible for any whose own experience hath not informed him to describe, or fully to understand, the injuries, blood, and violence, the depredations and fire, the imprisonments of prelates, the burning, slaughter, and robberie committed upon holy persons and religious houses, and a vast multitude of other barbarities, which that king execute on this people, without sparing of any sex, or age, religion, or order of men whatsoever.

But at length it pleased God, who only can heal after wounds, to restore us to libertie, from these innumerable calamities, by our most Serene Prince, King and Lord, Robert, who for the delivering of his people and his own rightful inheritance from the enemies hand, did, like another Josua, or Maccabeus, most cheerfully undergo all manner of toyle, fatigue, hardship, and hazard. The Divine Providence, the right of succession by the laws and customs of the kingdom (which we will defend till death,) and the due and lawful consent, and assent of all the people, made him our king and prince. To him we are obliged and resolved to adhere in all things, both upon the account of his right and his own merit, as being the person who hath restored the people's safety, in defence of their liberties. But after all, if this prince shall leave the principles he hath so nobly pursued, and consent that we or our kingdom be subjected to the king or the people of England, we will immediately endeavour to expel him, as our enemy, and as the subverter both of his own and our rights, and will make another king, who will defend our liberties: for, so long as there shall but one hundred of us remain alive, we will never subject ourselves to the dominion of the English. For it is not glory, it is not riches, neither is it honour, but it is libertie alone that we fight and contend for, which no honest man will lose but with his life.

For these reasons, most Reverend Father and Lord, we do with most earnest prayers, from our bended knees and hearts, beg and entreat your Holiness, that you may be pleased with a sincere and cordial piety to consider, that with Him, whose Vicar on earth you are, there is no respect nor distinction of Jew nor Greek, Scots nor English, and that with a tender and fatherly eye you may look upon the calamities and straits brought upon us and the Church of God by the English, and that you may admonish, and exhort the king of England (who may well rest satisfied with his own possessions, since that kingdom of old used to be sufficient for seven or more kings) to suffer us to live at peace in that narrow spot of Scotland, beyond which we have no habitation, since we desire nothing but our own; and we on our parts, as far as we are able, with respect to our own condition, shall effectually agree to him in every thing that may procure our quiet.

It is your concernment, most Holy Father, to interpose in this, when you see how far the violence and barbarity of the Pagans is let loose against Christendom for punishing of the sins of the Christians, and how much they dayly encroach upon the Christian Territories: And it is your interest to notice, that there be no ground given for reflecting on your memory, if you should suffer any part of the church to come under a scandal or eclipse (which we pray God may prevent) during your time.

Let it therefore please your Holiness, to exhort the Christian princes, not to make the wars betwixt them and their neighbours a pretext for not going to the relief of the Holy Land, since that is not the true cause of the impediment: The truer ground of it is, that they have a much nearer prospect of advantage, and far less opposition, in the subduing of their weaker neighbours. And God (who is ignorant of nothing) knows, with how much cheerfulness both our king and we would go thither, if the king of England would leave us in peace, as we do hereby testify and declare to the Vicar of Christ, and to all Christendom.

But, if your Holiness shall be too credulous of the English misrepresentations, and not give firm credit to what we have said, nor desist to favour the English to our destruction, we must believe that the Most High will lay to your charge all the blood, loss of souls, and other calamities that shall follow on either hand, betwixt us and them.

Your Holiness in granting our just desires, will oblige us in everie case, where our dutie shall require it, to endeavour your satisfaction, as becomes the obedient sons of the Vicar of Christ.

We commit the defence of our cause to him who is the Sovereign King and Judge; we cast the burden of our cares upon him, and hope for such an issue as may give strength and courage to us, and bring our enemies to nothing. The Most High God long preserve your Serenity and Holiness to his holy Church.

Given at the Monasterie of Aberbrothock in Scotland, the sixth day of April, in the year of Grace MCCCXX. and of our said king's reign, the XV year.

Notes

p.iii   'Ringan' is Scots for Ninian; Norse, Rinan. Ringan was a common forename in the sixteenth century and later, and the fact that Ninian was the earliest known Christian missionary in Scotland may have led Galt to use it. 'Gilhaize' may be a version of Gilhazie (pronounced Gilhayes or Gillies), or Gilhagie.

p.3   The Covenant here may denote both the National Covenant of 1638 and the Solemn League and Covenant of 1643, which were often run together and referred to simply as 'The Covenant'.

p.3   The great elder worthies, or Lords of the Congregation, were those Protestant members of the Scottish nobility whom John Knox, when he was for a short time in Scotland in 1555–56, had organised into a political and religious group.

p.5   George Wishart (c. 1513–1546), a native of Angus, left Scotland in 1538 after being charged with heresy. He probably spent some time in Germany and Switzerland before returning to England and then Scotland in 1543. His preaching attracted attention at Montrose, Dundee, Ayr and elsewhere. John Knox became his disciple. Arrested as a heretic and handed over to Beaton, he was burned at St Andrews on 1 March 1546. It is not known whether he was involved in any of the plots to assassinate Beaton.

p.5   David Beaton (c. 1494–1546), Cardinal Archbishop of St Andrews, was murdered at his castle there on 29 May 1546 partly in retaliation for the burning of Wishart.

p.7   Luckenbooths were booths or shops that could be

locked. A famous row of them stood in the High Street to the north of St Giles church. They were demolished in 1817. The States, or Estates, are the Lords Spiritual, the Lords Temporal and the burgesses, the three Estates, which made up the Scottish Parliament.

p.7   The Dolphin or Dauphin, the heir to the French throne, was Francis, son of Henri II of France. 'Our young Queen' is Mary, Queen of Scots. On 14 December 1557 the Scottish Estates acceded to the request of Henri II that commissioners should be sent to France to conclude the marriage agreement between Mary and the Dauphin. Mary had been in France since 1548 when the marriage agreement was made.

p.8   The Dowager Mary of Guise, also styled Mary of Lorraine, was the mother of Mary, Queen of Scots. She ruled Scotland as regent from 1554 until her death in 1560.

p.9   The reference is to Archibald Campbell, 4th Earl of Argyle. The church was concerned at the spread of reformed preaching and Archbishop Hamilton expostulated officially with Argyle for entertaining a preacher influenced by Lutheran teaching. The Archbishop of St Andrews was John Hamilton, promoted from Dunkeld on Beaton's murder. Hamilton was the illegitimate half brother of the Duke of Chatelherault. John Douglas was at this time principal of St Mary's College, St Andrews, and a Carmelite Friar, but had come under Lutheran influence. Knox (I, 138) says Argyle 'caused him preach publicly in his house, and reformed many things according to his counsel'.

p.21   Wishart's words, as reported by the seneschal, are taken from Howie's *Scots Worthies*, and Galt's description of Wishart corresponds with Howie's.

p.30   The account of the trial of Walter Mill is based on Howie's chapter on him.

p.30   These details taken from Howie, who concludes

his chapter on Mill: 'The death of this martyr brought about the downfall of Popery in Scotland; for the people in general were so much inflamed that, resolving openly to profess the truth, they bound themselves by promises and subscriptions of oaths, that before they would be thus abused any longer, they would take arms and resist the Papal tyranny; which they at last did.' Galt gives the burning of Mill the same significance. From now on the religious sympathies of the many characters Gilhaize meets are indicated by their reaction to news of the burning.

p.46   In passages like this, full of circumstantial details about the closes, bows (gates) and buildings of the old city of Edinburgh, we see why Galt insisted in letters from London, written on 13 and 31 January 1823 during the composition of *Ringan*, that his publisher, George Boyd in Edinburgh, should send him Maitland's *History of Edinburgh*, which reproduces a map of the old town that lay on either side of the High Street between Holyrood House and the Castle.

p.49   Joseph resisted the advances of Potiphar's wife. See Genesis XXXIX.

p.79   The Earl of Eglinton was 'the head of the Montgomeries'.

p.81   Lord James Stuart, 1531–1570, was the eldest of James V's bastard sons, and therefore half-brother to Mary, Queen of Scots. Mary conferred on him the title of Earl of Murray or Moray.

p.84   The Protestant preachers were cited to appear at Stirling on 10 May 1559. See Knox, *History*, I, 159.

p.86   For his part in the murder of Cardinal Beaton in 1546, Knox was sentenced to a spell in the French galleys. On his return he became a Protestant preacher at Berwick, and later London. During the reign of the Catholic Mary Tudor he went to Geneva, but spent a short time in Scotland 1555–1556. In January 1559 he left Geneva for the last time. Donaldson says: 'Knox, in common with the rest of the Marian exiles, had regarded Elizabeth's accession as a signal for his return, but the queen declined to have in her realm the author of *The first blast of the trumpet against the monstrous regiment of women* . . . Had he been acceptable in England he might have picked up the threads of his earlier life there and never seen Scotland again.' (*Scotland: James V to James VII*, p. 92.) Knox was only about fifty at this time.

p.104   Archibald Campbell, 5th Earl of Argyle, son of the Argyle of earlier chapters who died in 1558.

p.104   John Willock, because of his religious views, had fled to the Continent from England on the accession of Mary Tudor. He returned to Scotland in 1558. For a time he was minister at Edinburgh when it was too dangerous for Knox to stay, and was later superintendent of the west.

p.127   James Hamilton, 2nd Earl of Arran, as heir presumptive to the Scottish throne, was Governor in Queen Mary's minority until 1554. He was granted the French duchy of Chatelherault in 1549 for having among other things helped to secure the consent of the Scottish parliament to the marriage of Mary and the dauphin, and the conveyance of the child queen to France. A figurehead of the revolution of 1555–60 he rebelled against Mary on her marriage to Darnley (1566), and was in exile till 1569; he was then a leader of the Queen's party until 1573.

p.129   Ian B. Cowan thinks the moderation of the Scottish Reformation one of its most striking features. In spite of frequent assertions made from 1560 to the present day, the destruction of the Religious Houses was not in most cases due to the Reformers, although they cannot be absolved completely, but rather due to English military operations, sheer neglect in the pre-Reformation period and the indifference of later times. See Cowan, *Blast and Counterblast* (Edinburgh, 1960.)

p.136   In his MS Galt shows no hesitation about the name of the mailing given to Gilhaize, Quharist ('whaur is't?'). Readers who know the 'vicinage' of Eglinton may enjoy trying to plot the location which Galt had in mind. The clues are many but I have reluctantly concluded that Galt enjoyed setting us a puzzle that may not admit of one solution.

p.141   For Knox's words compare McCrie pp. 173–74 and Howie's chapter on Knox. Galt's material may be largely borrowed but it nevertheless provides one of the debates on the use and abuse of authority, and the right of the individual to resist absolutism – the theme which runs all through the novel.

p.147   Loch Leven Castle stands on a small island in Loch Leven just outside Kinross. It was held at this time by Sir Robert Douglas, stepfather to the Earl of Murray, but is best known as the place of Mary's imprisonment, 1567–68, after her defeat at Carberry Hill.

p.148   Alexander Gordon was consecrated Archbishop of Glasgow in 1551 but, failing to gain possession, was appointed titular Bishop of Athens in compensation. He was nominated Bishop of Galloway in 1559 and served the reformed church as bishop.

p.152   Mary herself remained a Catholic, and recognition of the new kirk was yet far from complete. The Reformation Parliament of 1560 had acted illegally in abolishing the Latin mass and papal supremacy and in authorising a reformed Confession of Faith, and Queen Mary had refused to ratify its acts. All she would commit herself to was an announcement that the state of religion would remain as it was when she landed in Scotland – which was highly ambiguous. The Reformers hoped for a Protestant marriage and a Protestant heir, partly as being more likely to secure succession in the future to the English throne. Rizzio had come into Mary's service from that of the Savoy ambassador (see Buchanan, Bk. XVII) and became her French secretary in 1564.

p.154   Henry Darnley, son of the Earl of Lennox, was through his grandmother, Margaret Tudor, a claimant, like Mary herself, to the throne of England. He had little to recommend him but 'physical charm and athletic prowess' (Mitchison), but Mary was attracted. Buchanan (Bk XVII) makes much of the role of Rizzio in promoting the union: 'turning every stone, Rizzio at last succeeded in hastening the celebration of the marriage though the Scots were not much for it, and the English were much against it'. It took place on 29 July 1565. Elizabeth of England was displeased that her agreement had not been sought when both parties to the marriage were related to her, and were also claimants to her throne.

p.154   The good Earl of Murray's raid, also known as the Chaseabout Raid, describes an ineffective revolt, of a few months' duration, against Mary and Darnley by a number of Protestant nobles. Murray's part in the rising lost him Mary's trust. (The earl is invariably referred to nowadays as Moray rather than Murray, though both forms appear in the sixteenth century.)

p.154   Mary had married Darnley at the end of July 1565, without waiting for the papal dispensation that their cousinship made necessary. Darnley quickly lost favour with Mary, and allied himself with some of the nobles also out of favour for their part in the Earl of Murray's raid (see above). Their resentment of Rizzio's gaining the Queen's confidence led them to murder him almost in her presence in March 1566, when Mary was six months pregnant.

p.154   Prince James, who became James VI of Scotland and I of England, was born in June 1566.

p.157   Some historians claim that an apparent reconciliation with Darnley was politic since Mary may have been pregnant again in the summer of 1567, but whether Mary committed adultery with the Earl of Bothwell before Darnley's murder remains controversial.

p.158   This looks like historical licence. Galt may have given Mary a French guard to facilitate the introduction of his next point, but it is highly unlikely that she had one.

p.160   James Hepburn, fourth Earl of Bothwell (c. 1535–78) was attached to the Reformation but hostile to England and loyal to Mary of Guise. He began to find favour with Mary Queen of Scots after Murray had raised his rebellion.

p.160   On Darnley's murder, see Buchanan Bk XVIII, and McCrie pp. 226–27. Darnley, largely by his own folly, had made many enemies among the Scottish nobles, and many were suspected of complicity in the plot against him. Mary wished him out of the way, but did not wish a divorce lest her son's legitimacy be impunged. The Earl of Murray was conveniently absent, and Darnley was killed when the house at Kirk o' Field was blown up on 10 February 1567. He was evidently suffocated or strangled; it has been suggested that he was responsible for storing the gunpowder under the house with intent to blow up Mary and that when he awoke to sounds of movement or smell of burning he fled hastily in his nightshirt only to encounter his own enemies outside. Mary may not have known the plan of the murder but her very indiscreet behaviour after the event brought suspicion upon her.

p.163   Cf. McCrie p. 227. On 15 May 1567 Bothwell became the third husband of Mary Queen of Scots after highly precipitate divorce proceedings. His wife was Jane Gordon, sister of the Earl of Huntly.

p.164   After the National Covenant of 1638 and the Solemn League and Covenant of 1643 many writers anachronistically came to apply these titles to sixteenth-century documents (as here) in order to imply continuity and respectable antiquity. These misleading annexations of the titles are responsible for much confusion.

p.166 Sir William Kirkcaldy of Grange (c. 1520–1573) was one of the early leaders of the Reformation who later fought in France where he gained the reputation of a gallant soldier. He fought for the reforming party in Scotland from 1559, opposed Mary's marriage to Darnley, and in 1567 joined the lords who rose against Mary and Bothwell. To him Mary surrendered at Carberry. He fought at Langside with Murray, but did not approve of Mary's being imprisoned and compelled to abdicate. Murray had made him captain of Edinburgh Castle, and in 1571 he declared for the exiled Mary. He held the castle until 1573. After its fall he was hanged. From the field of Carberry Bothwell fled, narrowly excaping capture by Kirkcaldy of Grange, and made his way to Norway where he was imprisoned by the kinsmen of a Danish lady whom he had earlier seduced. He died a prisoner in the Castle of Dragsholm, in the north of Zealand, and a body reputed to be his is to be seen in the nearby church of Faarevejle.

p.166 See Buchanan, Bk XVIII. Those whom Darnley had antagonised now turned on Bothwell and sought popular support by exploiting the upsurge of moral indignation against him and the Queen. Mitchison (p. 132) calls their banner 'a piece of outrageous double-faced propaganda'. The truth was that since there was now an heir, the Queen was expendable.

p.166 Mary's forces were defeated at the battle of Langside on 13 May 1568. Murray was made regent, after Mary was imprisoned at Lochleven Castle. His elevation was resented by some of the nobility, and particularly by the Hamiltons.

p.168 The Regent Murray was shot in Linlithgow in January 1571, by James Hamilton, a nephew of the Archbishop of St Andrews, who had lain in wait for his passing, concealed in a house belonging to the Archbishop.

p.182 Charles IX of France on St Bartholomew's Eve, 24

August 1572, began the massacre of his Protestant subjects on the occasion of the marriage of Henry, King of Navarre, to Charles's sister.

p.184 For the reference to Elijah, see 2nd Kings I-III. Matthew II tells of Herod's slaughter of the Innocents.

p.189 Judith by cutting off the head of Holofernes, after she had made him drunk, saved the city of Jerusalem to which he had laid siege. (See the Book of Judith in the Apocrypha.) Holofernes here, of course, denotes Philip of Spain.

p.189 After the defeat of the Spanish Armada the Spaniards made for home by sailing round Scotland, but a gale left some of their vessels wrecked round the Scottish coast. A ruined castle stands on Portincross ('Pencorse'), a headland on the Ayrshire coast, just south of Fairlie.

p.190 Galt is here being deliberately vague and using emotive language. James VI of Scotland and I of England had been fairly successful in controlling the Presbyterian wing of the Church of Scotland. The Church was administered by the General Assembly, but the King called its meetings. By shifting the time and place of these, James emphasised that the Assembly met when he chose. In 1617 however he provoked ill-feeling when he introduced some new religious observances – the most unpopular of which was kneeling to receive the sacrament. Opposition to the innovations showed him that he could not hope to change the liturgy, and he did not try. The 'molestation' that Jenny Geddes is said to have suffered 'in her worldly substance' may explain the virulence of her animosity, but seems to be of Galt's devising. Although the riot took place in 1637, Janet or Jenny Geddes does not appear in any of the accounts of it before 1670. In 1637 Charles I insisted that a new liturgy was to be read in all Edinburgh churches. When it was read in St Giles, riots broke out. The incident Galt uses of Jenny Geddes hurling the stool and crying out is traditionally the best known.

p.191   The English Civil War had begun in 1642, and in January 1649 Oliver Cromwell had the King executed. Galt moves swiftly here over twelve years of troubles in church and state from the first reading of the liturgy in St Giles in 1637 to the death of Charles I in 1649. The Covenant, however, to which Ringan in 'his green years' was a party, was the National Covenant of 1638, signed first in Greyfriars Church in Edinburgh at the end of February, and then in churches throughout the country. Gordon Donaldson describes it as a manifesto to consolidate opposition to Charles I's innovations in worship, the 'corruptions of the public government of the Kirk' and the 'civil places and power of Kirkmen'. Rosalind Mitchison (p. 196) says: 'At times its language became, like the Declaration of Arbroath, a trumpet call to unity and action. Through it all ran the Old Testament analogy, the concept of a nation binding itself in a special relationship to God'. The Solemn League and Covenant was the alliance by which the Scots in 1643 agreed to assist the English Parliamentarians against Charles I on condition that England would in effect adopt (and encourage Ireland to adopt) a Presbyterian Church system. As its title indicated, it was a civil 'league' or treaty as well as a religious convenant. Galt has obviously found it convenient to regard the two convenants as one.

p.193   These Blackcuffs and dragoons were soldiers of the Scots army employed to suppress religious dissent in the Restoration period (1660–88). John Graham of Claverhouse (1648–1689) served as a volunteer in the French and Dutch armies. After his return to Scotland in 1677 he was appointed Captain of one of the three troops of horse commissioned to act against the conventicles which were by then meeting in the south-west. He also acted against

the Covenanters in that area between 1682 and
1685. Hated by them, he was known always among
them as 'Bloody Clavers'.

p.194 It was in fact James VI and not Charles who had
put 'the prelates upon us'. James VI had revived the
powers of the bishops and successfully combined
elements of episcopacy and presbyterianism in
church government in Scotland. It was Charles
I's determination to exalt the former elements at
the expense of the latter that in the end convinced many that the two were incompatible. See
Stevenson, *The Scottish Revolution*, p. 23.

p.195 Arminianism was the doctrine of the Dutch Protestant theologian Arminius (d.1609), who opposed
the views of Calvin, especially on predestination.
'Arminian' tended to become a loosely used term
of abuse for all religious trends which were disliked,
but the fear of Arminian tendencies was none-
theless real and influential. See Stevenson, *The
Scottish Revolution*, p. 44. Laud was Archbishop
of Canterbury and was consulted by Charles I
about religious policy in Scotland as well as in
England. This speech of Nahum Chapelrig is the
only sample Galt gives of the kind of Presbyterian
rhetoric which its critics found objectionable.

p.195 The wording of his argument shows the spreading
social awareness that political liberty is indissolubly
linked to the religious liberty specifically referred
to. Ebenezer Muir's speech here is the first apologia
for the best of the Covenanters, seen always as heirs
both of those who struggled for religious liberty
under the Lords of the Congregation, and those
who earlier fought for national independence under
Wallace. These views are repeatedly expressed
throughout the rest of the novel (see for example
pp. 144–45).

p.196 Psalm CXL asks for God's protection from violent men.

p.201 The burden of Psalm LXXVI is that God will judge
and save the meek.

p.208   Although almost every place in the novel is actual (see the maps on the end-papers), the parishes of Garnock and Stoneyholm are fictitious.

p.211   Psalm XLIV recalls favours done by God in days of old and complains of present evils, against which only faith can help. In the Scottish metrical version, the fifth verse reads:

> Through thee we shall push down our foes,
> that do against us stand:
> We, through thy name, shall tread down those
> that ris'n against us have.

p.215   The bloodless raid of Dunse Law of 1639 is also known as the First Bishops' War. Because the king's troops were disaffected and badly organised, the royal castles of Edinburgh, Dalkeith and Dumbarton fell to the army of the Covenant. At Berwick the king decided to negotiate, promising a Parliament and an Assembly. The Scots claimed victory but it was against a collection of English troops that did not wish to fight. 'Raid' means simply an expedition, and does not imply that any fighting took place.

p.216   In the Second Bishops' War of 1640 the Covenanters' army led by General Alexander Leslie, later Earl of Leven, occupied Newcastle. Peace was made at Ripon mainly because the Covenanters forced Charles to summon the Long Parliament which attacked and then destroyed his principal servant Strafford. Control in Scotland was in the hands of a Parliament which had been prorogued and had illegally reassembled as a Standing Committee of Estates. It made the Covenant compulsory. The Covenanting party in Scotland at this time was supported by the young Earl of Argyle, one of her biggest landowners.

p.217   The Civil War had broken out in 1642. The Solemn League and Covenant had been signed in 1643, and in 1644 the Scottish Covenanters, allied with the English Parliamentarians, won the decisive battle of Marston Moor against the King's forces.

p.217   The Whig(g)amore expedition or raid of 1648 was a move by the more extreme 'Kirk Party' faction of the Covenanters, and overthrew a moderate-covenanter / moderate-royalist regime in Edinburgh. Argyle was the most prominent of the Kirk Party nobles. The raid itself marks an advanced stage in the growing distrust of the nobles as leaders. The word Whigamore or Whig was later extended to mean any Covenanter.

p.218   The extreme Kirk Party proclaimed Charles II king of England, Ireland and France as well as of Scotland. Proclaimed King in Edinburgh after his father's execution Charles was not invested with authority or allowed to set foot in Scotland until he had accepted the Solemn League and Covenant, and promised to implement it. For the humiliations he underwent at this time, the king detested the Covenanting religion. Charles II was crowned at Scone on 1 January 1651. Defeated at the Battle of Worcester later in the same year he escaped abroad.

p.221   James Graham, 5th Earl and 1st Marquis of Montrose, a skilful soldier, had tried to raise support for Charles in the north but was defeated. The king had to accept the Covenant and disown his dealings with Montrose, who was to be executed before Charles II reached Scotland from Holland.

p.221   The Remonstrance was a paper put forward to the Committee of the Estates by the Covenanters of the West of Scotland 'which showed openly that their concept of monarchy was a conditional one: the king was to be owned only 'so farre as he owns and prosecuttes the cause'. Doubting, probably with reason, the sincerity of Charles II's adherence to the Covenant, they demanded his removal from power'. (Mitchison, p. 231.) Covenanters of the west so distrusted him that they formed their own army of the Western Association that refused to obey his regime's orders.

p.221   Cromwell established military control of Scotland with citadels at Ayr and four other strategic towns.

p.224   On the face of it Argyle was tried and condemned for co-operation with Cromwell's regime, but he was in fact put to death for the hostility he had shown to Charles II and his father. The 'colour' of Ringan's own 'political animosities' should be remembered when they lead him so completely to whitewash the house of Argyle.

p.224   May 1660 saw the restoration of Charles II. James Sharp (1613–79) had been sent as a delegate from a meeting in Edinburgh to the restored Charles in London to ensure that Presbyterianism would become the established religion. The King instead restored Episcopalianism in Scotland as well as in England and appointed Sharp as Archbishop of St Andrews.

p.225   Although there is no record of it in the Town Council minutes, the Covenant is said to have been publicly burned at Linlithgow.

p.230   In Psalm XCIV. 23 the Psalmist, calling for justice, complains of tyranny and impiety, finishing with the hope that those guilty of iniquity will be cut off in their own sin, and slain by God. Swinton's text from The Lamentations of Jeremiah reads 'Remember, O Lord, what is come upon us'. Swinton goes onto quote from Psalm CXXXVII. 5.

p.230   Psalm CXL asks deliverance from the evil man, and preservation from the violent.

p.237   Sir James Turner (1615–?1686), a professional soldier, was knighted at the Restoration. In 1666 he was made commander of the forces operating against the Covenanters in the south-west. Gilbert Burnet described him as 'naturally fierce' and 'mad when drunk, and that was very often', but added that he was 'a learned man'. Wodrow says he was 'very bookish'. Nevertheless Turner's severities were blamed for the outbreak of rebellion and he fell from favour when the government adopted milder measures.

p.247 Nehemiah X records the sealing of Israel's Covenant with God, but because it is largely a list of Hebrew names it makes 'unedifying' reading. In *The Entail* the Bible is open at this chapter when Girzie makes a show of reading it. On the same page of that novel Girzie refers to a cousin Ringan Gilhaise, the Mauchlin malster. *Ringan* was much in Galt's mind as he wrote its predecessor *The Entail*.

p.252 I am grateful to Dr David Stevenson for pointing out that 'Ringan's spells of passivity followed by bursts of action characterise also the conventiclers' reaction to persecutions throughout the 1660–88 period – reluctant obedience or passive resistance alternates with episodes of active resistance and denunciations of the regime growing ever more extreme. Thus Ringan's personal development closely parallels the general trend.' For comment on the way Galt shows Ringan's obsession gradually impairing his judgement and alienating him from the real world see Patricia J. Wilson, '*Ringan Gilhaize* – a Neglected Masterpiece?', in *John Galt* 1779–1979, edited by Christopher A. Whatley (Edinburgh, 1979), pp. 120–50.

p.255 Captain Learmont was Major Joseph Learmonth. Colonel James Wallace of Auchans died in exile in 1678. Many of the military leaders on both sides in the 1660s had by coincidence served together in the Scottish Army in Ulster in the early 1640s.

p.257 General Dalziel: Sir Thomas Dalyell of the Binns, (c. 1599–1685), was a professional soldier who had seen service even with the Czar. Charles II recalled him and gave him command of the forces in Scotland (1666). He was a staunch royalist who made and kept a vow never to cut his beard after the execution of Charles I.

p.266   Arthur's Seat, an extinct volcano, rises 822 feet from Holyrood Park, in Edinburgh. The Covenanters were defeated at Rullion Green on the eastern slopes of the Pentland Hills in November 1666, at what became known as the Pentland Rising.

p.271   Cromwell had defeated Charles and a Scottish army at Worcester in September 1651, after which Charles escaped abroad. For the quotation, compare Job XIV. 1.

p.317   Tales such as this of the laird of Ringlewood are common in Covenanting lore, but Galt uses it to show how distrust and fear were breaking the ties that traditionally had bound the community together.

p.328   The island of Great Cumbrae, on which stands the town of Millport, lies directly opposite Largs and Fairlie, in the Firth of Clyde. The Wee Cumbrae lies a little further south.

p.330   Sir John Murray is an error for Sir Robert Moray, a well-known soldier, politician and scientist who had played a leading part in founding the Royal Society a few years before. He was one of the moderate royalists who wished to try to settle religious dissent in Scotland by conciliation. The extreme royalists had argued that persecution was necessary to prevent rebellion, but instead it had provoked it in 1666 and they were therefore discredited.

p.332   John Maitland, 2nd Earl and 1st Duke of Lauderdale, had originally been one of those arguing for moderation, but was driven back to advocating persecution when concessions failed to restore religious unity.

p.332   The idea that the regime tried to provoke rebellion to have an excuse for decisive action is almost certainly untrue, but many believed it.

p.333   Mitchison (p. 263) writes that the government 'put into action the strongest legal weapons it had, making landowners responsible for the behaviour of their tenants, fining those known to attend conventicles, and using the fines to reward their local enemies.'

p.339   Sharp was killed outside St Andrews on Saturday 3 May 1679 by a group of armed horsemen who had been lying in wait for another enemy, when Providence, as it seemed to them, delivered Sharp into their hands. The identity of those who did the deed and their subsequent fate are dealt with in great detail in much Covenanting literature, and Scott portrays the ringleader, John Balfour of Kinloch or Burley, in *Old Mortality*. The killing divided the country into those who condoned the deed out of hatred of the oppressive regime Sharp represented, and those who abhorred it as criminal and unlawful. The Archbishop's murder became a matter of reproach to all Presbyterians and was for years used as a handle against them when they were subjected to questioning.

p.340   Galt quotes here the best known lines from the Declaration of Arbroath of 1320, and he reproduces the whole text as a Postscript to the novel.

p.342   Galt probably had Walter Scott in mind among the 'discreet historians'. To the Covenanters James Graham of Claverhouse was always 'Bloody Clavers'.

p.344   On 29 May at Rutherglen ('Ruglen') a declaration was read out against the Acts of which the extremists disapproved. Copies of the Acts were publicly burned, and the bonfires lit to celebrate the anniversary of the King's restoration extinguished.

p.346   Wodrow says that Claverhouse, captain of a new levied troop, was granted large powers and marched on Saturday 31 May against those who had published the Declaration at Rutherglen. Wodrow says Claverhouse could never forgive the baffle he met with at Drumclog, and Galt adds the incident of Claverhouse being unhorsed and almost seized by Ringan.

p.347   The Duke of Monmouth, illegitimate son of Charles II, was in command of the King's forces in Scotland which overwhelmingly defeated the ill-equipped and untrained Covenanters at the battle of Bothwell Brig. The detention of prisoners in Greyfriars Kirkyard, and the foundering of the ship bound for the plantations are facts.

p.370 The Sanquhar Declaration of 1680 was an extremist document, the work of Richard Cameron from whom the Cameronians got their name. 'The Covenanting movement was [now] openly political in aim, and clearly a minority affair' strongest in Galloway and Dumfriesshire. (Mitchison, p. 265.)

p.380 James, Duke of York, became Commissioner in Scotland when Lauderdale fell from power after Bothwell Brig. In July 1680 there was a small but bloodthirsty encounter between Government cavalry and Cameronian extremists at Airsmoss (or Ayrs-moss) in the parish of Auchinleck in Kyle. At it Richard Cameron was killed.

p.382 Donald Cargill had become leader of the Cameronians after the death of Richard Cameron at Airsmoss.

p.386 Cargill quotes from Luke, VII. 9, then from Matthew, V. 12. Ringan quotes from 2nd Samuel, XVIII. 33.

p.394 Psalm CIX has 31 verses, the sixth of which reads in the metrical version:

> Set thou the wicked over him;
> and upon his right hand
> Give thou his greatest enemy,
> ev'n Satan, leave to stand.

This is the same Psalm in which, in Hogg's *Private Memoirs and Confessions of a Justified Sinner*, the Rev. Robert Wringhim seeks 'scripture warrant' before he prays for vials of wrath to be poured on the head of the unnamed Laird of Dalcastle.

p.398 The King's brother, James Duke of York, was next in line of succession to Charles II. Feeling in Scotland did not favour the accession of a known Roman Catholic.

p.399 The Earl of Argyle was in exile in Holland after

opposing official religious policy, and having been condemned to death.

p.399 William of Orange, Stadtholder of the Netherlands, was nephew and son-in-law to James, Duke of York. William's wife Mary was (as James's daughter) heir presumptive after James.

p.403 Galt seems to bring forward the return of James Renwick from Holland. He did not return till 1683, but here he reappears just after the capture and execution of Donald Cargill, which was in 1681.

p.403 Galt seems to ascribe to Ringan the Apologetical Declaration of 1684, usually said to have been composed by Richard Cameron's successor, James Renwick. The Apologetical Declaration was an extremist document which threatened death to all engaged in proceedings against the Cameronians. Refusal to disown it was made punishable by death.

p.413 Charles II was not poisoned. Galt's wording is skilful. We feel that Ringan wants to believe the current rumour, and therefore states it as fact, but immediately undercuts it.

p.420 The Duke of Monmouth, illegitimate son of Charles II, was proposed as king in preference to James VII & II only by the most bigoted opponents of the accession of a Roman Catholic sovereign, but he landed in England in 1685. By an arrangement made between them in Holland, Argyle was to make a landing in Scotland while Monmouth invaded England.

p.422 Wodrow, IV, 297. Argyle found little support, for King James had been generally accepted in a flush of loyalty to hereditary monarchy, and the Covenanting dissidents, although they did not acknowledge James, would not support Argyle, who was not himself a Covenanter. Argyle was executed in 1685 in terms of the sentence passed on him in 1681. He had suffered a previous death sentence after his father's execution at the time of Charles II's restoration.

p.424   There was a night of rioting in Edinburgh, follow-
         ing the mobbing of the wife of the Earl of Perth
         after mass by the Edinburgh apprentices.

p.425   The Indulgence of February 1687 offered toleration
         to Roman Catholics and Quakers. In June this was
         extended to Presbyterians.

p.430   The birth of a son promised a Catholic succession
         and those who found this unacceptable turned now
         to William of Orange, nephew and son-in-law of
         James II.

p.433   James had called his Scottish troops south but as
         he had then fled to France, they were not involved
         in any fighting.

p.435   The conventiclers who remained active were be-
         coming known as 'the society people', their meet-
         ings as 'prayer societies' When it was known that
         the Prince of Orange had landed and that the regu-
         lar troops had marched to join the English army,
         the disaffected Presbyterians flocked to Edinburgh.

p.436   Sir George Mackenzie of Rosehaugh (1636–91),
         founder of the Advocates' Library in Edinburgh
         and author of *Jus Regium: or the Just and Solid Foun-
         dations of Monarchy in General, and More Especially
         of the Monarchy of Scotland* (more familiarly known
         as *A Vindication of the Reigns of King Charles and
         King James*), was hated by those of Convenanting
         sympathies. He was Lord Advocate and chief
         prosecutor in the trials known in Covenanting
         lore as the 'killing time'. This was the period that
         saw the response of the government to the Apolo-
         getical Declaration of 1684 (usually attributed to
         James Renwick but by Galt to Ringan). Mitchison
         (p. 268) writes: 'After the *Apologetical Declaration*
         the Covenanters began to fulfil their promise of
         systematic murder, and in reply the government
         insisted that anyone not abjuring the more blood-
         thirsty sections of the Declaration when asked,
         should be shot out of hand. Suspects, even if they
         passed this test, should be sent up to Edinburgh
         for trial.'

p.438   James II's flight to France had left the Royalists in confusion. Edinburgh was full of Covenanters from the south-west, and the Convention of Estates there was so strongly Whig and Presbyterian that Claverhouse (Viscount Dundee) rode north of the Tay with his troops to where he could count on finding others with Jacobite sympathies. (See the text of Scott's song 'Bonnie Dundee'.)

p.442   2nd Kings VI. 2-17.

p.443   The bayonet was a new weapon and was still the 'plug' bayonet which had to be inserted into the muzzle of the musket. This meant that bayonets could not be fixed until after the musket had been used as a firearm.

p.447   Psalm CXXXII. 1.

p.447   Compare 1st Chronicles XXIX. 2.

p.447   Claverhouse met his death at Killiecrankie in the moment of victory, and with him, for the time being, resistance died in Scotland; a fact that was recognised by King William, who, when he was asked to send additional forces to Scotland, replied: 'Armies are needless: the war is over with Dundee's life'. Galt does not make use of the common myth that the devil had granted Claverhouse immunity to attack from any but a silver bullet. To have used the familiar legends or superstitions would have detracted from the seriousness with which Galt has depicted his Covenanting hero.

p.448   Galt saw Scots as an extra weapon in his artistic armoury, pointing out in his story 'The Seamstress' that Scottish writers possess 'the whole range of the English language, as well as their own, by which they enjoy an uncommonly rich vocabulary'.

p.449   John Wilkes (1727–97), an English politician and journalist, founded *The North Briton*, a weekly periodical, in 1762, in opposition to *The Briton* which Smollet was conducting in the interest of Lord Bute. Wilkes's paper purported ironically to be edited by a Scotsman who rejoices in Lord Bute's success and the ousting of the English from power. In 1764 a libel in the paper led to Wilkes being expelled from Parliament and outlawed, but four years later he was re-elected and his outlawry reversed. The usual view of Wilkes is that, although a man of dissolute character, he nevertheless did much to make people aware of the need for Parliamentary reform, and helped establish the right of the press to discuss public affairs.

p.449   Galt here draws on a very old Scots national myth, whereby Scotland is depicted as a never conquered nation of free men; the English were conquered by Romans, Anglo-Saxons and Normans, and their acceptance of such conquests demonstrates their natural servility; the Scots had fought off all these conquerors – and of course the long attempts at English conquest. The myth's attraction as a source of Scots pride never recovered from the Cromwellian conquest of the 1650s which demonstrated clearly that Scotland could be conquered.

p.449   Colonel Stewart is Major General David Stewart of Garth, author of *Sketches of the Character, Manners and Present State of the Highlands of Scotland; with Details of the Military Service of the Highland Regiments*, 2 vols, (Edinburgh, 1822).

p.449   Otherwise known as the Declaration of Arbroath of 1320, the Remonstrance is reproduced in facsimile in Sir James Fergusson's *The Declaration of Arbroath*, (Edinburgh, 1970). The 'sacred original' was not in fact restored to the Register House until August 1829 (Fergusson, p. 43). The translation Galt uses seems to be that of Sir George Mackenzie of Rosehaugh. It probably pleased Galt to use the translation of the Covenanters' 'Bluidy Mackenzie' as a further indication that the sentiments of Ringan are not his, 'nor at all the colour of the piety with which the enthusiasm of the hero is tinged' (*Literary Life*, I, 251).

Glossary

Note that the curtailed past participle was a common feature of Scots verbs ending in 't' or 'd'; e.g. connect: connected; consecrat: consecrated.

aboon: above, beyond
ae hue: one shade, one little bit
afterings: results, consequences
ahint: behind
airt: direction
almous: alms
aneath: beneath, below, under
anent: concerning, about
arles: an earnest or foretaste of something more to come
assoilzied: found not guilty, acquitted
aught: possession ownership, charge; anything
aumrie: cupboard, pantry
ayont: beyond

bail(l)ie: magistrate
bakiefu': bucketful
ban: curse
bannock: flat cake
bating: feeding
bawbee: halfpenny, 1/2d
beck: bow, curtsey
bedstock: strong beam of wood that runs along the front of a bed

beek: bask
beglamour: bewitch
ben: in or to the best room (in cottages in Scotland there were only two rooms: the 'but', the outer or kitchen, the 'ben', the inner, or parlour)
benweed: ragwort (believed to have been used by the fairies and witches to ride on, hence *benweed ponies*)
besom: broom
bickering: fighting, quarrelling
bide: dwell, wait, stay
bide awee: wait a little
bield (beild): protection, shelter
bien (bein): well-to-do; cosy, comfortable; hence 'bienly' (adv.) and 'bienest' (superlative adj.)
big: build
bigging: a building
bilf: a blow, thump
bir(r): force, energy, enthusiasm
black-avised: of a black complexion, swarthy

478

blate: modest, diffident

blethering: foolish talk

blithemeat: something given to those in attendance at a birth

blithened: gladdened

bout-gait: a roundabout way

bowne: bound

boynes: tubs

braird: first shoots or sproutings of grain, turnips etc. Also used fig.

branders: gridirons

brattled: rattled

brechans: bracken

buirdly: stalwart, well built, powerful; hence 'buirdliest' (superlative)

bunker: a chest; 'window seat', bench, pew

buskings: decorations, ornaments

buskit: adorned

but: out; into the kitchen (see 'ben')

by-common: out of the ordinary

ca'ing: driving

calks: debts (literally *chalkstrokes* showing the number of drinks consumed)

callan: lad, boy, hobbledehoy

camstrarie: unmanageable, perverse

cannily: gently, carefully, skilfully

cantrips: tricks

canty: lively, cheerful

cap: cup

carl: man, fellow

carlin: old woman

carnavaulings: revellings

(found only in Galt)

carry: cloud drift

carse: low and fertile land, gen. adjacent to a river

castendown: downcast

causey: street laid with cobblestones

causey, crown of the: centre of the road

chapped: knocked, struck

chappin: liquid measure = half a Scottish pint

chiel: man, fellow

chimla, chumla: grate, hearth, fireplace

chimla-lug: fireside

chimla-nook: chimney corner

churme: murmur

clachan: hamlet, village, gen. containing a church

clampering: making a heavy or clattering noise when walking

claught: caught

clishmaclaver: to gossip

clishmaclavers: idle talk

cloks: beetles

closs: a narrow passage or alley

clout(e): rag, cloth

clouting: mending, patching (clothes)

Cluty: the Devil

cod: cushion, pillow

collek: collect

collop: thickish slice of meat

collop-tangs: tongs for roasting slices of meat etc. before a fire

conceited: imagined, thought

condumacious: contumacious

contrarious: contrary, perverse (Galt only)

contumelious: insolent
  (Galt only)
corbie: raven
cotter: tenant who leases a
  cottage and attached plot
  of land
couthie: agreeable, friendly,
  sympathetic
couthiness: kindliness
cowan boat: fishing boat: see
  Notes, Page 303(b)
crack: conversation
crack sae croose: talk so
  boastfully
cranreuch: hoar-frost
creel: wicker basket
cried fair: fig. in a state of
  stir and bustle (literally
  a previously advertised
  fair and therefore a
  crowded one)
crouse, croose: bold
cruisie: oil lamp
cuff: nape or scruff (of
  the neck)
cuif: fool, simpleton
cushy-doo: term of affection,
  literally, wood-pigeon

dark, darg: a day's work, task
daud: strike so as to shake
dauner: to stroll, saunter
dauner: a stroll, a slow walk
dauty, my: my dear
deacon: an expert
dead-ill: mortal illness
dead-thraws: death throes
deg: dig
den: to hide (oneself)
den't: hid
diet: died
dinle: tremble or tingle as
  with pain
dints: blows

dippet: dipped
dirl: rattle
doddard: foolish old man,
  dotard
doited: in one's dotage
doless: lacking in energy,
  improvident
dominie: schoolmaster
do-na-good: good for nothing
donsie: unfortunate, luckless
door-cheek: door-post
doos: pigeons
dotage-dauner: foolish journey
douce: sedate, sober,
  respectable
doucely: sedately
douceness: sedateness, sobriety
  (suggesting circumspection
  and cautiousness in a
  person)
dour(e): hard, stern, severe
dourly: with dogged reluctance
dow: to be able to
dowie: sad, dispirited,
  melancholy
dram and snap: small drink of
  liquor and a bite to eat
dreed: endured, suffered
dreigh: protracted, dreary,
  hard to bear
drouth, drowth: thirst
drumly: muddy, dark, gloomy,
  sullen; thick (of the voice)
dub: puddle, muddy pool
duds: rags, ragged clothing
dule: grief, sorrow, misery,
  suffering
dunt: knock
dwam: swoon, faint
dyke: wall

e'en: even
egget: incited, urged
eild: old age

ell-wand: a measuring rod

Enbrough: Edinburgh

ends and awls: bits and pieces (from shoe making, *ends:* thread ends)

enew: sufficient, enough

entry-mouth: entrance to a narrow lane or passage

erles, arles: earnests, pledges

ettle: try, strive

ettler: striver

eydent: diligent, industrious

fainness: liking, love

fash: to fret, vex, trouble

fear't for: afraid of

feckless: ineffective, spiritless

fee: a servant's wages

fek: value

fell: acute, keen; sharp, cruel; also *feller, fellest*

fell't: felled

fend: contrive, manage (past participle *fenn't*

ferrier: blacksmith, horse doctor (English *farrier*)

fey: doomed

fin': perceive with the senses, feel

fine-levers: exactors of fines

finger-stool: finger-stall

fisle: make a rustling sound, whistle

flit: remove, shift

flitting: removal

flyting: scolding, railing

for(e)nent: opposite (to), in front of

forgatherit: assembled, gathered together

fother: fodder

frien': relation by blood or marriage; friend

frith: firth

frock: a sailor's or fisherman's knitted jersey

frow: a big, buxom woman

fykie: restless, fidgety

gaberlunzie: beggar

gallows-knowe: hillock on which the gallows stood

gar: to make, cause

gardivine: wine bottle

garnel: granary, meal bin

gaucy, gausie, gawsie: plump, fresh-complexioned and jovial-looking

gaud: bar of iron, especially one used in forging

gauntrees: wooden stand for barrels

gear: possessions, effects

geizen't (keg of sobriety): dried up, withered (i.e. *gizzent*, from *gizzen*); *or* sated, saturated

gett: offspring, progeny, child

gif: if, whether

giglet: girl

gilly: young lad

gin: if

gir(d): hoop of wood or metal

girn: snare, trap

glaikit: roguish (of the eye)

glaming: gleaming

glamoured een o' fear: eyes bewitched or dazzled with fear

gled: literally, a kite (the bird); figuratively, one who preys on his fellows; a plunderer

gleg: quick, keen of perception

gloaming: twilight, dusk

gloom: to grow dark

gludder: a dull splash

good-willy waught: a hearty draught, a generous drink

gowans: daisies

gowk: fool, simpleton

greeting: weeping, crying

grewed: shuddered (from cold, fear or repulsion)

grouff, on his: prone (only by extension 'stomach')

gude, guid: good

Gude: used as a substitute for God

gude-brother: brother-in-law

gude-mother: mother-in-law

gude-man: husband

gudewife: landlady

gurged: swelled, surged

gurl: to growl

gurly: stormy, threatening

hack: hay-rack

hae't: have it

haffets: sidelocks

hale: healthy

Hallowe'en: eve of All Saints' Day; the festival of witches and the powers of darkness

han'let: handled

happing: plashed, bobbing up and down

harled, harl't, harlt: dragged, pulled, hauled

hass: throat, gullet

haver: talk foolishly, speak nonsense

havers: nonsense

haws: hawthorn berries

heck and manger, live at: feed without thought of cost (from cattle with free access to hay-rack and manger)

heel: end of loaf of bread

heft: haft, handle

hempies: rogues deserving hanging, i.e. destined for a hempen rope

heritors: landowners in a parish, responsible for upkeep of the local church

herret: plundered

herry: harry, plunder

hirkos: he-goat (Latin *hircus*)

hirple: limp, hobble

hirsled: slithered, shoved himself along by the hands in a seated posture

hobbleshow: uproar, tumult

hogget: hogshead, large cask

Hogmanae: last day of the year

holden: held

holm: a green islet, a river flat

hoor: whore

Horney: nickname for the Devil

horse-setter: horse hirer, job-master

hovered: tarried, paused

howdy: midwife

howf: place of resort, public house

howk: dig

huxtry (shop): huckstery (shop), general store

hyte: crazy, in a highly excitable state

ilk: same

ill: evil, wicked; poor in quality

ill-e'e: evil eye

imbrued: deeply dyed, imbued

ingrowth: increase

inkling: trace, hint, slight indication

jawping: splashing, spilling over

jealous, jalouse: suspect, guess, surmise

jelly-flowers: gilliflowers

jimp: scarcely, hardly, barely

jink: turn quickly or move nimbly (to escape notice)

jinkie: chink, narrow opening

jo: sweetheart; a term of endearment

jow: single stroke or pull of a bell, or sound of such

kail: cabbage; soup made with cabbage

kail-blades: colewort-blades

kell: coating of dirt or grime (here used figuratively)

kep: catch

kerns: foot soldiers

kist: a chest

kit: a wooden vessel

kithe: to manifest; manifest itself

kithings: manifestations

kittling: tickling

knelled: struck, rang

knotless: aimless, futile, ineffective

knowes: hillocks, slopes

laddie: boy

laigh: low

lair: learning, education, lore, doctrine

laith: loath

lambie: diminutive of lamb (term of endearment)

lamiter: cripple

lanerly: alone, lonely

langsyne, lang sincesyne: long ago

langnebbit: having a long neb or nose

lave: the rest, remainder

laverock: lark

lawin: tavern bill, reckoning

lea: shelter, or sheltered side

left to themselves: misguided, led astray in their judgement

leil: loyal, faithful

libel: specify in, or by means of, a libel or indictment

limmer: woman of loose character

linn: waterfall

lintie: linnet

lippy: a bumper, a full glass

list: ready, quick, eager

list: to wish, desire, please

litherly: languidly, lethargically

lockit: locked

lookit: looked

loon: rogue, rascal

losel: scamp, rascal, loafer

loun, lown: windless, calm, still

lounder: heavy blow, wallop

loup: leap, jump

low: reddest part of a fire

lown: see *loun*

luckenbooth: booth or shop which could be locked

lucky: landlady; a familiar form of address to an elderly woman, often prefixed to a surname

lug: ear

luggie: small wooden dish or vessel with one or two handles

lum: chimney

maddent: maddened

Mahoun(d): a name given to the Devil

mailing: a farm

mak away wi': kill, murder

malversations: breaches of trust, acts of duplicity

Malvesia: Malmsey
manger: see *heck*
Marymas: feast of the
  Assumption of the Virgin
  Mary held on 15 August
  (Old Style)
maun: must
maunna: must not
mei(c)kle, muckle: large,
  big; much
merks: silver coins
midden-heid: topmost of
  middle part of a dunghill
mill-lade: mill-race
mind: notice, concern
  oneself with
mindet, mindit: have in mind
  to, intend
mirk: dark, black, gloomy,
  obscure
misdoot: doubt, distrust
misdooting: lack of confidence,
  distrust
misfortunate: unfortunate,
  unlucky
morphosings: changes of
  form (Aphetic form of
  metamorphosings)
mort-cloth: funeral pall
muckle: see *meikle*
mutchkin: a liquid measure =
  approx. 1/4 pint Scots or
  3/4 pint imperial
mutchkin cap: cup holding a
  mutchkin

napery: household and
  other linen
napery press: linen cupboard
neb: point or nib of a pen
ne'erdoweels: good-for-
  nothings
New'ersday: New-year's day
nieve: fist, clenched hand

no canny: unnatural
nodge: nudge
notour: notorious

observes: remarks, comments
o'ercome: refrain or burden
o'ersea: foreign
off-gett: illegitimate child
outgate: exit
outstropolous: rowdy,
  out-of-hand
overly: excessively
oxter: armpit

Pace: Easter
paction: agreement, bargain
pad: soft saddle used by ladies
pattle: to stroke, fondle
pawkie: wily, sly, cunning;
  astute
pawkily: shrewdly,
  resourcefully
pawk(e)rie: trickery, slyness
pay-way: farewell
peeseweep: lapwing
pen-gun: a kind of pop-gun
  or pea-shooter made
  from quills
pen-gun at a crack: a
  chatterbox
penny-fee: cash wages,
  earnings
pet day: a day of sunshine in
  the middle of a spell of bad
  weather
pitty-patty: used onomat. to
  indicate the sound of quick,
  light footsteps
plack: a small coin
plaid: rectangular length
  of twilled woollen cloth,
  often of a checked pattern,
  worn as an outer garment
  or shawl

plaiding: material of which a plaid is made

play-marrow: playmate

plenishing: goods, gear, effects

plenishment: stock, supply, outfitting

ploy: light-hearted enterprise, frolic

pock: bag or pouch

polemic: argument

pomated: dressed with pomade

poopit: pulpit

poortith: poverty

precentor: an official appointed by the Kirk Session to lead the congregation in praise

press-head: top of a free-standing cupboard

primed: pinned

propugnacious: quarrelsome, extremely pugnacious (only in Galt)

puddock: frog

puddock-stool bonnet: flat cap resembling the head of a toadstool in shape

puzhened: poisoned

queen: female, sweetheart, lass

quire: choir

rabiators: plunderers; bullies

rackses: set of bars used to support a roasting spit (mistaken double plural of racks)

rampageous: furious, wild, unruly

ranting: roistering, uproarious

raspet: rubbed, grated

red(d)e: advise, warn; think, reckon

ree: tipsy

reeking: having smoke coming out of the chimney and therefore inhabited

remede: remedy, redress

residue: one left alone, (here) window

rigs: strips of ploughed or planted land

rone: gutter or spout to convey water from a roof

rowals: rowels

rugging: pulling roughly

runkled: creased, crumpled

sair: causing pain or distress; trying; severe

sall: shall

sawn: sown

scad: a quick glimmer, gleam, glimpse

scaith: damage, harm

scaithless: unharmed

scant: short, stinted

schimmer: reflection

schore: a chieftain

scoff't: scoffed

scog: conceal, hide

scogging: concealing

scomfish't: exhausted

scowthert: burnt, scorched

scroggy: bushy, covered with undergrowth or scrub

selt: sold

servitude: casement, obligation attached to a piece of land

shavling-gabbit: having a wry or twisted mouth (also used by Galt in 'The Howdie' and 'The Jaunt')

shelvy (skelvy): shelving, forming a shelf or ledge

sib: related by blood

sicker: safe, secure

siller: money

sincesyne: since then

siver: gutter

skail: scatter, disperse

skayled: dispersed

skelf: shelf

skelp: smack, slap

skirring: scurrying about, travelling rapidly

sklinter: a splinter

sklintered: splintered, broke off

skreigh: shriek, scream

slae: sloe

sleekit: plausible, ingratiating, sly

slippit: escaped

slockening: quenching, extinguishing

smeddum: spirit, mettle, energy, drive

smiddy: smithy

sneck: latch, fasten

snell: severe, harsh

snodly: neatly, tidily

snool: humble, bully

sole: sill

solemneezed: solemnised, rendered grave

sookit: sucked

soople: ingenious, wily, cunning

sorned: idled, loafed, lazed

sorner: idle fellow (only in Galt with this meaning)

sosherie: sociability, conviviality (found only in Galt)

sough: sound of the wind

spae: foretell

spark in my hass: lit. particle in my throat; euph. for a craving for liquor

spean: wean

speats: floods

speir, speer: ask

spicerie: slight touch, trace

spicin: sprinkling

splurt: a sudden movement, a small fracas

spring: quick, lively tune

spunk: spark of fire

stabler: stable keeper

sta(i)nchers: iron bars forming part of a grating

stang, ride the: to be subjected to a form of mob justice by which the patient was borne shoulder-high astride a pole

steading: piece of ground on which (usually) houses are built (here Elspa suggests Marion is building on sand)

steeking: closing

stoops: supporters, staunch adherents

stoppit: stopped

stoup o' sherries: sherry cask

stour(e): dust

stoury: dusty

straemash: uproar, commotion

stravaig: wander idly

swankies: strapping young fellows

swappit: exchanged

swatch: sample, specimen

sweart't: swear to it

swee: movable rod on which to hang cooking pots over a fire

swither: be in two minds, doubt, hesitate

syne: ago; so, hence, then

tack: lease, tenancy

taiglet: delayed, waited

taigling: delaying

tak the door on your back: leave [the mill] closing the door behind you

tawnle: bonfire (particularly

one of wood and kindled on a hill on the eve of the Wednesday of Marymass fair in Irvine)

telt: told

temming: thin woolen cloth

tent, take tent o' her cantrips: beware of her tricks

tethert: tethered

thacket: thatched

thegither: together

thir: these

thole: endure with patience or fortitude, tolerate

tholed, tholet: past tense of *thole*

thrang: busy; crowded

thumbikins: thumbscrews

til't: to it

timeously: in good or sufficient time

timerarious: nervous

tirling at the pin: working the handle of the knocker

tocher: dowry

tod, tod lowrie: fox

tolbooth: jail or prison (in small Scottish burghs the Tolbooth incorporated the Town Council offices, the magistrates' court, and the jail)

toom: empty

toop: ram, tup

tormentors: tongs for toasting oatcakes etc.

toupie: toupee

trance door: passage door

trench: encroach

trintled: caused to roll or flow

tron(e): market place (because of the trone or weighing machine that was there)

trot-cozey: warm outer garment consisting of a heavy coat or cloak with a capacious hood

twalpennies: a shilling Scots or one penny sterling

uncanny: not safe to meddle with, mischievous

unco: strange

unco, in a state o'– : in a state of amazement and hubbub

uncos, the – of the town: strange sights

unharnished: unharnessed

unjealoused: unsuspected

untimeous: unseasonably late, inconveniently late

upsides, be – with: be even or quits with

vent (of smoke): to find its way out

vera: very

vilipendit: disparaged

virl: small narrow collar

virled: furnished with ferrules

vivers: provisions, victuals

vogie: vain, pleased with oneself

vouts: vaults

wae: sad, grieved

waff-like: feeble, weak, exhausted

warrandice: warrant, authorisation

warsle: wrestle

wastage: place of desolation

wastrie: wastefulness

waught: see under *good-willy waught*

waur: worse

weans: children

well e'e: spring

whigamore: Covenanter:

whilk: which

whin: gorse, furze

whisht: to silence; hush!

whisking: switching

whorl: small wheel

whumplet: complicated, involved

wicket-hole: loophole in a wall

wight: valiant, bold

wile: coax, entice

willease: valise, portmanteau

willy-waing: bewailing, making lamentation

winna: will not

winsome: pleasing, charming

wis: wish, wish for

wised: led, directed

wist: knew

wouldna: would not

wrack: flying clouds

wrang: wrong

writer: lawyer

wud: mad

wuddy: gallows rope; gallows

wuddy-worthies: rogues deserving hanging, gallows-birds

wynd: lane

wyte: blame

yestreen: yesterday evening, last night

yett: gate

yird: ground, earth

yird and stane: symbols of infeftment (Scots law); the act of giving symbolical possession of heritable property (used here metaph.)

yirded: buried

youthy: youthful esp. in appearance as belying one's years

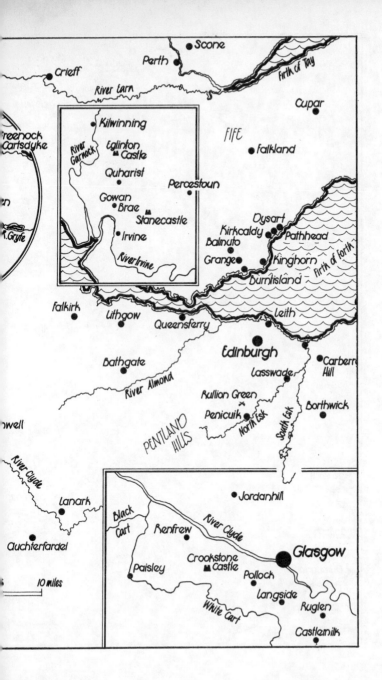

Scone

Perth

Crieff

River Earn

Firth of Tay

Cupar

Kilwinning

FIFE

Falkland

reenock
Cartsdyke

River Garnock

Eglinton
Castle

Quharist

Percestoun

Gowan
Brae
Stanecastle

Dysart

K.Gyle

Irvine

River Irvine

Kirkcaldy
Pathhead

Balmuto

Grange
Kinghorn

Burntisland

Firth of Forth

Falkirk

Lithgow

Queensferry

Leith

Bathgate

Edinburgh

Carberry
Hill

River Almond

Lasswade

Rullion Green
×
Penicuik

North Esk

Borthwick

South Esk

*PENTLAND
HILLS*

well

River Clyde

Lanark

Jordanhill

Auchterfardel

Black
Cart

Renfrew

River Clyde

Glasgow

Crookstone
Castle
Polloch

10 miles

Paisley

White Cart

Langside

Ruglen

Castlemilk

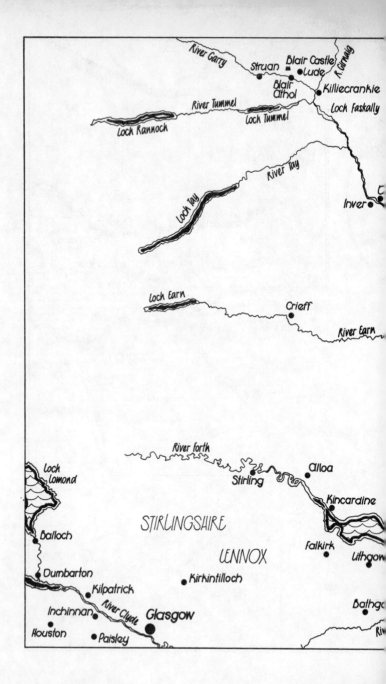

Robert Louis Stevenson

Pictures of the Mind

Many highly talented and famous artists have lent striking imaginative interpretation to Robert Louis Stevenson's most powerful writing. This elegant book celebrates the diverse range of art inspired by this much loved author and is the perfect testimony to his ability to entertain.

"a lovely book...glorious illustrations"   *The Herald*
"a wonderful tribute to Stevenson'   *The Independent*
128pp (120 colour plates)   086241 492 X   £14.99 P

The Strange Case of Dr Jekyll and Mr Hyde

Stevenson's chilling study of the conflict between good and evil is an all-time classic, superbly brought to life by Robert Trotter in this best-selling audio version.
"One of the best voices currently recording in Scotland"
Gramophone Magazine

2 Cassettes (2hr) 1 85968 082 8   £7.99

Travels with a Donkey in the Cevennes

In September 1878, Robert Louis Stevenson set out from Le Monastier to tramp through through the wild region of the Cevennes - his only companion was a donkey.
"A beguiling mix of vivacity, warmth and humour" *Good Book Guide*
2 Cassettes (2hr 24min) 1 85968 065 8   £7.99

The Body Snatcher and other stories

The Body Snatcher - By night sinister figures deliver shrouded burdens to Dr Knox's assistants, Fettes and MacFarlane, and although some of the bodies are suspiciously 'fresh', few questions are asked.
Thrawn Janet and *The Tale of Tod Lapraik* - Two terifying tales in Scots
2 cassettes (1 hr 39min)   1 85968 067 4   £7.99

All Canongate titles including those listed above are available direct from Canongate Books, 14 High Street, Edinburgh, Scotland, EH1 1TE. Tel 0131 557 5111
Postage and packing free on all orders within the UK.
Our current catalogue will also be sent on request

Lewis Grassic Gibbon's

A Scots Quair

(ISBN 086241 532 2   £4.99 pbk)

Chris Guthrie, torn between her love of the land and her desire to escape the narrow horizons of a peasant culture, is the thread that links these three works. In them, Gibbon interweaves the personal joys and sorrows of Chris's life with the greater historical and political events of the time.

Sunset Song, the first and most celebrated book of the trilogy, covers the early years of the century, including the First World War. Chris survives, with her son Ewan, but tragedy has struck and her wild spirit subdued. In *Cloud Howe,* as the minister's wife, Chris learns to love again, and we witness the cruel gossip and high comedy of small village life until once again, Chris suffers a terrible loss. *Grey Granite* focuses on her son Ewan and his passionate involvement with justice for the common man.

For Chris, with her intuitive strength, nothing lasts – only the land endures.

'It would be impossible to overestimate Lewis Grassic Gibbon's importance... A Scots Quair is a landmark work; it permeates the Scottish literary consciousness and colours all subsequent writing of its kind.' David Kerr Cameron

A complete listing of our Canongate Classics
is available upon request.

CANONGATE CLASSICS